THE FRUIT

OF THE

DENDRAGON

TREE

Paul H Deepan

Outskirts Press, Inc.
Denver, Colorado

This is a work of fiction. The events and characters described herein are imaginary and are not intended to refer to specific places or living persons. The opinions expressed in this manuscript are solely the opinions of the author and do not represent the opinions or thoughts of the publisher. The author has represented and warranted full ownership and/or legal right to publish all the materials in this book.

The Fruit of the Dendragon Tree
All Rights Reserved.
Copyright © 2010 Paul H Deepan
v4.0

Cover Photo © 2010 JupiterImages Corporation. All rights reserved - used with permission.

This book may not be reproduced, transmitted, or stored in whole or in part by any means, including graphic, electronic, or mechanical without the express written consent of the publisher except in the case of brief quotations embodied in critical articles and reviews.

Outskirts Press, Inc.
http://www.outskirtspress.com

ISBN: 978-1-4327-5670-3

Outskirts Press and the "OP" logo are trademarks belonging to Outskirts Press, Inc.

PRINTED IN THE UNITED STATES OF AMERICA

Dear Becky – Thanks so much for your love, support & friendship. Know it is all returned to you in deep friendship always. — Paul

This book is for Rajindra and Kamal

6/28/2010

Prologue

"There are no new stories, child," said Keffyldyn, "and the most beautiful, powerful and sad ones repeat themselves through the circles of time, like a tree that loses its leaves every autumn, lies quiet in winter, and blooms again in the spring. The blossoms and leaves of the tree are always unique, yet reveal their own unmistakable nature, just as the characters in stories do. But the tree remains the tree; it simply grows a little every time a fresh yet familiar story passes through its branches.

We are all leaves in a story that will end, then begin again, on a tree that never dies, a tree that grows because we have lived and died. Today's bloom is always earmarked for a fall, and tomorrow's death always for a new life.

So thank the spring, for its joyous rush of life. And thank the dead of winter, for its hidden promise."

(The Dynfarch Wisdom, Book 1: Dialogues of the centaur)

I knew sleep would elude me; I should have known I couldn't elude my son. The wood fire was blazing and I had settled onto the sofa, scotch in hand, gazing at the flames. I was too tired to face Jake, but he found me anyway, coming into the living room a few minutes after I got there. He was tall in the firelight, and his shadow danced around the room like a boxer looking for a fight.

"Hi, son," I tried, but the glare I received told me how things were going to go.

"How come you're so late? I told Meg to go home. Mom was asking where you were."

Meg was the palliative care nurse who stayed with Mary during the days. My wife lay upstairs, dying by inches, but at least she was home. I'd looked in on her earlier, but hadn't wanted to disturb her sleep.

"I was at the campus," I said. "I told you I had to do my exam tonight."

"Why couldn't someone else do it for you?"

I sighed. "I've already told you, I've asked Joan and Cary to cover for me way too many times already." Joan and Cary were two married colleagues of mine in the Owen School of Management at Vanderbilt University, where I taught. They'd been incredibly supportive. "I only had to go in for a couple hours to run the exam, and then come back. But the traffic was a mess with the snow, you know these people here can't drive in it."

When I'd first moved to Tennessee from Canada I had joked with Mary, herself southern-born: how the schools would close with even a snowflake in the forecast. As a northern transplant, it was axiomatic with me that Southerners couldn't drive in the snow. Mary had chuckled at my rants. We'd laughed together about many things, right up until the day that her breast cancer was staged, and we realized she probably wasn't ever going to get better. After that, nothing seemed funny anymore.

I knew what Jake was thinking. He was wondering if I'd stopped anywhere else on my return home. I decided to meet him head on. "I didn't see Erin, if that's where you're going. I told you, that was never anything." Erin Wood was another colleague in the Biz School. I hadn't known her well, but she'd injected herself into my life after Mary's diagnosis, coming by to check on me, phoning several times a day. One afternoon a month before, I'd been in my office, staring into nothing, and Erin had stopped by. I stood to greet her, and after one look at my face she said, "You need a hug," and proceeded to give me one. But she'd wanted more than a hug. She nestled into me, and raised her mouth to mine. I jerked back, but Jake had walked in at that precise moment, and I couldn't seem to convince him that I hadn't wanted her kiss, that my retreat from Erin had been rejection of her advance, and not guilt at his own. I had recently told him that we had to accept the fact his mom was going to die, that we'd have to move on, that she would want us to move on. As a result of what he'd seen, though, he saw my rationale for such acceptance in a whole new light, as if I had already replaced Mary with Erin. As if I could replace her with anyone.

I realized afterwards that I'd been a fool to even let Erin into my life, let alone get so close. I'd discovered she had a reputation, and that her sudden interest in me was more probably sparked by her predatory sense of my vulnerability, and not compassion. But I knew Jake didn't care about any of that. He didn't want a vulnerable father, he wanted someone strong he could lean on, and now he felt betrayed by the loss of two parents, not just one. If I had known after that night all that would follow, I might have tried harder. But fate is inexorable, and anyway I didn't. I was too wrapped up in my own misery to work out what to do about my son's.

Now, back in our house, Jake shook his head, and gave the kind of scornful exhalation patented by teenagers. "Y'know, it really doesn't matter where you were. Mom needed you here. She could die any day now, remember? You told me so yourself. What if she'd gone while you were out? How would you have felt then?"

"I would have felt like crap!" I exclaimed. "But what was I supposed to do? I had to give my students their exam. Nobody else could do it. It's my job! I didn't think I'd be gone this long, but the snow held me up." My excuses sounded weak even in my own ears; God knew how they sounded to Jake. Suddenly exasperated, I slammed the tumbler of single malt onto the nearest end table and it smashed, spilling twelve-year-old McCallan onto the rug. A shard of glass lanced into my left palm, immediately drawing blood. "Damn!" I cried, and threw the thing at the fire.

There was a time when Jake would've asked me if I was ok. He was that kind of kid. But that time seemed to have flown away between us, and he continued to exude contempt. "You just wanted a place to hide," he said. "You can't face being here, so you thought you'd leave for awhile. You've given up on Mom, given up on us, and you're just waiting for her to die so that life with Erin can go on. You're pathetic."

There it was. I couldn't believe the pain his words caused me. And as was my habit when wounded, I went on the attack. "Pathetic? What about you? Sitting up there night after night, doing these stupid internet searches for some miracle cure that you aren't going to find! How is that for not wanting to face reality? Grow up, why don't you? Your mother is going to die, and there's not a damn thing either of us can do about it!"

He looked stricken for a moment, before proving he was my son. "At least I want to do something!"

I realized we'd gone too far, that we'd turned our pain fully upon each other, which was the last thing I'd wanted, and I knew Jake well enough that he wouldn't have wanted that either. I took a step toward him, but he backed away, that single piece of body language more powerful than any words. I stopped in my tracks, fighting for air, for the words to reach him. "Look," I said, as calmly as I could. "We're both upset. Let's talk in the morning. It shouldn't be like this between us."

"Whatever," was all I got in reply, and then he was gone.

I had to be told a lot of things that happened after that night, as I didn't witness them first-hand. So my words won't be the only ones you'll encounter in these pages. If I get the details wrong, no doubt they'll change them as they see fit. My memory may be faulty, but it's all I have, and all I need.

The wise say that death is just a doorway. I, not being wise, always taught my soldiers not to go charging through doorways just because they are open. But the young are in a hurry for everything. Sitting here, I can remember Jake vividly as he was then, poised on the edge of manhood, waiting to take the plunge into that dangerous pool. I loved him so, but in those days it seemed as if we spoke different languages when it came to love. He was deaf and I was mute and the one who translated for us was dying in her bedroom. How often does such awkwardness exist between a father and a son?

I remember my own father, the physician: loved by so many, an enigma to me. Only after he died did I feel the terrible vacuum where his love used to be. I didn't want that ignorance for Jake, but I felt unable to reach him. So I lay on the couch nursing my hand, and stared at the flames while my son sat upstairs at his computer. We were two islands; victims of an emotional drift from the continent of what had been a family, split apart by the knowledge of Death's inevitable visit. Jake was just furious at the prospect. He raged against his mother's passing and poured himself into his hopeless Internet quest, searching for some miracle cure that would keep her alive. And I did not do those things, and so betrayed him, in his mind. Even if I'd never met Erin Wood, I'd still accepted that Mary was leaving, and he had not, and to Jake my capitulation to Death was treachery of the worst kind. I didn't know what drove him, although now I do understand. But then all we could do was circle each other, like two stray dogs wondering when the next kick would find us. That last argument had been the worst; had cut both of us the deepest. I needed to find a way to bind the wounds we'd caused each other, so that we could heal together once Mary had left us.

Time is fluid. It pours through your body like rain, washing away your youth. For you, it wasn't very long from now, and not very far away, that our white moon peered through ragged clouds and lit up the snow, swirling in the gusty wind. The blizzard that had arrived that afternoon was nearly over, yielding to the mass of cold Canadian air moving in behind it. In the morning, Nashville would waken to a fresh white blanket, sparkling like pale fire in the sun, melting rapidly as snow does there. But now it was still dark, except for glimpses of moonlight, and my neighbors slept, insulated in snug houses from the capricious winter. And the boy who would not see that morning's sunshine was awake upstairs, oblivious to the abating storm outside.

This is his story, and mine. And if you love enough, it could be yours too.

Chapter 1

*And why the pentangle is proper to that peerless prince
I intend now to tell, though detain me it must.
It is a sign by Solomon sagely devised
To be a token of truth, by its title of old,
For it is a figure formed of five points,
And each line is linked and locked with the next
For ever and ever, and hence it is called... the endless knot*

(Sir Gawain and the Green Knight)

Ureth the Crone stood on a grassy hillside, lost in thought under the light of two moons. She was ready now, ready to bring the boy Jake from his world to hers, but she could not suppress a shiver at the enormity of what she was about to do. "It's time, Jake," she whispered to the night. "We need you now." But the quickening was not there: the skin-crawling itch that meant you were partnering with another witch had not yet assailed her, and she shook her head once in mounting impatience. What was keeping the girl? Ureth had told her the proper spells to say. That's what you got when you put your faith in amateurs. She looked at the sky. The moons were in their proper position; soon it might be too late. To quell her exasperation, she looked downhill.

Below her in the town of Marfold, lights twinkled through windows like stars come to light the earth, and she could imagine the warmth of family suppers on rough wooden tables. But no such warmth awaited

Ureth: the Crones were her only family now, as they had been for most of her life. When she was only three years old, Ureth had seen her first vision in the flames of her father's hearth. Her mother had cried, for fear of what her daughter's life would become: a girl without love's first kiss, a woman without a child's first smile. Ureth had cried too, for in her vision her mother had died, and then her vision came true. Her father had tried to keep Ureth's power a secret, but such things cannot be hidden forever. One day, while playing with friends, an older boy had pushed Ureth too hard, landing her unceremoniously in a muddy puddle. The boy Gareth had started laughing, which made things worse for both of them. Ureth could still vividly remember that day, Gareth laughing at her, her tears running down her hot cheeks, red with embarrassment.

"Go on Ureth, get up you baby, don't lie in the mud like a pig!"

Her dress was muddy, and her hands. Ureth hated getting her hands dirty. Then Gareth had snorted like a pig, and anger had flashed in her mind like a lightning bolt.

"Stop laughing at me, Gareth! Stop it! Stop it, you jackass!" and she'd *thought* he was a donkey (though to be fair her own little donkey was much nicer than Gareth), and to her horror Gareth's laugh had become a bray that went on and on, it seemed like forever, though it could only have been a few seconds before he stopped, horrified, clamping his hands to his mouth. It didn't last, of course, that kind of power was only suggestive. The other children had thought that Gareth was just being funny, but Ureth and Gareth knew the truth. She could see the fear in his eyes and she'd felt compassion for him, and a weird sense of resignation for herself, and she'd said, sadly: "It's all right, Gareth, you're only a little boy." And although Gareth had immediately gotten his normal boyish voice back, the first words out of his mouth were: "You witch!" and he'd run home to tell his mother.

The Crones had heard, of course. They always managed to find those with any Craft, which was a good thing for everyone. Any psychic power could cause grave damage, not least to those that wielded it, and the Crones provided the proper discipline. They interviewed

Ureth, then tested her, then took her as one of their own. She'd had a choice: she could reject the power, and through their spells, at which Ureth was now more than adept, the Crones could leach it out of you. But few chose this path; those who refused their Gift were listless, and died young. Most chose the Craft, and the ecstasy of thought and vision that could be attained, though the price was very high. For once initiated fully, the novice surrendered any physical beauty, her voice cracked and her flesh withered, even if she was still young. So Ureth had paid the price all Crones paid: she looked ninety, though she was only nineteen, and what man would look past that to see the young woman hidden within? The Crones learned solitude early, and tonight Ureth felt more alone than she had ever been, since that far off day when her father had left her with the witches she knew he despised.

Sometimes, Ureth secretly wished to hold a man, to be held by a man, to give birth to a child. But these things were not for the Crones. They alone had the Craft, the source of their strength. And in return for this power, only they could call upon the fire of the Dragon. The power of the Craft was its own reward: the Crones, more than anyone, helped shape history, at least so far as the Dancer allowed. It had been that way for a thousand years, and, if Ureth had anything to say about it, it would remain that way still, even if she had to take matters into her own hands.

So Ureth stood alone, in the wind that keened at her ears and strained to part her cloak like an unwelcome lover. Low in the sky behind her left shoulder, the full Dragon moon glowed red, casting a fiery glow over the frost that covered the grass. Ahead of her, across the river Marfell, the golden Warrior moon was also full, though higher in the sky. The dual moon-glow was captured by the swift waters of the river, curving from west to south to wrap Marfold in its powerful embrace. And in the middle of the river stood the castle Marfang, seat of the Duke Coegun, the man who had brought Ureth to this desolate hillside, on this night of two full moons.

Ureth knew, despite what he might say otherwise, that the Duke of Marfang wanted to be the king of Taumar, jewel of the world of

Tiramonde. The young king, Endil, ruled Taumar due to the sudden death of his father in a hunting accident the year before. But Duke Coegun was experienced, charismatic, proven in battle, wily in counsel, and deep in her bones Ureth knew he was not above using magic to further his ambition. For there were those who disputed the exclusive right of the Crones to wield the Craft; they would seek, unguided, the power of wind and rock, river and flame, and fall into the Darkness that waited to twist their desire to its own ends. Ever they fell, but never before they wreaked the havoc of their unbridled arrogance.

But Coegun was hailed as Taumar's protector, for her enemies had tested her borders soon after the new king's coronation. While the Duke was engaged on the northern frontier in skirmishes with the Ice People, the Sacours from the Southwestern Desert had attacked, desiring the castle Marfang and the treasure it guarded. But Coegun had defeated the Icemen, and hurrying south also humbled the Sacours, convincing them to revert to their usual status of quiet, if not well-intentioned trading partners.

Coegun had saved the kingdom from invasion not once but twice, covering himself in glory, his star outshining that of the young king Endil. And now, Ureth was certain, Coegun was abandoning his oaths of loyalty to a monarch who was weaker than he was. She had taken her concerns to the Council of the Coven, but they had been no help. Though young, Ureth had earned a place on this Council through her undeniable gifts, but try as she might she could not prove to them any wrongdoing on the Duke's part. Whatever Coegun's magic, it shielded him from discovery, and though Ureth's clarity of Sight was unmatched, she could offer the Sisters nothing more than the feeble premonitions of a fireside psychic. The Council, several of whom were jealous that one so young had as much power as they, remained unimpressed, and secretly glad of her difficulty.

"What exactly would you have us do, Ureth?" they had asked. "When we ask what Coegun has done wrong, you give no evidence of anything. Nor can you offer a single vision of any evil he may commit in the future. And even if he is truly our enemy, do you really expect us to move against him now, at the height of his power and popularity? The people would not stand for it. The king himself would not stand for it. We will be watchful, as we respect your insight, but we can do nothing yet." She had been dismissed like a mere novice, which had stung her pride (of which she still had plenty, may the Dancer forgive her). But she was right about Coegun and the evil he aspired to, of that she was sure. More than that, she was desperately afraid. Something had to be done, Ureth knew, and she was on that hillside, on that night of all nights, to do it. She was breaking about three hundred rules to be there, and possibly risking her life, but what else could she do? Nobody else saw the danger, and even if they did they chose to ignore it.

He must be stopped. The wind whispered the thought in the grass about her feet; the waters of Marfell whispered it against the stone piers of the town. Even the moons above whispered it in the heavens, in an alignment not seen for a thousand years, not since Kildraig the Dragon was first entombed. The Pendraig had to be summoned. Long had she sought him, and far from her world, as the prophecy dictated. Though to be truthful, her help in that other world had been less adept than she would have liked. And as for Jake, he didn't really seem to know what he was getting into. But he met the right criteria, unlikely as that seemed: He had offered his death for a life, for a mother who had risked her own death for his life, and he had the purity of spirit to command such a bargain. *Jake must be the one,* Ureth told herself for the hundredth time. She needed him to be the one, for she was out of time. And if he were, at least the kingdom would not go to Coegun, whatever else might happen.

2.

Completely unaware of Ureth's urgency on his behalf in another world, seventeen-year-old Jake Patel stared at a computer screen in his. Tall and slender, with black hair, and blue eyes that gazed into nothing, his long legs disappeared under the computer hutch while his hands lay motionless on the keyboard. A black high school jacket with red and gold letters for swimming and track hung on the back of his chair. The jacket to a karate *gi* lay on his bed, the black belt snaking through the loops. The pants lay crumpled in a corner, contributing to the disarray.

A framed photograph of Jake and his parents, standing beside the computer monitor, revealed Jake's resemblance to his mother. Like him, she had black hair, blue eyes and a tall, slender build. Dad was dark and stocky, with intense black eyes. Like Mary, Jake loved music, and reserved his athleticism for individual sports, not team games like ice hockey, which Dad still played. But all of them had loved to laugh together; they were laughing in the picture, which had been taken the day before Mom's diagnosis.

Jake knew he should sleep, but sleep came hard, and staying asleep came harder. For the past three nights, he'd had a recurring dream, one he could not completely recall, but which filled him with dread. He remembered an old woman who looked like a witch, holding out a withered hand to his face, calling to him. The language she spoke was at the edge of knowledge, but in the place where the dream occurred, he knew she was addressing him by some title. But he had no title; his family was middle class American melting pot: Scots-Irish Dixie mixed with Anglo-Indian Canadian. So the dream made little sense, yet somehow he knew the witch offered him a terrible choice.

Jake didn't particularly like computers; he preferred long runs in the woods. But he was too tired to run and anyway it was freezing outside. At least the virtual world contained in the box on his desk seemed better than his dream world, and certainly better than the real one. And sleeping was beginning to frighten him a little, which was embarrassing. He told himself it was only a dream, after all. So he was online again, looking for any new websites, and not in bed, tired as he was.

The monitor was the only source of light in the room, and its glow threw jagged shadows among the chaotically strewn belongings of teen-aged boy. Jake ignored the clutter. One of the extremely few benefits of having a dying mother was that nobody nagged him to keep his room clean. Like many people inching toward a slow death, Mom had good days and bad days. Lately, the bad days outnumbered the good ones. Jake knew that his father was right: Mom was going to die. But to Jake such acceptance was surrender, and Jake had never been one to give up. Life had been great. His parents were happy and they loved him. He had friends, swimming, karate, track, and vacations overseas. He and his mother were particularly close. One day she'd found a small lump, not painful, but which still carried a dreaded label: Breast Cancer. That had been a year ago. And Mary had fought for her life every day since. But now it appeared her fight was going to end. And Jake had learned that there were certain battles for which no amount of brains, money or prayer would be any help.

Running had helped, at first. Running fast, to outpace the fear that shadowed his heart: long, risky runs in the woods at the dead of night, his feet dancing in turn with the changing seasons over bare earth, dead leaves, the occasional snow, exhaustion helping to sublimate the fear he could never defeat. But three days ago the dreams had started, and the wakefulness. Now he was too tired to run. He had nobody to talk to. His father had withdrawn into an emotional cocoon after Jake had found that blonde bitch kissing him in his office. Deep down, Jake knew his Dad hadn't been looking for that kiss, but reminding him of it was a good way to pay him back for giving up, to hurt him. And Jake sure as hell wanted to hurt someone.

None of his friends knew how to help him. Having him around made them uncomfortable, Jake believed, so he had simply stopped talking. His computer was his only companion, now. With it he could talk to unknown people all over the world, asking questions. Jake had flogged the Internet to research what was happening in the area of breast cancer treatment. He knew how to classify a breast tumor, and what the standard and experimental treatments were for each kind. His mother's tumor had been an invasive "Stage 2". Stage 2 was a lot more serious than Stage 1. She'd had surgery, radiation and chemotherapy, which had respectively disfigured, burned and poisoned her. But the cancer was now in her bones and liver. His mother wasn't going to get well, and Jake knew there was no miracle cure for her.

Three nights ago, Jake had started playing games online, without telling Dad. He liked the role-playing ones best, where he could be an elf warrior, and combat demons who conveniently died when you did all the right things, and didn't rip your heart out, no matter how scared you were, how hard you tried, or how many bargains you whispered to God in the dead of night.

Jake sighed and took his fingers from the keyboard. He was in no mood for games tonight. Better get to bed now and do his homework in the morning. His grades had slipped, but not badly, and his teachers were taking pity on him. Jake hated that pity: it made him feel weak. He wished there was no reason for them to pity him. He wished his mother were well. He wished he could find something to make her better, but in all the world there was nothing to stem the flow of life that dripped out of her, a little more each day. Maybe there was a place where he could find a magic drug to make his mother whole again, to sit and laugh and sing with him once more. If there were, he had vowed, he would find it, no matter what he had to do, even if he had to die. No matter who had to die.

Something fluttered at the edge of his vision and he heard a soft thump against his window. "What the heck was that?" he muttered, though he had an uneasy suspicion he knew the answer to his question. He looked at his window. A dense circle of snow smeared against the pane, at odds with the drifts that had accumulated in heaps in the corners of the sill. Something whirled outside in the dark, and the glass thudded once more. Jake crossed to the window and opened it quickly, sticking his head outside. A third snowball, because that's what someone had been throwing to get his attention, caught him square in the middle of his forehead as he did so.

"Damn!" he swore, wiping the powdery white stuff quickly away. He looked down, and of course it was her, as he'd thought it would be. Jenny Blackwood, prowling the neighborhood in the middle of the night. He groaned inwardly. Great. "The school ghoul," they called her, and apparently now his personal stalker. Jenny always dressed in black, which matched her hair and contrasted with her pale skin. Her eyes, he remembered, were deep blue, and he guessed she was pissed off about that, because it detracted from the vampire motif. Jenny was weird, to say the least. At school, to match her black clothes, she wore black mascara and black lipstick, and painted her nails black too. But her eyes were blue.

"Jenny! What do you want? Go home!" Jake hissed, trying to whisper his outrage yet stay quiet, to avoid waking his mother. In recent days, Jenny had started taking an unwelcome interest in his affairs, as if he were a pet project. She sat near him at lunch, followed him home from school. And now she was throwing snowballs at his window in the dead of night. Crazy.

"Jake! I need to talk with you about your mother! We can help her!"

"Are you nuts? It's late! I can't let you in now! What about your folks, do they know you're out?"

Jenny shrugged, dismissing all parents as irrelevant. "I don't want to come in! I was sent to get you. I know it's late, but it's not too late, not for you, not for your Mom."

"What did you say?" he gasped. Fury at possible manipulation, and impossible hope surged together in one breath, expelled like water-smoke in the moonlight.

"You heard me. I can help your Mom. But you have to hurry: it has to be tonight! She told me."

"What has to be tonight? Who told you? You aren't making any sense!"

She looked up at him for a moment, her eyes intent on his. He looked in them, and was lost.

"Please, Jake, I'm freezing!"

Jake wanted to ask why, if she were cold, she didn't conjure up a bonfire like any self-respecting witch, but he didn't. He suddenly realized that in all the time his mother had been sick, not one person had offered to help get her better. Some doctors had quoted statistics, presented with admonitions to be brave and strong. Others had been optimistic that his mother was a "fighter" and would "pull through this thing". But not one person had offered real help. Not that Jenny could do anything. Everyone knew she was a flake. She had no friends. But that didn't mean much. Jake didn't have many friends anymore either. People didn't know what to say to him. But what if she said she could help, and somehow she really could, and he ignored her? What if he subsequently discovered there might have been a way, however unlikely, that he could have helped his Mom, and he hadn't? It didn't bear thinking about.

"Just a minute," he said, and ducked back inside. He crept downstairs, remembering what Jenny had said about being cold, and grabbed an extra jacket for her from the hall closet. It was one of Mom's. From where he stood, he saw the firelight flickering in the family room. His father was in there, Jake knew. Hopefully, he'd fallen asleep by now. Better not wake him; he'd only dismiss Jake for attempting a wild goose chase. And he'd probably be right: he nearly always was. Which was part of the problem. But Jake had to know for sure. Dad might have given up hope, but Jake hadn't. He couldn't blame his father, not anymore. He knew that Dad the business teacher was just playing the numbers. And Mom's numbers meant she was lucky, if that was a word that could be applied to her, to still be alive.

Jake regretted accusing his father of weakness for giving up hope; knowing Dad in turn would regret labeling him as weak for refusing to face facts. But despite all the evidence, despite the fact that he saw her dwindling every day, Jake could not let himself admit that his mother would die. So he had to follow every desperate chance, in case some miracle happened, something not in the normal way of things. Dad was Dr. Logic. If you couldn't prove it, it wasn't real. Mom was different. She believed in the intuitive flashes Jake sometimes had, the things he knew would happen before they did. It occurred to Jake that she would understand Jenny's desire to explore magic, though she might not do it herself. Mom liked mysteries, didn't think that logic could explain everything. Jake wondered, not for the first time, what spark had drawn and kept his parents together.

He lingered a moment in the hall, feeling sad, torn by the conflicting emotions that sneaking away from his father to help his mother were stirring up. He wanted to tell Dad he wasn't mad at him anymore, that he loved him; that they'd be there for each other no matter what happened. But now wasn't the time.

"I'll tell him tomorrow," Jake promised himself, as he slid out into the freezing night to join the strange girl in his back yard. She took the spare coat from him with murmured thanks. The clouds were all but gone now, and the full moon shone brightly, lighting the snow-covered lawn.

"Where are we going?" he asked, for Jenny had already turned without another word, shrugging into his mother's coat as she walked through the newly fallen snow towards the woods bordering the rear of Jake's property. She didn't answer, so he clutched her arm, and was about to repeat his question when she turned and looked at him. In the moonlight, he noticed for the first time that she was beautiful. He felt awkward with this realization, which the effect of daylight on her ghoulish makeup had kept from him. Jake also saw that Jenny resembled him: slim, dark hair, blue eyes. He could be her brother; though there was nothing brotherly about the instincts she was arousing.

"Do you believe in magic?" she asked, her voice low. Jake realized he liked her voice, too.

"I don't think so," he said, though as she looked down in disappointment he hurried to add, "But I want to, if it'll help my mother." And that was true enough, though he'd never thought about it before. But what had all his midnight sojourns been, in the woods and on the computer, if not a quest to find a healing magic that could save his mother's life?

Jenny stared at him a moment, then said: "I don't know if it matters whether you do or not. It just might make it easier for you to cooperate if you did. Come with me, say nothing, and do as you are told. OK?" He nodded, and she turned again, walking back along footprints he realized she must have already made on her inbound journey from wherever she was now taking him.

Jake's house was the last in a cul-de-sac, carved from virgin woodland deep in Williamson County. Jake's father had built it there fifteen years ago, to Mary's design. It was too big for three people, but it was supposed to have held more. Other hoped-for children had never arrived, and now it looked as if only two people would be living there soon. Jake shook himself. *Stop it!* He concentrated on following the girl.

The lawn, blanketed with snow, ended at the edge of a wood, the immediate paths of which Jake knew from dark runs when sleep mocked him. Jenny headed straight to the rear of Jake's property and took him into the wood, leading him through the columns of hickory, laurel and oak. The air was still and it was less cold among the sleeping trees. About fifty yards into the wood, the ground sloped uphill. The girl attacked the incline, moving with very little sound through the newly fallen snow. It was light enough for Jake to see the little puffs of breath that streamed up and behind his guide. He followed easily, his strong runner's legs not tired now, as he grew ever more curious about their destination.

This they reached soon, at the crest of the second hill they climbed, where an open space admitted the full light of the moon, now sailing in a star-sprinkled sky. The snow in the small clearing had been packed down, as if someone had walked repeatedly over the space. In the middle of the clearing, a five-pointed star had been gouged into the snow pack, the points of the rough furrows ending at wooden stakes driven into the snow. The five stakes looked like torches. A circle had been scored around the star, linking each of the stakes.

Jenny stopped just outside the edge of the pentagram, waiting for Jake to catch up.

3.

The skin on Ureth's arms twitched, and she sighed with relief: the quickening had begun. *Finally*, she thought. Behind Ureth, at the summit of the hill, was the ancient Stonering. Nobody knew who had built the Ring, not even the Crones who knew all the lore of Tiramonde. It was, simply, a relic of the Old Ones who had come before. Ancient and powerful, the Ring was a hallowed place where one went to cast the most urgent spells, the spells of the Dragon. It was time. Ureth turned and started walking uphill. When she reached the top, the gusty wind died down. The monoliths stood in a perfect circle, twelve in all, joined on their top surfaces by huge lintel-stones. Each lintel-stone was curved, so that together they formed a perfectly circular bridge around the tops of the upright monoliths. In the center of the Ring, a huge granite altar lay bathed in the double moonlight, red on one half, golden yellow on the other, daring the foolhardy to tempt its power for the wrong ends.

Could she do this? Ureth shivered again. She had the right: Taumar was in peril, no matter what the rest of the Council said. She had the right, but did she have the ability? She had brought three trusted acolytes to the Stonering, novices she had mentored herself. They would do as she asked, but would they be enough? Ureth looked over to where the girls stood whispering, at a respectful distance from the altar stone. She could read their thoughts as clearly as if they were her own, and didn't need the Sight for it either. For a single member of the Council to come here in secret, with only three acolytes to help could only mean desperate need, or desperate folly. Much could go wrong. The acolytes were fearful for Ureth, and for themselves. They were afraid the spell would go awry, and possibly most of all they were afraid of getting caught. Ureth didn't blame them: she was afraid of those things too. But she had no choice: she could permit no mistakes, and no retreat.

Ureth's skin began to crawl in earnest now, as in his world Jake joined Jenny at the edge of the pentagram. The witch may be inexperienced, Ureth thought, but words have their own power, and the words Jenny had learned in her dreams from Ureth were among the most powerful of all. She approached the young women, their faces still smooth with novitiate youth, but with telltale lines around their eyes and mouths that showed their training had begun. "Thanks for being here," said Ureth. "Though they don't know it yet, the whole world owes you a debt. Please spread yourselves outside the Stonering. Engage the Perimeter of Fire. And for all our sakes let nothing escape the Ring."

But the whispering of the acolytes had already proven damaging to Ureth's plans. Ariana and Mina would not meet her gaze. However the oldest, a beautiful girl of sixteen named Naomi, who looked approximately thirty-five, spoke up: "Sister Ureth, we don't know if we should help you. Who are we to come secretly to the Stonering when even the Adept tremble to come here?" Naomi was no fool, Ureth knew. She had realized how strange this circumstance was, and how the Council would view the night's activities, though she knew nothing of what was to come.

"Naomi, we've been over this. I need your help. You are loyal, and gifted. A dreadful danger threatens us all, but the Council is blind to it, and deaf to my warnings. Even I, with all my powers, can barely sense this shadow, and everyone else basks in the sunshine of victory. But the threat is real; I feel it as I have felt nothing before. We have to act alone, because no one will believe me. We four hold the fate of the world in our hands. So please help me: if I could do it alone I would, but I can't. I especially chose you for this desperate task. Have you ever known my aim to be anything but pure?"

They had not, for Ureth had always dedicated herself to the health of the land and its people, faithful in her duty. So when the quickening came upon them also they did as she asked, despite their misgivings, and stood outside the Stonering. They conjured the Perimeter of Fire, and held their fear in check. And Ureth stood at the altar, bathed in the light of the red moon and the gold, and chanted the spell that would forever change the fate of her world.

4.

"Jenny, what is this place?" Jake was whispering, without knowing why. He pointed at the pentagram. "Did you draw this symbol? Isn't it some kind of black magic thing?"

"This is the place I was told to prepare for you, Jake. I come here sometimes, when I want to be alone. I have seen you pass by, in the night, when fear for your mother has driven you out of the house.

Tonight, though, this is more than a place of quiet. It is a place of magic, a place of power. As to whether the pentagram is for dark magic or light, symbols don't mean the same thing to everybody all the time. Your deepest wish can be granted here. I think we both know what that is. But be careful of what you wish for, and how, in case the price is higher than you want to pay." Jenny's gaze was steady, not at all like the elusive girl at school who wouldn't make eye contact. She'd just spoken to him more in the past twenty seconds than in the whole past year.

"Why are you talking so funny?" he asked. "You're saying that this place of yours can grant my deepest wish?" His skepticism was apparent, but Jenny wasn't fazed.

"I didn't say this was my place, Jake. I didn't say the magic was mine, either. I was simply told to bring you here, and that if you were brave enough your deepest wish could be fulfilled."

"What are you talking about? Who told you? Why would you do such a thing? Do you think I'm a flake too? My Mom's sick, OK? We both know I'd do anything to change that, but this… I don't see how this can help her."

Jenny remained calm in the face of his growing hostility. Her authority in fact seemed to grow every time she spoke, Jake felt with some surprise. And he was aware, too, that despite his irritation he was attracted to her; there was something about Jenny in the moonlight in the woods that was a lot more appealing than Jenny the wannabe witch in school.

"I'm doing this because I was told to do it, and when this person asks, you don't ignore her. And in return you can help your mother, if you are willing to face the risks that follow. What do you have to lose?"

It was the same question he'd asked himself. God knew he'd sacrifice his own or anybody's life to save his mother's. He'd said that aloud often enough.

"But who told you?" he insisted. Jenny gave him a keen glance, and apparently came to a decision.

"You've been having dreams, haven't you Jake? Dreams about an ugly old woman?" Jake nodded, dumfounded, as Jenny continued: "This woman needs your help. If you help her, you may be able to help your mother." Her glance softened. "Besides, you must know I care about you. And I want to help you." And she looked again like the unsure high school girl he had seen, scuttling by in the hallways, but always seeming to find his glance in the crowd. Jake realized that he had noticed her noticing him, and now felt a twinge of shame that he'd ignored her. That, he knew, would change after tonight, no matter what else happened. Secrets could make you lonely, he knew. But secrets bound people together, too, and Jake knew he'd be friendlier to Jenny now. He made up his mind.

"What do you want me to do?" he asked.

Jenny smiled, her face pretty in the moonlight. Jake wondered what it would be like to kiss her. But only briefly. She was all business again, and anyway, that wasn't why he was here.

"Stand in the middle of the circle. Don't leave it until I say!"

He did as he was told, feeling foolish. He'd better be getting back soon, before his Dad missed him. Meanwhile, from a bundle of branches piled nearby, Jenny pulled a wooden torch, about two feet long. She muttered a few words to herself. Jake stiffened. He knew without a doubt that the language, though strange, was the one the old woman used in his nightmare. He stood in the circle facing Jenny, who passed her left hand over the top of the torch and held it high above her head. For no reason that Jake could see, the top of the torch erupted in flame, orange and gold in the moonlight. Jenny lowered her hands, stretched wide apart and to her sides, until they were about shoulder level. Flame leapt from the torch she was holding to the stake closest to Jake. The top of this torch lit up also, then a line of flame danced from stake to stake, until each was alight in turn, surrounding Jake in a ring of fire, flowing around the circle, connecting the tops of the torches. Beyond the flames, Jenny thrust her own brand into the snow. The dancing ring of flame, roaring in the night, was suddenly extinguished, leaving the five torches at the points of the pentagram crackling merrily in the night. Jake caught the scent of sulfur. How had she done that?

Jenny's eyes were fixed on Jake, standing in the middle of the pentagram. She placed her palms on the front of her thighs, closed her eyes, and began to chant in the unknown language. Jake admitted to himself that he was getting a little spooked. He wasn't scared yet, of course, he was after all a karate black belt, and this was only a single girl. But his palms were becoming sweaty, as was his forehead, yet there was an icy knot in the pit of his stomach. OK, so maybe he was scared. But who wouldn't be? Perhaps he should go. Thanks Jenny, but no thanks. Moonlight rituals were not going to cure his mother. Nothing on this earth could. Yet part of him still hoped he was wrong. Jenny, entranced by her incantations, was not looking at him. Jake turned to go, but found it difficult to move. His feet seemed rooted to the ground, the cold feeling in his stomach radiating down his legs. He tried again, but it was no use. What was this? He tried to yell at Jenny, to get her to stop whatever the heck she was doing, but his voice had flown. Terror closed his windpipe and stifled anything he might have said.

As he fought for breath, a stab of lightning cleaved the clear night air directly overhead, forking into five branches that poured elemental flame into the five burning staves. The thunderclap crashed into him instantly, a torrent of sound that hurled him on his face. He lay there stunned for a few seconds, dimly aware that the smell of sulfur was stronger now. He could move his legs again, and began to crawl away from the center of the pentagram. The brands burned ever more fiercely in the night, almost as if they were alive, and for some reason he was thinking of dragons. Or rather, a single dragon, black in the night, descending upon him with outstretched claws. He heard Jenny's wild chanting, high and keening now in the sudden rush of wind that enveloped him. He didn't care what she had said; it was time to get the hell out of there.

The instant he breached the boundary of the pentagram, the sky fell in. A brilliant green light flashed through the clearing. All five staves exploded simultaneously upwards: a volley of wooden missiles from a forest silo, consumed before they reached the treetops, with only some ineffectual sparks to mourn them. Jenny was screaming: "The Dragon, the Dragon!" But he couldn't see her: everything was black, the light must have blinded him. Somehow finding his feet, he tried to run back to the edge of the clearing, but he tripped over a root and sprawled facedown. Something plucked his shoulders, and he felt himself lifted off the ground. Disconnected thoughts crowded his mind as he floundered in the snow. His earlier rage at his father had been a mistake, he saw. In fact, Dad would be a welcome sight right now. His breathing was coming in great, ragged gasps, as if he'd just run a marathon. *Mom's in a marathon now*, he thought. *And there's only one way for her to finish*. His mind going in circles, he tried to breathe, but instead fire filled his lungs, just before a great roaring filled his ears. His feet kicked wildly in mid-air. Where was the ground? He thought he would throw up. Then the whole world went dark and he felt nothing more.

Chapter 2

The Hour of Doom is drawing near, and the moon is cleft in two…

(The Q'uran)

Deep within his castle of impregnable stone, the Duke of Marfang came fully awake.

He is here.

It was a thought fully formed, as if spoken aloud, yet without meaning. Who was here? And why did the thought of this unknown presence cause an icicle of dread to form along his spine?

Coegun lay silent and still in his vast bed, waiting. His hand closed over the hilt of his sword, three feet of faithful steel that never left his side, even in bed. *Especially in bed*, he thought, and smiled grimly to himself. His eyes roamed the bedchamber, taking in stone floors and walls, with tapestries and rugs forming deeper squares of shadow in the room. Light from the torch fixed to the wall outside his room seeped under the heavy wooden door. As his eyes adjusted, they confirmed what his body already knew: he was alone.

With a fluid motion, the Duke threw off his coverlet and stood, sword in hand, naked by his bed. The faint light showed a powerful figure: tall, broad shouldered, narrow hipped, ready for any threat. What had awakened him? Had it been a dream? He closed his eyes and relaxed, searching his mind. But his sleep had been deep and dreamless, except for the echo of the idea still whispering in his mind:

He is here.

Coegun crossed the room and opened the door. His chamber was at the top of a flight of stairs, at the rear of a semi-circular landing. Three of his men guarded the landing, one awake and two asleep in shifts. The guard standing at the top of the stairs, sword in hand, whirled around as the door opened behind him. Fast as he was, the man sleeping across the threshold was faster. He was already moving as the door opened, rolling to his feet, unsheathed sword already lifting, as his companion's had been. The third guard was also upright by the time the Duke stepped through the doorway, and all four men faced each other, silent and wary as cats.

Coegun's men were all hardened soldiers, and his personal bodyguard rotated through the elite of his force. These three were especially deadly, the Duke recalled.

"Rand, did you hear anything?"

The guard still standing at the top of the stairs, to whom this question was addressed, became if anything more alert. The Duke was a formidable taskmaster, full of tricks to keep his men on their toes. He shook his head.

"No, My Lord, nothing untoward inside. There was a noise like thunder outside, a few moments before my lord opened his door. I trust your sleep was not disturbed?"

"A vain trust, as here I am." The Duke's voice was deceptively gentle. "Thunder? I didn't hear that. The sky was clear when I retired."

"As you say, My Lord. But there was a noise like thunder a few moments ago." Rand began to sweat. It was never wise to contradict the Duke, but worse to tell him what you thought he wanted to hear.

"Did you two hear anything?" Coegun asked the other guards.

"No, My Lord." They spoke in unison, not looking at Rand, unwilling to be associated with him until this unusual situation became clearer. The Duke normally retired until dawn, often alone, sometimes with a woman. Most times the woman emerged alive. But not always. The Duke had certain…moods, but that was his business. The dead ones were never missed by anybody. In any event, danger wasn't supposed to arrive from behind the door of the man they guarded.

The Duke was becoming irritated when there was a sudden commotion on the staircase below. Someone was approaching, making a great deal of deliberate noise. While still out of sight below a curve in the broad stone steps, a voice called upwards.

"Rand! Rand! It is I, Jasper! Are you awake up there? Don't run me through, you bloodthirsty wolves! Wake the Duke; I have tidings he needs to know! Do you hear me? Rand! Answer me, you rogue!"

The four men at the head of the stairs relaxed a little, and Rand permitted himself a small smile. The voice belonged, as advertised, to Jasper, the Duke's councilor. At least he would be no threat. Rand looked to the Duke.

"What are you smirking at, you fool? Answer him! Tell him to meet me in my chamber, but wait a minute until I find something to wear. If he sees me like this, he may get excited."

The three guards grinned at each other. Jasper's proclivities were well known. Though occasionally the butt of some barracks humor by the fighting men, his sexual orientation was tolerated as the price of a brilliant military mind. It had been Jasper who had devised the plan that repelled the Ice King and made the North March safe again. Jasper, too, who had advised the Duke's army to such effect against the Sacours. Though he looked ridiculous holding a sword, and would never lead men into battle, he had his place. After a suitable interval, Rand admitted him into the Duke's presence, and resumed his station outside the door.

"Well, Jasper, why are you also disturbing my sleep?" Coegun saw no need to mention his premonition. In any case, Jasper often provided answers to questions he was not asked.

"My Lord, my deepest regrets, but there is urgent news. You would berate me more if I let you sleep."

"I'll be the judge of that," growled the Duke. "Well, what is it?"

"Tonight, just a few minutes ago, a fireball plunged into the river Marfell and extinguished when it hit the water."

"You woke me to describe some astronomical disturbance? This could not wait until morning?"

"My Duke, you may not like to believe in heavenly portents, but this event may be significant. But no matter," Jasper continued hurriedly, catching Coegun's impatient glance, "As you may know, tonight both the Dragon and Warrior moons were full in the sky at the same time. And the guard who saw the fireball also saw two other things."

"Well?"

"Er…yes. The first thing was a brilliant white light around the hilltop at Stonering. I fear the Crones may have been up to something."

"Perhaps. And the other thing?"

"The other thing, Lord, and I don't know how to interpret this yet, I am merely a conduit of information-"

"And a cursedly long-winded one at that."

"Yes my Lord. I regret my failing. The guard also noticed the fireball came out of the Dragon Moon, straight out of the moon mind you, then over the Stonering, over Marfold and into the river."

He is here.

The Duke heard the words again in his mind, as if someone had spoken aloud. Who was here? What was this premonition? Alone of all the men in Taumar, Coegun possessed the Sight, a secret, among others, so far hidden from the Crones. This matter warranted investigation, it was true. And there was something else.

"Jasper, isn't my privately commissioned barge due to return tonight?"

"Yes my Lord."

"Then go and receive it at the pier. I am curious to know Scarth's version of events on the river tonight. And send the guard who made this report to me. I would question him myself. Take Rand with you. He lacks imagination, which may be helpful on such a strange night. Make haste."

"Yes, my Lord," said Jasper, as he bowed out. The Duke raised his sword. It glowed in the faint light of the torches on the balcony, fine steel, with a golden hilt, beautiful and deadly. Not a ceremonial sword, but one that had been bloodied in battle, a bane to flesh and bone. Marfang was its name, like the castle it defended, a long tooth with which to take a bite from any enemy.

He is here.

Why was he afraid?

2.

It was black and cold and wet and Jake realized he was underwater holding his breath. If he didn't breathe soon, he felt, he'd drown. He hadn't swallowed any water yet, but was extremely confused. *Where am I? Remember!* Jenny was there… a walk in the woods, a fiery pentagram, then… nothing. But he was awake again now. It didn't feel as if someone had knocked him out and dumped him in a river. He shook his head. *Death is not an option.* This had become his mantra over the past year, a pearl of stubborn courage to deny his mother's passing. He looked up and saw moonlight glimmering on the surface. He kicked upwards, the water icy against his naked skin. *Why am I naked?*

His head broke the surface, lungs devouring air. He trod water for a few moments, panting. Above him, a pale yellow moon lit a wide river, flowing past a steep hillside, crowned with trees. He turned to face the other bank, and stopped breathing. A second red moon hung low above the hills on the opposite bank. He looked frantically back and forth at the two moons, then at the sky. There were too many stars for home. Not to mention too many moons. *Where am I?* He came to the edge of panic, fought it down. There were lights on the far side of the river, the bank below the red moon. There must be a town there. Hopefully, he wouldn't get arrested when he asked for help. *Yes, ma'am, I'm naked, but I'm unarmed.* Maybe they shot first and asked questions later. But maybe they didn't have guns. That was an encouraging idea. Thoughts whirling, he started swimming towards the lights. His stroke was choppy, uneven in his disorientation, but his mind shied away from facing his sense of dislocation. That way lay madness. He put his poor form down to the cold, and the current that fought his passage. It was safer that way. Wherever he was, he couldn't stay in the middle of the freezing river. As he swam, he made out a dark shape upstream, moving towards him. It looked like a barge, like the ones he'd seen on the Thames River in London that holiday before... well, Before. In Jake's mind, time was divided into two eras: Before his mother became ill, and After. London had been Before. He and Mary had walked along the Embankment, all one golden afternoon while Dad had been at a conference. They'd walked forever through the city, it seemed, and he knew at the time he'd remember that walk for the rest of his life. It was one of those rare perfect days you get to spend with a parent. His mother, Tennessee born and raised, had met his father in London during college. Mary loved the city, probably for that reason, and knew more about the place than most natives. She had told him there weren't as many of the old barges on the busy Thames as there used to be, delighting in sharing her bits of trivia with Jake. He didn't think he'd have another day like that with her.

This barge approaching him now seemed huge from his vantage point low in the water. There were men on board, he could hear them talking, and he was relieved to discover the voices were unmistakably human. He couldn't make out the words, however. He splashed his arms in the water and cried out: "Hey! Hey! Over here! Help! In the water!"

"What in the name of The Dancer was that?" Marwyn the boatman made the warding sign against evil. It was an ominous night, with two full moons in the sky. He'd never seen such a sight. Legend said that two round moons foretold a crisis, a time for Dragons to fly. *Old wives' tale*, he told himself, but still, not a night to be afloat. The fireball had appeared suddenly from the red moon, ripping the air above Marfold before plunging into Marfell's deep waters downstream from his barge. His barge, though the owner was aboard on this trip. Marwyn did not know the nature of the cargo he was carrying, and didn't want to. He guessed it must be valuable, as it was guarded by six of the Duke's men. He also guessed it must be secret, as it was being landed under the cover of night. That by itself was enough to make anyone nervous, without omens in the sky. He did as he was told, closed his eyes when he had to, and made his livelihood. A captain's job was to guide his ship, even if it was an ungainly barge. A merchant bought and sold, and paid for services he couldn't perform himself. Though this merchant did share the voyage as a crewman, and if he had a stateroom he also took a turn at the helm when needed. Scarth the owner was indeed at the helm, and Marwyn had been readying to relieve him, so as to bring the heavy barge alongside the pier, when fire had torn the air with red light and thunder.

"Did you hear a splash, Master?" asked the boatman.

"No, Marwyn, but I was too startled by that flash to notice. Did you hear one?"

"Not then. But I hear several now. Sounds like they're coming from dead ahead. Let me have the helm, I'll turn us so we drift more slowly. The men will have to pull to make it back upstream to the pier, but it can't be helped."

Scarth relinquished the tiller, and the massive barge, abeam to the flow, slowed perceptibly. All the crew could hear Jake's shouts now, and even those who had been below, and so missed the fireball, made the warding sign when they heard his voice from the water. Everyone knew not to swim the Marfell here, so close to the legendary prison of the dragon.

Jake saw the barge turn, and swam towards the dark hulk, his stroke more even now that rescue was at hand. A thick line snaked down into the water as he approached the side, and he caught it as it floated nearby. The rope felt fine and silky in his hands, not the coarse painter he had expected. But he was glad to get out of the cold water, despite his nakedness, and the strange softness of the rope. He began to rethink his relief as he began climbing up the side of the barge. The air was much colder than the water, and he was shivering uncontrollably as he clambered over the gunwale. Several men stood around him in the dark. Some were muttering to one another in a language he didn't understand. Nobody looked very friendly. One man, wearing a fur coat, offered him a blanket, which he wrapped around himself, eyes darting from face to unsmiling face.

"Thanks, M-m-mister," stuttered Jake. "I don't know where I am. Do you have a phone? Does anyone speak English?" *Idiot! Stop babbling!* He had no idea what to expect, but was still completely taken by surprise when a man standing next to fur-coat pulled a sword from somewhere, and, hissing a string of unintelligible but unmistakably venomous words, pressed its point against his throat.

3.

Life gradually seeped back to Ureth's stunned senses, and awareness returned. The cold grass pricked her naked body where she lay facedown in the middle of the Ring. *Why am I naked?* Her thoughts echoed those of Jake's. The acrid scent of charred cloth gave her understanding: the Dragonfire had burned her clothes away. She was naked, and glad to be so. She felt pure, and cleansed by fire. She sat up.

The wind breathed over the high grass and she shivered, though she had long since inured herself to physical discomforts. It was still night, but dawn could not be far off. She searched her memory, trying to piece events together. She had sung to the Dragon Moon, and asked for the means to awaken the Dragon, to deliver the Pendraig, a feat that no Crone had ever dared before. But she was alone on the hilltop. What had happened?

The incantation had begun well, she remembered. The words, memorized in the hope they would never be uttered, spilled out of Ureth at first like a routine spell of the sort used to light a campfire, on a rainy evening far from home. But then a vibration entered the air, a magic outside the words, intruding into the ritual. The Dragon Moon shone brighter, until it was almost scarlet, and the Warrior moon dimmed in turn, as if awed by the majesty of its partner. The Perimeter of Fire became a roaring torrent of white flame, and the three acolytes trembled with a nameless fear that demanded they run away and hide. But they stayed, their love for Ureth and for Tiramonde buttressing their Craft, and the Perimeter held, for a time.

The Fruit Of The Dendragon Tree

Ureth had continued the chant, which was the prayer for the Pendraig, the Deliverer of Tiramonde, the request which she made alone, with no authority save her love of justice. But the magic flowed too strong even for her, the most adept of her kind. Little wonder: it was the most pure of the Dragon spells; it desired the Dragon's freedom, and the plunging of the kingdom into chaos.

Why did she choose chaos? In the dark years that followed Ureth often asked herself that question. But she remained ever convinced that the price of her choice, given the alternative, was worth it in the end. So she summoned the power of the Dragon. It flowed through her, and the ecstasy was so profound that the long years of discipline were all worthwhile for the incandescent moment when the Flame touched her soul. The Dragonfire pulsed and writhed like a living thing through her breasts and her loins, and she gasped and shuddered in pleasure and in pain, yet stayed the course of her chanting. The acolytes, however, were not so strong. As the prayer ended, a final pulse of magic caused their Perimeter to flare. Their Craft was not enough to hold it, and Ariana and Mina, already doubtful of their task, broke off in terror and fell to the ground. Naomi stood a moment more, but couldn't hold the Perimeter on her own, and was overwhelmed as the Dragonfire sought her out. The Perimeter failed, and a ball of crimson flame roared at them from the Dragon moon, passing overhead with a thunderclap that pinned Ureth and her acolytes senseless to the ground.

Had they failed? No, Ureth thought: the Dragon Moon *had* answered, she was sure of it. She remembered the ecstatic power flaming in her mind, in her heart, and even in her loins, which as a Crone she ritually ignored, but as a woman could never totally forget. The lift of great wings, the breath of flame, had poured through her for an instant, and she had soared as an ember from an open fire, to spend herself like ash in the darkness.

In that moment she had felt no bounds to her powers of creation or destruction. Not a sense of intelligence, or of magic, or of physical strength. Rather a fountain of angry, ruthless joy of being alive, an unapologetic fact of vigorous existence in a sea of timidity and inhibition. It was the consciousness of the Dragon. So it was to fly, and breathe fire at the stars while a moon named for you reflected your glory over the whole world. How contemptible to be human, to tread cold earth on slow legs, to grope for gold, to mate, to die toothless and alone, while grasping for an impossibly elusive power over an inevitable death. Ureth had felt the Dragon's power, and she knew with a desolate sense of loss that she would never again be as she was before drinking at that wellspring of life.

She looked up. The red glow of the setting Dragon Moon cast hints of pale blood about the Stonering. The grass was burned where she stood, and her clothes were gone, but her body was unmarked. Her acolytes had vanished. The wind whistled through the huge stones, an echo of Ureth's desolation. She sighed. She needed to find the acolytes, to calm their fear before they blurted to the Council what they had witnessed.

With a small groan she stood, looking for the girls' footprints. Outside the stones nearest to the castle, three sets of tracks converged and pointed the way back home. They could have returned by now: Ureth had no idea how long she'd been senseless. But perhaps she could overtake them. She sent an inquiring thought down the hill, along the path revealed by the bent grass. Yes, there they were, three quivering psyches radiating fear like a beacon in the night: a novice could have found them. Ureth suddenly had no doubt she could catch them. Some ember of the Dragon's touch flared in her soul, and rushed down the hill, a breath of flame in pursuit of her sisters. In her mind, she became the north wind, fleet, cold and unwelcome. *Wait for me girls*, she thought with a grim smile. *Wait for Ureth*. She blew away down the hill, so intent on being the wind that she never noticed her flying feet: not bending the stems of grass, but burning their tips as she sprinted downwards. Nor did she notice that she was warm now, with a heat that was not completely her own.

Chapter 3

If the eye could see the demons that people the universe, existence would be impossible.

(Talmud, Berakhot 6)

"That's enough, Marwyn." Scarth's voice rumbled out of his barrel chest, through the fur coat he wore. He was a big bear of a man, and his deep voice was one other men would instinctively obey.

Marwyn was loyal to Scarth, had served him as a soldier, now as the captain of his river fleet. But a superstitious dread had seized him when Jake had spoken. A man, using the language of the Crones! Coegun's law spelled death for any who spoke their tongue, and with reason. Who knew with what magic a man might be tainted, who knew enough about Crones to talk to them? "This lad might know enough magic to turn us all into toads!" he cried. The men clustered around muttered agreement.

"Think, Marwyn," replied Scarth. "If the boy could do that, you'd be croaking by now!" The men chuckled, and Marwyn, feeling slightly foolish, removed the point of his sword from the boy's throat. A small ruby of blood welled up from where the sharp steel had nicked Jake's neck. Marwyn kept his blade raised, however, and without moving his eyes, spoke to Scarth. "Master, you pay me to be careful. There are two full moons in the sky, for the first time in a thousand years. A fireball, hurled from the Dragon Moon, has crashed into Marfell. And then we find a strange young man swimming naked in the river at midnight. And he speaks the tongue of the Crones!" He spat, to ward off magic. "So forgive my itchy sword hand, but I say kill him now."

The men murmured their agreement once more. "Marwyn is right, Master," said one. "This is an ill-omened night. The boy could be an evil sorcerer come to plague us. And the law says-"

"I am the law on this boat, gentlemen," said Scarth. "And my first duty is to the king's laws, not Coegun's. I will not make an ill-omened night more so by spilling the blood of an unarmed boy on the deck of my ship. Look at him, naked and afraid! What sorcerer would place himself at such a disadvantage? I grant you it's a strange night. But this boy is no danger to us. Do we kill him because of how he speaks? If he only knows the Crone's speech, then we will have one of them ask him his business. But we will not murder him. Sheath your sword, Marwyn, that's the end of it!"

Marwyn obeyed. But as he did so, one of the armed men standing near Jake spoke up. He was a tall, well-made man, with a dark cloak, fastened at the left shoulder by a metal brooch that glinted in the moonlight. Jake couldn't see that the brooch, wrought out of red gold, was fashioned in the likeness of a dragon, writhing on its back underneath a castle. It was the insignia of the Castleguard, the Duke's elite troops, men of noble birth and skill at arms. "My master will be interested to hear your opinion of his laws, Mister Scarth," said the man. "What will you do with this boy after we land? Surely you will allow me to bring him to the Duke?"

Scarth looked at the Duke's man, who had been sent to oversee the safe delivery of the cargo. Despite his silky speech, Scarth knew that, as a member of the Castleguard, such a man was a formidable warrior. But he wasn't going to surrender his catch so easily. The law was on his side, and he still had one or two friends in high places, who remembered his own abilities as a fighting man. He did business for Coegun now, but that didn't mean he trusted him. Scarth had a strong premonition that this boy's life would be very short if he handed him to Coegun. And for some reason that he didn't understand, Scarth was feeling protective of the lad, still shivering on the deck.

"No, my Lord," Scarth replied. "Any salvage is mine, by law of the King. The boy will stay with me as my guest. But be assured I shall escort him to your master to pay his respects when he has rested."

But the noble would not let go so easily, though his voice remained soft. "The salvage is the Duke's, Mr. Scarth. You are on his commission, and any salvage is thereby his to receive. I again request that you allow the boy to accompany me when I disembark, and I will secure him an audience with the Duke myself."

Behind the polite words, Scarth knew, lay a formidable challenge. For the request implied a command from the Duke himself, and Coegun's commands were not lightly ignored. But he would not be cowed on the deck of his own ship, where by law only the king could overrule him. "Sir, I agreed to deliver cargo for the Duke. And this I am doing faithfully. But the vessel is mine, the river belongs to Taumar, not Marfang, and any salvage is therefore mine unless the king wishes it otherwise. By that law, this lad is now my guest, and I intend to make him comfortable." So saying, Scarth removed his heavy fur coat and wrapped it around Jake's shaking frame, over the wet blanket. Then, speaking to a couple of his own men-at-arms, he said: "Take him below, to my cabin, where he can rest until we land. I claim him as my salvage. I will gladly surrender him," he said, bowing to the nobleman, "If the King's Council orders me to do so. Until then, he remains in my care." And with these deft words, Scarth knew he had bought some time, but he also knew that Coegun was now an enemy. And unless he was very, very careful in future, the boy's life was not the only one in jeopardy.

Jake hadn't followed any of this dialogue. The language sounded vaguely Scottish to him, but none of the words made sense. When the man had pulled the sword on him, he'd been terrified. Marwyn had moved so fast. But the big man who had given him the coat had obviously told the swordsman not to harm him. However, he didn't need to speak the language to see that the dangerous-looking man with the brooch on his cloak looked murderous. Who or what did they think he was? More to the point, who or what were they? *Just where the hell am I?* His brain felt as if it was freewheeling out of control, like a truck with no brakes careening downhill under a load of fear it couldn't handle. Maybe the whole thing was a bad dream. But he felt the cold keenly enough, and was embarrassed by his nakedness in front of these rough, unknown men. He had no more time to think, however. At a few words from the bearded man in charge, two of the hands began to lead him below. At the hatchway to the lower deck, Jake turned to look at Scarth, knowing that he owed the big man a debt: quite probably his life. He drew a ragged breath.

"Thank you, sir," he said, his voice shaky. "Thank you."

There was a pause while Scarth gave him a keen glance from under bushy black eyebrows. Jake received the distinct impression he'd been understood. Finally, Scarth inclined his head in the briefest of nods. But he made no reply, in his or any other language.

Jake allowed himself to be led down a short, steep staircase to a narrow passage below-deck. It was much warmer below. Oil lanterns in wall sconces lighted the passage. His guards led Jake aft, passing several solid-looking wooden doors on either side. One of the guards opened the door at the very end of the passage and motioned Jake inside. Jake entered the cabin, illuminated by an oil lantern on a small table in the middle of the room. A large chest lay on the floor underneath an oval porthole. A small cot, neatly made, stood against the starboard bulkhead. There was no other furniture in the room.

His guards left, and Jake sat on the bunk. A pleasant aroma like sandalwood emanated from somewhere, but did nothing to quell his fears. *Mom, where are you? I need you! I want to come home!* It had been a long time since Jake had let himself need his Mom. *Dad?* Jake suddenly ached for his father. What would Dad do? He could hear him now: "Make a plan if you can. If you can't, relax until you know enough to do so." *Good advice, Dad, but what do you do if you don't know anything?* Nothing made sense. He wasn't dreaming, but how could this be real? Completely bewildered, he unconsciously did the most practical thing possible. He dropped the damp blanket on the floor, lay on the bunk, pulled the fur coat more tightly around him, and aided by fatigue, shock and disorientation, escaped into sleep.

2.

"I can't believe you were so reckless!" It was the Mother speaking, Marah the chief Crone, and she was furious. Naomi looked on, trying not to be noticed. They were in the Council Chamber, the apex of the tower that housed the Coven. The Mother was a tiny woman who barely reached Ureth's chin. Wrinkled and stooped, her plain black robe hung loosely to the stone floor on her bony frame. The robe had a broad hood, cast back to reveal Marah's silver hair, and was gathered at the waist with a rope belt, from which hung a small leather pouch. In her left hand she held a gnarled wooden staff, dark with age. She looked like a market beggar woman, but Naomi had long since learned to discount physical appearances, especially amongst the Sisterhood. This was only the second time she had been this close to the Mother. She shivered, remembering the first time Marah's eyes had searched her own, looking for any sign of the Gift. She had felt her soul laid bare on that occasion, and Marah had only been giving a cool, detached assessment. Now she was angry, and Naomi prayed to the Dancer that she would escape close scrutiny. The aura of the Mother's power filled the room like a living, breathing presence, seeming to compete for air in the close quarters of the chamber. Naomi wanted to cry, to confess, but to what she didn't know. She wanted to look down, but against her will her eyes were locked on the Mother's, pinioned by her gaze, and thus she waited for the storm to pass.

Marah's costume was unadorned, but its very color proclaimed her rank: only the Mother, First of the Council, could wear the black robe. The acolytes wore shorter, sleeveless red tunics, shapeless burlap bags that hid their aging figures. Those who had suffered the rites of passage, and attained the ability to tap into the Sight at will, wore white robes and were addressed as "Sister." Sister Ureth was one of these.

But Ureth was also one of only five Crones, including the Mother, admitted to the Council. The four other Council members, known behind their backs as the "Aunts," typically wore blue robes, and were women of varied and profound powers.

The three other Aunts were seated at a small table behind the Mother, against the far wall of the small room, staring at Ureth. The tall one on the right was Sister Hane, who could understand the thought of any animal or bird, and subdue it to her will. The short one in the middle, Sister Elbeth, for all her pleasing plumpness, could achieve the same effect with humans. Sister Rathe, pink-faced and gray-eyed, was a Healer, and conversed with the Dead during their voyages beyond the stars. Many a wounded soldier owed his life to this woman, sitting with sedate dignity on her hard wooden chair. But none of the other Aunts could match the sheer power of Ureth, still naked and mud-stained, standing defiantly in the middle of the chamber. Ureth was the Fire-Wielder, the Destroyer. She could summon lightning from the summer sky, and cleave the ground upon which one stood. And she could do everything the other Aunts could do too. She had been, at least until this night, the apparent successor to the Mother's black robe. For the Mother needed to be adept at all the skills of the Gift, though not necessarily to the level that each of her lieutenants possessed within her own specialty. Of course, all the Crones, even the acolytes, possessed the Sight Premonitory, the ability to envision potential future events and, if possible, thwart or prepare for those that would be most catastrophic. It was the presence of the Sight, even if raw and untutored, that marked them in the beginning from other little girls and brought them to this place. But the Sight was only the first Gift; Naomi, who knew she did not yet possess the skill to light a campfire in the rain, shivered at the power in the room, and stayed silent.

"How could you be so…arrogant?" Marah nearly spit the word. "The Pendraig is not something you call on a whim! We have vowed never to call him, unless the whole world was in dire peril, and the whole Council united to bring him from the Dragon Moon!"

The Fruit Of The Dendragon Tree

"But Tiramonde is in peril!" cried Ureth. "More peril than has ever been known. And this Council," she waved a contemptuous hand, "will never agree to any course of action that I propose, simply because it is I who propose it!"

"And why is that, do you think?" Marah had recovered some of her composure. "You are headstrong and impulsive and rash. Taumar is at peace. Our borders are more secure than they have been in a generation. The people have enough to eat. Trade is stronger than ever. What in this causes you concern? The Dancer alone knows what disruption you may have caused tonight."

"I may be stubborn, Mother, but I am not rash, nor did I act without thinking. I have never felt such a sense of danger to Taumar, to Tiramonde, as I do now. I cannot say why, at least not in a way that will sound convincing. But when have we ever been able to explain our intuitions to the skeptical? If I cannot gain consensus in our Council, is it truly because I am impulsive, or because I breed jealousy?"

Marah paused before answering. Ureth had touched a nerve with her colleagues, she saw. Sister Hane in particular was struggling to contain herself. And, truly, at least some of the antagonism Hane bore to Ureth was due to jealousy, from which destructive emotion Marah knew even the Crones could suffer. Nobody of Ureth's age had ever been so advanced in her training and skill, let alone possessed a seat on the Council. Ureth had been invited to join as the Fire-Wielder, for that was what was needed when Marah had donned the black robe, assuming the weight of leadership when her predecessor had gone to her dance behind the stars. But Ureth had been chosen as the new Fire-Wielder barely two years after first joining the Coven, an unheard-of rate of progress. But she could have taken anybody else's spot on the Council by then as well, and everyone knew it. Ureth could tame a wild bear with a gentle word, and heal a sword thrust with a touch. As for her suggestive powers, it had been comical to watch when, for play as an acolyte, she induced Coegun's soldiers to obvious infatuation with her old woman's body. But such mischief was frowned upon once the red tunic was turned in for the white robe, let alone the blue of the

Council. So it was true, Ureth, possessing so many gifts, did threaten her colleagues, who each struggled to master just one. It was almost as if the Coven offered Ureth too small a scope, which was a sobering thought, for in all Tiramonde where else could she go?

"Ureth," the Mother's voice was gentle. "You are the most powerful among us. Who can deny it? But power without discipline merely leads to the evil you say you wish to avoid. We have rules to protect ourselves. We have rules to protect the kingdom of Taumar, and the larger world of Tiramonde. Our rules even protect you, powerful as you are. Tell me truly, were you not overcome tonight?"

Naomi stole a glance at Ureth's face. Their eyes met, remembering. The blaze of flame had coursed around the Stonering, rendering Naomi and the other two acolytes breathless. Naomi had been terrified. The flames had been reaching for her, licking greedily at her scanty garment, when she cried out and fell to the ground, breaking the Perimeter of Fire. With the Perimeter broken, a river of flame had cascaded into Ureth. In the flash before she lost consciousness, Naomi had seen her mentor's form jerking spasmodically in the fire, and believed her dead. After the fireball had passed, the three acolytes, not daring to enter the Ring, had gathered together in terrified silence. They had gazed at each other in mute horror for what seemed like minutes, but in reality could only have been a few seconds, when, with one unspoken agreement, they had turned and fled down the hill towards home.

The wild run down the hillside had been torture, every inhaled breath a flame, each footfall a shard of glass into the belly. But fear was a sharper goad, and on they ran. They were almost at the secret door to the Coven when Ureth's voice had snaked over them from behind.

"Stop, you fools," she'd hissed, and Naomi had looked behind to see a naked demon woman, hair streaming behind her, feet flaming where they brushed the grass. She screamed, trying to run faster, but to no avail. Ureth had caught her easily, grabbing Naomi by the shoulder with fingers as hot as tongs. She had cast her acolyte to the ground, and tripped in turn the other two who also ran gibbering in their fear, all reason and training vanquished that night of the Dragon.

"Naomi! Mina! Ariana! Stop! It is I, Ureth! We need to speak together. For the Dancer's sake, be still and listen! This is no time for blubbering!" Ureth helped Naomi to her feet, scraped and bruised but none the worse for wear.

"Sister Ureth, where are your clothes?" Naomi used the formal tone address, and Ureth nodded with satisfaction. Good. They hadn't meant to abandon her. They were simply scared. Perhaps all was not yet lost.

"The Dragon burned my clothes, Naomi, as he has burned me, though no mark on my body would tell you so. I fear because the Ring broke," a glare at Ariana and Mina, who could not hold her gaze "that he has not answered my call, but we need to speak before we return to cloisters."

"I think you have spoken enough with these children for one night, Sister Ureth." The disembodied voice came out of the night, quivering with restrained anger, and something else.

"Mother Marah!" The three acolytes dropped to their knees, foreheads to the ground, in the salute for the Mother.

"Get up!" said Marah. "Get up and come with me, you foolish girls. You too, Ureth, you have some explaining to do."

Naomi and her companions had been escorted home in silence, back through the dark orchard, silvered with frost, through the secret underground tunnel to the stone tower they called home. In silence, they followed Marah to the Council Chamber, where the other Aunts were already waiting. When they arrived in the Mother's chamber, Ariana and Mina exchanged sidelong glances with Naomi, as if for moral support, but it quickly became evident that they were not the focus of the Mother's attention. That honor was reserved for Ureth, and now they neared the heart of the matter.

"Was I overcome?" Ureth repeated the question. Suddenly, all her pride left her. She looked down, and her shoulders slumped. When she spoke again, it was in a much more subdued tone. "Yes, Mother. I was overcome by the Dragon's breath. My clothes were scorched from my body, and my senses scorched as well. I was lost in his fire, and my thoughts left me. I awoke naked and alone in the Ring. Alone, I say," and here she looked at the Mother. "Alone, and therein lies the proof of my failure. For although against your command, and the wishes of the Council, I uttered the spell to summon the Pendraig, he did not come. I felt the power of the Dragon burn through me like a flame, but when I awoke, I was alone."

The room was quiet. Naomi was stunned. Ureth had attempted that? Calling on the Dragon essentially by herself, with only three acolytes to help her? No wonder she had sworn them all to secrecy! Sister Hane looked as if she wanted to strangle Ureth. An ember fell in the grate. Through the small window, Naomi could see the first blush of dawn in the night sky. Time for chores, soon, she thought, resignedly.

Finally, the Mother spoke. "Leave us Sisters, Daughters," she said. "It has been a trying night. There is much to think about. Daughter Naomi, Daughter Ariana, Daughter Mina, you are charged to tell no one what happened this night, nor what you have heard of Ureth's folly in this chamber. Council Sisters, thank you for your attention. I will speak now with Ureth in private."

Naomi could scarcely believe her ears. Ureth had attempted to dare the most serious taboo of the Coven and here was the Mother, not even giving them a slap on the wrist. It was true they'd been tricked into helping, but this was not the outcome Naomi had been expecting. Naomi would have thought that a week of solitary confinement with no food or water would have been just the starting point. A covert glance showed the other acolytes and Council members thought so too. Sister Elbeth looked as if she was about to burst. Sister Hane, last to leave, started to say something, but a stern glance from the Mother quelled her objection, and she trooped out into the corridor with the rest, shutting the door behind her.

Ureth was now alone with the Mother. Weak with relief, Naomi felt a twinge of sympathy for her erstwhile heroine. But this was quickly replaced by a searing anger that she and the others had been used in Ureth's designs. Once back in her cell, Naomi lit a small forbidden candle, a stub of wax, that she had hidden under her bed pad.

The Fruit Of The Dendragon Tree

The acolytes were not allowed candles, or baths. Oh, Dancer! What she would give for a bath! Her only compensation was that the wrinkled skin of a Crone retained no odor, so she never stank. Naomi had been discovered late by the Coven. Indeed, she was almost too old to be an acolyte, and her skin had not yet acquired the gnarly quality of her peers'. The candle was a forbidden indulgence, but Naomi was a rebel. She lay on her straw pallet and tried to compose her mind.

Most young women of her age would be getting married and having babies. Some might be artisans, merchants. Some, high born like herself, would have even larger responsibilities, and the freedom to come and go as and with whom they pleased. There had been a boy, not all that long ago, who had looked at Naomi with longing, and picked apples for her from his father's orchards. He rode a beautiful gray mare because his father was a wealthy nobleman. But one night Naomi had dreamed the mare died, and then it did. And she had told the boy about the dream before the fact. He became fearful, and the Crones had come, and not even her family's position could stop them. Now here she was, bound by a grinding discipline, learning humility the hard way, for she had led an indulged life. It was not so strange, therefore, that when Ureth had befriended her, and recruited her for her secret plans, that she was grateful and flattered for the attention. She felt appropriately exalted, as if she had recaptured some of her lost status. Naomi had tried to believe she had acted to save Tiramonde, but deep down she really knew that all she wanted was to feel special again. It had sounded grand, the way Ureth had inspired them: only a chosen few with the courage to act decisively! About what, had never been made clear. A moonlight escape, and a secret incantation at a sacred place: but things had never seemed right, and everybody had been scared, even Ureth, she now saw, and then the fire had come, and she simply couldn't hold on to the Perimeter alone. Her terror had overcome her, and Ureth's plan, whatever it was, had been foiled. And, worst of all, they had been caught. She had to leave: being a Crone wasn't for her. But how? She dreaded the muted existence of a woman stripped of her gift. Naomi began to cry silently in the dark, an island of self-pity in a cell of cold, indifferent stone.

3.

For a time I lay in the dark, cradling my sadness. The fire had become low embers in the hearth and the room was warm. Outside, the wind had died and the moon peered in, its soft white rays reflecting through the windows from the undulating blanket of snow outside. I had heard Jake leave the house but hadn't heard him return, and that was troubling. Without warning, I felt that tidal surge of love, mingled with worry, that often accompanied my thoughts about Jake. I knew about his late-night rambles, and I hadn't interfered: the boy needed to let off steam. His mother was dying, possibly by becoming a mother. Doctors had warned us of this, given that her family was rife with Breast Cancer: mother, grandmother, sister. We'd learned that high estrogen levels were a big risk to such people, and pregnancy sends your estrogen levels through the roof. But Mary had wanted a child, her child, more than anything, and I could never refuse her when she had her heart set on something. We'd wanted more kids, but even one had been a risk, and now her doctors said she'd be dead in a few days at most. Doctors. They knew nothing helpful.

They'd been sympathetic enough when I asked to bring her home, to meet Death on something resembling her own terms. They'd seen it all before, and would again. It's a hell of a thing to speak dispassionately to people who are going to die, to speak with their families about expectations and the degree of heroism everybody wants to use to delay the inevitable. It's the hardest part of their job, I would suppose. No wonder half of them turned to drink or drugs. But nobody really knew what was going to happen to Mary, or when, but they gave odds as if they were bookies. And we'll try to skew the odds in her favor as much as we can, David, but there's really only so much we can do, and you should know that.

I looked at my watch. It was nearly 2 a.m. I must have fallen asleep and Jake had come home without me hearing him. I'd better go and see check. It wouldn't hurt to stick my head around Mary's door, either, though the monitor would have alerted me if anything had changed. I'd moved out of the Master bedroom; that place where we'd had so much happiness was now where Mary waited to die. I'd moved to the guestroom, but usually slept on the sofa in the family room downstairs. That is, if one counted three or four restless hours of tossing as sleep.

Mary's night-light was on, casting a dim yellow glow near the bed. The chair where Meg sometimes slept looked inviting, maybe I should stay here for the rest of the night. My wife slept with difficulty, needing increasingly high doses of morphine to make her comfortable. Her body was so ravaged by surgery and disease that she didn't look anything now like the beautiful woman I'd married. Unable to eat, she was gaunt, with large black circles in the ever-deepening hollows of her eyes. She didn't bother with her wig anymore and the thin stubble of hair that remained on her scalp looked like a cornfield after harvest. I'd loved Mary's hair. When it all fell out, it had been as if Death had come early to a party and left a calling card to say he'd be back. Events had proved my premonition correct: Mary always said I was more intuitive than I allowed myself to be, but who wants to be right about stuff like that?

Soon it would just be Jake and me. Somehow, we both had to come to grips with that. I knew he thought I was giving up on his Mum too early and I just didn't see how she could survive. I'd never managed the easy closeness with Jake that Mary had. Perhaps it was because I'd always worried that having kids might be a bad idea for her. Mary had loved Jake passionately from before he was born, while I was busy being afraid for both of them.

Jake was a special kid. I often felt ready to burst with love and pride when I was around him. He was smart, athletic, and a good person, but I probably didn't tell him that often enough. I'm not a demonstrative man by nature, but I'd always been sure my son knew I loved him. Maybe he didn't. Maybe I'd have to change, perhaps arrange some counseling after Mary – well, afterwards. Yes, that would probably be a sensible thing to do. Staying sensible in a crisis, in my English-tinged family, was a prized attribute. Stiff upper lip, and all that. What bullshit. Bullshit: what a great American word. So many ways to say it, so few times I could do as I wanted. I wanted to scream "Bullshit!" at the top of my lungs at half my students, whining about grades as my wife kept dying. I had to keep working though; this was America, where health care was only as good as your insurance or your bank balance. And cancer was expensive. Actually, work gave me something to keep my mind from dwelling on Mary's situation, while she clung to life with a tenacity that had surprised everyone except Jake. She was never going to be well again, so why did I feel such guilt when I prayed for her peaceful end? Yes, counseling would be a good idea, for me as much as anyone.

This small decision made, my despair lessened somewhat. From the door, I could see Mary's head on the pillow, eyes closed. Her breathing was quiet, but steady. I'd sit with her once I checked on Jake. I pulled the door to, and padded down the hall to his room. The bed was made for once, though the rest of the room was a shambles, and the computer was on. Jake wasn't there. So he hadn't come back home unnoticed after all. He'd never been out quite this late before. I noticed his window was open. That was strange. The half-open blinds rattled faintly in the intermittent breeze. The snowstorm had stopped, and the moon shone from a clear sky into my son's room, augmenting the glow cast by the computer monitor.

I crossed to the window and looked out. The automatic outdoor lights were on; someone must have triggered them within the last ten minutes, which was how long they stayed on: Elementary, my dear Watson. I saw a set of footprints in the snow outside, leading up to the house just below me.

From there, these footprints led over to the kitchen door, which opened onto the back yard. These two sets of prints in turn led straight across the back yard, to the woods at the rear of our house. So did someone come to get Jake? And did Jake then leave with them to go for a midnight jaunt in the woods without telling me? Holmes, you're a genius. But why had he gone off like that? As if we didn't have enough to worry about, without him running around in the middle of the night with some unknown person. Up till now, he'd always let me know when he was out by himself. I could feel my irritation building again. I loved my son dearly, but often didn't understand him. I knew I'd better start soon, though. Because the day I'd be his only parent was not far off, and his mother wouldn't be there to buffer our mutual exasperation. I closed the window, my heart racing with the gut-wrenching anxiety that only comes to parents who don't know where their children are, and wondered what to do next.

I'd just decided to call the police when the doorbell rang. He must have forgotten his key. The breath I didn't realize I'd been holding came out in an audible gasp of relief. *Thank you, God. I'm going to kill him.*

With these two conflicting thoughts sparring in my brain I ran downstairs as quietly as I could.

Chapter 4

Those who verily depart from this world, to the moon, in truth, they all go.

(Kaushitaki Upanishad)

The lantern still burned on the trunk, and in its low light Jake retrieved his scattered thoughts, shepherding them home from the edge of insanity. He hadn't been awake long. When he'd first opened his eyes, his first thought was: *Wow! What a crazy dream!* But then he realized he wasn't at home. His own bed was large, with a soft mattress and a duvet. This berth was hard, narrow, and higher off the ground than he was used to, very different from his, but very tangible. When he sat up and dangled his long legs over the side, his feet didn't touch the floor. He was completely naked as well, and that wasn't how he usually went to bed. And as the large fur coat that warmed him slid from his shoulders he fully remembered that wherever he was, it was far from home. He found it hard to breathe, and bit his lip to stop himself from crying. The pain steadied him

So where was he? What had happened to him? And, most disturbingly, why had people wanted to kill him on sight? His mind veered once more to the edge of panic, and he bit his lip harder, drawing blood. As far as he could tell, everything around him was real. Those men on deck had been real, too, and so had the sword. Gingerly, he felt his throat where the sword point had nicked his skin. Yes, it was still sore. So how had he gotten here? He'd gone out into the woods with Jenny. He remembered the fire, and shuddered. He'd been terrified, but of what he couldn't say. There had been something else there in the clearing, more than just the fire. What had she been screaming? "The Dragon!" What did that mean? And now, suddenly, here he was, wherever here was. He shook his head. *Don't lose it now, dude. At least fur-coat hadn't wanted you hurt. Better stay on his good side, because some of those other guys really don't like you, for some reason.* Encouraged by the fact of stringing together three coherent sentences in his mind, he felt a bit more calm and began to take stock of his surroundings.

Water lapped outside his cabin bulkhead, but the barge was not moving. Over the faint smell of the river came the pleasant scent he had noticed when he first came below. Above, he could hear men's voices, and the sounds of heavy loads being shifted. *Dad, I hope you aren't too worried about me; I'm fine, at least I think I am. Better not tell Mom I'm gone, though, she doesn't need that, especially now. I'll try to get back home somehow, as soon as I can.* But he had to admit he had no clue how that was going to happen. *How do I get back home from here, when I don't know where here is?* He felt ill. The cabin door opened, and the big man who had loaned Jake his coat stood in the door, holding a bundle of cloth. He said something unintelligible. When Jake did not answer, he looked annoyed, and repeated the phrase sharply, beckoning the boy towards him.

"I don't understand," said Jake. "Do you want me to come with you? I don't have any clothes."

"Wear these. Give back coat," said Scarth, tossing Jake the bundle he'd been carrying. When Jake unfolded this, he found a long-sleeved, dark green fleecy tunic and matching leggings. The outfit was a little like a sweatshirt and pants, although the tunic came almost to his knees and the leggings, with no elastic waistband, had to be held up with a length of rope that passed through loops of cloth sewn into the waist. There was no footwear. The man looked away modestly while Jake dressed, and Jake was nearly ready before he realized that he'd understood him.

"You speak English!" Jake was so excited by this that he took a couple of steps towards his rescuer, only to see the man's hand flash to his sword hilt and half pull the blade from the scabbard. The boy stopped short. *Man, everybody is so jumpy here.* There was a brief silence, as the man looked him over. Jake had seen that exact look on doctors' faces when dad asked them difficult questions about his mother's condition. He suddenly realized he would have given anything to have his father with him at that moment.

"Speak…Crone, yes," Scarth whispered. "Daughter teach. You meet her soon, I think. I Scarth. You?"

"I Jake, I mean, I'm Jake, my name's Jake". *Stop babbling, moron. He's a guy with a sword, not some girl you're asking to dance.*

"Jake. Good. You talk not. No more talk. You tell not I speak… Crone. We make understanding? Finish clothing. You come me now."

But Jake couldn't stop his questions as he finished pulling on the warm clothes. They were a little big for him, but not too bad, he thought. "You don't want anyone to know you can speak to me, is that it? How come? Man, I'm going to look like Robin Hood in these! Is it a crime to speak English around here? Are we in Quebec? But no, you guys aren't speaking French. So where are we? Do you have a cell phone?" The stream of questions threatened to become a flood, but Scarth held up his hand, a thunderous look on his face, and Jake checked himself. The face behind the hand was dead serious, the eyes cold, and Jake noticed the sword was still half out of its scabbard.

"You deaf? I say no more talk!" Scarth was still whispering, but he answered at least one of Jake's questions. "Is…crime, yes, for me speak like you. Crime for you too. Keep quiet. Let Scarth talk. Stay by me. Life or death you listen. Understanding?"

Jake nodded. Scarth pierced him with another glance from his black eyes, drew a deep breath, and nodded in turn. He picked up his coat from the floor where Jake had dropped it in his haste to change, and put it on. The heavy fur made him look even more bulky, and he seemed to fill the small space. "Come," he said softly, and left the cabin.

The Fruit Of The Dendragon Tree

Jake followed, the wooden floor cool under his bare feet, trailing Scarth down the passage. He thought again of his father, how he would worry when he found him gone. "We may only have each other, soon," he whispered to himself, as his father had done. But unlike David, he pushed that thought away. His mother wasn't dead yet, and wouldn't be, if Jake could help it. This place, wherever it was, was somehow mixed up with that desire. Maybe there was a way here to save his mother's life. Wasn't that what he had asked for?

He climbed the steep stairs at the end of the passage, following Scarth up onto the deck. When he came out into the open, a cold wind stirred his hair, and he was glad of the warm fleecy clothes. In the gray pre-dawn light, Jake saw the barge was tied up alongside a stone pier. Men were unloading the contents of the deep hold onto four broad, flat wagons, each harnessed to a team of six of the largest horses Jake had ever seen. They were like Clydesdales, he thought, only even more massive, and they were all black. The top of the hold had been covered last night, Jake remembered, he had walked over that space as part of the deck. The precut timbers and squares of board that must have served to make the top deck one solid plane stood neatly stacked on the larger aft deck. Three large beams crossed the hold from port to starboard, at intervals of about ten feet, making the hold about thirty feet long. These must act as support for the removable deck timbers when the barge was under way, Jake realized.

He walked over to the starboard side, the pier side, to watch the unloading. The river smell was stronger now, a combination of dead grass and dead fish. Gray gull-like birds scrabbled for food scraps on the pier, or wheeled overhead with mournful cries. Scarth had descended to the pier, where he was talking to two men. Both these newcomers were armed with swords. One was very large and strong looking, with a long, dirty blond ponytail. The other, short and fat, was doing most of the talking, punctuated by frequent hand gestures. Like Jake, the two wore dark green tunics that fell to mid-thigh, but their sword belts were silver. Dark green leggings disappeared into brown leather boots tied below the knee. The mincing fat man kept glancing at Jake, pointing at him for emphasis, his voice raised.

But Scarth was obviously refusing whatever they were asking, shaking his head, palm towards the fat man. He barked out some words that sounded final to Jake, folded his arms across his broad chest, and glared at the two men in green. The fat man grew red in the face, and spluttered, and the big man with the ponytail grabbed the hilt of his sword, but at a sudden sharp word from Fatso left it where it was. Ponytail said something sharp to Scarth, which drew no reply, and the pair withdrew a few steps, with Fatso muttering urgently to Ponytail. Eventually, they walked off down the pier, and boarded a waiting launch manned by several swarthy men in leg irons.

"Everyone seems pretty touchy around here," muttered Jake to himself. *I wish I could understand what they were saying*. At that moment, the sun came up behind him, illuminating the deck. Feeling its warmth upon his neck, he turned to face it. And that was how Jake caught his first sight of Marfang Castle, standing between him and the rising sun. Mighty and proud rose the fortress, atop the flat hill which it crowned, upon its craggy island in the river's midst. Immediately across from Jake, two broad stone towers, hundreds of feet apart, climbed into the air a hundred feet or more, joined by a stone wall more than half their height. Two other towers, completing a quadrangle, loomed behind these, no doubt connected by similar walls. Massive and square, yet with battlements so high above the water level they seemed like cliffs, impregnable Marfang clove the river, indifferent to the waters that bathed its feet. On the island itself, green terraced fields and orchards flowed up to the gray stone of the castle, all dappled by the rising sun. A sense of square but lofty symmetry, of a guard never breached, radiated from the structure as if it were a living entity, serene in its own strength, yet ever watchful for any enemy.

Even to Jake, who knew nothing of its history, the island fortress looked imposing enough. He looked around in the sunlight, taking stock of what lay around him. *You're going to have to tell Mom about this, when you get back home*. The thought unaccountably cheered him, as if he could

The Fruit Of The Dendragon Tree

deal with his new reality more easily by envisioning a successful return to his old one, and he continued his visual inventory, the activity further settling his mind. The barge was moored to a stone quay that ran north and south along the riverbank for two hundred yards in each direction. The buildings of a large town, quiet in the early morning, spread up the hill that dominated the view immediately to the west. The river itself curved out of sight to the west farther upstream, among green hills on the western bank, and green fields to the east. A hand fell on his shoulder. Startled, Jake turned away from his sightseeing and looked up into Scarth's face. The big man could move very quietly, and Jake somehow knew that he'd had a lot of practice at it. The merchant looked a little concerned, but that was all. The men in green obviously did not frighten him.

Scarth whispered to Jake hurriedly: "Go my men, now. They take you my house. Stay there. I come later". He gave the boy a questioning look that clearly asked: "Do you understand?" Jake nodded, and walked down the gangway and along the quay with three tall men, all dressed in black and wearing long swords. He felt many eyes upon him, but did not look around.

His companions, like Scarth, were broad as well as tall, and looked like they could deal with trouble if it came their way. They did not speak to Jake, and he, remembering Scarth's instructions, followed silently. They left the quay and the warehouses that lined its shoreward side, entering the town behind. Despite the early hour, there were some folk abroad, who glanced their way with open curiosity. They were not emboldened to speak, however, and Jake guessed his guards did not exactly invite conversation. The people were dressed in different colors, like uniforms, Jake thought. Poorer folk with unkempt hair and dirty hands wore ragged tunics and overcoats of brown. These, like Jake, were unshod despite the chill of the morning. More prosperous-looking people wore crimson, or black, or dark blue. These individuals were generally cleaner in appearance, and all of them could afford (or were allowed to wear? Jake wondered) some type of footwear. The buildings they passed near the waterfront were wooden; brightly painted or stained a rich red brown.

Jake's guards led him uphill, away from the waterfront. The streets, narrow and twisty at first, gave way to broader straight avenues near the crest of the escarpment. Jake wondered early on if they doubled back a few times, but could not be sure if his guards were checking to see if anyone was following, or if it was merely the twisty streets that directed their progress. In any event, he was glad when they breasted the hilltop and reached more level ground. Their upward and westward progress away from the rising sun (*at least there's only one of those so far*, Jake thought, smiling to himself) brought them to an obviously more affluent part of town. The houses that were crammed together near the river were farther apart here, framed by lush green lawns sparkling with dew in the morning sunshine. The houses up here were of stone, and roofed with red clay tiles, unlike the thatch coverings of the dwellings closer to the water. A woody creeper plant with dark green leaves embraced the walls of many of the stone houses. Occasional purple flowers, the first to celebrate the spring, decorated some of these vines, but Jake did not recognize them. They passed several large dogs in the streets, one of which bared its teeth and growled at them. To Jake, they all seemed of a type: mostly black, with large heads and stocky bodies.

A horse-drawn cart clattered by on one of the streets, its wheels loud on the cobblestones. Jake paid little attention to the driver, who was slouched down, his face hidden by a large hood. But he noticed the horse. It was a fine bay animal, large-boned and strong, with a proud carriage that belied its humble task. Jake found the presence of animals he could recognize very reassuring. Wherever this world was, Jake thought, it was in many ways very similar to his own. The air on the hilltop was cold and fresh. It was a beautiful morning, no matter where he was, and Jake suddenly felt amazingly awake, alive and strong. He felt he could run forever, and as he recognized the amazing vitality flooding through him his sense of extreme dislocation greatly diminished. Though things were far from normal, it was difficult to remain scared and confused when he felt so vibrant and healthy. *I wonder if people get sick here?* He thought.

The Fruit Of The Dendragon Tree

As he walked, he stole occasional glances at his rangy, silent companions. All three of them had deep-set brown eyes and black hair. They were dressed alike too, in loose-fitting black tunics and leggings of the same fabric as Jake's borrowed clothes. They wore supple leather shoes with some kind of sole that allowed them to walk very surely and quietly along the uneven cobbles. Their golden sword hilts protruded from jeweled scabbards, and glinted in the sunshine. The scabbards themselves were attached to plain leather belts, black like the rest of their garments. They were in uniform, Jake realized, and so was everyone else he had seen here. The whole town wore clothes that denoted their social position. It was an insight he gained with very little evidence, but was correct for all that. Jake wondered at his growing calm acceptance of his situation, and the realizations that flooded him as certainties. But he marveled most at his increased sense of physical well being, and that his bare feet were not cold at all, though they carried him over stones that had not yet warmed in the early sunshine.

Presently, Jake's little group arrived at a stone wall, some dozen feet high, that fronted the road for a considerable distance on their right hand side. After walking next to it for roughly fifty yards, they came to a gate of wrought metal. The wall ran past this gateway for several hundred feet again, before curving to the right out of view. At a soft word from one of Jake's guard, the gate was opened by another man inside the compound, similarly armed and dressed in the dark uniform of Scarth's retinue. Closing the gate behind them, this fourth man gazed curiously at Jake and asked a question of the man who had given the password. After a brief conversation, the house guard returned to his post by the gate, but not before fixing Jake with a hard, unfriendly stare.

Why the heck does everyone look at me like I'm some kind of worm? Then he brought himself up short. *They think I'm a Crone, whatever that is. And whatever a Crone is, they don't like them very much. And they think I'm a risk to their Master. So stop being a baby and figure out a way to let them know you aren't a Crone.*

His escort was now leading him up a well-manicured gravel drive to a large, two-story stone mansion separated from the road by a wide swath of beautiful emerald-green grass. The color of this lawn was richer and deeper than any Jake had ever seen. The stone wall, which they had breasted from the road, seemed to surround the entire grounds, roughly a hundred yards square. It was by far the largest piece of private property that Jake had yet seen. They reached the house, and the leader knocked on the wooden front door with a curious rhythm that Jake presumed was another password. Yet another guard opened the door, and they entered a spacious, airy foyer lit by the morning sun, streaming through large, heavy-paned windows above the door. The inside guard opened another door on the left-hand side of this foyer and gestured Jake inside. *What the hell,* Jake thought, *they haven't hurt me yet.* He entered the room, the door closing behind him.

Inside, hundreds of books, of varying shapes and sizes, lined shelves that rose from floor to ceiling around three sides of the large chamber. The books were covered in red or brown or green leather, with titles embossed in gold leaf. Jake glanced at a few, but couldn't read the language. On the fourth side of the room, large windows looked northwards into the sunny garden. A sturdy brown sofa sat in front of these, its back to the glass so the reader could catch the light. The only other furniture was a solid desk, with scrolls and more books stacked in neat piles, in front of a leather-covered chair in the middle of the room. It was a very quiet and peaceful in this library, which is how Jake immediately thought of it, and Jake could almost believe he was back in his father's study at home, except for the alien golden language that hid the books' contents from him.

Jake assumed he'd been deposited here to wait for Scarth, and despite the room's beauty he soon fretted to be gone. But he was only there a few minutes when he heard voices raised in the hallway outside. The commotion ended when the door to the study burst open, and a pretty girl about his own age, with a parting retort over her shoulder to the guards outside, slammed the door behind her and turned to face him.

The Fruit Of The Dendragon Tree

2.

"Would you like some tea?" Marah did not wait for a reply, but poured for herself and Ureth from a porcelain urn warming on a tripod table by the iron brazier on the floor. The Aunts and acolytes had left the turret chamber, leaving Marah alone with her gifted but wayward protégé.

Ureth nodded her thanks as she sipped the hot, bitter brew, feeling it warm her from the inside out. *What are we, that we should so often deny ourselves these small pleasures?* she thought to herself.

"I didn't realize how cold I was," she said aloud.

"Yes, a cold night. But it is passing now." The Mother was right, Ureth realized. Through the window, the sky was pale with incipient dawn. The Dragon Moon no longer cast its red glow, nor the Warrior Moon its gold. Only a few lonely stars showed their remote light, distant and indifferent to the concerns of Tiramonde. Ureth looked at the floor.

"I am sorry I was angry with you, Ureth. No, do not speak," for Ureth had opened her mouth to do just that. "You were foolhardy. But you were also brave. I know you understood the risks you were taking when you attempted to summon the Pendraig. Who better than I knows that you have the courage and determination to do the most difficult tasks? Though sometimes I take you to task for your judgment."

"Courage or not, Mother, I have failed." Ureth felt suddenly weary. What was this all about? If there were to be a penance imposed, why couldn't the old witch get on with it?

"Have you? Failed, I mean?"

Ureth looked up sharply. What was this? "Yes, Mother, I failed. The fireball roared over me, not into the Ring, where it was supposed to go. Even then, I was nearly consumed. I endangered the acolytes. I broke the Rule, and all for nothing. The Pendraig did not appear. I should be punished." *So hurry up and get on with it*, she didn't add. Nonetheless, there was defiance in her tone that belied the submissive words.

"Yes, Ureth, you did all that. Yet even so, perhaps the Dragon answered your hope. Perhaps not, it is too soon to tell. We already have news of the strange fireball from the sky. It plunged into the Marfell. And the Duke's barge apparently picked someone up."

"Picked someone up? What do you mean? And how do you know this?"

"You forget yourself!" The Mother did not often lose her temper; she rarely had to. She could persuade or induce behavior in all but the most strong-willed simply by couching her desires as suggestions. But when angered, her voice could crack stone. Ureth flexed her psyche, sleek and powerful, and with wonder perceived the aura of the Mother, not debilitated and confused as she had supposed, but a hitherto cloaked force, burning with fierce heat.

She is stronger still than I supposed, Ureth thought. *What other miscalculations have I made this night?* She looked into Marah's eyes, and saw there the fierce pride, necessary to the rigors of Motherhood, but always needing to be controlled. She knew then that Marah had been incredibly forgiving of her, not just tonight, but for the many years of their association she'd endured her immense but brash talent.

"How is it you need to ask such a question?" asked Marah. "I am the Mother, possessed of all the gifts of the Craft, and still your superior despite the fact that you chafe under the guidance of any will save your own."

And for the first time that night, now rapidly becoming day, Ureth felt truly contrite, acknowledging the truth of the Mother's words. She did indeed chafe under discipline, even her own, secretly desiring the abandonment of restraint and the exercise of raw magical power. The soaring ecstasy she had felt at the Ring, far from being the touch of the Dragon, may after all have only been the wanton indulgence of her own thirst for liberty, the wild freedom forever placed beyond her reach, not only by her wrinkled and ugly body, but by the iron oaths of the Coven.

"Forgive me, Mother, I understand. Of course, you have seen this with your Sight."

The Fruit Of The Dendragon Tree

"You understand nothing! By the Dancer, sometimes you are as dense as a scullery novice! Forget the Sight and your desperate yearning for a magic answer for everything, and use your mind!" The Mother caught herself with an effort, taking a sip of tea to prevent her tongue from lashing out further. She closed her eyes, and drew a deep breath. Then belying her own command, she began to speak in the monotonous chant of a Crone reciting a vision.

"The fireball came out of the Dragon Moon and neither you nor the Ring were enough to contain it. It roared overhead, into cold Marfell, which alone could douse its heat. Deep, deep, it dove, into the icy cold dark of the Dragonwater, and when it was spent a naked boy was swimming for his life, lungs bursting, up to the night of the twin full moons. He is from another world, and the fire that hurled him forth came from the Dragon Moon, on the first night in a millennium when he has been full in the sky with his rival, the Warrior Moon. A night when, using the Dragon's own fire, you called for the Pendraig, and felt the hot breath of the Worm heat your very loins."

Ureth blushed with shame. Was nothing secret from this woman? She hadn't sought the climax on the Ring. As a Crone, her sexuality was something she sublimated in the search for a greater power. She had been too young to think of such things when she'd had her first interview with the Council, and since her days as an acolyte such matters were not taboo, so much as ignored. The premature aging of the body no doubt helped. The acolyte was spared the hormonal fluxes of a normally awakening sexuality, and her appearance did little to attract attention from those who experienced desire. Also, the spiritual ecstasy of the Craft rendered the physical sort prosaic. Just as the goldsmith did not work with iron, the sensual distractions of the body were irrelevant to the purposes of the Sight. But Ureth knew that the psychic communion with the Dragon's Breath had nearly shattered her with an ecstasy felt everywhere in her body. The physical sensation had been beyond her experience, profoundly intimate and private. To hear Marah describe it in the succinct tones of a psychic witness was almost a violation.

The Mother ignored Ureth's discomfort and droned on: "Who is he this boy? If here at your summons, does that mean the Dragon delivered him to us in a place of his own, and not your choosing?"

Ureth was confused. Was the Mother suggesting that Jake had indeed arrived? Had the spells, hers and Jenny's, worked after all? But a naked swimmer? That was hardly an awe-inspiring description of the one who would fulfill the ancient prophecy, the one who would unleash the might of the Dragon, ensure the rule of the rightful King of Taumar, and destroy the usurper. Then she remembered her own nakedness on the hilltop, and felt her heart begin to beat faster.

"And where is this boy now?" the Mother continued. "He sleeps on the merchant's barge, the trader called Scarth, soon to walk the streets of Marfold, beyond the Ring, beyond the Cloister, beyond Marfang's walls. He is, indeed, still beyond the orbit of all who would attempt to bend him to their designs, or destroy him for the danger he posed. I see him in the streets, clad in borrowed garments, protected by the guards of the merchant who found him, walking with the common folk. And what are we to do with this knowledge? For we will not be alone with it for long: it will spill and spread, as the fire that brought him spilled, though others may use more common methods to gather it than we have done." The Mother fell silent for a moment. Then, the chant of vision over, she asked in her normal voice: "What are we to do, Sister Ureth?" And Ureth was surprised to realize that the Mother's question was not rhetorical. She really did not know what to do. And who could blame her? There was no precedent for this, not for all the centuries the Coven had existed. Ureth wasted no time in answering, and so consecrated a fate that had been sealed when she had begun her chant at the Ring.

"We must find him and bring him here. We must discover if he truly is the Pendraig." The two women were silent for a time. A coal slithered in the brazier, and a ray of light knifed through the window as day pierced the cold chamber. A cock crowed in the distance. To an outside observer, the two witches would have seemed to be two immobile old women, saying nothing. But a world of meaning was shared in the silence that passed between them, as if silence itself was a living entity.

Marah finally stirred, though Ureth already knew what she would say. When she spoke, it was with a resigned compassion. "I agree. It is our only option, though I wish it had never been thrust upon us. Or upon you, dear Ureth. Don't think that your heart will escape unscathed from this night's work. I see grief for you, in more ways than you can imagine. Go to the house of Scarth the merchant, and bring the boy here. Then we shall see what we shall see."

Chapter 5

Seeking and learning is all remembrance

(The Dialogues of Plato: Meno)

The girl watched Jake intently. In the brief time she was still, Jake realized he'd been wrong. She wasn't just pretty, but incredibly beautiful: of medium height, with thick shoulder-length auburn hair, and eyes a dark but brilliant green. Her skin was cream, and her cheeks were flushed. She wore a sleeveless calf-length dress of midnight blue, with a pattern of golden leaves woven into the fabric. Her feet and arms were bare, save for a thick gold band on each wrist. She smiled a sudden, dazzling smile and came towards him: hands extended forward, palms down.

"Ola-da! Huisma du by?" The incomprehensible words were so obviously welcoming that Jake instinctively relaxed, and raised his hands to meet hers from below. She smelled like strawberries. She squeezed his hands, then released them and stepped back. She still smiled, but now had a quizzical look on her face as she waited for his response. Jake realized she'd greeted him, probably *"Hi there who are you?"* he thought. The cadence of her speech was like his own, but the words were different, familiar but veiled.

"Ola-da," he managed, surprised he'd gotten that far. "I'm sorry. I don't know what else you said to me."

The effect of his short reply was dramatic in a way that was by now becoming funny. The girl gasped, and brought a hand to her mouth.

The Fruit Of The Dendragon Tree

Her fingers were long and tapered, Jake saw, and it surprised him that he noticed; there seemed to be some *difference* here that made him experience everything more keenly, as if not only he, but this new world itself, was more alive, more receptive to who he was. But it was the girl who surprised him next, for she replied in his own language.

"You speak Crone! How? Who taught you? Who are you?'

"My name is Jake. Where I'm from, everyone speaks this language. Crone, right? A crone is an old lady or witch or something, right? We call it English. I've noticed people here think it's bad, or something."

"English? What part of Tiramonde is that? Are you all Crones there? But no, you are not a woman. You're right, the Crones are old, or at least seem so. It is the price they pay for their art. But you are not old. So where is the place that you can openly speak this language and not be killed?" She was eager to know, Jake saw, and certainly wasn't hostile, unlike Scarth's soldiers.

"I can't tell you where it is," Jake replied. "It's all so freaky. One minute I was outside in the woods, the next I'm here, swimming in the river. Where am I? How do I get home?"

"Why, this is Tiramonde, which we call the part of our world that was saved from the Dragonfire. We are in the North Kingdom, or Taumar, in the city of Marfold. You are in the home of Scarth the merchant, and I am his daughter, Sathryn. Be welcome here. But be careful to whom you speak. It is forbidden to speak Crone in our March, by orders of the Duke, unless you belong to the Sisterhood. Coegun does not love the Crones, though he must tolerate them, and they him." A shadow passed over her face, and she fell silent, looking down. Jake liked the sound of her voice, and wanted her to keep talking.

"Scarth is your father? He rescued me from the river, then sent me here. You speak my language much better than he does. Are you a Crone?"

Sathryn laughed at this. "No, by the Dancer, I am not one of them! But I enjoy learning foreign tongues, and it pleased me to learn English, as you call it. It has some advantages, I confess." She smiled, a little sadly Jake thought. He still had no answers to his questions, but the beautiful Sathryn did make him feel better. He was seventeen, after all.

"Who taught you to speak Crone?" he asked, thinking that if there was someone who could teach English, they might tell him where he was, how he got there, and, most importantly, how he could get back home.

Sathryn tilted her head sideways and gazed at him seriously. "Strange. I have not been asked that before. Perhaps because nobody has ever guessed the truth. My sister taught me. Now you are here, a stranger, and you know my most dangerous secret. Are you a danger to me, Jake?"

"I would never want to be," Jake replied. And that was true, he realized. He had only just met her, but being with Sathryn had already made him feel more peaceful. For months, all he had in his mind was the fact he was going to lose his mother. He had erected walls inside, behind which neither his father nor his friends could reach him. He had not let them. But Sathryn, with her beauty and vulnerability, had just walked right through them.

"I believe you," she replied. Yet we are often accidentally dangerous to each other, even to the ones we love. Sometimes especially to the ones we love." She gazed at him some more, searching his face for an answer to a question he had not heard. She shook her head suddenly, not finding it, and muttered to herself: "No, I don't have the skill. No doubt the Dancer will reveal all in time." Then to him, "I am sure, Jake, that you will meet my teacher. Yes, she will want to meet you. And she has a habit of getting what she wants."

Jake could tell Sathryn found no happiness in this certainty, and wondered again at the keenness of his insight, that complemented his feeling of vitality and strength. Whether the girl's concern was for herself or him, he didn't know. Without knowing why he reached out and hugged her. To his pleased surprise, she hugged him back. *I don't understand this,* he thought. *Am I dreaming? But she feels so warm and alive I don't see how I can be!* Aloud he said, "I will never hurt you."

She leaned back, still in his embrace, and gave him a crooked smile. "I know," she whispered.

And that was how her father found them.

2.

When I opened the door, the cold forced its way into the house and bit me. It wasn't Jake on the doorstep, but a young girl, dressed all in black under Mary's coat, wearing dark makeup that made her look like a witch. My eyes took her in, the way they always do with people. Too thin, no visible body piercing, nose red from the cold. Eyes red, too, but then she'd been crying. She looked scared, as if she wanted to run away. But that wasn't all that strange, when one considered she was going around in the middle of the night ringing doorbells.

"Yes?" I barked at her, couldn't help it, I was beginning to really worry about Jake, and didn't need this distraction.

"Dr. Patel?" She asked. She had a nice voice, and was pretty and vulnerable in the moonlight. "You're Jake's Dad, right?" immediately getting my attention, and I said yes and motioned her inside. But I'd obviously been too abrupt, as I often am with Jake himself, and so she hesitated for a moment, shivering with the cold.

"Come in, come in. I won't bite!" sounding even to myself like some sort of stage Englishman, though I must have seemed harmless enough, for she finally crossed the threshold as I gladly shut the door behind her, beginning to shiver myself in the chill.

"Is Jake here?" she whispered. And I realized it wasn't me she was scared of.

"Bit late to be paying a social call, isn't it?" Immediately regretting my sarcasm I had a sudden insight. "Has he been with you?" A nod. "But he's not anymore." A slight hesitation followed by a shake of the head. Earrings shaped like small silver crosses glinted in the soft light of the hall. She was very pretty, and I could see why Jake might have wanted to spend time with her. I realized that it was Jake's and this girl's footprints that I had seen, leading from the house to the trees at the end of my property. I asked as much, to confirm my guess, and got another nod in reply.

"Well, he hasn't come back home, Miss, er, what's your name, by the way?"

"Jenny, Jenny Blackwood. Dr. Patel, I'm so worried about Jake. One minute he was with me, and the next…" She stopped, obviously not knowing how to continue.

"Yes, and the next?" I was more gentle now, the compassionate professor, eliciting information from a self-conscious student.

"He was gone!" And her fear, of some unknown dread, cut through my visions of uncomfortably cold but harmless hanky-panky in the woods, and imparted itself to me as if blown on the wind outside.

We stood looking at each other. The wind picked up again, making the branches of the holly tree pluck at the window behind me. It was a lonely sound, for a lonely hour, though there were two of us standing there.

"Perhaps we'd better go and look for him, then," I suggested mildly. "Why don't you show me where you were?"

She looked at me, still frightened, but nodded her head and said, "OK".

3.

"I see you've met my daughter."

Jake hadn't heard Scarth enter the room, so softly did he move. Jake started with surprise, but Sathryn turned to her father, a glad smile on her face, nothing furtive or guilty in her eyes.

Scarth noted Jake's discomfort, however, and it did not displease him. Wherever the lad was from, he clearly had the same instincts as any young blood of Scarth's experience, and by definition would bear watching.

"*Ola-da, husige du?*" Sathryn asked her father, and although Jake could follow the words now, he still could still not understand their meaning. Scarth replied in the same language.

"I was delayed at the dock. Coegun is very interested in this young man. The nature of his coming, and the omens in the sky last night, suggest someone has brewed strong magic. Though I doubt the boy is a mage, everybody else seems to think he is, and I have little hope of him surviving Coegun's hospitality if I surrender him."

"Why? Why would the Duke want to hurt him? Where did you find him anyway, and how did you keep him from Coegun?"

To Jake's surprise, Scarth answered her in English. "I found him floating in the Marfell, last night. There were two full moons- did you see them? I claimed salvage rights on him, which did not please Coegun's men, and invoked a Royal Council to determine his fate. That didn't go over very well, but they had to agree, of course. At least for now."

"Floating in the Marfell?" asked the girl incredulously. "How in the name of the Dancer did he get there?"

She turned to Jake, "Jake, how did you get here?"

Jake didn't know how to answer, and in any case he had a question of his own. "You speak much better English here than you did on the boat," he said to Scarth. "How come?"

Scarth gave him an amused glance from under his deep-set brows. "It's not always wise to show how clever you are, young Master. Perhaps this is a thing you haven't yet learned. I was more careful, on my boat, surrounded by perhaps many enemies, to be less learned in a forbidden tongue than I need to be here, in my own house, in front of my daughter and a guest I have twice saved from sure death."

"What do you mean, saved from death?" asked the girl. "Why would anyone want to kill him?" Sathryn sounded really upset at the prospect, Jake thought, liking her more each moment.

"There were Duke's men on the barge with us last night. If you have not already found out, this young man speaks only the forbidden tongue. That by itself was enough for my own men to want to kill him, let alone the Duke's. But I've never sanctioned the kill first, ask questions later mentality, as you know."

Jake felt an indescribable relief at knowing people in this strange place who could actually talk to him. But in a strange way, this made him feel more alone. Sathryn and Scarth spoke English as a foreign language. Their accents were strange, and the cadence of their speech, so similar to his when they spoke their own language, changed when they spoke "Crone".

"Look, Mr. Scarth," he said. "I'm really grateful for everything you've done for me, but I need help. I really need to get back home, and I don't know how I'm going to do that, because I don't really understand how I got here. I don't even know where here is. Sathryn said this was the North Kingdom of Tiramonde, but that doesn't mean anything to me. There is no such place on my world, so that doesn't help me get any closer to figuring out where I am, how I got here, and how I'm to get back home."

"But you already know that, or at least you should." The voice came from behind Scarth, whose bulk hid the doorway from view. He stood aside, revealing the speaker. A thrill of fear went down Jake's legs. The old woman from his dreams, the witch who had been calling to him, stood in the doorway! If Scarth had moved silently, then she had simply appeared. She was dressed in blue and looked unutterably old. Jake gasped, and looked around for an escape. Sathryn just looked disgusted.

But Scarth only looked resigned, and said, "Hello. You seem to be just in time, as usual."

Jake looked at the old woman, and suddenly the name "Crone" made sense. He could tell that this was indeed a real witch. She had spoken to him in English, using the language the way he did, as if she spoke it all the time. She had haunted his dreams, but once he'd gotten over his first shock, she didn't look so frightening in the daylight. The eyes that gazed out at him from under gray brows were a keen and youthful blue, making her look younger than her face. Jake thought she was tall for an old woman, then realized this was because she stood erect, despite her wrinkled face and spotted hands. Her young eyes pierced him as if they could penetrate his inmost heart.

The Fruit Of The Dendragon Tree

Jake found it hard to hold their gaze, and that he was again having trouble breathing.

"You are here because I called you. And you agreed to come," she said.

"Your name is Ureth," he replied. And he wondered how he knew.

Chapter 6

*The shadow of his loss drew like eclipse,
Darkening the world.*

(Alfred, Lord Tennyson: Idylls of the King)

Jenny wanted to look for Jake on foot, but as she hadn't seen him on her return to our house I thought he might have tried to come back by road. It was getting colder, and that worried me. I knew the spot where she said she'd last seen Jake. We'd been up there together a few times, when he'd still wanted my company, and I knew where the road curved close to the hill she'd described. I decided to drive the SUV.

Distracted, I turned the key in the ignition, forgetting that I'd already done so, and winced at the grinding of the starter motor. Jenny looked at me, and I saw the essential kindness in her eyes, whatever other issues she had.

Our breath fogged the windshield as the heater struggled. I was frantic with worry about Jake, and confused by Jenny's story. She'd told me about coming to the house, and getting Jake to follow her with an idea about helping his Mom. That part sounded true, at least. If anything could persuade my son to do something foolish, it would be an appeal to help his mother. He simply would not accept she would die, and I knew he blamed me for "giving up." But I couldn't wave a magic wand and change reality. People died of cancer every day, and loved ones grieved before Death came, just as I did. Some families wanted the going to be peaceful, while others wanted to try every intervention, no matter how invasive or toxic. In my limited experience, it seemed that those who wanted the most done often felt the most guilt, but I couldn't comprehend what guilt Jake might feel, to fight so hard.

So he'd left with this strange girl, who had lured him with hope.

Where had he gone? And what was I going to tell his mother?

The Yukon skidded as we pulled out of the driveway: the fresh blanket of snow had started out as rain, and the rapid drop in temperature that had turned rainstorm into blizzard had carpeted the roads with a treacherous sheet of ice under a downy cover that softened the world's edges. I was mindful I wouldn't do Jake any good if I went off the road. Beside me Jenny looked tense, staring straight ahead. Outside, the moon lit the night with silver fire.

"It was supposed to be a great gift," Jenny said suddenly. "A magic gift. If I found her a man with a true warrior spirit, she would grant his heart's desire."

"What are you talking about? Who would do this? You know Jake is no warrior."

"She said he didn't have to know how to fight, just be pure in spirit. He had to have a burning desire for something, be willing to pay the ultimate price for it. Her magic would take care of the rest."

"Well, Jake is pure in spirit." I felt a burst of pride in my son as I said it. "But who exactly told you all this nonsense about magic? What's her name, and where do we find her?"

I braked as I spoke, taking my eyes off the road, and the heavy vehicle skidded. *Just something else to worry about*, I thought.

Jenny gasped as I corrected the skid but didn't answer. I tried again. "Jenny, do you know what it's like to love someone more than you love yourself? That's how I feel about Jake. That's how I feel about his mother. That's the only magic I know, the only magic worth knowing. I'm going to lose my wife. I don't want to lose my son as well. Please tell me, who told you these things? If we can find her, maybe we'll find Jake."

Jenny held onto the dashboard to steady herself, and when she spoke she wouldn't look at me.

"She said her name was Ureth. And we don't find her, Dr. Patel. She finds you."

I didn't know what to make of this, and it was my turn to fall silent. A minute later, I found the curve I was looking for, and pulled the SUV onto the shoulder, skating to a stop on the snow-covered gravel. We hadn't passed Jake, and he was nowhere in sight. I turned off the ignition.

"What now?" I asked myself, but Jenny answered this one.

"I'm going to tell you something that will be hard for you to believe." She still wouldn't look at me.

"I'm listening," I said, sounding calm and wanting to shake her.

"I'm a witch," Jenny said, finally looking at me. I withheld the look of ridicule she must have seen before and held her eyes. "I mean I'm a real witch, not just somebody who dresses up as a Goth and pretends to be a vampire. I can SEE things before they happen. And sometimes I make things happen, just because I want them to."

"OK," I said again, still carefully impassive. *Humor her*, I thought, *she might be crazy, but she's probably not dangerous*. At least I hoped so, just what had she done with Jake, anyway? "So you cast a spell to help Jake's Mom?"

"Yes, but it wasn't MY spell. It was hers, Ureth's. She's a really powerful witch, the real thing. She comes to me in dreams sometimes. She helps me when I get discouraged. Jake's been dreaming about her too, for the last few nights. She really needs him and has been calling him. When he wouldn't answer her, she got me to talk to him. She told me that if Jake helped her, she would grant his heart's desire. And we both know what THAT is." Jenny's dark blue eyes caught the moon and held its glow for a moment. She was a beautiful girl. I understood again at least one reason why my son might have followed her into the woods.

"Yes, we do," I answered. "He wants his mother to live."

"Yes, he's desperate for her to live. So she, Ureth, told me in my dreams how to get him ready, and how to get him to her, how to get him to WANT to go, because you have to want to, you can't be sent against your will. So I brought him to the clearing up there, and I said the spell, and I guess he must have gone, but I didn't really think anybody could do magic like that, least of all me, and I'm scared because I don't really know what's happened to him, if he's safe, or even really where he is. And I'm not sure he really wanted to go, as I didn't tell him I was sending him anywhere, but I think the magic worked, because something came while…"

I interrupted her. "What do you mean, send him anywhere? Where is she, this Ureth? Another country?"

"No, No, it's more than that. She's in another world."

I'd had enough. "That's the craziest thing I ever heard! I'm going to look for Jake! If you can't help me young lady, at least let me do that without wasting my time! He could be freezing to death!"

She went still then, and looked away. I hadn't meant to get so upset at her, but my fear for Jake overwhelmed me. Maybe she didn't like being called "young lady," I had even winced to myself as I said it, but she didn't seem upset, just quietly determined, as if I was a wayward child with whom she was trying to be patient. "OK Dr. Patel," she said softly. "What if I prove it to you?"

I hesitated. They say he who does so is lost. Certainly, looking back now, something changed forever in that moment. Jenny sat there in the passenger seat of the SUV, gazing straight ahead into the middle distance. Her dark hair framed her face, and accentuated the paleness of her skin in the moonlight.

"Why don't you try and start the car again?" she said in the same soft voice. "If you can, we'll head back to your house, and you can call the police to help you look for Jake. But if you can't," and here she looked at me again, making sure my eyes held hers, "then come with me up to the pentagram, and I'll try to help you call him home."

I remember thinking at this point that she was a complete lunatic. Who did she think she was, bargaining with me like that? This had gone far enough. I was going to go home and call the police anyway, so I reached forward and turned the key in the ignition.

Nothing happened. I tried again, and the engine still refused to turn over. I glanced furtively over at Jenny, who was now staring at me. She didn't look triumphant or mocking, but merely watched me with her eyebrows raised, as if to say "You see?"

But I didn't see, not yet. I gave the engine another try: still nothing. I undid my seat belt, and tried to open my door. Immediately, all the locks clicked, and the door wouldn't open. I began to feel impatient, not wanting to believe that my always-reliable vehicle would suddenly not start, nor let me leave it when five minutes before it had been a perfectly functioning automobile.

"What the hell is wrong with the God-damned truck? Sorry." This last was to Jenny, in apology for my language. But she didn't seem in the least put out, and for the first time I thought I saw a flash of enjoyment in those blue eyes.

"Dr. Patel, why don't we have some music?" The radio came on, the Oldies station that I listened to, blaring out Credence Clearwater Revival's "Bad Moon Rising." How perfect. Jenny still hadn't touched anything, and I shivered.

"You know, that's actually a pretty cool song," said Jenny. "But I think something more modern would be better." The digits on the radio dial raced, and stopped at a rap station to which Jake would sometimes listen. I often told him that rap music was an oxymoron, but I don't think he'd appreciated my sarcasm. A song called "Gold Digger" was playing, and it was clearly late enough for the uncensored version. We listened for a few seconds, then Jenny said "That's probably enough," and the radio turned off.

She was still looking at me, no trace of mischief anymore, and I had to admit she had my complete attention. "How did you do that?" My voice came out as a croaky whisper, and I realized I was scared.

"I'm a witch, Dr. Patel, like I told you," said the pretty girl in the seat beside me, who looked just like any other suburban kid pretending to be a vampire. "I wish I was a good enough one to save your wife myself. I really care about Jake and I'd love to see him happy. But I think I might be strong enough to help you find him if you really want. I sent him; I think I can bring him back. We may still have time." She paused, as if listening to something I could not hear, and when she spoke again her words were rushing over themselves once more. "Yes, we still have time, but it's your choice. If you want to help him, you can, but you have to act very soon. Jake left to save his Mom, or die trying. I know I'm not powerful enough to cheat death, and I'm not really sure it's even a good thing to try to do. Even Ureth, who's ten times more of a witch than I'll ever be, can't do that. For that, you need magic greater than any one person can make."

She made a small gesture with her hand and the keys turned in the ignition. The SUV started effortlessly. I seemed to be free to drive home, though I think I already knew I wouldn't. But I didn't yet know I wouldn't see that home again. Jenny opened the door and stepped out, never taking her eyes from mine.

She was still looking at me when she said, "For that, you need a Dragon." And then she closed the door.

I didn't understand everything then, and still can't completely explain the reasons why I chose the path I did. But I knew I loved my son more than my own life and would not let him risk his own without my help, if I could give it. Perhaps the siren song of blood was all the reason I needed. I reached forward and turned off the SUV. When I got out of the car, the cold speared me, almost freezing the breath in my lungs. The wind had died, but my worry was not less. Part of me still thought Jake was out here, and we had to find him fast.

"This way, Dr. Patel," said Jenny, already walking, and I followed her into the ditch and up the other side, climbing the steep hill that bordered the road. Underfoot, the snow had settled in drifts upon the folded hillside, and I sunk knee-deep in some of these. Why did I follow? What choice did I have? I knew, somehow, that to return home would have been to say goodbye to my son forever. There was something else, too. My logical mind could not explain away what had happened to the SUV's ignition and radio. If there was such a thing as magic in this world, then maybe there was still hope for a miracle, both for my son and my wife.

Hope. When it finally dies, when all expectation of a better outcome is extinguished, when you know the darkness is going to find you, with no promise of light, it's strange, but life almost seems to get easier. Hope is such an anxious indulgence, with its obsessive reliance on "maybe," that its absence can make reality easier to bear. I realized I had been without hope for a long, long time. But as I panted up the hill, I realized that my hopelessness was merely an anodyne, numbing my pain but wounding my soul. Floundering after the beautiful girl who held the key to my son's whereabouts, I felt the sudden, sick anxiety of hope hit me so forcefully I could hardly breathe. *Mary could live, after all.* The truth of this thought flooded my limbs, making them tremble. Hopelessness had made my whole body rigid: seemingly strong, but really only unbending and brittle. And in the defenselessness of this new, violent hope, despite the shaky feeling in my muscles and the fluttering of my heart, I felt oddly resourceful, as if my very vulnerability to hope was lending me a flexible durability to whatever might happen next. I was breathless when I caught up to Jenny, and not just because I was middle-aged and out of shape. Though I don't think either of us was concerned about my vanity at that point.

"I'm glad you came." She was matter-of-fact, with no hint of triumph.

"I didn't feel I had a choice," I replied, still panting from exertion, and from hope.

"You ALWAYS have a choice, Dr. Patel," she said, but kindly, her eyes soft in the moonlight.

"It felt like the best choice, then," and I heard the truth in my voice.

"I think it was," she said, with a little smile. "Follow me. We have to hurry, and luckily we aren't too far from the clearing here. Be careful though, it's tricky underfoot."

"Tell me something I don't know."

She smiled and moved ahead of me, more slowly this time. She seemed to know, somehow, where to put her feet, and she rarely sank into the snow farther than her ankles. After tripping over a hidden tree root just to the right of the path she had made, and sprawling headfirst into a mercifully soft but deep drift, I decided that the best course of action was to literally follow in her footsteps, and I trudged after her deeper into the woods, our way still lit by moonlight.

Intent on not missing my footing, I had my head down when a change in light made me look up, and I realized that the clearing had opened up around me. The moonlight pouring into the glade revealed the disturbed snow just ahead. I looked at the sky. The moon was sinking, but was still above the treetops, huge in the sky, reflecting the light of our sun upon our planet in the night. It had no light of its own, no warmth. It was merely a cold, dead mirror of the splendor it witnessed across the heavens, a counterfeit star that provided nothing to life. I was suddenly reminded of Plato's idea that what we experienced as reality was only a distorted reflection of the real truth that shone from elsewhere, outside the caves in which we hid our hearts and minds. The real truth always beckons us to find it, and we struggle towards it, yet do so love our caves.

The trees stood in stark relief against the sky, jagged black arrows thrusting heavenwards among blue-white stars that glittered like diamonds. My breath, condensing in the frigid air, wafted up like smoke and disappeared. *Just as I would disappear one day*, I thought; just as we all are as substantial as smoke, unless we leave a child behind us. I didn't know what I had expected, but my skin shivered as I examined the ground, and not just from the cold. I took it all in: the rough pentagram drawn in the snow, the burned out torches lying askew, and a myriad of footprints, several of which led to and from the dell in the direction of our house. Presently, one set of footprints caught my attention: a single track, leading away from the pentagram and curving towards the trees on the farther side of the dell, in the direction, as a crow would fly, of home. The prints in this track were muddled, and I realized that the person who had made them had been crawling. They ended suddenly, before they reached the trees, as if their maker had suddenly sprouted wings and flown away.

This last set of tracks really bothered me, even more than the crude remains of a fire, and the residual sour smell that still permeated the clearing. I had a sudden desire to shake the girl, to go on shaking her until she told me what had happened. But I knew if I did that I would get no answers at all, and I was desperate to find Jake, especially if he was alone out here in this deadly cold.

I controlled myself as best as I could and said, pointing to the mysterious tracks that struck me as an accusation: "Are these Jake's tracks?"

"Yes," Jenny said, sounding frightened again.

"Well," I asked, fighting for composure, "Where did he go from here? What happened to him?"

"I'm not really sure."

"Well, did you see anything?" She gave me a quick up and down jerk of her head, a flash of defiance in the dark blue eyes, and then the look away, as if she was scared of something. Then she looked at me again, and I could tell she believed what she told me, though the answer made no sense to her either: "The Dragon took him." And she started to cry.

I realized that Jenny had involved Jake in something over his head, and the sick, crawling feeling that comes to every parent who thinks they have lost a child returned, snaking its way under my rib cage, ravaging my heart. But neither her tears nor my fears would help him.

"Jenny," I said, still forcing myself to be calm. "You need to tell me what to do." And I was terrified she would.

"Dr. Patel, I know it sounds crazy, but it's true," said Jenny, drying her eyes on the sleeve of her borrowed parka. "I saw Jake disappear from the clearing. A dragon, or something that looked like a dragon, but I don't know because I'd never seen one before, and who really knows what dragons look like? But it was huge and had huge wings... anyway, this thing flew into the clearing and snatched him up and flew away, and I think... I think he is now in Ureth's world." She sniffed once, and rushed on: "But I still believe we can call him back, if we hurry. Stand in the middle of the pentagram, and close your eyes. And please don't move until I say, no matter what."

The Fruit Of The Dendragon Tree

"OK, but what are you going to do?" I asked, doing as Jenny said, watching as she gathered brush from the edges of the clearing, depositing a little pile at each blackened point of the star. I didn't know about dragons, but despite my bias against the paranormal I could feel magic at work.

"I'm going to pray for fire, and chant the summoning spell. I want you to close your eyes, and think very hard about Jake. Hopefully, between us we can call him back. I know it sounds crazy," she said again, as I opened my mouth to protest, but this really is the only chance we have, you must believe me."

I still didn't know what to believe. I knew my wife was dying. I knew my son was missing. I knew I loved him well beyond the value I placed on my own life. I could feel these truths in every cell of my body, but so much had happened so quickly. In the space of under an hour I had missed Jake in the night and followed a young girl into the woods to look for him. There I had come across signs of arcane magic, in which I was surprised to find myself ready to believe. And oh yes, the girl who brought me here had confessed herself a witch, told me she had sent my son to another world, shown me some inexplicable influence over the machinery of my vehicle, and announced that the only way to get Jake back was for us to summon him together. Using magic. It was a lot for your average suburban Anglo-Indian to deal with.

But: "OK, I'm ready," was all I said, and even looking back now I couldn't, and wouldn't, have said anything else.

I closed my eyes and breathed in. The air was so cold I could feel it drying out my nostrils. I thought of Jake. I saw his face clearly in my mind, and tears threatened to spill from underneath my eyelids. "Please, bring him back safe to me, Lord," not knowing to which Lord in question I was praying. Krishna or Christ, it didn't matter, and in those moments of frantic desperation I think they're the same person anyway.

Jenny had started chanting in a language I didn't know. I heard several soft pops and could tell from the light pressing on my closed eyelids, the sound, the heat and the scent of pine needles that at least some of her little piles of brush must have caught fire. Well, that was one prayer answered. I struggled to keep my eyes closed, to keep faith with spells that my mind had forgotten, but that my body knew existed. The crackle of fire grew louder. The sense of nearby heat and light intensified, but the image of Jake's face faded in my mind. He was becoming a shadow, and I struggled to keep seeing him. Jenny was chanting louder now, yet seemed farther away. I was sweating from the proximity of a great fire that I felt surround me. Suddenly, I knew I couldn't bring Jake back; it was too late. There was only one other choice, and I think I'd always known what it would be.

Despite Jenny's command, I opened my eyes. Flame was all around me. I looked down, and at first I thought I was on fire. Then I realized: I WAS a fire. Where my legs should have been, two columns of flame poured into the ground. Flame roared in my head. I felt light, weightless. I was burning, yet I was not burned. I was on fire, but I was not consumed. I was one with all fire ever conceived. In some unimaginably far-off void I could hear a young girl wailing, a single, high, never-ending "NO!"

I looked up at the adamantine stars, deep beyond the night. Then I leaped from our Earth, into the waiting darkness.

Chapter 7

*For perhaps he therefore departed for a season,
that thou should receive him forever*

(King James Bible: Philemon, v15)

Ureth smiled, and Jake caught a glimpse of healthy white teeth in a mouth that seemed somehow too young. She crossed to Jake, moving like a woman much younger than her face. Ureth was clearly not an average old lady. She grabbed his left shoulder and her eyes blazed at him with a terrible intensity, not of anger, but as he said to himself later, "with a burning desire to *see*." He could not look away. But he suddenly found he wasn't afraid of her, and knew this surprised both of them. He noticed that her eyes were the same blue color as his own – the same color as his mother's. He could feel the writhing psychic power within her, but simply accepted it, as a surfer accepts the power of the wave. After all, what else could he do? Her hair was white, but her brows and lashes were golden. A faint odor of dried flowers emanated from her, and she seemed somehow wholesome. Though he could not have said why, he trusted her already, and his earlier fears of her while dreaming now seemed ridiculous.

"Yes, my name is Ureth," she agreed. "And yours is Jake. I'm glad I found you." She regarded him a bit longer, but with a palpable reduction in intensity, as if she had dimmed some psychic high beam. She turned to Scarth and Sathryn.

"Greetings, Sathryn, Scarth. You have done well, to keep this lad from the Duke."

"Greetings, Ureth," the merchant replied. "I have asked for a Royal Council to decide his fate, but I think Coegun will insist on holding him until the Royal Envoy arrives, and I have a nasty feeling he'll have an accident if I turn him over to the Duke's men."

"You're right. We must leave immediately," said Ureth.

"Excuse me," said Jake. "Can you tell me what you're saying? I can understand you when you speak English, but not when you speak this language, whatever it is-"

"That won't do at all," muttered Ureth. Before Jake could react, she placed the heel of her right hand against his forehead. He felt something gently pop in his brain as she regarded him and his awareness was suddenly heightened. Curious, he waited for her to speak.

"Ureth, what are you doing?" cried Sathryn, moving to Jake's side.

"It's alright," he said to her. "I'm not hurt. And- I can understand you perfectly!" And Sathryn was amazed too, for Jake was speaking in her own tongue. He found the thought ineffably reassuring, as any explorer would who could speak the local language. He smiled up at Ureth in relief. "You can't do that with Calculus, can you?" he asked, in English. "It's a bitch."

Ureth looked at him quizzically, not understanding the reference. But she had no time for jokes. She extended her hand again, grasping his elbow. "Say, goodbye, Jake, we must go."

"Where are you taking him?" asked Sathryn, "Surely you aren't going to try and sneak him in to that pile of old stone on the river. Father, tell her she can't."

"When has anyone ever been able to tell Ureth what to do?" asked Scarth. "Besides, Jake will probably be safer there anyway."

"Well, then, I'm going too. I don't want Coegun hurting him, but we can't just leave him to the witches. Who knows what they'll try and do with him? Besides, how do you know they'll let him in?"

Ureth made as if to protest, but Jake, catching the beseeching look that Scarth gave her, felt he could hear their thoughts. *He knows he*

The Fruit Of The Dendragon Tree

can't go with us, Jake thought. *And he's scared for Sathryn. He thinks she'll be safer with Ureth, and Ureth knows that too, although she's not happy about it.* And he realized not only that Scarth and Ureth shared some kind of psychic bond, but that his own powers of intuition had also grown, possibly much more than Ureth intended with her spell. *She is impatient,* thought Jake. *And I'm not the first one to think so.* But he stayed silent, and if the others felt his thoughts as he did theirs, they gave no sign.

"Are you a virgin, boy?" Ureth asked.

"What?" he stammered.

"You heard me. Are you a virgin? Have you ever lain with a woman?"

"Yes… no, I mean… I haven't…" Jake fumbled, confused and embarrassed by the questions.

But Ureth was all business. "Good," she said. "Then you may claim sanctuary with us. See that you behave yourself." But the hard look that she gave to accompany her last remark was directed not at Jake but Sathryn, who though she glared back defiantly could not prevent the crimson flush that seeped from her neck to the roots of her hair.

"There isn't much time," said Ureth. "If this boy is who I think he is, then he needs my protection, and the Crones won't argue, at least not much. But you know the rules, Sathryn. No man who has lain with a woman may enter the cloister, nor remain there should he violate that rule while he is our guest. For Jake's protection, leave your appetite at the door if you come with us. Don't think I don't know what you do."

Scarth stirred uneasily, and looked as if he might speak, but Sathryn beat him to it. "Don't you act all high and mighty with me, you withered old hag. At least I'm living my life, not frittering it away, old and wrinkled before my time. Why, you don't even know what it's like to be kissed."

But if Sathryn wanted a fight from Ureth, she was not to get one. "I am sorry," Ureth said. "It's been a long night and an uncertain morning, and I shouldn't chastise others for their indiscretions when the Dancer knows I have committed enough of my own. Very well Sathryn, come with us if you will abide by our rules. And now, we really must go. The Duke's armed escort is on its way here. And their intentions are not friendly."

Jake turned to go but Sathryn, incredibly, began to argue with Ureth again. "But what if I don't agree to your stupid rules?" she demanded. "Are you going to make me live on bread and water? And I don't have anything to wear, and I'm not going to go around in some burlap sack like you!"

But here Scarth intervened. He grabbed Sathryn by her shoulders, making sure he had her attention. "Listen, you little fool," he hissed. "You are in great danger. The Duke's men are coming here for this boy. He won't be here. They will question me as to his whereabouts. If they find you here too, they will take you, either to make me tell them what I know, which is little enough, but also to make me do what they want and to punish me for what they will call my disobedience. If I refuse them, they will torture you and kill me, after arresting me on some pretext when I try and stop them, as they know I will. Even if I help them, they will still hurt you. For that is Coegun's way. He sees power only as a club or a sword. You would soon have no clothes at all if you meet his men. They'll strip you naked before they bring you pain, and that's not counting any other games they might want to play with a peach like you. So you *will* go, now, and you *will* abide by the Crones' rules, you *will* wear what the Crones wear and eat whatever they give you to eat. You must blend in, and the finery I have spoiled you with is not going to help you do that. You do whatever Ureth tells you to do, and do not show your face here again until I have expressly told you it is safe to come back. Am I clear?"

What was clear to Jake was that Scarth had never before spoken to Sathryn like that. She stood, blushing crimson, not knowing where to look. But he had no time to feel sorry for her "Can we get going?" he asked. "You guys might be in danger and I need to get back home!"

Ureth nodded. "You are right, Jake. Come with me, both of you." She turned and left the room, as swiftly and silently as she had appeared. Sathryn stumbled after her, biting off a sob. Jake was about to follow, but he stopped and gazed back at Scarth. The big man regarded him seriously from under his bushy eyebrows.

"Thanks, Scarth," said the boy. "Thanks for saving me. Not just from the river, but from the Duke too. I think I owe you my life. I know I do. I hope you're OK." He felt tears unaccountably prick his eyelids and he was ashamed.

"Dance with the Dancer, my young friend," Scarth's replied. "We will meet again, I feel it. In the meantime, take care of my daughter for me."

"I'll try," said Jake. He followed Ureth and Sathryn out of the room, catching up to them as Ureth started down a hallway towards the rear of the mansion. Jake noticed rich tapestries, mostly of red and gold, lining the walls of this corridor. Vast chambers, with high ceilings and many windows to let in the streaming sunlight, opened up to the left and right of them as they passed, wooden floors polished to a golden sheen. The middle of the passage was covered with rich, soft carpet runners, also of red and gold, that deadened the noise of their hurrying feet, and the overall impression was one of solid wealth. But Jake's newly heightened perceptions received only distant echoes of true happiness, as if wealth was attempting to substitute for laughter, and as if elegance could bandage grief. It was not a feeling he could put into words, but rushing through Scarth's mansion he sensed loneliness, and a deep emptiness that no riches could fill.

Eventually, the trio came to a large wooden door at the end of the long corridor. This opened directly out into the sunlit garden, where the sudden flood of light after the dim corridors caused Jake to blink rapidly. The air was still cold, but shone with crystalline brightness, reminiscent of the northern January mornings his father loved.

Ureth didn't let him admire the view.

"This way," she said softly. There was no mistaking the urgency behind her words, though Jake couldn't tell if he was feeling her mind, or simply hearing her tone of voice.

"OK. I'm with you," he said, and Ureth shot him a look of grateful surprise before running lightly across the grass to the high, vine-covered stone wall that circled the grounds. Jake and Sathryn followed. Ureth scrabbled behind the creeper, which bore the small purple flowers Jake had noticed before. Her hands found what they sought: a wooden lever set into the wall, which she pulled down sharply. A small door of stone, camouflaged by the ivy, opened silently to the broad street beyond. They stepped out, Ureth pulling the door shut behind them. Jake did not catch the words she then muttered, but when he looked again at the wall he could see no sign of the door.

"Cool," was all he could say.

Ureth smiled at him, her young eyes and teeth gleaming out of her wrinkled face.

"A door for leaving and not for entering," she said. "You'll see more of these while you're here, Jake. We should be safe now, but should still hurry." She turned and began to lead them at a fast pace away from Scarth's estate, along the wide, quiet avenues of the wealthy.

They did not immediately descend into the lower, busier sections of the town, but instead kept to the higher parts that ringed it. Jake occasionally caught a glimpse of the brooding stone castle, grim even in the cheery morning sunshine. From a distance, the towering gray walls seemed to promise security, and freedom from invasion. But the stern battlements, and the danger he was in, spoke volumes about the steep price of that security, and Jake felt he understood Scarth a bit better now. Perhaps, for Scarth, an unjust ruler and surrendered freedom was too steep a price to pay for an uneasy peace. Though he had to admit, although everyone seemed to think his life was in great danger, he felt wonderful. *Maybe the air here does something to you*, he thought. Perhaps he should bring his mother here; maybe she'd feel better. But then he had another thought.

"Why are we going to the castle?" he asked Sathryn. "Isn't that where the Duke is?" he asked.

Sathryn chuckled. "You don't understand, Jake," she said, not unkindly. "We're going because the Crones also live there, in their own tower, which even Coegun does not dare enter. No doubt Sister Ureth has some plan for getting you inside, but I'll be interested to hear how she explains you to the acolytes, not to mention the Mother."

"Why do you call her Sister Ureth?" asked Jake. "Is she a nun, or something?"

Sathryn looked at Ureth before answering, but the Crone stalked ahead of them along the sunlit avenue, not speaking. "I call her Sister, because that is her rank, which she attained within the Coven by years of discipline, and her own great talents. I may not like her much, but I do respect her abilities. But I also have another reason."

"Sathryn," Ureth had stopped, and turned to face them. But Sathryn ignored her.

"I mean the word literally," said Sathryn. "Ureth is my sister. Scarth is our father. And our mother is dead." Her lip quivered, and she bit it hard, fighting back sudden tears. Jake felt a sudden wave of compassion for her. Sathryn had already suffered what he had vowed to prevent. But Ureth was impatient, and had no time for sympathy.

"Look, we don't have time for this," Ureth said. "Coegun's men are already searching our father's house for us. We must get inside the castle before they return." She turned and walked on again, leaving the other two little choice but to follow.

At least someone else is in a hurry, thought Jake. *I wonder how soon the Crones can send me home.* He thought of his father, probably worried sick, and of his mother, dying, and he hurried his stride to keep pace with the witch.

They had headed mostly southwards across the upper town, before turning onto a long avenue that cut straight downhill towards the water. There were more people about, but Jake paid them little attention. Presently, they came to level ground, and the buildings they passed were smaller and closer together. The street they were on gradually petered out until it ended in a sweet-scented, lightly wooded space, on a level with the river. Ureth led them nearer to the water, which Jake could glimpse now and again through the trees. The bulk of the town was to the north on their left, the river straight ahead, and Jake realized that Ureth had led them in a wide arc that had brought them to Marfell below the city and its island fortress.

From this approach, Jake could see Marfang, cleaving the River Marfell into a natural moat that swirled swiftly round on either side. The two streams merged once more as the river veered from northwest to south. The river pressed the town of Marfold against the steep escarpment they had just descended, the lower houses of laborers and artisans giving way to wealthy mansions as one's eye ascended the hill.

Despite the invigorating air, Jake was finally feeling tired, and worse, hungry. He trudged along just behind Ureth, glad of the lack of conversation that saved his breath for walking. The leaves of the trees among which they passed sheltered pale golden fruit, incongruous in the cold air. The sun slanted through the dark green leaves of the orchard, turning the puffs of their breath into small iridescent clouds. The grass underfoot was heavy with the dew of melting frost. Jake could hear the dull roar of falling water, and as they approached the bank he saw that here the river fell into a cascade of rapids much different from the deep level waters only a short distance upstream. Black jagged rocks jutted from the water like broken teeth, and in the spray small rainbows caught the morning light with a precision at odds with the fluid chaos that gave them birth. To his right, about half a mile downstream from the castle, the rapids ended, and Marfell flowed smoothly onward again.

"Lucky I didn't land here," Jake muttered to himself. Those rocks would've killed me for sure." And suddenly he felt the fact of being alive with every fiber of his being. For the first time, he fully believed this place, where he magically found himself, was real. No matter how strange it was, he could finally accept that truth. But he also recognized another truth: he had no hope of finding his way home without Ureth. Without her, he had no other path to follow. Bone weary and hungry, he wondered again how his disappearance was going to affect his father. And his mother too, if she still lived.

They came to a clearing near the water's edge, at a point just upstream of the rapids. Here the river was a sinewy course of swift water, several hundred yards wide. To their left, the huge gray castle loomed on its green island. Nearby, on their side of the river, set back from the bank at the edge of the trees stood a low stone building, flat-roofed and six-sided. The structure had no windows, and was featureless save for a recessed alcove set into the westward wall directly facing them, shadowed from the morning sun, still climbing into the sky across the water.

At their approach, three tall men came out of this alcove, swords in hand. They were clad in green, but their sword belts and scabbards were golden, set with red gems that caught the sunlight and reflected pinpoints of ruby fire. The men were cloaked and booted, and the hoods of their cloaks were thrown back to reveal strong, regular features, brown eyes, and dark yellow hair. Each man wore at his shoulder the golden dragon-clasp of the Castleguard. The blades of their swords glinted as the men lifted them towards Ureth and her companions.

"Uh-oh," Jake whispered to Sathryn. "This doesn't look good. What do we do now?"

"Silence, you two. Stay back" said Ureth, completely unfazed. And she walked on.

She approached the men without hesitation. They watched her come, impassive, but keeping their swords towards her. Jake couldn't let her face them alone, no matter what she said. He shrugged off Sathryn's hand, which was clutching at his sleeve. It wasn't as if he thought it was such a great idea to look for trouble with these men. But there was definitely something in the air here…

"Good day, Lady," said the leader of the men to Ureth. "What do you seek here this fine morning?"

"I come to pay respects to the Mothers who have passed, to meditate and pray at the site of their rest." Ureth was in front of the man now, gazing up at him with her clear blue eyes. Jake was standing next to her on her right, Sathryn, foregoing her reluctance, a little behind her left shoulder.

"And these?" The man's sword traversed Ureth's body, back and forth, to indicate first Sathryn, then Jake, in front of whom the point lingered like an accusing finger.

"These are my acolytes, come to assist me while I pray."

"Is that so?" asked the man softly. "Since when do the Crones accept boys as acolytes? And I must also tell you Lady," he went on before Ureth could respond, "We have orders from the Duke to detain all males who are traveling in the company of Crones." And he spat to one side as if the word was unfit for his mouth, the spittle wetting Jake's bare feet in the cold morning air. The sword point moved again, so that for the second time since his arrival Jake felt the press of cold steel against his throat. *This could get old in a hurry*, he thought, as he looked into the man's eyes.

"Take him," the other said.

Chapter 8

A Prince, whose character is marked by every act which may define a Tyrant, is unfit to be the ruler of a free people.

(U.S. Declaration of Independence)

"Open in the name of the Duke!" Rand's anger at being balked by Scarth on the pier poured into the merchant's door through his mailed fist, causing the hinges to shiver. Scarth, having sent his retainers and servants away, opened the assaulted portal himself.

"You don't need to abuse my door or waken my neighbors, Rand, the Duke's men are always welcome here," he said. But Rand pushed past him into the rich foyer, followed by the six men who accompanied him. These were tough-looking customers, and Scarth could feel the menace they brought into his house.

"May I help you?" asked Scarth.

"Silence, Merchant," sneered Rand. "Where is he?"

"If you mean the boy, he is not here."

"Why not? I have a warrant for him signed by the Duke. Fetch him now, or I will let my men search your house, and I cannot vouch for how they may treat your fine furnishings."

"You forget yourself, Rand," said Scarth quietly, his hand drifting to his sword hilt. "I have served in the Castelguard too, in my time. My word is still as good as any man's here. If you do not wish to take it, you are welcome to search, of course, but your Duke will receive a bill for any damage done to my home. If my furnishings are too fine for your taste, perhaps you should confine your part in the search to areas in which you may feel more comfortable, such as my outbuildings?"

Rand flushed at the insult, and drew his sword, as Scarth had intended. *Seven to one*, he thought, as he drew his own blade. *Well, I've faced worse odds before*. But none of Rand's retinue had drawn their weapons, and seeing this, the Duke's man thought better of leaping to the attack. In doing so he saved his life.

You Dancer-cursed son of the Dragon, Rand thought. *I may hate your guts, but I'm not stupid enough to fight you alone. Yes, I know your reputation Scarth, though now you are only a money-grubbing merchant. My master is possibly the only man in the kingdom who could defeat you, which is why I serve him. Your time will come. Oh yes, and I will wait for that day, and laugh as he spills your guts onto the ground*. But he kept his thoughts to himself, and aloud he only said over his shoulder: "Is there any reason why I don't have your support here, Guardsmen?"

One of the men behind Rand spoke up, and Scarth's eyes narrowed as he realized that this was the true leader of the group, both in rank and brains. *How devious Coegun is*, he thought. *If Rand had attacked me and died, I would have been charged with his murder, as he came with a lawful warrant. If I'd died, they would have said I was killed resisting a lawful search.*

"Our orders were to execute a search, and not a man, Captain Rand," said the tall, dark-eyed man who stood amidst the others. He stepped forward now. "Master Scarth is a loyal vassal, often entrusted with important shipments of cargo. I suggest you put up your sword and let me do the talking from now on."

Rand flushed again, but Scarth could see he was relieved to do as he was told, holding his rage in check as he lowered his weapon. "My apologies, Colonel," he said. "Please forgive my rough haste."

"Haste in doing your lord's bidding is always laudable," said the Colonel. "Scarth, our master the Duke requests that you hand over the boy you rescued."

"And if I refuse?" Scarth growled. His weapon was still out.

"Then Captain Rand will issue you with a warrant directing the boy to be placed in the Duke's custody, and allowing us to search your house for him. We will of course," he went on, "take care to disturb your home as little as possible."

"You don't need to serve your warrant Colonel," said Scarth, lowering his sword but not sheathing it. "The lad is not here. I have already sent him to Marfang with my daughter."

"The mistress Sathryn? Why did you not tell us this? That boy may be dangerous. He certainly should be well guarded while we decide what to do with him." The tall colonel was annoyed, but also relieved. He knew that Scarth would not let them search his house. Blood would spill first. *Too much blood for one young boy*, he thought privately. But his orders had been clear: "Come back with the boy, or don't come back," Coegun had said. However if Scarth had already sent the boy to the castle, then all was well. The colonel, whose name was Eoin, did not doubt Scarth's word for an instant. The erstwhile soldier's honor was as legendary as his skill at arms.

"I had little chance to speak when you arrived," said Scarth with a grim smile. "Several powerful people seem to be interested in this boy. But apparently it was the Crones who sent for him." The men murmured at this, and Eoin himself looked uneasy. Only Rand's face did not change, Scarth noticed, almost as if he already knew Scarth's revelation. "I wouldn't want to mislead you, Colonel," he went on. "Although my daughter Sathryn is with the boy, I sent him to Marfang with my other daughter. It was the Crone Ureth who brought the boy to Taumar. I thought that if anyone had a right to him while his fate was decided it was the Crones. I sent him to Marfang, but not to your section of the castle. He has gone to the Coven. Let Coegun serve his warrant on them."

There wasn't anything left to say, and the men of the Castleguard filed back out into the street. Rand went with them, but Eoin lingered in the foyer. He clasped Scarth's right arm with his own, hand to elbow in the salute of the Guard. "The Dancer protect you, Brother," he said.

"And may the Dragon sleep forever," said Scarth, in the traditional reply. He closed the door as the men marched away, sword hilts glittering in the sunshine.

The colonel looked back once as he trailed his men. "You're a dead man," he muttered sadly under his breath. "Why do you care so much about one lost boy?" Nobody heard him. A raven croaked from a tree nearby. It took flight over their heads, and also headed for the castle, alighting there well ahead of them, at a window in the Crone's tower. A gnarled hand reached from the darkness within to stroke the glossy black feathers. It was Sister Hane's hand. And the bird and the Crone had much to say to each other.

2.

Jake watched helplessly, sword at his throat, as the two other men moved towards him with ropes in hand. Behind him, Ureth cleared her throat quietly and said, "Stop." And the men did, standing perfectly still a few feet from Jake, the ropes dangling uselessly. Their leader drew his sword from Jake's throat, and pointed it at Ureth, grabbing Jake roughly by the shoulder as he did so.

"That's enough of your parlor tricks, Crone! Release my men or his belly will taste three feet of cold steel for breakfast!"

"I think not," replied Ureth, still quietly. You instead will put up your sword, and let us pass." She raised her left hand above her head as she spoke, and the swordsman gasped. His face contorted with strain as he tried to stop himself, but his right arm lifted up above his head, sword pointing harmlessly at the sky. "Release the boy and kneel!" Ureth spoke louder this time, pointing now to the ground. Jake felt the man release him, cursing weakly as he sank to his knees, sweat pouring from his face, helpless in the face of Ureth's power. She turned to Jake and Sathryn, and pointed at the alcove in the ivy-covered building. "Go and open the door you'll find there, hidden behind the ivy." Jake followed Sathryn to the low stone building, where they indeed found an iron door pull, set into the wall behind the creeping leaves.

The Fruit Of The Dendragon Tree

There was no sign of an entry, but as he and Sathryn pulled on the heavy ring, the round outline of a doorway appeared, and next the door itself opened silently on unseen hinges.

It was a heavy portal, a foot thick, made of the same stone as the rest of the building. The space behind it was very dark, and smelled like a damp basement. Jake turned back to see what Ureth was doing with the men, but she had already joined him and Sathryn, hustling them inside and closing the door behind her. Jake caught a last glimpse of the men, two of them standing perfectly still with ropes meant for him, the third kneeling, sword pointing uselessly at the sky.

"How long will they stay like that?" he asked, as the door swung shut. There was the grate of stone upon stone, and then the light was gone, leaving them in pitch darkness. There was something wrong about the men being so helpless, he felt, even though they had meant him no good.

"As long as they want," replied Ureth, raising aloft a stick with a flaming tip. They now had some light, at least.

Jake forgot about the men. "What's that?" he asked, meaning the light. "Where did you get it?"

Ureth turned to him. "Do you really not know?" she asked softly. "Even on your world they still know about witch's wands."

Jake said nothing to this. He nodded, his mind reeling. *She does know about my world*, he thought. *I've got to get her to send me back*. But as if she had read his thoughts, Ureth went on. "I have conversed with witches in your world, Jake, but they have become pale shadows of what they once were. But powerful as I am compared to them, only the power of the Dragon could bring you here. Only that can send you back."

While speaking, Ureth had moved to a stone slab, about three feet square, set into the earthen floor of the building. There were several of these dotted around the floor, he noticed. He was still curious. "I don't get it. If you've never been to our world, how did you talk to anybody there?"

"I spoke to them in their dreams, as I did with you. As I did with your friend Jenny".

"She told me that, yes. But how did you get into our dreams?"

"She used a Waterstone." There was a note of awe in Sathryn's voice. "Even though it is forbidden. Ureth, what were you thinking?"

Ureth did not reply. Lips tight, she pushed down lightly on the slab with the lit tip of her wand. It gave a little, and she lifted it up like the trap door it was. She motioned to Jake and Sathryn. "Inside, you two. We don't have time to debate my wisdom now." She glared at Sathryn. "Unless you would rather stay for the men outside to find you."

Sathryn didn't speak, but moved quickly to the trapdoor and began climbing down a wooden ladder set into one side of the narrow shaft. Ureth motioned to Jake to go next, and he followed the girl, trying not to step on her hands as she descended below him. Ureth came last, pulling the trapdoor behind her, sealing them inside the earth.

The ladder went down about twenty feet, Jake thought, and ended on an apron of rock. From this, a pathway of stone extended along a black tunnel that led away from the base of the shaft. The air here smelled clean, even though they were deep underground, and in the distance from around a bend in the tunnel came a flicker of orange light, as if from the glow of a torch.

Ureth took the lead, holding her wand above her head to light the way for the other two. The tunnel sloped downwards for a time, before curving gently to the left. It was wide, high and completely dry. The walls and ceiling were of black stone, glossy and smooth like glass. As they went round the bend, Jake saw that a lit torch was indeed flaming from a sconce in the right hand wall. As they drew closer, Jake noticed that the metal sconce depicted a dragon climbing up the wall. Its mouth was open and pointed upwards, and the flame coming out of it made it look as if the dragon was breathing fire. As they passed it, the flame went out, but another one some distance ahead flared into life, beckoning them along. Ureth put her wand away, as they now had enough light to make their way.

"Where are we?" Jake whispered to Sathryn, who was staring hard at Ureth's back as if she could bore holes in it with her eyes.

The Fruit Of The Dendragon Tree

"We're in a Draighole, one of the secret tunnels of the Crones. No doubt this one will take us under the river to the castle."

"I still don't get how it's safe there, if that's where the Duke is."

Sathryn gave a tired smile. "One quarter of the castle belongs to the Crones, given them by the king a thousand years ago. No man may enter their precincts, unless he still is a virgin. This enclave is the Coven, where all the acolytes are trained, before being sent out into the world to do their work. Marfang is not only the strongest castle in Taumar. It is the center of the Crones' power. Despite their proximity to the Duke, I doubt you could be safer anywhere."

Jake fell silent, thinking. Jenny HAD seen Ureth. And so had he. Ureth had gotten him here somehow, but why? They continued along the obsidian tunnel, which again descended a steep slope and then leveled out for several minutes, before climbing once more. Jake realized the slopes must have been to take them underneath the river and up again the other side. He had counted about thirty dragon torches, and they were climbing when he asked Sathryn, "Who made this tunnel?"

She looked at her sister, but Ureth seemed content to let them talk among themselves. "It is said that the Dragonfire made these passages, long ago when the Dragon ruled here. It is said that his breath melted the very rock so that he could forge his way underground almost as easily as he could fly."

"The Dragon," said Jake. "And what happened to him? Did he dig a bit too far and drown in the river?"

But Sathryn missed his sarcasm, or chose to ignore it, because she gave him a straight answer. "It is said he lives still, imprisoned by the Crones and the Eldervolk, deep below Marfang. And that he will come again to purge Taumar, in the hour of our greatest need."

"Why would he do that," asked Jake, "if you guys put him down there? I'd think he'd be angry, imprisoned underground." Another thought struck him. "And what are the Eldervolk, anyway?"

But Sathryn had grown impatient with his irreverent tone and told him sharply: "You ask too many questions! I'm sure the Crones will tell you all you wish to know. When it suits them."

Jake was too curious to be silent. "You seem to know a lot, though. Are you a Crone too?" Sathryn gave a bitter laugh. The tunnel had ended at the foot of a spiral stone staircase. This was of a pale color that contrasted with the blackness of the tunnel walls. Jake could see it twisting up into darkness overhead. Ureth was looking at Sathryn, and Jake realized she too was waiting for the answer.

"No," said Sathryn, looking at her sister. "I am not a Crone. I have some Sight, but not enough for their purposes." And as they began to climb the twisted stairs in silence, Jake didn't know if she was happy or sad about that.

When they got to the top, Ureth opened another trapdoor above their heads, and they climbed out onto the floor of a small room. When she closed the trapdoor again it was completely invisible. Ureth opened the door of the room, which was a small chamber at the base of a wide stone staircase. There were no other people about. Ureth led Jake and Sathryn up the stairs, along empty passages, up more stairs, more passages, higher and higher until they came to a small wooden door at the end of a short narrow corridor. It was the door to the same Council Chamber that Ureth had left earlier that morning. Entering the room behind, Jake could see that it was bright with daylight, and the sunshine and the still-lit brazier made the space invitingly warm.

Jake followed Ureth and Sathryn into the room, feeling as if every cell in his body was drinking in the warmth and light. As he shut the door behind him he heard Ureth murmur a greeting to someone inside. He looked around, and saw an old woman sitting in the corner.

"I'm glad you made it back safely," said the Mother, for it was she. "I take it this is the young man?" Jake started to speak, but a quick glance from Ureth kept him quiet. *NOT YET.* He heard her thought in his brain. It was her voice, though she hadn't spoken. She wasn't making him be quiet, as she had forced the men by the river to do her will. Jake relaxed, waiting to see how this next meeting would play out. Ureth was amazing, he realized. He would just have to trust her. And he definitely didn't want to annoy her.

3.

"Tell me again how you let them get away." Coegun's voice was soft, and everyone knew this was a very bad sign. The three men who had been guarding the stone crypt that Ureth, Jake and Sathryn had used to gain access to the castle knelt in front of him. Their leader, Rethe, had finally gotten tired of holding his sword arm above his head and when he had realized this it had dropped of its own accord. He had shaken his head to clear it, shaken his arm to regain some sensation, then started to bark orders to the other two, breaking the spell on them as he did so.

"Let go of the Dancer-cursed rope and follow me!" *A fine set of fools we shall look when we return home with this story. We'll be on latrine duty for a month, I shouldn't wonder!"*

They had searched the crypt, but were unable to open the stone slab around which the earth had been disturbed. Eventually, they trudged back to the pier, and caught the ferry over to the castle. There, they had made their report to Eoin, the Colonel of the Guard, the same who had returned empty handed from Scarth's house, arriving too late to capture Jake before Ureth had spirited him away. News of Jake's arrival in the Crone Cloisters had somehow preceded them. And the nature of the boy's arrival, narrowly avoiding a search party and brazenly walking past three veteran soldiers, without a drop of blood being spilled, was unsettling. Worse, it was embarrassing. And Coegun did not like to be embarrassed.

"It is as I said, Lord," Rethe said nervously. His knees were aching from the marble floor. From his position he could only see the Duke, pacing back and forth in front of him and his two men, kneeling on either side of him. There were others ranged behind him, Rethe knew, he had seen them when he had first entered the chamber, and their rank and reputation made him uneasy. Jasper was there, and Captain Rand, who seemed nowadays to be always near his master. His colonel, Eoin, was there too, to speak for him if necessary, and to hear and implement any punishment. His presence was somewhat comforting, but something didn't feel right, and suddenly Rethe knew that he and his men were facing more than a mere dressing-down. The Duke's sword was out, and he was tapping its point gently on the floor at intervals as he paced back and forth in front of the three kneeling men.

"She used the Power on us," said Rethe, knowing better than to look up. "You know what she can do. I told Ion and Dori to bind them and she froze them like stone. I had my sword out, but then I couldn't move either. She made me kneel to her. They entered the crypt. We searched it after the spell wore off, but there was no sign of them, nor of the entry to the tunnel they must have used. We came back here to report."

The Duke continued pacing, silent now in his black felt boots, his sword point no longer tapping the marble. A bead of sweat dripped from Rethe's forehead onto the grey stone of the floor. It was so quiet in the room that he heard the faint splash. The soldier could smell the fear coming from the two men flanking him. He wondered if they could smell his. It was a scent, he knew, that could drive men mad with lust in battle, or render them helpless, like grass to the scythe. Another bead of moisture dropped from his brow, this time onto his upper lip. Rethe licked it away nervously, tasting his fear as it mingled with his salt.

"She *made* you kneel? Look at me, all of you," commanded the Duke. The voice was soft, and Rethe looked up, relieved, to meet his lordship's eyes. They were gentle, almost sad, and too late Rethe remembered Coegun's reputation, that he was never more deadly than when he seemed most kind. He glimpsed a sword flash to his right, but he was dead and past seeing anything before it finished passing through his neck.

It was a tremendous blow, thought Rand. The Duke had lifted his sword hilt across his chest and, with a single backhand stroke, had sliced through two of the necks in front of him before his blade stuck in the throat of the third. This last was Ion, now gasping for air, and breathing only blood. Rand knew his role. He stepped forward and dispatched the dying man with a single thrust in the back, his loins singing with the familiar, engorging ache that the sight of blood aroused.

"My Lord, what are you doing?" This was from Eoin, the colonel, spattered with the blood of his men. The verdict upon them had been so final and so swift that he literally gasped the words. Rethe's head had rolled behind his body, one open eye staring at his colonel like an accusation. But Eoin felt Jasper's warning hand upon his shoulder, and restrained himself with an effort.

"Are you questioning my judgment, Colonel?" asked the Duke. "They made obeisance to a Crone!" His voice even now was almost tender, though he grimaced slightly as he dislodged his blade from Ion's neck.

Eoin chose his words with care. "My Lord, they did their duty as best they could. They were three of my best men, but they were only men, as are we all. We have no defense against the art of the Crones, if they wish to use it upon us. They were loyal and true to you my Lord. They would have lain down their lives for you."

"I think they just did, Colonel. And if you do not wish to join them in that honor then I suggest you hold your tongue."

Eoin made as if to reply, but felt Jasper's fingers dig into his shoulder more urgently. He shook himself free, but bowed his head to the Duke. From somewhere far off, as if he was listening to someone else utter the words, he heard himself say: "Your word rules us all, my Lord."

"Yes, it does," growled the Duke. "And anybody who forgets it will pay the price in blood. Now heed my words. Rand, get someone to clean up this mess. Set the heads on stakes and have them look to the Crone tower, so that Ureth can feel the sting of these deaths on her conscience. I will forget your impudence this time, Colonel, as I know your loyalty to your men, and to my person. But just a word of advice: Do not grow too fond of those whose lives you have to spend in battle, they will not thank you if they are overrun by the enemy as a result. You are dismissed. Jasper, a word. Rand, why are you still here? Stop gawking and get this mess cleaned up as I commanded." The Duke turned on his heel and padded silently out of the small chamber. Jasper hurried to catch up, stepping daintily to avoid treading in the blood of the three dead men now pooling over much of the floor.

Eoin followed more slowly. Blood licked his boots as he quit the room, but the stains it left there were nothing compared to the one he felt in his soul. How would he tell Rethe's widow what had happened? How would Ion's son, who wanted to follow in his father's footsteps, feel when he saw his Da's head raised on a stake? This had been an evil deed, no matter his oath, and the ripples from it had only just begun to spread.

Rand, the last to leave, smiled and inhaled deeply once he was alone. The scent of blood was intoxicating, even more so than the scent of fear had been. Once he had overseen the cleanup crew, he would need a woman. Lust inflated his loins. The wind from his cape stirred the hair on Rethe's head as he exited the chamber. Behind him Ion's body twitched, rippling the viscous red pool on the floor.

Chapter 9

And the dragon stood before the woman

(Revelation 12:4)

"I see you've brought your sister," Marah said into the silence. She stood beside a stone pedestal near the open window. A huge crystal rested on the pedestal, catching the sunlight streaming inside. The refracted light cast small rainbows over the otherwise gray walls of the circular tower room. Jake's heart lifted at the spattered beauty. The Mother moved towards Sathryn as she spoke. "How are you my dear? It's been many years. You have become a beautiful young woman."

Sathryn flushed. "It beats the alternative, I suppose, and with respect I'm not your dear. You didn't want me, remember? I wouldn't look like this if you..." She trailed off, flustered.

The Mother waited a beat before replying. "If we had taken you? You are right, of course. But Beauty has its own power, as you may have discovered. Ours is a power of a different sort, and we sacrifice whatever beauty we may have to possess it. Be happy with who you are, Sathryn. You would not have been happy with us."

Sathryn remained silent, though two points high on her cheeks remained red, with some emotion Jake was unsure of.

"Forgive my manners," the Mother went on, glancing at him. "I so rarely entertain young people. Would you care for some tea? It is cold outside, and you'll have had no breakfast, I'd guess."

"Thanks," said Jake, "You're right, I'm starving." He took the cup the Mother held out to him. Ureth looked on bemused. A young man sipping tea with the Mother in the Crone Tower. She was willing to bet such a thing had never happened before. "It's good," said Jake, and it was. He felt the warmth creep through him, and something else besides, whether from the tea or the Mother's presence, a feeling of peace that augmented the general sense of his own inner power that he felt here. His hunger vanished. "I don't mean to be rude," he went on, but I need to get back home. Can you help me?"

The Mother smiled at him as she handed Sathryn some tea. "You are an honest boy, Jake. Honesty is a thing we could do with more of here." She glanced at Ureth, who blushed and looked away. This wasn't going at all like she'd thought it would.

Jake was aware of the undercurrents in the room, though he didn't understand them. But getting home was the only thing that mattered. "Thank you Ma'am. My Dad always taught me to be honest." His voice caught when he mentioned his father, and he found he couldn't continue. He paused, and looked at the Mother. She regarded him steadily, and he was surprised that her eyes were also moist.

"Yes, he did," Marah said gently. "So let us be honest with each other. Tell me why you came."

"You'd better ask Ureth," Jake replied. "She's the one that's been invading my dreams."

Ureth said nothing, but was aware of an increasing sense of loss. Surely Jake was not the Pendraig. He was too young and inexperienced. Worse, he seemed to have no idea of his purpose here. *The Dancer help us all,* Ureth thought. *Something has gone terribly wrong.*

"Ureth?" asked Jake. "Tell me what you want with me, then let me go home!"

"How is it that you are here, and do not know how or why?" Ureth kept her voice gentle, despite her astonishment.

"Look, I don't really know how I got here. One second, I'm outside in the woods back home, the next I'm here, swimming in a river with two moons in the sky. Two moons! That's one too many! And when I get pulled out of the river, people want to kill me because I speak English! This whole thing has been freaky, but I really have to go home, my Mom-"

"But you wanted to come for her sake!" cried Ureth. "You must have done! Nobody can make the journey for you... nobody can come here from your world unless they wish it, and even then, few are successful. Tell me, did you not willingly stand in the gateway, the pentagram? Didn't Jenny cast the spell? Do you not remember your dreams?"

"Well, yeah, she did, and she said you had told her what to do." But then Jake remembered his departure and his voice trailed off. He looked around. When he spoke again his voice was much more subdued.

"Yes, I remember the dreams. But I could never understand you. And when Jenny made the pentagram in the snow, I thought she was just a flake, but then I got scared and tried to run. Who are you Ureth? Why did I know your name when I saw you, and why did I dream about you?"

But Marah interrupted. "You think his arrival is a mistake," she said to Ureth, still holding her tea between the fingertips of both hands.

"I don't know what else it could be," admitted Ureth. "He had no real wish to come here. The invitation was given, as required by the spell, but Jake did not understand it, or its significance. He did not come to save Taumar, and Tiramonde, as I had hoped."

"To save Taumar?" asked Marah. "Perhaps not. But he did wish to fulfill some desire. Intention is the most important thing, always. Tell me Jake," she continued, "What is the wish closest your heart? What desire did you declare you wanted before you arrived here?"

"Well, Ma'am, I, that is, my mother is very sick. In fact, she's dying. And Jenny knew my wish is for her to live."

"Hmm. A noble enough aim, though perhaps misguided. Doesn't everyone die eventually, on your world as well as this?"

"Yes, they do. But, she's still so young, and she, she's my MOTHER! I mean, she has breast cancer, and it's horrible, and she was so beautiful, and even if she wasn't nobody should die like THAT. And I love her and I don't want her to die, no matter how many people say she's going to, and there's nothing to be done." And he stopped, mostly because he didn't want these women to see him cry, as he knew they would if he kept talking.

"And so," said the Mother gently, "You had been trying to find a way to save her life, is that it?"

Jake nodded.

"And you've explored many avenues, and seen how all of them would come to nothing, and when Jenny offered her help, you thought you'd give it a try, with no understanding of the power you were embracing, because it was camouflaged in a girl you saw every day. And you might have been willing even if you did know the danger of that power, no matter how unlikely the chance seemed, because perhaps, just perhaps, this was the ONE chance out of a multitude that could save your mother. Am I right?"

Jake nodded again. It was all he could do. Marah's compassion had brought the tears to the very brim of his eyelids. He wanted to hide his face.

"Tell me Jake," whispered Marah, "What promise did you make?"

"Promise?" Jake suddenly had an uneasy feeling in the pit of his stomach, for no reason he could name.

"Yes, promise. Or bargain, perhaps. These things are never free. There is always some promise or exchange that must be made. One does not bargain with the Dancer; you didn't make your bargain with Him, though you might have thought you did. What did you declare you would be willing to sacrifice in exchange for your mother's life?"

Jake looked at Ureth, but saw no guidance there. And though Sathryn looked sympathetic, he knew she couldn't help him either. He cleared his throat. "I said I would give my life, that I didn't care if I died in her place," he answered, his voice low, and now he couldn't look at the Mother, those young eyes in the ancient face, looking right into his soul.

"But that's not all, is it Jake? You've promised more, haven't you, in the still watches of your nights?" The Mother's voice was still soft, but implacably insistent on the whole truth, no denying that there was indeed more, more than Jake had allowed himself to remember until that moment.

He cleared his throat again. "I said, 'I didn't care who might have to die'." It was his turn to whisper, but both Crones heard it, and a sharp look passed between them. Jake didn't notice. The wet spot on the floor, where one of his finally escaping tears had fallen, was taking up far too much of his attention.

2.

The darkness began to recede, and I became aware of myself once more. Stars wheeled all around me, and I seemed to be flying through space. I could feel no wind, nor hear any sound. It occurred to me that if I was really flying through space without a pressure suit, I should explode, but I wasn't as afraid of this happening as I ought to have been. I tried to breathe, but there was no air. I looked, and could not see my body. I tried to peer backwards along my path, but somehow this was very difficult to do. I could only manage it for a second before my vision snapped back to what was ahead of me. But in that second I did see something that scared me. Where my body should have been there was only light, as bright as the sun. I had been reduced to an eye at the head of a miniature sunbeam as I hurtled through the stars. I blinked, and passed by a moon. I blinked again, and passed another. I don't know how I knew they were moons, nor did I know how I blinked with no eyes, but that's what it felt like.

Ahead, an unknown planet loomed in my path. Its sun was to my left, and on that side the sphere shone blue, as beautiful a blue as pictures of Earth are from space. But it was not Earth. There was even more ocean than we have, and at first I thought there was no land at all. In the southern ocean, a massive cyclone whirled, and I briefly wondered about the effect of so much water on the planet's climate. Then in the northern hemisphere I noticed an island continent, about the size of Europe, rotating into the night side of the planet. Its northern part was white, while most of the southern reaches were desert brown. An irregular patch of green spread from the middle of the continent out to the west coast, and beckoned me towards it.

I hit the atmosphere of that world and my flame expanded, becoming a gash of fire across the sky. The roar of my passage trailed behind me. I was the breath of the Dragon, and I was returning home.

The green patch of the continent was larger now, darkling into night. I came low to the ground, and the lights of a town flashed below me. A river rose to meet me, its banks clad with forests, its waters swift and deep; I was strangely familiar with this place I had never seen before. I plunged into the middle of the river, at a place where it flowed between steep hills. Down I went, into the depths, my flame extinguished by the engulfing waters. My body took form around me once more, and the cold would have taken my breath away, had I any to spare in my lungs.

Some animal instinct saved me from trying to draw breath underwater. My lungs were tight, craving air, and I kicked upwards. I suddenly remembered Jake as a little boy, teaching him how to swim underwater. "The surface is where the bubbles go," I had told him. Heeding my own advice, I kicked harder, racing the bubbles as my blood clamored for oxygen.

My head broke the surface like a champagne cork and I devoured bucketfuls of air in deep, greedy inhalations. Once I could stop panting, I became acutely aware of the cold, and knew I had to get out of the water. For no particular reason, I struck out for the left, or western bank, the current carrying me downstream to the south as I swam. The riverbank came gradually closer, but it was steep and overhung with spiky conifers, and I began to wonder how I would get ashore. Fortunately, this problem was solved as the river curled around a low bluff, thrusting into the middle of the stream from the western side. In the moonlight, I saw a small beach that the water had carved from the hillside, and working with the current my increasingly tired strokes brought me to the soft shingle. I stumbled ashore, shivering violently in air that lanced right through my wet naked body.

The Fruit Of The Dendragon Tree

I collapsed on my back, gasping in sheer exhaustion, and watched the stars overhead. They were brilliant and clear in a deep blue sky, and I recognized no constellations. Low in the east, a yellowish moon just off the full was sinking, while overhead a huge crimson moon glared down upon me, turning everything on the beach a pale shade of pink. Two moons. So I truly was no longer on Earth. I felt no shock. My equanimity surprised me, and I sought to explain it to myself. I *am* half English: stiff upper lip and all that, able to hide my feelings so well that I can sometimes forget I have them. Which was probably the source of a lot of my trouble with Jake. *And*, I thought to myself, *maybe when you've been changed into pure energy and back again little things like interplanetary travel don't faze you.* There it was: my sense of irony, that failsafe prophylactic against insanity. Or grief. Besides, I knew deep in my bones that only one thing motivated me: finding Jake. And the single-minded purpose of finding a lost child makes a lot of things, which would otherwise be important, seem trivial.

I roused myself, and stood on shaky legs to take stock of my surroundings. I was drier now, and the wind felt less keen, but I was still very cold, and knew I couldn't stay still. In the rosy moonlight, I noticed a path from the beach angling steeply uphill into the woods. Thinking it might be warmer among the trees, and that a path might lead somewhere helpful, I crossed the beach and followed it upwards. The air was fresh, and redolent with the scent of pines. Among the trees, a carpet of needles cushioned my feet, and the rushing noise of the river was dampened. The wind was less also, and eventually my teeth stopped chattering. Something that sounded very much like an owl hooted close by, but otherwise there was only the quiet of the woods at night. I had gone about halfway up the slope, enjoying the peace, when a sound like an angry hornet buzzed in my ears and a sudden vibration in the ground just ahead showered my right foot with a dusting of pine needles and earth, stopping me in my tracks. I looked down to see a long black arrow quivering between my ankles. My inner calm evaporated, and I was suddenly extremely self-conscious of my nakedness.

"Stay still," said a soft voice from the trees ahead.

"Unless you wish to die," said another, just as soft but slightly deeper.

"Cover me Coblyn," said the first voice, "While I see what the river has brought us."

"The sky, you mean," said the deep voice, supposedly Coblyn's. "His trail burned in the air as he plunged into the river from above."

"I believe you Brother, but whatever flame he brought with him is now quenched. It remains to be seen who he is and why he is here, now of all times."

"Then be careful, Dynan," said Coblyn. "And stay out of my line of fire."

"I will," said Dynan, and a tall shadow, that had until that moment been part of a tree, detached itself from the trunk and glided down the path towards me. I didn't know how I had missed him, as a pale glow like starlight shimmered around his head. The sword in his hand glinted red in the moonlight, but the light around his person was silver. His hair was silver also, and his skin was very pale, but his eyes, even for nighttime, were deep and dark. He wore a dark tunic and leggings; on his feet were soft boots that made no sound as he walked. A dark cape hung straight down from his broad shoulders. The cape had a hood, but this was pushed back, and I could see him clearly. It occurred to me that, hooded, his silver light might be invisible.

Despite the arrow in my path, and the sword in his hand, I sensed no malice in him, merely a wary curiosity, and a confidence in his own ability to deal with whatever came his way. I felt strangely glad to see him, as if he too was familiar, and on some impulse I bent to pluck the arrow from the ground, holding it out to him feathers first.

"You might want this back," I said, in a language I didn't know I knew, but though he was now close enough to take it from me, he didn't.

"It is my brother's," he said. "But I am sure he will be glad of it. He thinks an arrow shot in warning is a wasted arrow. I'm a little surprised he didn't shoot you when you moved to grasp this one. If you live long enough you can return it to him yourself."

"I can hardly seem a threat, in my current state," I said; glad to note my voice was steady even though I was shivering.

"Perhaps you are a threat, perhaps not. But we can't be too careful here on the edge of our own lands, and at the edge of these times."

"And what lands would those be?" I asked, still trying to control the tremor in my voice, though I knew any answer would only lead to further questions, along the lines of where in the heck could I be, if I was in a place that had two moons. It wasn't just the cold that was making me shiver.

"As to that, the stranger should introduce himself first," Dynan replied, with a small smile. "But perhaps you could do this in a less shaky voice if you weren't so cold." So I hadn't disguised the tremor after all. But he unfastened his cloak and handed it to me, though I noticed he somehow managed to keep his sword pointed at me the entire time.

I decided not to feel too bad about the apparently obvious tremble in my voice at that point. There's something about standing at swordpoint naked, wet, and freezing after unexpectedly traveling to a strange world that just takes the fight right out of you. Try it sometime and see. I didn't know until much later the strange parallels between my arrival and Jake's, and I am still unclear why I understood everybody immediately upon landing, and he did not. Ureth told me later it was because I truly desired to come and he did not, but there it is. Not all magic can be explained, which I suppose is the whole point. I took the cloak gratefully and wrapped it around myself. It was wonderfully soft and warm and I stopped shivering almost at once.

"Thanks," I said. Then, after a brief silence during which Dynan looked deep into my eyes and saw almost everything inside worth seeing, I added, "My name is David Patel."

He nodded, as if I had just agreed with some inner expectation he had. "So, you have come too," he replied, but the torrent of implications behind his words flooded my mind, and I felt unexpected tears prick my eyes under the light of those alien stars.

"Too? You mean, is Jake… here? Is he safe?" I asked, hoping for the right answers, dreading the ones I might hear.

Dynan looked at me again, and this time I felt the force of his compassion, somehow not at odds with the sword in his hand. "He lives, as far as we know, but his life is in danger. If he can come to us, as we hope, he may be safe for a time. Although safety is not why either of you are here, so that time may be short-lived. But enough talk for now, you need food, and rest, and warmth, and Coblyn and I will share what we have with you, this night at least. Follow me, and take your ease while you can. Your journey is dark, David Patel, and more dangerous than you know."

He turned on his heel and left me standing there, still clutching his brother's arrow. I looked around, and heard the breeze whispering in the pines. Their scent told a story of a wild and lonely place. With a certainty I could not explain, I knew I could trust Dynan, and probably even his bow-happy brother. I settled the cloak more firmly about my shoulders and set off after his silent shadow, drifting up the path ahead of me.

3.

Ureth knelt in her cell, her insides on fire. Sweat poured from her face, and her arms trembled as she clutched herself, elbows tight against her sides, fingernails digging into her palms. Her buttocks pressed upon her heels as she knelt, while her head bowed over almost to the floor. Never in all the rigorous initiations of the Crones had she felt such pain as this. What was its cause? Why was it happening?

This was no disease brought on by bad food or water. She had eaten nothing, as a penance for her arrogance, for her pride, for working alone with magic beyond the scope of her powers. Wait, the Mother had given them tea that morning, could it have been that? No, the Mother would never do that to anyone, least of all Ureth whom she loved. Besides, Ureth knew, she would have tasted the taint of any poison, no matter how small a dose, and the tea had been just that, the warming, rejuvenating Dendragon tea of the Crones. So what was this?

This is life. The words came into her mind from nowhere. *This is life. This is birth. Life is pain. Birth is pain. Welcome to life.*

The Fruit Of The Dendragon Tree

"Who are you? Who is in my mind?" She spoke aloud, but her voice was barely a croak.

You don't know?

"Mother, help me," she whispered, and it was to Marah she pleaded, the only Mother she had ever truly had. The stone walls of her cell absorbed the plea, but offered no help. She moaned softly, the pain excruciating. *Go away pain, you do not exist.* But it did; it could see her, it had found her, it was all the pain she had ever managed to avoid. She was tempted to scream, but didn't know if she could. Even if she did, nobody would come. She had banished herself to her cell, with the approval of the Mother, so nobody would dare come near her. If she screamed, it would be just more evidence to her enemies that she was unhinged.

"Listen to Ureth howl," they would sneer. "Listen to the reward awaiting those who dare to summon the Dragon." So she bit her lip till she drew blood and was silent, blinking back tears she did not know she was shedding. Sweat dripped from her forehead onto the floor, one drop, two, and a third that hissed softly when it met the stone, disappearing in a tiny puff of steam. It took Ureth a moment to understand what was happening. Her sweat was burning hot! This was magic, not disease, but whose?

Mine, fool. The thought came unbidden into her brain.

"Who are you?" she whispered.

I am he, came the reply inside her brain.

"I don't ... understand," she managed, her breath jagged. The pain grew less acute, but a sense of surrendering to something larger than herself began to conquer her, magnifying her while rendering her helpless at the same time.

Do you not? asked the voice in her mind. It was a sibilant voice, male, raspy, unutterably potent. *I am the one you have awoken.*

"Go back, I did not call you," she gasped, her voice croaking like a frog that had lost its pond.

Yes you did, was the answer. *And now we are forever linked, you and I, always one.*

"We are not," she whispered. "Not after the Ring. We took the oaths again, to make sure. None of us would dare call you again."

Nobody here, perhaps, but you have whispered into many ears, Ureth, in more worlds than this one. And you did not bind all of their lips with your renewed promises.

Dancer! thought Ureth. *What have I done?* That girl, the one with little power and less training, the one who had helped send Jake from his world. Jenny, that was her name. Jenny, who could hear Ureth in her dreams; Jenny, who loved Jake, and wanted to help him, who had been used by Ureth to send a young man to save Taumar, in exchange for his heart's desire. *Jenny, what were you doing?*

She was trying to bring Jake back home. The voice in her mind had a smile in it.

"She would have needed help," said Ureth. Her voice was almost normal now, her sweat no longer hissing as it struck the floor. The heat within her body had subsided into a pleasant warmth. She felt unaccountably drowsy, and surrendered to the feeling, lying on her side in the fetal position.

She had it, said the voice. *The boy's own father called for him.*

"His father?" Ureth's voice was dreamy, and she couldn't seem to think properly. The voice in her mind was telling her something significant, but she didn't know what. For all their power and wisdom, for all their insight and magic, the Crones by their very nature could never fully understand the bond between a father and a son. Its very maleness defeated them.

Yes, whispered the voice. *I was tempted to let the boy go, he had no true desire to be here after all. Your invitation, offered in dreams, was too ambiguous for him to comprehend. But you woke me, and I know you thought he'd be useful, so I kept him for you. Besides, he might yet complete the task, and I am tired of my prison. So enjoy this, now, as my little reward. You deserve it.*

"What happened?" Ureth asked, but in truth she barely cared anymore. She was wonderfully warm, and a delicious heat was spreading from between her legs. Her thighs began to twitch slightly. She rolled onto her back, knees up, her feet flat on the floor. The stone felt so warm and comfortable. She knew she was wet, there, in that place, where the Crones decided not to feel anything. *No wonder we do that*, she thought, *we'd never get anything done, otherwise*. She tried to move, but her limbs wouldn't obey her. She was liquid gold, she thought, as pliable and as heavy. The heat between her legs was pulsing now, and really, nothing had ever felt this pleasurable in her life. She remembered what had happened to her at the Ring, and her sense of anticipation grew, heightening her pleasure.

The father is here as well, said the voice. *Now there are two, and one of them is the Pendraig. Now you know how much I care for you.*

"Mmm?" moaned Ureth, but it was a question to which she already knew the answer. "Yes," she sighed, but not in answer to any question. Something exploded softly inside her, her buttocks lifted off the floor as her hips thrust rhythmically upward for more, and more, and more. Her fingers scrabbled against stone, trying to hold on, but she was in abandon. Spasm after spasm shuddered through her. This was the part of life that the Crones had abdicated, but it was no man that made her feel this wild pleasure, as profound as the pain he had brought her. Her shuddering finally abated, and she lay spent on the floor of her cell.

"Who am I?" asked the voice, male but no man.

"You are Kildraig the Dragon," whispered Ureth, and fell asleep.

Chapter 10

From that first tree forth flowed as from a well
A trickling streame of Balme, most soveraine…
Life and long health that gratious ointment gave,
And deadly wounds could heal, and reare againe
The senseless corse appointed for the grave

(Edmund Spenser: The Faerie Queene)

On the morning after his arrival in the Crone Tower, Jake awoke in the small cell that had been allotted to him as a special guest of the Mother. He had a thin blanket and a thinner mattress, which, though he didn't know it, was more than most of the women in the cells around him had. Ureth knocked on his door with two small bowls of gruel. He was halfway through the second one before he realized it was supposed to be hers, that she had come to share a meal with him, and that he was eating her breakfast too. She had waved away his apologies with a small smile. The Crones didn't eat much, certainly not to the scale of a teenaged boy, but Jake had never been so hungry in his life.

Sathryn arrived later to keep him company and Ureth left, leaving his door carefully open. Jake was lonely, and Sathryn was pretty, and curious about him. She even made him laugh a few times. She was irreverent about the Crones, lovingly exasperated at her father, whom she seemed to think of as a giant teddy bear, and sympathetic about Jake's desire to heal his mother. "There is no miracle the Dancer cannot grant," she had said, "if your desire follows the steps of your dance. If it does not, no amount of desire will alter His will." But she would not be drawn into a discussion of what that might be.

It seemed odd to Jake that such a lively girl would talk so freely about God. But then everyone he had met accepted the existence of God, or the Dancer, as a self-evident fact. "Do you have religions here?" he had asked, and when the question had drawn a blank stare, had attempted to explain. Sathryn thought the whole notion ridiculous, and the idea of religious conflict beneath contempt. "So, people in your world actually hate and kill each other because of differences in how they worship the Dancer? That's insane!"

He had no answer for this.

Ureth brought their lunch (more gruel) herself. "Would you like to go for a walk?" she asked Jake, pointedly not including Sathryn, who pouted. But Jake was happy to accept the offer.

"Sure," he replied, and left his cell with Ureth. They wandered along wide corridors, and up several flights of stairs. A few acolytes, with young-looking bodies and old-looking faces, bowed in deference to Ureth as she passed, and stole covert looks at her companion. Jake tried to ignore their stares and suppressed giggles. He didn't have the best sense of direction indoors, and at first thought they were heading back to the Mother's tower room. But they didn't climb high enough for that, and presently Ureth was guiding him along a covered stone promenade, open to the air on their right hand side, the roof supported by intricately carved stone pillars set into a curving stone balustrade. Their walkway was curved as well, and moving to the outer edge Jake could see that they were actually high up the inner face of one of the four massive circular towers that bounded the keep of Marfang castle. They came to a low stone bench, set with its back to the balustrade, and Jake had a sudden desire to sit down and rest. He slowed his pace and looked over the edge as his guide followed suit.

"So this is the Stronghold of the Coven?" he asked, surprising Ureth with his use of the formal name.

"Sathryn has been educating you," Ureth replied. "Yes, this is the home of our order, and we live here under the king's protection, and our own." She had a formal way of talking that irritated him slightly, but he let it go: she probably didn't get out much.

"Well, she told me some stuff, yes," he said. "But I don't really understand what you are. I mean, I saw how you put a spell on those guys by the river, but I got the feeling you didn't really like doing that to them. Are you a witch? Are all the other Crones like you? And if they are, why don't you just take over? Sathryn told me you hate the Duke. Why don't you run the show?" The questions tumbled over themselves in his thirst for understanding.

Ureth smiled, the first true smile he had seen on her face. Then she actually laughed, her eyes twinkling in the morning sunshine, and placed a gentle hand on his arm. "I'm not laughing at you," she said, looking into his eyes. "I just haven't heard so many questions from anyone but me in so long. You sound like the person I was when I arrived here, full of curiosity, driving to find things out, to know what others could teach me." Her smile faded, but her voice was still gentle. "It took me a long time to realize that the one with the best answers to my questions was myself."

Jake looked baffled, and she smiled again and touched her hand to his face. He was expecting the papery touch of an old woman, but the warmth from her hand told a different story. "I'll try not to confuse you with riddles," she said. "You are a handsome boy, and sometimes it comes as a shock to realize I am not that much older than you, in the way that men count years." She dropped her hand and looked again over the edge of the balcony. He followed her gaze downward into the vast square courtyard below. The quadrangle was green with early spring grass, sectioned by grey paths of crushed gravel that tracked between the outbuildings, nestling against the massive inside walls. The sunlight made the crisp air seem warmer than it really was. Bread was baking somewhere, and the aroma made Jake's mouth water.

There were a few people below, walking about with purposes known only to them. Near the north end of the quad was a round pool of green water, bounded by a low wall of flat stones. On an island in the middle of the pool stood a tree, already in full leaf. The wide trunk of the tree was chocolate brown, wrinkled and twisted around on itself like a corkscrew. Huge, flame-colored blossoms were bursting out of the dark green foliage of its canopy. Jake could not say why, but the tree seemed young and old at the same time, beautiful yet forbidding.

"What kind of tree is that?" he asked. "I've never seen anything like it." He looked at Ureth, and saw her eyes were wide, as she too looked at the tree as if seeing it for the first time. "Is something wrong?" he asked, but she just shook her head.

"Let me answer your earlier questions first," said Ureth. "Then, when I tell you about the tree, you will perhaps better understand why you are here." She motioned for him to sit on the bench, and he did so gladly, his stomach rumbling again.

"We care for Tiramonde," said Ureth, "which is our name for our world. We Crones are for the most part healers and are always female. All of us possess to some degree the gift of the Sight, the gift that sometimes allows us to see beyond the limits of time and space. The Sight is how I visited you and Jenny in your dreams. It is also an important part of how we heal. We go out into the world to work for the health of the world. We heal the farmer who injures himself. We help his wife bring forth her children. We bless the planting and the harvest. We settle disputes over land, marriages, theft and the like. If someone commits a crime, we use our discernment to discover the truth of things, and to bring compassion to the measure of justice. Our powers are therefore tolerated because of our usefulness to a community.

"We vow to the Dancer to protect Tiramonde, our Mother, from all danger. Our people's ancient history was one of war, and the enslavement of subject races, and the Crones will not allow such a situation to arise again. But the use of extraordinary power for the greater good demands great discipline and focus, without distraction from worldly ambition or sensual pleasures. So what we gain in psychic power we voluntarily lose in the guise of youth, physical beauty, and the pleasures of the senses. But the Sight is its own reward, because with it we may voyage beyond the prison of the senses.

"Some of us are able to discern the thoughts of others, or even bend their actions to our will. Others are more skilled at healing animals or people, even from terrible wounds, while yet others have the gift of growing crops in barren ground. Am I boring you?" Ureth almost snapped the last question, as Jake's eyes had wandered and he stifled a yawn.

"No, ma'am. It's just that I'm very tired, and I don't understand what this has to do with me."

"Hm. Well, I can feel you are tired, and I am sorry for it. But do try to stay awake, I promise I am getting to the part that concerns you. Give me your hand." Jake did so, and once again the warm vitality of Ureth's touch, coming from such a seemingly ancient body, served to confuse him. She paused for a while, and his hand grew warm in hers. The warmth traveled up his arm, into his chest. Soon, he felt warm all over, wide-awake, calm, and not a bit hungry. She let go of his hand and smiled. He smiled back. She had not done anything to him, he felt. She had merely led him to someplace within himself that filled all his needs. He wondered if she could do that for herself. He wondered if she could teach him to do it for himself.

"We have another role," Ureth continued, "as teachers of those blessed with the Sight. We raise them here, training them in the Craft in a long apprenticeship, which readies them to be of service no matter where they go. It is sometimes difficult for parents to relinquish their children to us, and often difficult for children to face the harsh physical life here, especially if they are older, and have to unlearn the habits of softer usage. But there are compensations, such as the peace I have just shared with you. And the alternative, to have the Sight, yet not be part of the Coven, is anyway forbidden. A mystic, with no exposure to the rigors of spiritual and physical discipline, eventually becomes a pawn of evil. And evil exists in this world, just as it does in your own.

"This portion of the Citadel of Marfang was ceded to us a thousand years ago, so that we could have a place to teach our Craft to

The Fruit Of The Dendragon Tree

those with the Sight. These we find by our work in the world, and send them here, to be properly trained. Our precincts are sacred, and none will dare violate them, 'while the castle stands and the Dragon sleeps' as we say."

"So where do I fit in?" asked Jake. Ureth didn't answer right away, but stood up again, and leaned over the parapet of the balcony. Jake moved to join her, looking at the tree once more. There were many people standing around the pool now, as if something significant was happening. A faint hum of excitement echoed around the walls of the keep, and more people kept coming to look at the tree.

"What's going on, do you think?" asked Jake.

"It's the tree," replied Ureth. "I'll tell you in a moment." She began to speak more quickly, as if the background she had started to give him now had a deadline for completion, the activation of which had just happened in a way he did not understand. It had to do with the tree, he thought, and why all the people down in the quad were gathering round it. He gave Ureth his full attention, knowing somehow she wasn't a teacher who cared to repeat herself.

"It was foretold at the building of this castle that one day Taumar, and perhaps wider Tiramonde, would again need the power of the Dragon imprisoned beneath it. An evil of the world would have grown sufficiently strong that only the Dragon's power could defeat it. Nobody born of Tiramonde can release this power: the legend is that only the Pendraig, called from another place, can do so. The Pendraig will come here in order to satisfy his heart's desire, which will be granted when the Dragon is released. Legend says that the Pendraig will arrive when both our moons are full in the sky at the same time, which only happens once every thousand years. If the legend is true, then that time was two nights ago, when you arrived. I had already been trying to convince the Council that the time of greatest evil is upon us, but they were hesitant. To be honest nobody is really sure if the legend is true. If there was a dragon, does he still live? If he does, will he root out the evil for us? The dragons were supposedly evil themselves, and the one buried here was the most powerful of them all. But my fear for Taumar is great, so I performed the summoning spell of prophecy without the blessings of the Council, and brought you to us."

"You mean I'm here to fulfill some legend you don't even know for sure is true? You think I'm this Pendraig? Are you crazy?"

"I've been accused of it, believe me." Ureth gave a rueful smile, gone almost as quickly as it came. "But the signs are unfolding, though they are coming true in ways that nobody has expected, including me. So though you may be granted your heart's desire, it may not happen in a way that you expect." Jake didn't reply; his mind was reeling.

"You will be safe now until after the Royal Council," Ureth continued. "But whatever they decide, I promise I will not let the Duke have you."

"Why?" asked Jake. "What'll happen if he gets me?"

"He will kill you," said Ureth, looking straight into his eyes, and Jake felt a cold shiver run down his back at the truth of her words.

"But why?" he asked again. "I haven't done anything to him!"

"Why do men kill those who have done nothing to them? He fears you, Jake, so he will kill you, if he can. He has his own magic; I can feel it, even though my Sisters cannot. He is evil, he is cold, he cares only for his own power, and wantonly spends the lives of those who serve him to get it. Yet, they do serve him. Like many evil people, he is very charismatic. He is skilled in arms, a brilliant general, and has defeated those who continuously harass our borders. And I am convinced, though I have no proof, that magic has helped him do this. In our world, magic is forbidden to men. It corrupts them. But his is growing, and the time is coming when he will not fear us. There are evil powers in this world, with whom he may forge unholy alliances, using them until he rules all, and makes an abomination of all creation. Then all Tiramonde will be at risk. But whether or not you are the Pendraig, just by being here you represent magic more powerful than ours, or his. So if he can kill you, he will gladly do so."

"So what do I do? Kill him first?"

"No, nothing like that."

"Then what?"

The Fruit Of The Dendragon Tree

"You have to pluck a piece of fruit from a tree. That tree down there, in fact."

"That's all? How hard can that be?"

"Well, it certainly just got easier. Do you see those red and orange blooms? They weren't there yesterday. That tree hasn't bloomed for a thousand years, since the castle was built. But you arrived, and the Dendragon tree has bloomed, and its fruit must follow soon." Ureth laughed, but there was more wonder than mirth in the sound. "And somehow, unlikely as it seems to both of us, I believe you will stand by that tree, and take its fruit, and so fulfill your destiny, and ours."

2.

"The Tree has bloomed!" Ureth burst in upon the Mother, Jake in tow, to tell her the news. Marah calmly held up her hand, as if to stem the flood of words she knew Ureth wanted to spill. As she took a sip of her ever-present tea, Jake wondered if she had been sitting there the whole time since yesterday, waiting for them to return.

"Naomi, some tea for our guests," Marah said, as if she knew what he'd been thinking. Jake noticed a petite, dark-haired acolyte near the small brazier where the tea was brewing. She still looked young, he realized, and wondered if she hadn't been in the Coven long enough to look old. The girl blushed when her eyes met his, then she turned away to do as Marah had asked. When she gave him his tea, her fingers brushed his own, and she looked at him shyly again from eyes that were deep dark pools, holding some message for him he could not read.

"Thanks," he said, and though she did not look at him again she blushed once more as she handed a cup to Ureth, who nodded her thanks and looked from Naomi to Jake. She looked as if she was going to say something to them, but then Marah spoke again, and the moment passed. In the future, Ureth would look back on that first meeting between Naomi and Jake, and wonder if she should have followed her instincts. But to follow them where, she could never say. Sometimes the steps of the dance simply have to be danced, for destiny to have its way. For much good did eventually come of this destiny, even though much pain intervened. Besides, there was too much else happening to make too much of a single glance between two young people. Priorities, as well as appearances, can deceive.

"Yes, my Dear, it has indeed," said the Mother, not needing to ask which tree. "The Dendragon tree has flowered after a thousand years, and you are bursting with questions. But I believe the most important one for you is whether you still believe that Jake's arrival was a mistake." She sipped her tea again, and Jake did likewise, again feeling the immediate banishment of his hunger. Whatever was in there, he thought, would fetch a fortune back on Earth as a diet drink. And he felt again the strangeness of being here, alone except for these magical women who seemed to care about him. He sipped the tea again, trying to quell the anxiety that threatened to become panic.

If Ureth was surprised that Marah already knew her news, she hid it well. As she explained to Jake long after, "The most amazing thing about her was how hard it was to surprise her, but then it was her business to never be surprised. I had great power while still very young, but I have yet to match her in wisdom, and don't know if I ever shall." Ureth suppressed her excitement, sipped her own tea as well, and took a deep breath before responding.

"I suppose it is not, a mistake, that is."

"Gee, thanks," said Jake, but a look from Marah quieted him.

"I think we should proceed as if he is the Pendraig," Ureth continued, "even if he is not what I expected."

"Ah, yes, expectation," Marah replied. "That double-edged sword between hope and disappointment. You expected a hero of heroic proportion. But I have often found that heroes are ordinary people whose proportions become embellished after the fact to fit the stature of their deeds. So tell me, Jake," she said, turning her gaze upon him, "Do you feel like a hero?"

He didn't have to think about it. "Well, no, ma'am, I don't."

The Fruit Of The Dendragon Tree

"Good. Had you said you did, I would have known you were not one. On the other hand, feeling you aren't a hero only lets me know that you could be one, not that you are one. It's very confusing isn't it? Hardly worth considering with the gruel we've been feeding you. Naomi, please stop looking at Jake as if he were chocolate, and bring him a meal more suited to a possible hero than what he's had so far."

"Yes, Mother," said the girl, as she blushed her way out of the chamber.

"Thank you, my Dear," said the Mother to the closing door. "Now, Ureth, help me stop babbling and tell us what's whirling around in that brilliant mind of yours."

"It's as if Jake's arrival has set in motion events I didn't anticipate, possibly because I didn't really believe, deep down, that the old spells would work. I was frustrated, and desperate, and rebellious, and cast the spell at the Ring with Naomi and the other two acolytes because I felt the most urgent need to do something, anything, to force Coegun's hand. And now, I cannot see the end of what I have set in motion."

"Those are the most honest words you have spoken in some time, my Dear," said Marah. "How hard it must be for you to have all that power, yet restrain it, while those of us who have much less talent urge you to curb yourself. Is there anything else you'd like to tell me?" And Jake noticed she looked keenly at Ureth as she said this, as if the question was some kind of test.

"Yes, there is, but I don't know how."

"Well, start at the beginning, and walk me through to the end, and I'll ask you afterwards if I need anything explained."

"He came to me," Ureth started, and Jake wondered at first if she was talking about him, but then he saw the hunted look in her eyes, and knew she spoke of someone else.

"Ah, yes, and he would be…?"

"Kildraig, he said, or rather, I said it. It was the Dragon himself. He brought me pain and pleasure in the night, and told me that Jake's father had also arrived here."

"What? My Dad's here? Where is he?" Jake blurted out, before another glance from the Mother again quelled him.

"Jake, your father is here in this world," said Ureth, "but as to exactly where, I do not know. I did not call him; it seems as if your friend Jenny sent him here. I would have said she only has enough magic to be dangerous, but then one could say the same of me, arrogant as I have been."

"So how do we find him?" Jake was impatient, and had no time to hear Ureth's remorse.

"He is safe, for now," said Marah. "The ravens have had word of his coming from the Eldervolk. There is nowhere safer he can be for now, so we need to be patient."

"Who are the Eldervolk? Will they bring him here?"

"They are a different people to us," said the Mother. "You would call them elves, though labels like that mean different things to different people. As to whether they will bring him here, I expect that all roads will soon lead to this castle. But there I go, expecting something despite knowing better. What did you mean by pain and pleasure?" This last question was directed back to Ureth, who flinched as if she had been slapped.

"The pain was… it burned from inside, indescribable. He could have killed me, I think. The pleasure? Well, it burned too, but in a totally different way. He said we were connected, somehow, because I had called him."

"Hmm. Well, he's right, you are. But guard your mind from him! I am comforted that you told me of this conversation of your own accord. It means he has not influenced you to lie. But he poses a grave danger to you, my daughter. Remember, there is no pleasure he can give you that does not have ten times the amount of pain as its price. That is the way of the Worm, it always was so, and will ever be, even if only one still lives. They were all evil, submitting to no authority but their own, and having cold, empty spaces where their hearts should have been. They possessed great passion, but no compassion to temper their terrible strength, and a great heart that has been wounded is their most treasured prey. Kildraig was the greatest of them. He was imprisoned here; so long ago most only remember him now as an old wives' tale. But today his tree has flowered. The gift of its fruit will be life, and the price of it will be death, and that by itself is a sign that Jake is meant to be here, though nothing in any prophecy foretells the coming of another. That unanticipated detail clouds everything." She smiled ruefully at them, her eyes twinkling in the gnarled caverns of their sockets. "You see, my dears, it's one thing for our prophecies to be wrong, but quite another for them to be uncertain."

"So what should we do next?" Ureth asked the question that was in Jake's mind.

"We wait, of course. Oh, we'll think, and worry, and make plans, which will almost certainly be changed, and then we'll be forced to react to events as they unfold. And in the end, the Dancer's steps will be danced, as always. Ah, here comes the food." The door opened and Naomi came in balancing a tray, piled high with bread, and butter, and cheese, and coffee. Jake, with his heightened senses, could smell it all before he saw it, and magic tea aside he was ravenous once more. The bread was fresh, and still warm, and Jake wondered if it was the same he had smelled on the balcony outside. He fell to, and had never tasted food so wonderful in his life. It was several minutes later before he wondered, with a guilty frown, whether his Dad had also arrived naked, and if he was cold, and if the elves had food as good as this.

3.

"Oh, Jake, I think I will climb these walls soon!" Sathryn cried after Ureth brought him back. She had a point, as there was simply nothing to do. Sathryn was not an initiate, and Jake wasn't even female, so they were not allowed to go among the Crones in their Tower enclave. Within its walls flowed the rhythm of chores, of meditation, of prayer, of study. Secluded from those without the Gift, protected from the fear of the unsighted, the baser appetites of men, and the temptation of worldly pleasures, the Coven had no place for outsiders.

Left alone together once more, they started to speak to each other, in mutual loneliness and boredom at first, then with growing warmth, as they began to understand each other's pain, and the things that made them laugh. Jake had decided that Sathryn had a lovely laugh, and he tried his best to make it spill out as often as he could. This was easy enough to do, as he had an innate dry wit, and she loved to laugh. She was fascinated by his world, by his stories of technological marvels, of planes, and skyscrapers in huge cities, of television and computers, movies, and digital music and all the things he took for granted as part of his world that were now gone, leaving him with nothing but himself, and the company of a very beautiful girl who had lost her own mother, and so survived his own biggest fear.

For her part, Sathryn told Jake about her life, and the history of Taumar and Tiramonde. Of how, long, long ago, theirs had been a technological society too, one that had wrecked itself by valuing cleverness more than wisdom, and information rather than truth. How that world had nearly been destroyed, ravaged by wars and disease, almost as if the very planet itself had wished to eradicate the beings that populated her. Technology had all but died, and humankind with it. Then slowly, out of the ashes of ruined civilizations, magic had arisen to take the place of technology, magic both good and evil, playing out in battles in new kingdoms, until the coming of the Dragons, and the appearance of a new red moon in the night sky to herald their coming. This was the time lost to history, with no record of what had gone before; whole continents had disappeared, consumed by earthquakes and floods, as the world adjusted to the new entity in its heaven. Only legends and snatches of poems handed down through the centuries carried the rumor of how things once had been.

"The twelve Dragons changed everything," Sathryn said. "They were more powerful than anything we humans had ever seen, and only the most pure magic could stand up to them. Kings who dabbled in the dark arts quickly became their puppets, and lost their power, and soon the only good magicians left were women; the Dragons either had a soft spot for them, or else were better able to corrupt the magic of men. The Crones say that men are less able to use the Gift for the service of others; if they have power they usually want it for themselves, and no power can corrupt more easily than the Sight. Whether they are right about that or not, the male wizards either died or dwindled, fading to shadow creatures: hungry vampires, fit for nothing but furtive existence under the guard of the Eldervolk. Many of their undead vassals also remain, wolf-men also thirsty for blood. Endil, the first king of Taumar, was such a one who fell prey to the vampyrim. It is said he haunts the forest still, in thrall to his vampire overlords, ever wild, never resting, unable to join the Dancer in his Dance behind the stars. Meanwhile, the Dragons either fell to human magic or killed each other off, all except one, the greatest of them all. Kildraig was his name, and he was poised to rule the world."

"Sounds like a bad situation," Jake said, unsure how to process, in his mind, all the talk of dragons, and wizards, and other things he didn't believe in.

"Oh yes, Jake, it was. Human survival hung in the balance, but the female witches drew their magic together to defeat Kildraig. And this they managed to do, imprisoning that last, most evil worm under the river Marfell, under this very castle, built on top of his underground prison. It is said Marfang will never fall, while Kildraig lies entombed beneath it. And so the Coven resides here too, to make sure he never escapes, unless there is reason to summon the Pendraig from another world and so release him.

"Why would anyone want to free a Dragon they'd worked so hard to imprison?" asked Jake. He was fascinated despite himself, though still unsure if he believed everything he was hearing, and he could tell Sathryn wasn't sure either. But something magical had brought him to this place, and if some magic existed, he thought, maybe it all did.

"I don't know," replied Sathryn, "It must have something to do with the Undead, though. Everything is in balance, but if they somehow get free, then only a Dragon's power can hold them in check."

"What do you mean, 'get free', are they in prison too?"

"No. They were too many to be destroyed or imprisoned. But the Crones were able to force them into the great forest, many days travel from here. My people do not travel there. The legend says that the Undead are bound under the trees by the power of the Waterstones, whose magic sets the boundaries of their land. They cannot travel the sea, and they cannot cross the stones, to reach us. The Eldervolk have made sure of this, the legend says, for a thousand years. But nobody I know has seen any of the Undead, nor any of the Elven, and so, I think, the old tales are no longer believed. Nobody travels anymore past the borders of the old forest, and none to the feared lands beyond that to the sea. Those who go do not return. Today our worries are more that the Sacours will take our kingdom from us, so we are constantly fighting them, them and the cold ones that live beyond the northern mountains where it is always winter. And if I were one of these folk I would want what we have too! Rich land, and the medicine of the Crones, that comes from the Dendragon flowers, which grow only on this island where Marfang stands. They have great healing properties, and can prolong life."

"You mean you have flowers that can save lives?" asked Jake. "Why can't I just pick some of them and take them home?"

"I may have misspoken," replied Sathryn. "If you take a tonic of the Dendragon flower over a long period of time, then your life will be long, longer than those of most mortals, and healthy for the most part. But you will also end up looking like one of the Crones. Indeed in the initiation ceremony of the Crones, in which a young girl becomes a full-fledged acolyte, she drinks the pure essence of the Dendragon, to begin the live-extending magic that robs her of her beauty. And the petals can be ground up, and made into teas and other medicines that enhance vigor and health for long periods of time. These can cure lesser illnesses, but they would not work against the disease that consumes your mother, Jake. For that, I think Ureth told you the truth: you need the fruit of the Dendragon Tree itself."

"But the tree is guarded by the Duke, said Jake, "and the Duke wants me dead, so how do I pick the fruit?"

"I don't know," said Sathryn. "But Ureth is very powerful. I have never seen her fail at anything."

There was a touch of bitterness, as well as pride, in Sathryn's voice as she spoke about Ureth. "Must be tough, having a sister like that," he said. He stretched, and got up from the floor where he had been sitting. He crossed to the window, and looked out. Far below, in the courtyard, he could see some soldiers, practicing sword drill. His muscles yearned for some exercise. He looked back at Sathryn, who gave him a sad smile.

"Yes, it is," she said. He waited, but Sathryn said nothing else. He looked out the window once more. He thought he could recognize the leader of the sword drill as one of the men who had wanted to take him to the Duke from the dock. Even to his untrained eye, the man seemed to be an excellent swordsman. A sudden warmth at his side told him that Sathryn was standing near, and he looked quickly at her, then away. His heart beat faster. Jake cleared his throat, trying not to think about how beautiful she was.

"Can I ask you something?" His words seemed forced, unnatural, but Sathryn just smiled. He could see striations of green in the light brown of her eyes, and highlights of gold in the copper of her hair. The faint scent of strawberries came to him again, and he felt his pulse quicken even more.

"You can ask me anything, Jake, you know that." Sathryn placed her hand on his arm, and he felt as if he would melt under her touch.

"Why does Ureth want me to pluck the fruit from the tree? What's in it for her?"

"I don't know. The legend says that once the fruit is plucked, this castle will fall, which is maybe how she hopes the Duke will fall. But the legend also says that the sleeping dragon will be released when the castle falls. And I can't believe she wants THAT. There must be something else I don't know about."

A cold breeze gusted through the open window, and Sathryn shivered, spontaneously moving closer to Jake. "You're so warm," she said. He put his arm around her, his heart racing again. He tried to swallow, but his throat was dry. She moved to face him under his arm, and looked deep into his eyes, smiling softly. "You can kiss me, if you like," she whispered. And he did. It wasn't first time he'd kissed a girl, but it was definitely the best time so far. Her lips folded into his own as if they were meant to be there, his arms wrapped around her and held her close. Jake felt a whole bunch of delicious sensations all at once. His strong legs were shivering, almost wobbly, he was breathless, and most curious, he found it difficult to tell where his body ended and hers began and he knew intuitively that it was the same for Sathryn.

They kissed for what seemed a long time, but time had still flown too quickly when Ureth cleared her throat from the open doorway and demanded "Sathryn! Just what do you think you're doing?"

A cold bucket of water would have had less effect than this harsh interruption, and Jake broke away from Sathryn's embrace feeling flustered, and somehow guilty. Behind Ureth, Naomi caught his eye, and winked, and Jake flushed in embarrassment. But Sathryn whirled to face her sister, color high, and retorted, "I'm kissing a boy, Ureth! Maybe you should try it sometime!"

Chapter 11

Out of this wood do not desire to go.
Thou shalt remain here, whether thou wilt or no.

(William Shakespeare: A Midsummer Night's Dream)

The first thing I did when we reached Coblyn was to return his arrow. He chuckled softly in the moonlight, and his eyes glinted as he took it from me. "So it wasn't wasted, after all," he said. "Many thanks, David Patel, it's a good one."

"Aren't they all?" I replied. He chuckled again, but then grew serious and said, "Yes, they are. And I'm glad I didn't shoot you with it."

"Not as glad as I am," I said, and we both smiled. Dynan was rummaging in a backpack stashed on the ground behind a tree. He retrieved what turned out to be a pair of leggings and a tunic such as the ones he and his brother wore. A pair of soft felt boots followed these and he handed me the lot.

"Put these on, David Patel," he said. "We have a fair distance to cover, and you can't walk through the forest naked except for a cloak."

"Thanks," I said, and I meant it. "And you can just call me David; we don't use both our names except when we first introduce ourselves."

"Very well then, David it shall be. You may keep the cloak as well; I have another back at our campsite. Are you ready? Good, let us be off."

He started walking up the path, gesturing with his head for me to follow. Coblyn brought up the rear. Once we crested the hill, Dynan headed left along the ridge until we came to a rocky outcropping that was clear of trees. We were standing atop the promontory where I had beached, bathed in the light of the crimson moon. Below us, the river foamed as it broke and curved around the bluff upon which we stood, before flowing once more unimpeded away to the southeast. Across the river, a thick growth of trees pressed toward the water, but not far behind them was a gently rolling country, with few trees. This carried on for miles, smudged in the distance by a dark shadow that may have been mountains. On our side of the river, a deep forest hemmed against the water north and south for many miles. Away to the south I thought I could see where the trees ended, and open space began. Looking behind me to the west, I could see only trees, mostly pines that thrust up from the ground like the tips of spears, tinged with the blood-light of the moon.

"Welcome to Tiramonde, David," said Dynan. Though that may mean little to you yet. Away to the south are the villages of men, scattered about the veldt of the Taumarians. The castle Marfang, where your son is a guest of our friends the Crones, is on an island in the middle of this river, also many leagues to the south. Farther south still, this river, which we call the Marfell, eventually falls many, many feet, into the desert land of the Sacours, into whose lands it brings all life. To the east and north, across the river, lies the North March of the Kingdom of Taumar. On this side of the river is the South March; you are just outside the northern borders of that kingdom, at the edge of our lands".

"And who are you guys, again?"

They both looked at me with their deep, almond-shaped eyes. It was Dynan who spoke first, as I knew he would. "We are the guardians of the forest," he said. "We are what you might call elves, if your people remembered such things." I looked at them, unsure what to say, so I tried a feeble attempt at humor. "OK, well, thanks for the tour, what's next?"

Dynan laughed, the sound clear in the starlight. There could never be any mockery in a laugh like that. "You have a sense of humor, David.

That is a good thing. You may well need one while you are here. Look behind us, to the west." I did so, and looked again at the unending vista of trees. Above them in the distance, the full yellow moon rested, low and fat near the horizon. A dark line, far to the west, became a darker expanse beyond.

"This forest that stretches from the river nearly to the sea is called the Blutwald, or Bloodwood," Dynan said. "The Empty Ones live here, dark and twisted beings, recognizing no authority but their own, submitting to no other will, except the desire for blood, for which they have a constant thirst. They are hungry, these vampires, with a desire that cannot be filled, and they are growing bolder. Their minions, the werewolves, now travel in bands through the forest, and have become a constant threat to we who herd them. And now, we fear the whole kingdom of Taumar is threatened. And if they win that prize they will desire next Tiramonde the Jewel, our name for the gift of the Dancer, that knows no borders or kingdoms."

Dynan suddenly gripped my forearm, and looked deep into my eyes. I again sensed that he knew all about me. "Your son came here to help defeat this evil, though he didn't understand what he was getting into."

"Did he arrive the same way I did?"

"We think so, though the magic of the Crones is not known to us. But I can tell you this. The legend of his coming has been foretold. And the why of it is known as well. He comes to help Tiramonde, and to redeem his heart's desire."

My mind whirled. I knew Jake's heart's desire, but Dynan was right, he couldn't have bargained for this. I had to find him. "And me?" I asked.

"Your coming was not foretold, David, yet not completely unexpected, either. You are also here to redeem your heart's desire. And we will help you while you are with us; that much you can count on."

"Then let's go south; I need to find Jake."

"Yes, you do. But as for where to go first, we must take counsel, which we cannot do until tomorrow. Come with us tonight. Rest, eat, in the morning there will be news, I am sure. There is much danger abroad; much is happening, and sometimes the wisest course is not to act too soon."

"Better than acting too late," I retorted, flushing with impatience in the dark.

"Too soon or too late, neither is wise. But please trust me for now. We cannot go with you just yet, we are too few. And you would die if you tried the journey alone. The Undead are more perilous than you can possibly know. Jake is safe enough, at least for now."

It was maddening to accept Dynan's words, but there was not much I could do about the situation. I nodded at Dynan and Coblyn, standing there all elvish and silvery and serene in the moonlight, and chafed with impatience. But I knew my fate was in their hands for now. Dynan began walking again, and I followed him back into the darkness of the trees.

We walked a long way, that first night, before the second moon set. I was chilled at first; still feeling the lingering effects of my splash-down in the river, but the elven clothes and the pace that Dynan set soon warmed me. The forest was quiet, but the elves were quieter, and often almost invisible. If I hadn't spoken to them occasionally, I might have thought I was walking with a couple of shadows. Very comforting shadows, somehow, but not big on conversation. Dynan followed some path I couldn't see in the dark, and guided us expertly even through the thickest stands of trees. We crossed a small stream that I guessed flowed back towards the big river, though I was uncertain of my bearing in those strange woods, under those alien stars. Every so often, the utter strangeness of the situation threatened to overwhelm me, but then I would think of Jake, and the image of his face would serve to steady me enough so that I could bear down and concentrate on putting one foot in front of the other. Stiff upper lip, and all that.

We eventually came to a small hollow, bounded on one side by a low cliff. Dynan walked right up to this at his brisk pace and I was so sure that he was going to walk into the rocky wall that I almost shouted a warning. But as I drew breath Coblyn clasped my shoulder from behind and said, "Wait," and the next thing I knew Dynan had walked through the wall as if it had been a curtain. "Go where I push you," said Coblyn, as we approached the wall in our turn, and he shoved me gently towards the grey stone when we got there. I did shut my eyes at the last second, but never felt a thing, and when I opened my eyes I found myself in a small cave, lit with the fading moonlight. I turned around, and I could see outside, and could plainly see Coblyn as he walked into the cave as well.

"Well, um, just how did we do that?" I asked my hosts. Dynan kept a straight face, but Coblyn was grinning at my surprise.

"Just a little elf magic," he said. We can see out, but nobody can see in. Comes in handy if the wrong sort of people are about."

"Is the wall not real, then?"

"Oh, yes, it's real enough," said Coblyn. "But there's an invisible entrance through which we can enter, as you saw. And we can go in and out without having to take everything with us, which is convenient. We sometimes even leave the lamps on, though we didn't tonight as we were planning to stay out all night. That changed because of you, and I'm not sorry. Guard duty on the river isn't really my idea of fun." Coblyn was less serious than what my preconception of elves was like, though why I should have had a preconception at all was beyond me, as I'd never entertained the possibility of their existence before now.

"Well then, light the lamps brother," said Dynan, "and let our visitor get warm. Come, David, sit here. We have food to share, and wine. I know how strange all this must be for you, but you may as well take your ease while you can. It may be a long time before you are able to again."

So I sat down, dressed as a wood elf in a magic cave far from my world. The warm glow of the lamps did not spill outside, nor reflect back from the wall that allowed us to see out. I broke bread with my new friends, and better friends I have never had, in either world in which I've lived. Their wine would have put France out of business, and the bread was like nothing I could describe. Wholesome, and comforting somehow, but these words don't do it justice, and you will never taste anything like it, unless you come to that place somehow yourself. We didn't talk much, but I sensed that much was understood. When we had finished our light but amazingly satisfying meal, Dynan showed me to a berth carved into the rock, padded with a springy bedding like heather. He gave me a blanket of some material warmer yet lighter than wool and told me to rest.

"You love your son as a father should, David," he said, and I realized I had shared that emotion, without speaking, during the meal. "Rest now, and take what the daylight brings you." So I did, and fell asleep almost at once.

When I awoke, sunlight was dancing in the cave, through the magic wall, and my hosts were nowhere to be seen. I yawned, stretched, and felt totally calm, which I realized was very surprising, given the circumstances. I don't know why I felt like that; but I've since learned it is difficult to be around elves for long without feeling either restful, or uncomfortable, depending upon what you store in your heart, and they already knew what was in mine. I was anxious about Jake and Mary, but there was nothing I could do to help either of them right then, and this loss of control was somehow soothing, instead of anxiety provoking. I wondered if I had been emotionally transformed by my journey, if the quantum nature of being physically disintegrated and re-formed had somehow strengthened my spiritual outlook. I was half Indian as well as English, the two sides often in conflict, but often united in the ability to at least outwardly accept the fate that was brought me, whatever my own feelings. It was this ability to accept (the way, for instance, that I accepted Mary would die) that also drove Jake crazy. He didn't understand that I was scared if I let my feelings out, I might never be able to master them. But waking up in the elven cave far from my home world, unable to tend to my wife, unable to protect my son, feeling vulnerable yet resourceful, didn't feel like suppression. It felt like peace.

I shrugged these thoughts aside as being too deep a pool to dive into so soon after waking up. Retrieving the felt boots Dynan had loaned me, I shuffled my feet into them, and walked outside into the brilliant morning. It was cold after the warmth of the cave, but the air was refreshing and filled with the scent of the pines that pressed around the small clearing in which I stood. I wondered where Dynan and Coblyn had gone, but wasn't overly concerned; they weren't going to desert me, and I knew they could look after themselves.

There was a flat stump a few feet to the left of the cave entrance, which looked like an inviting spot to sit and wait, and I turned towards it. Before I reached it, however, a large black bird swooped out of the pines and alit on the stump with a loud caw. He looked at me with disturbingly intelligent eyes, before saying, "Good Morning, David."

I blinked. So much magic had happened to me already that I probably shouldn't have been surprised, but I certainly wasn't prepared for talking birds. I also understood the raven hadn't spoken aloud so much as formed the words he wanted me to hear in my mind, and the effect was disconcerting, to say the least. "Good morning," I managed in reply, but didn't trust myself to be intelligent much past that.

He looked at me, large and gleaming coal in the bright morning, and I could tell he was amused. "Don't know what to make of me, eh?" A series of soft croaks followed this question and I knew he was laughing. "Well, that makes us even, my friend, that makes us even. I can see your son in you. I know you've heard many times that he doesn't look like you. But you are stamped all over each other, no mistaking you for anyone else but his father. But why you're here, that's a different question. Yes, I've seen him, so hold your questions, but I'll tell you about that in a minute. I don't suppose you know where Dynan is, do you? I'd ask for Coblyn, but he's completely irresponsible, which takes some effort for an elf."

"Um, no, I don't," I replied, to this verbal torrent that seemed to know my questions before they even formed in my mind. I realized with a mental jerk that I wasn't speaking either: at least not out loud. "They brought me here last night and I've only just woken up and found myself alone."

"Hmph. Typical. Probably talking to the trees or something. Elves! They'll talk to anyone or anything that'll listen! Let me tell you…" But

I never heard what he was going to tell me, because at that moment my two hosts came back, materializing like ghosts at the edge of the clearing

"Good morning Dobrun!" cried Coblyn. "I see you've met our guest. What news from Marah do you bring us?"

The raven cawed in reply, just a normal bird-like sound, empty of any meaning as far as I could tell. He puffed out his feathers, and shook himself, and I realized that the silent approach of the elves had startled him. But I heard his answer in my mind, and knew the elves could hear him too. "The date for the Council has been set. They have already sent a rider requesting an Envoy from the king. But Marah doesn't trust Coegun, and begs your help. We are looking for Keffyldyn, too, though we haven't found him yet. Amazing how someone so obvious can hide when he wants to."

"Wait a minute, wait a minute," I said, out loud, my spoken voice as harsh as a crow's in the bright, still morning. "Tell me about Jake. You've seen him? Is he ok? Can you tell him I'm here? Where is he? How can I get to him?" The questions tumbled out of me, impatient, urgent. I had no idea who Marah and Keffyldyn were, but Dobrun had seen my son, and Jake was the only person I cared about.

"Patience, David," said Dynan's voice in my mind, and I could feel his great heart calming me once more. "Jake is safe, as I've promised you, at least for now. Dobrun's news of the Council touches him directly. What happens there will determine how and when you see him again. And you have a voice in that, believe me. Your son's life, and yours, may be forfeit if we go astray." He shifted his feet, and spoke aloud to the raven. "So Marah asks for our help, we who have not troubled the affairs of men for many a year. And Keffyldyn? If you find him, and he agrees to come, there will be many a man whose eyes will open wide when he appears. It's one thing to think old legends are quaint tales to put children to sleep, quite another when they stare you in the face. How long until the Council convenes?"

"The King's Envoy cannot arrive for a week or more," said Dobrun, "and the boy will be safe for that long. You should know, David," he said to me, "I have not spoken directly to your son. But I have seen him, and he is under the protection of Marah and the King. He is safe for now, rest assured."

"Yet Marah foresees a time when he is no longer safe, and therefore sends for Keffyldyn and the elves to safeguard the boy's life, and the prophecy." I was beginning to learn that Coblyn had a knack for plain speaking, but his words filled me with dismay.

"But why is Jake's life in danger?" I asked. "I thought you said the bad guys were in this forest. If Jake is safe in a castle, why is everyone so worried about him? And who is Keffyldyn?"

"It is as you say, David," said Dynan. "But we believe, and Ureth and the Mother Marah also believe, that the Duke Coegun has decided to align with the Undead, to fill his own desire for power. This is the same Duke of the castle Marfang, where Jake is. It is he who wants Marah to hand Jake over to her. He fears your son, because his coming may fulfill a prophecy that threatens the very heart of his power, that which he has already, and that which he seeks. And for those who crave power as he does, even the most unlikely threat must be ruthlessly dealt with."

"And as for Keffyldyn," said the raven, "He is simply himself, as you will see when you meet him. Old, he is, and wise, but as vigorous still as the first day he ran over the veldt. But he is the best help, perhaps even including Ureth, that your son could have."

"Ureth?" I said. "So she's real. She's the meddling witch that brought Jake here. I definitely want to speak to her. But how can we help Jake?"

Dynan smiled at me. "Ureth has been called many things in her time, but "meddling witch" has not been one of them. I'm sure your paths will cross before long. But for now, we should take you to a safer place, where there are more of our people to guard you. Then we will decide how many of us, and who, will travel to Marfang."

"Well, I have to go," I cried, "even if you don't! I came here to find my son and get him home, and that's what I'm going to do."

"Yes," said Dobrun. "You will find Jake, David, have no fear of that. But the how of it is dark to me, darker than my own feathers. So be patient in the meantime, as we all must be. Events will overtake us all too soon, I fear."

"And as for who will go to Marfang," said Coblyn, "That is not for us to decide on our own. We are guardians of our frontier, and cannot just quit our posts without leave. We have a Lord to answer to as well. And I should warn you that he may decide differently than you wish. If Dobrun is wrong, and Jake should die, you yourself will be the next target of the Duke's enmity."

"Your lord better not try to stop me," I said. "Where Jake is, that's where I am going."

"We'll have to see about that, child," said a voice, rich and deep and strong. I started, and turned around. Approaching me, as quiet as an elf, was a real, live centaur. "Do you wood sprites have any tea going? Or do I have to brew my own?"

2.

I discovered that it's very difficult to argue with a centaur. Apart from the fact that they are large and imposing creatures, they are wise, compassionate, and often very funny. Unless they are angry, in which case you should run. When you notice them looking into your heart, it is as if they have been standing there all along, chuckling gently at the deepest secrets of your soul. Dynan told me afterwards that they see everything so clearly, and feel so much of the world's pain, that if they didn't have a sense of humor they'd go mad. I really wanted to see Jake as soon as I could, but Keffyldyn, for he was the centaur, argued that he and the elves could get to Marfang much faster without me, and better handle any trouble they might meet on the way as well.

"David, you have to trust me," he said, between slurps of tea that the elves had made him. "As much as you want to help, you'll only slow us down. If we do run into a pack of screechy werewolves, or worse, and believe me child, there is worse, we can handle ourselves much better without worrying about you. Besides, whichever one of you is supposed to fulfill the prophecy, the first piece has to happen near the Blutwald, that men call the Bloodwood. And you're already here. For now, you need protecting as much as Jake."

However weird it was to meet a green and brown man-horse for the first time, there was no mystery about Keffyldyn himself: he was very plain spoken. The blow to my ego aside, I had to admit that life as an American suburbanite really hadn't taught me how to handle werewolves. The truth is the truth, and a centaur will never speak anything else, even if it ruffles your feathers. They didn't want me; I would slow them down, and be a liability if they ran into the trouble they were expecting. But fretting as I was in my desire to see Jake, I refused to let them talk me out of going with them.

Keffyldyn chuckled. "No offence, child, but you're a stubborn one. Come with us then to Kyphala-dyn, and make your case to Crionn the Elven lord. Who knows? He may even see things your way."

"He'd better," I replied. "There's no way anybody's stopping me from finding Jake."

Dobrun sighed. "That's the thing about centaurs, they're always in some argument. I'm off too, then, Master Elves. I'll return to the Crones to tell them you're coming. Make sure David comes to no harm. Do you have any message for Jake, David?"

There were so many things I wanted Jake to know that I couldn't think of where to begin. "Just tell him I'm here for him. Tell him... tell him I love him." I couldn't say more after that.

The raven looked at me with his wise old eyes. "Right then," he said, and was gone, leaving me with a pair of elves and a centaur. Which, if you're playing poker with your life in a strange forest, is not a bad hand to have.

I helped the elves tidy their cave, preparing for our own departure. They did not speak much, and Keffyldyn not at all, but there was nothing uncomfortable about the long stretches of silence between us. Coblyn put together a light pack for me, which contained some marching rations, and a spare set of clothes. Finally, he gave me a sword, with hilts wrapped in strips of black leather, and a scabbard bound with the same material. "You are not a warrior, David," he said, "but this sword knows what to do. "If you have to draw it, let it use you, rather than the other way around." I didn't ask him what he meant, but when I unsheathed the blade, and it shone silver in the sun, I felt it vibrate in my hand as it sought for an enemy, then lie quiet once it was reassured. I knew exactly what it was doing, and felt an immediate affinity for it. As I sheathed it once more, I saw Coblyn smiling at me.

"What?" I asked, but he didn't answer me directly. I came to know that this is a common habit of the elves. They prefer that you answer your own questions. Makes you mad, sometimes.

"Your ancestors' blood runs deep, David Patel. There is much more to you than you know." And the taint of fear that had been hanging around the edges of my mind, since Jake had gone missing, suddenly disappeared. I knew I would see my son again, and was content.

We walked all the rest of that day, barely speaking. The pine trees that lay closer to the river eventually gave way to tall, leafy hardwoods, awaking to the spring. I'm no botanist, but I recognized oak, and hickory and others that might have been ash. The scent of pines faded as we left them, and the bars of sunlight falling to the forest floor grew less as we moved deeper among the crowded hardwoods, so that our journey became darker as we went on. But the birdsong continued, as Bloodwood welcomed the warmth on its canopy. Once a deer crossed our path, with two fawns in tow. Coblyn had his arrow poised for flight almost before the noise of their passage had reached us, but a doe and her children were no threat to us, and an elf won't take that portion of life even if he is starving.

Late in the afternoon we crossed another stream, some tributary of Marfell that had wandered into the forest and happily gotten lost. Once over, we paused for a drink, and to fill our water-skins. By tacit consent, we rested for a while, munching on some of the dried fruit and nuts that we carried. Then we followed the stream as it flowed roughly westward, chuckling to itself in the solemn silence of the trees. The shallow watercourse widened until it was too far for a man to jump across, and its dancing laughter was subdued to a broader, whispering purpose.

The Fruit Of The Dendragon Tree

It was getting late. The sun was setting through the boughs of the trees directly ahead, and the dancing beams of light sent shafts of gold through the deep green veil. I was about to ask "Are we there yet?" when Coblyn, who was in the lead, pulled up short. Dynan and Keffyldyn were still as stone to my left, and my sword was in my hand of its own volition, questing forward for blood. There were eight of them, and they had chosen the place well. We were in a little clearing at the foot of a small hill, around the base of which the stream was flowing, temporarily diverted to the south. They had spread out in front of us so that our backs were to the water, and the only way forward was uphill through them. They didn't plan on letting us go anywhere. Our folk tales describe the wolf-man, but they don't prepare you for the reality when you find him up close in a forest in Tiramonde, even if you do have a magic sword in your hand.

They were all of a type, standing upright on hind legs that were animal in shape, with the backwards-facing elbows you find on dogs, their weight resting on massive paws like a kangaroo's with claws. All of them had huge, shaggy thighs, black with matted hair that swept up to their shoulders. Great arms, human in shape, hung from shoulders bunched with muscles like a gorilla's. Their hands also were mostly human, save for the savage claws that flared from every knuckle except those on the thumbs, a dozen claws per hand. Their heads were fully wolf-like, with red tongues and yellow fangs, bared in a unified snarl that seemed to freeze my very blood. They smelled terrible.

The leader wore a gold circlet around his head and was the only one who held a sword, its stone blade gleaming red in the light of the setting sun that filtered through the trees. He stared right at me. Part of me wanted to run, but a larger part took hold of me almost immediately. *It's fight or die, David*, I thought. Coblyn looked at me as if I had spoken.

Possibly both. I heard his words in my head. *But definitely both for them*. I felt his courage lift my heart, and I thought of Jake, and knew I would fight with everything I had to see my son again. There's nothing like a rumble with a gang of werewolves to give your life perspective.

"Kirr'em," the leader growled, and I knew what he meant, even though he couldn't speak properly out of his wolf's mouth. They howled, and lunged down the hill.

I remember vividly what I was not. Most of me seemed to disappear, as if I watched everything from a quiet room inside my mind. There was no fear. There was no anger. There was no Jake, no Mary, and no David. There was only a sword dancing in my hand, and I was its willing if inexperienced partner. The first werewolf lumbered towards me and died with Dynan's sword in his throat. His blood baptized me to my shoulders, hot and steaming under the cool green boughs and he died looking into my eyes with surprise. But he was monumentally heavy, and as he crashed into me I staggered backwards to the edge of the stream. This possibly saved my life, for I gained some space from a second werewolf, who had to jump over his falling partner to get to me. I swung wildly with my sword, and felt the blade sink deep into his neck. Blood again showered me, stinging my eyes. But none of it was mine, and as I backed to the right to get out of his way the second werewolf stumbled into the shallow river under the momentum of his charge and died in the water. His blood steamed the current with a hiss, and he gave an anguished scream, as if the water burned him, before subsiding.

I stood shakily by the water, and looked around to see what was happening. Six werewolves already lay dead, with Dynan and Keffyldyn attacking one to my left, snarling his defiance, and rage, and fear. But Coblyn was under attack from the last werewolf, the leader with the sword, and the clash of stone on steel rang out in the springtime woods. The wolf-man was heavier than the elf, and just as fast with his stone blade, and Coblyn's face was pale in the green and golden light. Dynan and Keffyldyn were too far away to help, and not knowing what to do I rushed to Coblyn's side, reaching him just as he fell backwards over a tree root, which had run down the little hill from the press of trees at its crest. The beast was poised to finish him, but I shouted and somehow parried his downward sword-thrust so that the point of his blade buried itself in the soft loamy earth of the riverbank. The werewolf snarled at me, with his yellow teeth bared and his breath of rotting meat, and as he pulled his weapon free he gave me a backhanded swat with his sword hand that sent me stumbling backwards again, this time into the stream itself. I felt the wicked claws on the back of his hand rend my face as he struck, and the blood started, though the pain didn't come until later. He left Coblyn on the ground and came after me, splashing into the shallow water and thrusting his blade towards my throat. Without knowing why, I dropped to one knee so that his sword point passed harmlessly over my shoulder, and my weapon flashed bright in turn as it lanced upwards from the ground, and laid the wolf-man's belly open. He rent the air with a howl of anguish, which went on until I stood and silenced him with a killing blow to the throat. He fell heavily into the water, twitched once, and was still.

I collapsed on my knees into the stream, my head ringing from the leader's blow, desiring nothing more than the cool of the water upon my wound. But the water burned like fire, and as I raised my head to scream I felt Coblyn's strong arms pick me up. "Upstream, David, upstream of the beast! His blood pollutes the water, and will taint your wound!"

I could see what he meant. The part of the river where I had fallen was red with the leader's blood. The water steamed and bubbled like a witch's brew as it carried the poison away. The werewolf's stone sword lay in the shallow stream, and Coblyn paused to pick it up before turning to me. I felt very faint, and Coblyn helped me upstream, and bathed my face. Here the water was pure, and cool on my wound. But the werewolf's blood had already mingled with mine; I could feel it snaking its way within me. The others had joined us, and at a word from Keffyldyn, Dynan cast around and found a type of purple moss growing on a rock near the stream. This the centaur tore into a spongy pad, which he spit upon, and gave to Coblyn to press against my shredded cheek. The moss and his saliva together held some kind of healing, he told me, and I could immediately feel it work, calming the fire on my face with its balm. But I knew even then that something of the wild wolf had already entered me, and would never leave. I carry him still.

Presently we heard someone call, and Coblyn's tired face transformed itself into a smile. The sun was very low by now, and the figures moving down the hill towards us were backlit, their features in shadow. But the faint glimmer of starlight that they carried with them showed they were elves. I lay against Coblyn as they approached, too tired to stand, while the moss soothed my face and put me to sleep.

They must have carried me from the riverbank, for when I woke up we were in a different place altogether, and I have no memory of the journey. I dreamed of Mary, healthy and beautiful and laughing with me on a beach, while Jake as a little boy splashed in the shallows. A Dragon came for him, black against the sun, and I would have thrown myself between them. But Mary moved to stop me, and when I turned to ask her why she was impossibly old: gaunt and frail and dying. But her eyes were young. When I looked back to where Jake had been, he was gone, and a black shadow was flying away into a deep blue sky. I ran into the surf as a wolf, howling my rage and grief into the stars of a sudden night, and only when the black speck disappeared did I turn back to the campfire that beckoned me from the desolate beach where Mary had stood. But she too was gone from me. Even in a dream, emptiness can fill your soul until you can't breathe.

Sleep faded, and I knew I was looking into a real fire, that flickered and spit and generally enjoyed itself. I was lying on a bed of springy material, in a stone alcove of what looked like another large cave. Tears wet my face, and the salt of them stung my wound.

"Shit," I said, wincing in the sudden pain, and Coblyn laughed from nearby.

"So the werewolf killer awakes," he said. "How do you feel?"

"Like a truck ran over me," I said, through a mouth that was fuzzy with the want of water. "Where are we?"

"We are safe," said Coblyn, and the surety in his voice calmed me at once. "We're several miles from where we were attacked, in the main stronghold of my people, deep in Blutwald forest, where no enemy has ever found us. We call this place Kyphala-dyn. Here is some water, drink it."

The Fruit Of The Dendragon Tree

I obeyed gladly, emptying the small bowl he held out to me in a single, greedy draught. I spilled some on myself, and noticed that someone had changed my clothes while I was asleep. A second bowl followed, refilled from a large wooden pitcher nearby, then a third, before my mouth unstuck from itself. I realized I was starving.

"That's better," I said. "How long was I out?"

"Nearly a day," said Coblyn, smiling at my surprise, before turning serious. "Many men would not have awoken from the wound you took, David, at least, not as a man. Even a punch from a werewolf can poison the blood; they lick their claws to make it so. We were lucky to have washed it and gotten the moss on it so soon." He looked at me searchingly. I met his gaze until he nodded sharply. "Good," he said. "You will not turn into one, I would guess. But am I right in thinking you feel the wildness inside?"

For a second I felt ashamed, and wanted to deny the truth. But if a centaur will not tell a lie, then an elf will not listen to one. "Yes, I can. I felt it even back at the river, like a shadow in my blood. What will it do to me?"

"That depends on the choices you make, my friend. Perhaps it will be a strength for you to lean on in battle; perhaps it will consume you with lust for blood. Perhaps neither, perhaps both. Only you can decide how you will dance with your shadow." He smiled again. "But you saved my life David, for which I am thankful, so it is my duty now to help you in any way I can."

"Well, where do you go to the bathroom in this place?" And laughing at my prosaic need he showed me to a little stone privy, cut into the rock above a stream of water that took my urine with it. There was no hiss of steam, I was thankful to notice. But then something else struck me, and I turned to ask, though as usual Coblyn was there first.

"Don't worry, I haven't given you polluted water, I filled your pitcher elsewhere. That stream empties underground, away from anything we might drink." His eyes left mine and gazed at nothing. "Besides, you are hard to kill now. Your wound has indeed strengthened you, and bound you to this world in ways that you do not imagine." He faced me again, and gave me his contagious grin. I smiled with him, not knowing what he meant, but glad to be alive, the blood singing in my veins and the wolf inside me running to its tune.

"Come, we have little time. I must take you to meet my Lord. We have to leave soon, and I know you don't want to be left behind."

I groaned inwardly. My face still felt raw, and my head ached. But I desperately needed to see Jake, and Coblyn was right: I wouldn't want to be left behind.

"Lead on, McElf," I said, feeling witty, and followed him out of the small chamber.

I never saw enough of Kyphala-dyn, and what I did see could be a story in itself. It was a complex warren of caves, set into a large hill not far from where the werewolves had accosted us. Of course, those fell beasts had had no idea of that; elven magic had protected the place from other eyes even in the ages of the world before the dragons came. But "cave" is a poor name for a place that partnered with living rock to make a haven such as that. Veins of crystal and gold glittered in the walls, and there was light everywhere, green and gold and white. I passed a cavern in which it appeared as bright as day, rich with trees and grass despite being underground. Another hall was at first glance as black as one would expect, yet I noticed the reflection of moonlight on water and a spray of stars seemingly high above. The sound of waves breaking gently on a shore came from this hall, and remembering my dream I would have gone in, but Coblyn took my arm and kept me on our path.

Other elves, who looked at us and smiled, began to join us from side passages. Some spoke to Coblyn, and I could tell his people held him with great affection. There were tall elf warriors, dressed like Coblyn and similarly armed, and beautiful elven women, some with swords, some with bows, all with grey or black eyes. Some of them had hair that looked to be made of silver, some of gold, but most were dark brown or black-haired. More and more elven people joined us as we walked, and our path led us straight along until it finally opened up into a huge, bright chamber carpeted with the greenest grass I had ever seen. The light was like natural daylight, as if we were out in the sun, yet when I looked up I could see a glowing crystal ceiling about twenty feet above. Unfamiliar trees with thick, slightly curved trunks and blue leaves, stood about at irregular intervals and there were elves in some of these. Someone in the distance was speaking in a raspy voice, and we made for the sound.

At the far end of the cave, three blue-leafed trees stood near a natural spring that bubbled out of the floor, creating a small lake. Keffyldyn and Dynan were there, standing next to a tall elf, richly dressed in robes of emerald and gold cloth, listening to a raven. The elf-lord's hair was as black as the raven's wing, and though I knew he never stopped listening to Dobrun, for it was he, his dark gray eyes fixed on me as I approached with Coblyn and stood before him.

"…So the Mother asks you send aid to the king, my Lord, aid such has not been needed since Kildraig was entombed alive. Coegun will likely declare himself soon, and without your help the king will be defeated, and woe betide us all should that happen." The raven stopped talking, and when the elf lord didn't immediately speak, he looked to see what had caught his attention. Seeing me, his eyes opened in surprise, then clouded with concern as he noticed my face.

"Hello, David Patel, what happened to you? Coblyn, I thought I told you to look after him."

But before Coblyn could reply to this, the Elf Lord spoke. "Welcome, David. My name is Crionn, king of my people, father of Dynan and Coblyn. I see that your wound is already much better. Are you ready to see your son once more?"

"Yes, absolutely," I said, my stomach growling. "But can I get something to eat first? I could eat a horse." Which, when I thought about it, was probably not the most polite thing to say in front of a centaur.

Chapter 12

"Every tree that bringeth not forth good fruit is hewn down, and cast into the fire"

(Jesus: Matthew; 3:10, 7:19)

Ureth glared at Sathryn as if lightning would bolt from her eyes, and Jake wondered if she could make that happen. The acolyte Naomi, who had accompanied Ureth, peeped round the door fearfully. Jake gulped, but took a protective step in front of Sathryn. "You don't have to be so mad, Ureth," he said. "We were just kissing."

"Just kissing? Just kissing? Do you not understand how badly such desire pollutes this place? But I forget, you are not of this world, and a man besides, so how could you know? This Coven is a refuge for the spirit, not a brothel! But she knows better!" Ureth cried, pointing at Sathryn. "She has defiled us! I knew she would do something like this!"

"Then you should let me go home!" yelled Sathryn.

"You insisted on coming here! And now it's far too late to let you go! Once you left Marfang the Duke's men would capture you and demand your release in exchange for Jake! Our father would never forgive me if I let that happen."

"What about Scarth?" asked Jake. "Couldn't they do the same thing with him?"

Ureth paused, and took a deep breath. Jake could feel her power recede from the air inside his lungs, could see the slight quiver in her body as she brought it back within herself. When she exhaled, she seemed much more in control, and he found he could breathe again.

"My father," she said to Jake, though still looking at Sathryn, "is a great warrior. If they sent enough men against him, they could capture him, but it is much more likely he would not be taken alive. And even if he were, he would never expect me to ransom his life with yours. He has saved you from them twice already; to surrender you even to save his life would be to dishonor that gift. But my sister is a different story."

"Why?" asked Jake, before Sathryn could. The acolyte Naomi had moved fully into the room now, and was staring at him intently.

"For the same reason that you would give your own life to save your mother's, Jake. Because Sathryn is the flower of his soul, the thing he loves most in all the world. Because it would wound him as surely as a sword in the heart if anything happened to her."

There was a small silence. "So how long do I have to stay here?" asked Sathryn.

"I don't know," said Ureth, and her simple, honest response surprised them all.

"But I do know," she went on, briskly, "that I cannot have you two kissing each other every chance you get. Naomi, take Sathryn with you now, and give her something to do. Are you not on kitchen duty? Yes, our kitchens might be a good place for both of you, given the way you also look at our guest. Jake, you come with me."

There was no argument, and Jake wondered if Ureth had used a persuasive spell to make that so. He caught Sathryn's eye, and she shrugged and gave him a small smile, which he returned. Naomi was still looking at him, he saw. There was a hungry look in her eyes. They really don't eat enough around here, he thought, and followed Ureth out of the cell.

Ureth didn't speak to him for a time, and thinking she was still angry he kept his silence too. They walked down the corridor to a large stairwell, which he realized must be in the center of the Crone tower. The stairway was circular, and wound down several stories. There were no railings, and Jake felt a small thrill of vertigo as he followed Ureth in her descent. But the stairs themselves were broad, and Jake found that if he kept his eyes on the witch's back he didn't worry about falling off to either side. When they got to the bottom, Ureth headed straight away from the foot of the stairs to a small door in the outer wall of the tower. She opened this, and Jake followed her outside. The door opened directly onto a deep green lawn dotted with red flowers and tall gnarled trees with dark brown trunks. They were outside the castle walls on the island of Marfang. It was a beautiful afternoon, with spring announcing her return in the angle of the sun, and the small purple blossoms on the strange trees. The air was full of birdsong, and rushing river. Jake looked back. Once again, there was no sign of the door they had passed through.

"Ureth," he said, "What are we doing?"

"Follow me," the witch replied, without looking back at him. And then she started to run.

Jake hesitated for a second, taken by surprise. But then he felt his feet move, and he was in full flight after Ureth. She ran well, he thought, light on her feet over the emerald grass, with none of the head bobbing that showed a runner wasting energy. He sped after her, surprised how long it took to close the gap between them. Even with a head start, Jake knew that he could beat almost anybody in a race. But Ureth ran as he did, with a combination of fierce joy and economy of motion that ate up the ground. He closed behind her, settling into an easy stride just behind her right shoulder. The grass, sloping gently downhill towards the river, was crisscrossed by paths that led among the trees and flowers. Ureth found one of these, wide enough to run in single file, and Jake stayed comfortably behind her, matching her pace easily. They were passing what looked to be a large vegetable garden to their right, the river on the left. A pair of ducks waddled across their path, quacking and flapping as the two runners breezed through.

The Fruit Of The Dendragon Tree

"Where are we going?" Jake asked. It felt good to be using his body, to be outside, not to be shut up in the cold stone tower. The air smelled of spring, young and fresh and full of life. The sense of vigor that he'd experienced on his first morning rushed back to him, and he felt wonderfully alive and strong. He laughed as he ran for the unexpected joy of it.

"Those trees up there!" called Ureth, laughing with him, with a quick gesture of her hand ahead and to the right. Jake looked and saw a dark cluster of trees about a quarter mile around the curve of the shoreline, close to the water's edge. The river had extended a small finger of water, about twenty yards long, into the island just before the trees, and someone had built a small wooden bridge across this. The dark copse of trees stood immediately past the bridge, a smudge of shadow in the sunlight.

"I'll race you to the bridge!" she said, and increased her pace.

"You got it!" replied Jake, as he found another gear, matching his pace to catch her.

They ran stride for stride, on either side of the narrow path, each tacitly surrendering any advantage offered by its harder surface. Jake realized that Ureth was an excellent runner. She was really pushing him, as hardly anyone ever managed to do. The bridge was coming closer. They were still neck and neck. He knew it would soon be time. A hundred yards to go. Fifty. And then, it was the moment.

Somewhere inside himself, Jake had a place. It was a place that he called on when he wanted to fly, the place that won him so many races. He called on it now, and it was there, in the air of Tiramonde, in his heart, in his soul, larger and more vibrant than ever. And he sped by Ureth as if she was standing still, timing his burst so that even if she was able to catch him, there was no more room for her to pass. She surprised him though. He was the first to reach the bridge, but barely. He saw her shoulder almost catch his own as they came to the inlet. They thundered in single file over the narrow span, slowing as they did so, catching their breath in the shadow of the trees on the far side. Ureth was hunched over, her hands on her knees. Jake was breathing hard, but the exertion had not touched his strength, he was sure he could have run all day at the same pace.

"You're not bad for an old witch," he said, still grinning.

She smiled at him, in return. It was the first gesture of real friendship she had yet given him, and the difference in her face was striking. Then, the wrinkled façade faded away, and he could see the young woman beneath. A woman even more beautiful than her sister, and not much older than himself. But she *was* older, he suddenly knew, and not just in years. She had made the sacrifice of the Crones, and embraced the ancient power. He could feel this power, pulsing between them. It hung about her like a cloak, camouflaging the vital young woman beneath, even more effectively than any outward sign of age. The vision of Ureth the young woman lasted only for a second, then the old witch's face returned once more. She was Ureth the Crone, and she had very nearly beaten him in a footrace.

"You are very fast, Jake. Nobody has ever beaten me before. Maybe there is more to you than meets the eye."

It was if she had taken the words from his mouth. And, Jake knew, with that shared exchange, and the look in her eyes, that he and Ureth became friends at that moment. Somehow, all the pain of losing her mother was there in her eyes, and he knew deep in his soul that she understood what drove him to save his own.

He thought for a moment of her beauty, of the vision that had just been before him. And he looked at her as she appeared now, wizened and wrinkled and old. "You paid a great price, didn't you Ureth, to become what you are?"

"Yes," she replied. "But then, everybody alive does that."

"You get, it, don't you, why I let Jenny bring me here?"

"Yes, Jake, I do."

"Do you think I'll be able to save my Mom?"

Her smile faded, not from displeasure, but because he could see she was taking his question very seriously. She turned, and looked up at the trees that encroached close to them here, and seemed to make a decision.

The Fruit Of The Dendragon Tree

"Let me show you something," she said, and walked under the branches of the small wood.

Jake followed her under the canopy of leaves, and immediately felt stifled. There were not many trees, perhaps a dozen standing in a ring, close by each other in the sunshine. But no sunlight penetrated here, and it was as if they had entered a cave. There was no grass underfoot, just bare earth, and Jake had a sense of a vast forest, of which these few trees were but a sample. Their bark was black, and their leaves such a dark green as to seem almost black too. There was no breath of wind under those branches, no sound of birds, and the laughing rush of the great river was suddenly muted to a dull hiss.

"Whoa, these trees are weird," he said.

"Do you feel them, Jake? They are the *Imperviata*."

"The what?"

"It means, in the old tongue, "impervious to life." Do you hear how quiet it is? They block the light. They buffer all sound. No bird will nest in their branches. Nothing can live under their canopy, not even an insect. They bar themselves from all existence but their own, protected from any natural invasion or connection. They risk nothing, and so have no true life. They are forever safe, and forever alone."

"That's kinda sad, don't you think?"

"Yes, it is. There are people like these trees, Jake. Beware of them." Ureth walked to the edge of a small pool in the middle of the copse, and knelt beside it. She patted the ground next to her, and said, "Come and sit here by me."

Jake did so. The water of the pool was also black, and had a convex surface. When he leaned over to look in, he could see no trace of his reflection. He felt himself powerfully drawn to the pool, and without thinking he reached out his hand and dipped it into the water. As he did this, he realized it was not a still pool at all. A current of icy water gripped his hand, and hungrily tried to drag it under. Startled, he pulled back, the current so strong that his hand made no ripple on the surface when it broke free.

"Holy... what is that?" he asked, looking at Ureth. She smiled at him again, indulgently as if he was a favorite little brother.

"If our legends are to be believed," Ureth replied, "and the evidence is mounting that they should be, this is an underground spring, fed by the river, that just breaks the surface here. It arches up here, and dives below again, thrusting deep, deep underground. The spring feeds a lake said to lie below this island, a lake that drains into Marfell on its other side, through a network of smaller, narrower springs. Anything that is placed into the water here is dragged below, presumably into that underground lake."

"And if you get to the lake...?"

"You find the Dragon in his prison."

Somehow, he wasn't surprised. "And you are showing me this because...?"

"Because I believe you were brought here to help us defeat the Duke Coegun, whose very name means "Empty One." If I am right, Coegun has shifted the boundaries of the Waterstones, and allied with the Undead, and even the magic of the Crones will not be enough to stop them. There is no power in this world that can stand against them, except the power of the Dragon. I need you to free the Dragon, so that he will defeat the evil we face."

"But Sathryn told me the Dragon was more evil than anything! And more powerful! Why would he help you? And why would you want him to?"

Ureth looked into the pool for a beat before answering. "As for the first question, I believe he will help us because the prophecy says he will defeat our enemies. As for the second... tell me Jake, with your mother's illness, what treatment did she receive?"

The question took him by surprise. "Well, I guess, everything, you know, we tried everything, radiation, chemotherapy, surgery, you name it."

"And she didn't get better."

"NO! You know she didn't! Why else would I be here?"

"I know. Please be patient with me. These treatments, did they themselves place a burden upon her?"

"Side effects, you mean? Hell yes. Chemo? That stuff is poison, made her puke, made her hair fall out, radiation burned the crap out of her. The surgery? Don't even ask. She cried for a month, especially when it didn't work."

"But yet all of you, your mother, father, you, her doctors, you all decided it was the thing to do, to poison her, burn her, cut her, in order to try to free her from her illness?"

"It was all we had! We'd lose her for sure otherwise."

"Yes, it was all you had. And yes, she would have died much sooner otherwise. The Dragon is all we have too, Jake. And we must free him. We will lose Taumar for sure, otherwise, and likely all Tiramonde, in the end. I am more sure of this than anything I have ever felt, though I cannot prove it to my Sisters on our Council. But sometimes, to cure a disease when there are limits to your wisdom, and to your power, you must use poison, or a knife, or a burning scourge. And you hope and pray to recover from the weapon that you must use, for you know that unchecked it can kill you too. But if you don't risk it, you know the alternative is a sure and terrible death. It is a monstrous choice, but your very limitations force it upon you. Do you understand?"

"Yes, I do," said Jake. And the strange thing was, he did. "But there is something I don't get."

"What's that?"

"Why me? I mean, really. I'm no warrior. In our world, we hang our swords on the walls for decoration. Nobody uses them to fight with. I sure don't."

"I'm not sure anymore, Jake, if in fact I ever was. All the legends speak of the one who frees the Dragon, the Pendraig as a savior from "another world." So I looked outside my world, into yours, where there is still some vestige of the connection between witches. I found Jenny, and she led me to you, and as I was desperate I brought you here. But here you are, and now it seems that freeing the Dragon requires no warrior training. I would guess that being a good swimmer would be as important as anything."

"Well, as it turns out, I'm a great swimmer," said Jake. But what is the Pendraig supposed to do?"

"He must dive in this pool, find the underground spring, and avoid drowning until the current carries him to the underground lake. When he emerges, if the Dragon does not kill him, presumably he will tell him how to approach the Dendragon Tree and pluck its fruit without being killed by the Duke's men. Then, the Dragon will be released, and will defeat our enemies, and the Pendraig will receive his heart's desire."

"Just like that?"

"Supposedly."

"And if you're wrong, and I'm not the Pendraig?"

"Then you will either drown, or be killed by the Dragon."

"Well, I'm glad it's not anything major."

"Yes. I understand," Ureth chuckled. "You are being funny. It is time we returned."

Walking back, Ureth realized with some surprise that she enjoyed Jake's company. He was a warm young man, with a generous heart and a ready smile, when he wasn't chafing with impatience to return home, finding his father, or curing his mother, or all three. She could see why both Naomi and Sathryn liked him so much: he was already handsome, and those blue eyes, so rare in Tiramonde except among the most adept Crones, would exert an almost magical pull for the two young women. Ureth herself had never spent so much time alone with a male who was not her father, and Jake's attributes were not lost upon her. But though not much older than he was in years, her Gift removed her from him more effectively than any guise of age. And besides, the other Gift, the one that had coursed through her at the Ring, and that night in her cell, had no equal among mortal men. Of that she was sure.

Kildraig's essence had suggested far more power than she would ever wield, yet he had clearly not surrendered any of the sexual potency she and her sisters had abdicated in their quest for spiritual purity. It was an intoxicating combination, and it terrified her as much as it had

The Fruit Of The Dendragon Tree

excited her. No, Jake was safe from her. She just hoped she was safe from the Dragon.

Making conversation, she asked him: "Will you give me a head-start if we race again?"

But he took her question seriously, and didn't answer for some time.

"No, I don't think you need one," he finally replied. "I think you have the same strength that I do."

It was the way he said it that made her pause. "What do you mean?" she asked, a cold snake of dread coiling in her stomach. Could he be empowered by the Dragon too?

"I don't know, really," Jake said. "I just know that I feel stronger here, more alive. Like there's some power in me that I didn't have before. Like I can do anything. And I think you're like that too. I think you could do anything. And it's not like you would be cheating by using magic. It's just that the magic is a part of you."

Ureth thought about this, knowing Jake was more right than he knew. The power of the Dragon still flooded through her; it amazed her that none had seen it, not even the Mother. Perhaps Jake sensed it where others could not. And what did that say about him? Had he, with his arrival, gained some of the Dragon's power? Was this the source of the sense of vitality he spoke of? Did they share the Gift, to a certain degree? She didn't know, but suddenly she was happy to be walking with someone who could relate to her. They came to a patch of brilliant red flowers that grew wild, scattered in numerous clumps, all over the island.

"These are the Dendragon flowers, Jake. They are the most coveted plants in the world. Their name means 'Dragon's teeth', after the shape of their petals. Each could grow into the full Dendragon Tree, but somehow they never do. There is only the one Tree. Yet even the flowers are the envy of the Sacours, who desire their medicinal and life-extending properties. More battles have been fought over them than I could tell you if I spoke until sunset. But only the Crones are entrusted with their harvest and usage."

"I asked Sathryn if they could cure my mother," said Jake.

"I doubt it. I'm sorry to say it, but your mother now rides too closely with Death. Only the Dragon's fruit itself can help her now, these flowers cannot. Go ahead, you have permission to pick one."

Jake realized she was serious about giving permission, and wondered what she would have done if he'd tried to pick one without asking. He reached down and plucked at the dark green stem of a flower, one that grew in a cluster near their feet. The stem came free of the earth with a satisfying snap, and an odor of something spicy. The flower was bright red on the top side, crimson on its under surface. As Ureth had said, the petals were triangular and sharp-edged, and looked very much like teeth. Black stamens laden with golden pollen thrust up to meet the sun, and to find the insects that spread their seed. These were a peculiar kind of black bee, which buzzed lazily among the red petals in the afternoon sunshine. Looking at the foreign insects, Jake suddenly felt the desire to return home so fiercely he stopped breathing.

"Are you alright?" Ureth's voice was gentle, for she had caught his sadness.

"I was just thinking: can we go inside the castle grounds and check out this tree?"

"Why not? You are under our protection, and I doubt anyone would want to pick a fight with me."

There was no self-satisfaction in Ureth's voice, Jake realized. She was simply stating the truth, confident in her own powers, and the ability to meet any situation as it arose. They turned up the nearest path that led to the main gates, and approached from the left, or western side. The guards at the gate knew who Ureth was, of course. The one on the left was closer. His eyes narrowed at Jake, and he looked as if he would speak. But when he looked back at Ureth he decided better of it, and drew up his spear to let them through. His partner on the other gatepost stayed looking straight ahead, almost as if he didn't want to know.

"He didn't look very happy to see me," murmured Jake, and Ureth agreed.

The Fruit Of The Dendragon Tree

"Three of his mates were executed because you made it safely here, Jake. Though they may be angry at the Duke for his harshness, they are more angry at you for their loss."

"Three...? You mean those guys at the entrance to the tunnel that day? They were KILLED? I mean, you're kidding, right, people don't get put to death here for that kind of stuff, do they? Why don't they get rid of the Duke themselves, if he's that cruel?"

"I wish I was kidding, Jake. As to why the Duke is allowed to still rule, our history tells us that people will often tolerate an evil ruler, if they feel he can keep them safe from a threat they believe is worse. I would bet your history is the same. The Duke has managed to convince everyone that the Sacours and the Ice People stand ever poised to invade our lands, ready to harvest our Dendragon flowers, and ravage our women, and that he is the only one who can stop them. Those who disagree with him are branded as traitors, or worse, and often end up like that." She pointed to a spot atop the castle turret diagonally across from the Crone tower where the heads of Rethe, Ion and Dori rested upon spikes set into the crenellated stone.

Jake hadn't noticed the heads; he'd been too busy looking around the courtyard itself. But he looked away quickly. All he said was, "That's twisted."

"You are right, Jake, it is twisted. Twisted is how the Duke thinks. His mind is like a snake. Twisted is also how he talks, and he curves men's minds into believing his lies, salting them as he does with enough truth for people to swallow them. That is the way of all successful liars."

They were passing through the main courtyard as they spoke, heading towards the Dendragon Tree, in its pool near the north wall. The Crone tower was behind them, set into the southwest corner of the keep. A group of soldiers were practicing sword drill just ahead, near the low wall that surrounded the tree's pool.

The afternoon sun was warm on his shoulders, but all Jake wanted was to get close to the tree. Perhaps he could pluck the fruit right now and get back home. *Great idea, genius. How's Dad going to get back?* He shook his head in frustration.

The group of men that had been practicing with their swords paused in their drill as the witch and the boy approached, and clustered loosely in their path, barring their way. Their leader was indeed Rand, Jake saw, looking very dangerous standing in front of him, stripped to the waist in the warm sunshine. The muscles in the man's arms and chest rippled as he lazily twirled his sword. Jake noticed a multitude of scars crisscrossing Rand's torso, and several gold rings were interwoven in the single braid of his long blond hair. All the soldiers were wearing their hair like this, Jake saw, tightly braided in a ponytail, with the occasional glint of gold bespeaking a trophy of battle. Jake understood he was in the presence of seasoned warriors, any one of whom would kill him at the slightest word from their leader.

Rand planted himself in front of Jake, but spoke over his shoulder to the men gathered round. "Well, well, my brothers. See who honors us with his presence. It is the river rat himself. Still hiding behind your witch's skirts, boy?" He grinned with scorn, and with his heightened senses Jake smelled death in the air. Rand's words were cold, and his sneer was full of hate. And the cold and the hate fell all the way down into Jake's heart, and therein found a mirror. A surge of anger went through him, like an electric current.

"I don't see how I can be hiding. I'm here, aren't I?" He spoke the words before thought could slow them. There was a lust in him that he couldn't name; he didn't know it was the ancient lust that men carry, the one that urges the spilling of blood. Rand saw it, though, and it surprised him, though he was too sure of himself to allow any doubt. The boy was clearly untrained, while he himself was the victor of many duels, a survivor of many battles.

"How about a little swordplay, then?" Rand asked, still with the insolent grin on his face. Jake glanced at Ureth, who was standing very still, staring at Rand. The warrior caught his look.

"Oh, we need Mummy's permission, do we?" he sneered. Pardon me, Rat, I thought you were supposed to be the legendary Pendraig.

The Fruit Of The Dendragon Tree

I must have been mistaken. Not even my lowest soldier takes leave of a woman for his actions. We follow our own desires." He turned his back. "Don't we, men?" he called to his band, who laughed as one, and roared their approval.

"The only permission I was asking was how badly I could kick your ass." Again, the words were out before he could stop them. Rand froze, still with his back to Jake, and slowly turned around. The smiles were gone from the men's faces. But Rand's still lingered, and was more satisfied than before, as if things were going just perfectly. The sun seemed hotter, and the courtyard was still. Over Rand's shoulder, the Dendragon Tree was emerald green in the still of the afternoon.

"*What* did you say?" He posed the question softly, but the threat in his voice was undeniable.

"Nothing! He is not himself." Ureth finally spoke, but Jake knew that she realized it was already too late, and was just going through the motions of stopping the inevitable.

"Then who is he?" asked Rand, and Jake thought that was the most reasonable question he had ever heard.

"That is for the Royal Council to decide. He is protected until then!" Why was she bothering? Jake wondered. *Something* was going to happen here, whatever it was.

"Ah, yes," said Rand. "But he just waived that protection. Unless he wants to hide behind that as well. Besides, I won't kill him: I just want to teach him some manners. He might bleed a little, that's all."

"You heard me, dickhead, I'm not hiding anywhere."

"Jake, be quiet. You have no skill with a sword. This is not going to happen. We're going." Ureth grabbed his arm, as if to draw him back. Jake shrugged her off.

"Don't lie to me Ureth. You want to see what happens here as much as I do."

"Besides, he called me a dickhead, whatever that is," said Rand. "And I can't believe he meant it as a compliment."

"You got that right," said Jake, and suddenly it was decided. His blood was singing, and all fear had left him. His strength was full, he felt the experience of a hundred warriors flowing through his body, and his heart felt like a, like a…

Like a Dragon's?

The voice came from nowhere, bursting inside his head. But "Can I borrow a sword?" was all he said.

One of Rand's men solemnly handed him his sword, and the men drew back, forming a half circle behind their captain. Ureth stood behind Jake. He turned to her, smiling an apology. "You know this is meant to happen," he said in a low voice.

"I know no such thing," she whispered back. "Why are you doing this?"

"I don't know," Jake replied. "I guess, if I'm who you want me to be, then he can't hurt me. If not, then I shouldn't be here. I suppose this way is as good as any to find out the truth."

"This truth can get you killed! Why choose this way?"

"Because it's the best way." And they were both surprised that Rand had spoken. "Have you forgotten the verse?

> *He who does the Dragon free*
> *Will a mighty swordsman be:*
> *No other can before him stand*
> *Once he raises sword in hand"*

"I know the verse, you idiot!" retorted Ureth. "Just because he *will* become a mighty swordsman, doesn't mean he is one *now*!"

"If he isn't one now, then he's not going to be much use to you anytime soon, is he… Crone?" Rand almost spit the last word. "I've spent my whole life becoming me. Are you going to wait that long for his becoming?" Rand turned his back again. Then it began.

"I said, I'm going to FIGHT!" yelled Jake, and with the flat of his sword flat whacked Rand in the rear. Rand wheeled in a flash, his own blade a blur in the sunlight. He knocked Jake's sword aside, the blow so strong that the boy lost his grip upon it. Rand thrust forward, but Jake stood his ground, his karate training taking over. He swayed his body backwards so that the killing blow went through the air where his heart had just been. Then he pivoted on the balls of his feet, turning his hip and shoulder into Rand's body, slapping down on his sword arm with his left hand, grabbed the man's crotch with his right, and completed the makeshift judo throw in one fluid motion. Almost before Rand hit the ground, Jake had danced backwards several feet to where his sword had fallen. He picked it up from the dust of the training ground, and held the hilts in front of his face. Suddenly, he laughed, and his laughter rang around the close. The watching men wondered at it, and at the young man who was revealed to them, young, and strong, and ready to mock death.

Rand wasn't laughing. He had picked himself up, catlike from the earth, his sword still in hand. "I'm going to enjoy this," he said.

"You must like being embarrassed then," Jake retorted, and they began to circle each other in earnest. Jake was vastly aware of everything. His world had become the arena of the immediate: two barefoot swordsmen facing each other in the sand of a training ground, under a brilliant spring afternoon. Yet he was also aware of everything orbiting this very small world. There was the intense attention of the men, some wanting his destruction, some just curious about how he would handle himself. There was Ureth, intently watching, motionless as only a Crone could be. The wheels of a heavily laden wagon creaked into the close. A raven picked at the eye of one of the beheaded men, high up on the wall. Another raven cawed overhead. The scent of hot sand wafted up from his feet and mingled with the male odors of the intent warriors standing around. He was immensely at peace.

From Jake's point of view afterwards, the thing seemed inevitable. Rand feinted to his right, then lunged the other way with a thrust to Jake's right shoulder. The blow was an ugly one, Jake knew, intended to incapacitate his sword arm. But it never landed. Jake took a sharp step backwards, and, rotating his wrist so that his sword described a tight clockwise rotation, dropped his right shoulder and leaned into Rand's thrust. Rand's sword passed harmlessly over Jake's shoulder, and Jake's blade slid down his opponent's while he dropped to one knee.

Surprised, Rand's momentum carried him forward and he stumbled, his sword arm fully outstretched. Quick as a flash, Jake stood upright once more and turned ninety degrees to his right, towards the killing space, like a matador teasing a bull. In one swift motion, he pulled his sword back towards his body, pulling Rand's sword hand against the same right shoulder he had wanted to pierce. Rand's right arm was now fully extended, right in front of Jake's chest. The boy continued to pivot with his hips, and shoved the heel of his left hand viciously against Rand's right elbow, pulling inwards against the other's sword as he did so. The snap of the warrior's arm as it broke at the elbow rang clear and loud in the still afternoon.

Thank you, Sensei Tominaga! Jake thought. He finished his spin, disengaging from Rand, who in rage and surprise continued to stumble forward. The man fell to his hands and knees in the dirt. His broken sword arm wouldn't support his weight, and he bellowed in agony as the pain shot up his arm, like a lightning bolt from the ground to his shoulder. He recovered enough to bear his weight on his left arm, but his head was swimming in pain and nausea. The mangled nerves in his elbow couldn't forward coherent signals to his hand, and without the proper instructions his fingers lost their grip on his sword, leaving it to gleam bright and useless in the sun. Somewhere in his torture he found the time to disbelieve his position. How had this happened? And so quickly? A tinge of fear: there must be magic at work! But Jake left him no time to ponder. In an instant, the boy was behind him, pulling his head back by its pigtail, and Rand felt the cold steel of the boy's borrowed sword pressed against his throat.

Nobody said a word. Jake stared at the faces staring back at him. Without exception, they registered varying degrees of shock and surprise at seeing their leader so quickly undone. Jake found Ureth's gaze. She was surprised too, Jake saw, but he saw something else in her eyes also. And then he knew. She was relieved, and inordinately pleased. He grinned at her, and pressed the edge of his sword a little more tightly against the man's neck, his eyes looking deep into Ureth's. As if in answer to an unspoken question, she gave him a quick shake of her head, and he released the tension of his sword blade against Rand's skin.

To everyone's surprise, Rand spoke first. "So, Rat," he gasped, "You think you have bested me? I grant it looks that way. But you had better pray never to meet me when your witch is not around to protect you with her spells. No mere boy could best me by himself! Do you doubt it?"

"No, Rand, he received no help from me," Ureth answered. "Believe what you will. It is you, I think, who should not hope to meet him again under arms."

But Jake was beyond words. Infuriated by Rand's continued contempt, even when beaten, he cast about wildly in his mind for some way to puncture the man's blind arrogance. The thrill of combat already receding, he discarded the idea of cutting his throat. And some part of himself, the part that had become small and remote in the heat and lust of battle, wondered how he could even consider doing such a thing in cold blood. He was not a murderer. Was he? Still, he urgently wanted to damage Rand's insufferable pride. There had to be a way. But none came to mind. In a burst of frustration, he did the only thing he could think of. With a jerk on Rand's ponytail that snapped his head back, Jake took his sword from the man's throat, and with an angry chop severed it halfway down its length.

He was totally unprepared for the result. With an agonized wail, Rand thrust himself upright on his knees, reaching backwards frantically for his hair with his left hand. Then, still kneeling, he lunged around and tried to grab his severed hair from Jake's hands. The wail went on and on, as if he had lost a child. Grasping his prize tightly, Jake took a few steps back. Glancing at the men, he saw they were even more stunned than they had been by his victory. They seemed to be collectively pale with shock, unnerved into inactivity. Suddenly, Ureth was by his side.

"Now you've done it," she hissed. "You've disgraced him. We need to leave, right now, unless you wish to fight all of them at once!"

"But why? What did I do?"

"You took his hair. Now shut up and run."

So they did, Jake dropping his sword, while some instinct kept Rand's hair, icon of its owner's manhood, tightly in his grasp. Ureth's fears were unfounded, however. She and Jake were able to retreat swiftly into the Crone tower, unchallenged by any of Rand's soldiers. And the great warrior himself remained where he was, kneeling in the dust of the training ground, his arm broken, his hair shorn, staring into nothing, while the gentle springtime sun kissed everyone it touched, whether they noticed it or not.

Chapter 13

Darkling I listen; and for many a time
I have been half in love with easeful Death

(John Keats: Ode to a Nightingale)

There is life. There is death. And there are the choices that lie between. Choose death, says one voice: it's easier. You will never climb out of that hole you are in. It is too deep, and besides, it was your choices that acted like a shovel, making it deeper. See the walls? They are too high, too slippery to climb, and that small patch of sky you see is the only remote sign of health and happiness you will ever again know in this life, to be glimpsed but never to be experienced. Let go.

Choose life, says another voice. Have courage; don't despair. The hole you have helped to dig is indeed deep, but it's not too late to gouge footholds in these slimy walls. The way will be messy and painful, but it is there. Upwards is the only direction to go when you have hit bottom. Start climbing, and one day that patch of sky above you will expand, and you will haul yourself out of that pit of disease and death. You will lie on the soft green pasture, feel the breeze upon your face, and embrace the sun as it smiles upon your tears.

There is a last choice, whispers a third voice: the one of not choosing. Of not dying, but of not living, not drowning, but not swimming. We can make this choice every day, until all power of choice is lost to us. But now, the time for not choosing has flown. Now there is only Death or Life. Burial or Ascent. Surrender or Struggle. Choose.

The sick woman stirred in her bed. Her dream teetered on the fulcrum of decision, her mind poised between the choice of sleep and wakefulness. Then a brilliant light, full of winter sun, and the reflections of fresh snow in the morning, crept in through the blinds and lit the room in bars of yellow. Mary felt the light kiss her closed eyelids, and she opened them slightly. Even this small motion took effort. The hospice nurse was not in her chair, which sat directly in her line of sight. What is her name? Oh, yes, Meg. And mine is still Mary, and I am still alive, God be thanked, or damned, I can't decide which.

The light enlivened the room, but Mary's spirits did not lift. How long would Death continue to ride leering alongside her at night, without lifting her onto his dark horse, the one whose very hoof-beats showered sparks of pain into her weary body? He came to her every night now, riding beside her bed, watching her intently. But every dawn he rode away without her, and now her pain had found its way into her very bones, and she wept in the daylight to find herself still alive.

Why am I still here?

It was because of Jake, she knew. He couldn't bear to lose her. And how could she leave a place where she was so loved? She understood that David had accepted her going. When they'd talked about having kids, he hadn't wanted them, saying the risks of her having a child were too high, given her family's history of breast cancer. "It's too dangerous," he'd said, "I don't want to lose you." "Everybody dies," she'd replied. "And I don't want to die childless." They'd gone round and round, and David had given in, as she knew he would. He always cared more about what others wanted. It was his weakness, and his strength. And now, here she was, dying of the dreaded disease itself, and he'd never even looked an "I told you so" at her, for he loved Jake with his whole heart. And what a son she had, too. Nobody could ever tell her that having Jake was a mistake. In the face of death, he was a symbol of life, of hope, of unrealized possibility. And she had borne him and birthed him and raised him and nothing, not even Death, could take that away from her.

So despite the pain, she hadn't yet surrendered to the idea that the son for whom she had risked so much would grow up without her. She couldn't yet allow herself to deal him so terrible a blow. But she doubted Jake understood how hard it was for her to stay. David did, she could see it in his eyes, poor man. But Jake, for all his wonderful qualities, still had the selfishness of youth. Life had been sweet, but now it was a constant, soundless scream of pain as the cancer ate its way into her very core. She knew she was near the end, no matter what anyone wanted. Her will, though indomitable, and her passion for her family, though unfathomable, could not delay the inevitable much longer.

And where were they, this husband and son who completed her dance? Very slowly, she turned her head to look at her bedside clock, this small motion in itself a marathon of pain. Seven o'clock. Both of them should have been in to see her by now.

"Dave. Jake." The two tiny whispers puffed from her lips. Her husband was not there, her son was not there, and she knew with an inexplicable certainty that they were not in the house, and she was suddenly filled with foreboding.

Where are you guys? But this time, the words formed only in her mind. Consciousness was fading, and she had no breath remaining save what she could use to retreat into sleep.

Mary closed her eyes, her face still wet with the tears she could not dry, and then, softly, she felt the warm touch of a tissue against her eyelids and thought that David must have come in after all. But when, after some effort, she opened her eyes again, she saw a young girl whom she didn't know standing by her bedside, dabbing at her as tenderly as if she was a piece of glass that might break, and holding her hand as gently as if she was her own daughter. And Mary was not afraid.

2.

Jenny Blackwood walked towards the dark circle in the snow as if she was approaching her own death. Terror clamped her throat, her jaw was tight, and she couldn't breathe properly. *Get a grip, girl. You're in the middle of the suburbs. There's nothing to be afraid of.*

Oh, yes. There is.

The unfamiliar voice entered Jenny's brain, ancient, mocking, and cold. She shook her head, as if to empty it of something, and tried to concentrate. She gazed at the ground, taking note of what it told her. Her daddy had called her the best deer tracker he knew, and she surprised herself with a sudden image of him, smelling his man smell, leaning close to him near a pine tree when she'd been about eight years old.

"The deer's that way, Daddy," she'd whispered, pointing, and he'd beamed his million-dollar smile, the one he could conjure when he wasn't drinking, and patted her gently on the shoulder. He'd let her drop that deer, it had been her first; she'd gotten her hands warm and bloody from the cleaning of it, and had been proud of the money they'd saved by not having to buy meat that winter. But Daddy's drinking had gotten worse as time had gone on. Momma left, and as Jenny grew, his hands had begun to wander down from her shoulders when he touched her. One day she'd pulled his own gun on him, and he'd seen the light of what she would do to protect herself in her eyes. He'd never touched her again. But he'd never smiled his smile again either, nor did she ever kill another deer.

Daddy wasn't a place to find comfort, after all. The memory faded, and Jenny saw once more the melted snow and blackened earth where David had stood before vanishing. She looked over to where Jake had disappeared, and wondered what had become of them.

They are where you cannot follow said the voice in her head.

"Yeah, I think I got that part," she said aloud. "So did they just fly away?"

They came to me. You helped send them. Their fate is in my hands, the voice replied: old, and cracked, and dark as the morning was light. It arrived this time with the force of a punch, and Jenny felt her knees sag with the power that hit her. The stench of burning grew stronger, mixed with a hint of sulfur, and bile rose in her throat. She gasped. She knew that voice, but from where? Somewhere she heard cold laughter, a trickle of freezing water down her spine. *Yes, you know me, my dear; everybody does, no matter which world you're from.*

She shook her head furiously. *Get out of my mind, you lying piece of shit.* The laughter in her head stopped as if a tap turned off. *OK Jenny, think!* The mental toughness that had allowed her to survive her father came to her aid, and she smiled at the easy banishment of the voice.

"I've dealt with a Dragon or two in my life," she said aloud, thinking of her Daddy's million-dollar smile.

Then she knew what she had to do.

She began running through the growing light, back to the car, her thoughts crowding her. She'd believed she wanted the power of a witch, but she hadn't. She'd really only wanted the power to cast minor spells: to catch glimpses of the future, to make Jake like her. Sending two people to a different world by magic was more than she had bargained for. Neither Jake nor his father had really understood what was going to happen, but then neither had she, and she still didn't. In fact, she admitted to herself, she hadn't really believed in the power she had used, until she had seen it work. Turning a car engine on and off, or changing the channels on a radio, that was the kind of trickery that other people might find freaky enough to respect you. But that magic was easy. Things that you could see and touch shared the same space and time as you, and you just became part of them and moved through them. And because they didn't have any wills of their own, not being alive, it was easy to imprint your will upon them and get them to do more or less what you wanted. But seeing a real live person disappear in front of your very eyes, and not know, not really know, what had happened to them, was just messed up. Then you began to laugh at yourself for using a phrase like "messed up" to describe it, when you really wanted to say something like "Holy shit!" over and over again. And THEN, and this was when the breath caught in your throat, and fear sent an icicle down your spine, *then* you thought that maybe the shit wasn't so holy at all, maybe it had been some pretty unholy thing that had swooped out of the sky, dragged off the guy you thought you might love, and turned his Dad, who definitely did love him, into a ball of flame that disappeared into the night sky, leaving no trace of either of them behind. If the voice in her head was any guide, what had happened was really evil, not anywhere near good; she had done something way over her head, and now what the hell was she going to say to the sick woman that both those guys had loved so much? Because Jake's mom would have to know something, that much was definite. Though she might want to, Jenny knew she couldn't run away from that. And that was perhaps the most terrifying thing of all.

Jenny's feet took her back to the SUV, but when she got there she found it hard to decide what to do next. She found it difficult to think logically, in sequence. She wasn't experienced enough to know that this happened often to those who had experienced or used powerful magic. Ureth could have told her that magic didn't operate in sequence. It happened all at once. The Crones knew this; it was part of their training. They called the type of thought that happened during everyday life "line-mind," while magic was "sphere-mind," and they knew it could be very disorienting for the novice to move quickly from one "mind" to the other. But whatever the connection that had existed between Jenny and Ureth, or whomever, was gone. Jenny could feel the loss of the power that had been with her earlier in the night, and despite her fear part of her mourned its passing.

She crawled inside the vehicle, shivering uncontrollably, her teeth chattering so hard they hurt when they clacked together. She couldn't remember what had happened to the keys, and she tried to turn the ignition with her mind. To her relief, the engine started. At least she hadn't lost the ordinary magic. She sat awhile, trying to calm her mind, forcing her thoughts away. Gradually, as the car heater did its own brand of magic, her shivering subsided, and she was able to think logically again. She had to drive to Jake's house and talk to Jake's mom. But what would she say? "I'm sorry Mrs. Patel, but I've accidentally sent your son and husband off to a different world, using magic. Why? Well, I sent Jake to try and find some medicine to save your life, and I asked Dr. Patel to try and call him back, but I think it must have been too late for that, and he decided to go and try and get Jake himself. Where have they gone? Um, I don't really know. How are they going to get back? Um, I don't really know that, either. Yes, I know it sounds crazy, but really, just because I dress like a witch and wander around in the freezing cold in the middle of the night causing people to disappear I really am very trustworthy, honestly." Somehow, she didn't think she would sound very believable.

But she would have to tell her something. Hopefully, the right words would come when she met the woman face to face. It was almost dawn; she had to hurry, before things started stirring in suburbia. Like, before a cop came by, and started asking awkward questions.

When she pulled into Jake's driveway, she parked the big vehicle, and waved a hand over the steering wheel. The engine stopped. Feeling like a murderer headed towards her execution, she got out of the SUV and walked up to the house. Jenny remembered David had left the back door unlocked, and she entered the house that way. Once inside, she crossed the kitchen, and began climbing the rear stairs. At the top of the staircase, she found her way down the hall to the master bedroom. This was set directly at the end of the hall, behind a set of white double doors. The doors were closed, but Jenny nudged one open, and peered inside.

She glanced at the bed, where a woman lay with her lips moving, seemingly trying to speak. In the growing light, Jenny could see the woman was very sick. She was pale, and thin, and her eyes lived in caves so dark that you couldn't tell if they were open or not. Jenny crossed to the bed. Bars of sunlight now lit the room, day had come after night, and the world, indifferent to the people it no longer contained, still turned. The woman on the bed was crying through closed lids, and Jenny took a tissue from the box on the bedside table and dabbed gently at the woman's cheeks. Mary opened her eyes, and looked deep into Jenny's own.

Who are you? Mary asked, though she made no sound in her weakness. But Jenny could hear her without the need of ears, and she grasped the lady's hand. She returned her look, knowing suddenly that she in turn would be able to speak without the need of words, and that no matter how strange it would seem, the truth would be believed. So as gently as she could she told Mary of all the things that had been done that night, for the desires of a pair of witches, for the greed of a Dragon, for the love of a son for his mother, and the love of a father for his son.

When it was finished, Jenny found she was crying, and brushed away her tears with her left hand, for Mary would not let go of her right.

"Are they both lost to me, then?" This time Jenny could hear the whisper in the room, not in her mind, and answered the same way.

"I think so," she said.

"You love my son." Mary excavated the words from her chest, the effort of each one as painful as a birth. She wanted to tell Jenny how she knew this astonishing fact, but she couldn't. Her eyelids fluttered closed, as she considered whether it was worth the effort to draw another breath. She was at the point where she could decide that question, she knew. So much pain, just to breathe. Her body would soon decide that the price of oxygen was just too high.

Jenny didn't know how to reply. Did she love Jake? She didn't know. Her heart lifted whenever she saw him. When she was near him, she was breathless. She cared for him too, cared about what happened to him, to his Dad, to his Mom. Was that love? Jenny took Mary's right hand in her own, feeling the fragility of the skin, the tenuous support the bones provided it, the ambivalent way in which the blood meandered through its vessels. Mary's spirit was indomitable, but her flesh had suffered so much. Her eyes fluttered open once more, and found Jenny's. She opened her mouth to speak again.

Don't talk, Jenny thought. *It's too hard on you. Just think what you want to say in your mind. I'll hear you.* Jenny smiled and nodded at Mary to reinforce the point. *Is this easier on you?*

Sure. Talking hurts so bad. Every little helps. I didn't know so much pain could happen to one person. A tear escaped Mary's right eye. Jenny dabbed it away with another Kleenex from its box on the nightstand.

The Fruit Of The Dendragon Tree

Can I get you something?

NO! I mean, no, no thanks. It helps, but I need too much of it now… this has to end.

Maybe I can help.

How? Sorry, it's hard to be nice when you want to scream and can't because it hurts too much.

It's ok, I understand. Close your eyes and hold my hand as tight as you can. Mary shut her eyes, and the pressure on Jenny's hand went from a feather to a silk handkerchief. Jenny raised her left hand, and stared at a spot just above the dying woman's head, then she too closed her eyes…

There was light. It was in the distance, but it was there. It was a light of love, of warmth, of forgiveness. Jenny opened her eyes. Sunlight streamed into the room through the half-opened blinds. But that wasn't the light she'd seen. She closed her eyes again. The light was nearer now: golden, warm. It touched Jenny's eyes behind closed eyelids, like a kiss. Jenny wanted to gasp, but the light stopped her mouth. She wanted to cry, but the light dried her tears before they could fall. Liquid gold fell into her mind, and poured down her spine. Every organ in her body awoke to its touch. The light cascaded around her head and face like laughing hair. It ran down her legs. It ran along her arms. It found her fingertips, where they met Mary's hand, and, like water filling an empty bowl, the light poured into the dark place of Mary's dying, and held her close.

A rattling breath escaped Mary's chest, and she was still. Jenny's fingertips, still tingling with light, closed the staring eyes.

Chapter 14

*"Think not that I am come to send peace…
I come not to send peace, but a sword."*

(Jesus: Matthew; 10:34)

When after long days it was finally time, they sent for him, and he met them in Marah's tower room. The Mother was there, and Ureth, and the other Sisters: Hane, Elbeth and Rathe. Naomi was there too, with Ariana and Mina, the other acolytes who had been at the Ring, for Marah felt they might be called as witnesses. A few acolytes, in their red attire, distributed tea and small cakes, and stole furtive glances at the handsome young man. Sathryn had gotten word to her father through one of the kitchen maids, and Scarth had sent Jake some clothes to wear for his audience with the King's Envoy. These were simple and comfortable, their only statement being the quality of their cut and the fabric. Jake wore a long-sleeved green undershirt, covered by a sleeveless beige tunic of soft cloth, warm as wool, but lighter and not as itchy. Fawn leggings of the same fabric flowed into sturdy brown leather boots that came to his knees. Everything fit perfectly.

He looked every inch a Taumarian merchant's son, or even a lesser noble. Sathryn was there too, of course, beaming with pride at his costume, and he smiled back, pleased she was so happy. Naomi noticed the smiles, and frowned. She maneuvered near Jake, and touched his hand. A shock went through him at the contact, and he blushed. But she quickly moved away, smiling to herself about what she had learned.

Jake quickly forgot this small undercurrent, however. He caught the excitement in the air, like a class going on a field trip, and he realized that the Crones never left their cloister en masse. Their forays out of Marfang were nearly always solitary, on quests for information or postings to distant villages. They might go out in twos or threes to work in the orchards or gardens on the island, but not like this, not all washed and combed, and dressed to attend a state visit!

The Envoy had arrived the night before, anxious to depose the matter of Jake as quickly as possible. There were already rumors that he would afford Jake the protection of the crown, and escort him to the royal palace at Marlona, the capital. If true, this would nicely deflect the Duke from his purpose of acquiring Jake, which even those Crones skeptical of Ureth's methods had come to regard as sinister. It would also remove his distracting male presence from the cloister. Marah, who missed little, noticed Naomi's eyes drifting towards Jake more often than was strictly appropriate. Finally, if Jake was a threat to Marfang, the Duke could hardly complain if the king took him to distant Marlona. Everything seemed poised to work out for the best. Which was why Marah was now wary.

Jake felt he would be glad to leave the cloister, though he would miss Sathryn, and Ureth too, he realized with some surprise. But if he gained an audience with the king, perhaps he could finally send to the Eldervolk for his father, and maybe together they could figure out a way to return home to his mother, if she was even still alive. He worried about this now a great deal. Mom had been very close to death when he had arrived in Tiramonde nearly ten days ago, and every day that passed the less likely was her survival. He also saw that if he went to the king's palace he might lose any opportunity to pluck the Dendragon fruit. Which was probably the point that would appease the Duke. The fact that he had so nearly mirrored the Mother's thoughts gave the lie to his relaxed posture as he and the Crones prepared for their audience.

He clasped Sathryn's hand as the delegation prepared to depart. "Thank you," he said.

She smiled back at him, her youth and beauty in striking contrast to the aged faces around her. "For what?" she asked, looking deep into his eyes.

"For helping me, for keeping me company while you could."

She laughed. "You're welcome," she said. "It was fun, in the end, but I'll be glad when I can go back home." Neither of them noticed the scowl Naomi cast their way.

"Yeah, me too," he replied. "My Dad too, I hope. I can't wait to see him." And Jake understood that in his heart he had turned an important corner in his relationship with his father.

"I'm sure you will soon. Whatever is said about the Duke, the king is supposed to be a fair and just man. I'm sure he will give you all the help he can."

"Which his Envoy cannot do if we keep him waiting," said Marah, who had overheard. And so the small procession of Crones, with Sathryn and Jake, made its way to the Council of the King.

During his time in Marfang, Jake had discovered that the Cloister of the Crones was a castle within a castle. The huge gated entrance to the keep stood in the south wall, and cut through a mass of stone twenty feet thick. A ground-floor passage within the wall itself led eastwards to the Soldier's Tower, manned by the officers and men of the elite Castleguard. A similar passage within the east-facing wall ran north and south, connecting the Soldier's Tower to the Banquet Tower, where the large reception and feast areas were. It was also where important visitors such as the Royal Envoy were housed, and where the traditional King's Feast would be held that night, after the business of the Council had been concluded for the day. The Royal Tower, where the Duke's quarters were, and where the Royal Suite was also housed, should the king himself ever visit, stood at the northwest corner of the keep. Yet a third passage within the north wall joined the Banquet Tower to the Royal Tower. So one could walk nearly three-quarters of the way around Marfang's keep within its walls. The Crone Cloister in the southwest corner was of course the exception.

No passages ran within the walls to join it either to the gate or the Royal Tower due north. Instead, the west wall was a honeycomb of rooms for the varied use of the Crones. Here were classrooms, and storerooms for herbs, the dining hall and kitchen (much smaller than the main one across the keep). Here too were the cells, dim little rooms, bare of any comfort, which offered only solitude.

"Not that they have much time to themselves," Sathryn had told him, before her relegation to the kitchen. "They're either cleaning their cells, gathering food, making food, cleaning up the dining areas, or sitting in classes learning strange lessons from the Sisters. You were very lucky to have had a cell with a window."

But Jake hadn't felt lucky at the time, though he did feel optimistic as the party made its way diagonally across the quadrangle to the Banquet Tower. They had exited the Cloister through the same doorway that Jake and Ureth had used to escape the wrath of Rand's soldiers, and the memory of his victory still burned brightly. He had since learned the significance of a Taumarian soldier's ponytail; that it was a sign of manhood tied with the rings of warriors its owner had killed in battle. It was a terrible omen to lose a queue. Worse, it was humiliating. No wonder Rand had wailed like a baby. So despite his impatience at delays he couldn't control, Jake's mood as he crossed the courtyard with his minders, and passed the dust of the training ground where he had bested the Duke's most infamous fighter, was decidedly jaunty.

All morning long, he had watched from his window the hustle and bustle in the courtyard as the castle folk had prepared for the Council. All Marfang was astir, from the great kitchen, where the night's feast was being prepared, to the smithies along the eastern wall, where furnaces glowed and hammers rang as repairs were made to the horseshoes and armor of the King's Men, who had made quick time from the remote fastness of Marlona in the northeast. The dozen or so horses themselves were standing in a group, just outside the stables that were also huddled against the east wall. They were large black animals, and one of them looked Jake right in the eye as he passed and nickered, as if to say "hello." And for a moment, Jake's anxiety about the meeting, and the waiting, fell away. He grinned at the horse, and sketched it a small salute, and the beast turned his attention back to his hay.

People paused in their errands as the procession of Crones and two young people passed them by. Several bowed to the Mother, and the women in blue, but as they looked at Jake their eyes said: *So this was what all the fuss was about. Doesn't seem that dangerous. That lass though, she's a real beauty.* But Sathryn had seen that message before, in too many eyes, to mind it now, and Jake didn't realize he was being evaluated as well.

The sun was high as they crossed the open space; spring had fully arrived, and the grass in the yard was a deep emerald green. The group passed close by the Dendragon tree, and Jake finally had the chance to see it properly. The tree stood alone upon its little green island, it's blossoms carpeting the ground, and the deep black water of the pool lapped gently at the low stone wall surrounding it. Up close, Jake could see how brilliantly red its blooms were. Like those of the flowers outside the walls, they resembled large red dandelions, with petals pointed like teeth. The gnarled black roots of the tree poked through the grass of the knoll, and crept to the water's edge like veins on the back of a hand.

The Banquet Tower held a large wooden doorway, which exactly faced the Crone Tower diagonally across the quadrangle. The doors themselves, which were open, were at least twelve feet tall, and shone black with age and lacquer. They stood at the top of a flight of four broad stone stairs. Two tall men of the Castleguard, draped in flowing black cloaks that were clasped at the shoulder by golden Dragon brooches, stood on either side of the doorway. Their swords were sheathed, but each held a long spear of ash, tipped with steel, that they held across the doorway in a large X, to bar entry to the uninvited. The fact that they did not raise this barrier as the group approached, forcing them to halt at the entrance, was not lost on Jake. The guard on his left, a fair-haired man with deep gray eyes, spoke to the Mother.

"Why are you here, Crone? The audience is for the boy alone. None of your kind is invited. Besides," he continued with a quick glance to his partner, who had begun to smirk, "you may not be safe in there. There are men inside, after all."

His companion snickered at the gibe, but Marah kept walking up the stairs until she stood just in front of the spears, not quite touching them. Jake and the others paused on the second step. "It is not because we fear men that we stay in the cloisters, Master Gareth, but because men fear us." The Mother's voice was soft, gentle with reason. Jake could see the surprise in Gareth's eyes at being called by name. "Come, let us pass," she continued. "It is unreasonable to think that having cared for this boy all this time that we should have no voice at the Council regarding his future."

"You do not seem to understand… witch," said Gareth. "Three of my brothers have already died for not keeping your kind out, and I myself have been demoted to guard duty for not avenging the loss of my Captain's hair. I have my orders, and I have no desire to end up like those three up there." He jerked his head in the general direction of the wall, where the carrion birds still pulled at the rotting heads of his three dead comrades. "They were my friends, and now they are dead because of witchcraft. Only the boy may enter. Everyone else needs the password. Let him come forward, then return to your tower. Whatever you may do to me with your magic, I fear my lord more."

"Very well," said the Mother. "If only those with the password may enter, then I will submit to that." She looked back at Jake with a soft smile, the young eyes in the old face full of liking. The guards had relaxed, Jake could see, knowing they had won.

Only, they hadn't. Whipping her head back around to the guards, Marah barked a single word. "Dendragon!" she cried, and to Jake's eyes the sun seemed to dim while the sound of the word echoed round the courtyard in a tide of power that pulsed in his head and chest, leaving him faint.

"What did you say?" whispered Gareth. "How did you- that word was a secret! How did you come by it?" Gareth looked wildly to his partner, who was smirking no longer.

The Mother pressed her sudden advantage. "The password for today is Dendragon, Master Gareth. Now put up those ridiculous spears and LET US PASS!" The last three words were said as a command, wielded with a force that brooked no argument. The spears snapped back, whether in obedience to the password or the Mother's will, and Marah passed through the doorway into the corridor beyond.

Jake followed the Mother inside with the others and stopped dead. There were people everywhere. People lined the broad corridor. They spilled up the staircases to the left and right of the entrance, a crush of people, brightly dressed, doing nothing in particular. After the quiet, sparsely populated tower of the Crones, the press of humanity made Jake claustrophobic. As he entered, the noise of a hundred different conversations died away. All eyes were on him, it seemed, and he realized they had been waiting for him to appear. A cold trickle of sweat snaked down his back between his shoulder blades. He tried to make eye contact, but there were simply too many eyes. They didn't seem friendly or unfriendly, just intently curious, but he felt like a bacterium under a microscope. Then the implications of the Crones' presence hit home with the crowd, and the chatter started up again, whispered at first, then louder, until the buzz of conversation was back in full swing.

The Mother had stopped just inside the entrance with Jake, Ureth and the others huddled around her. A broad corridor led directly away from them, straight into the bowels of the tower. The stairs to the right and left curved inwards, to join a common landing above the entrance to this corridor. From the landing, a single flight of seven steps opened onto an upper corridor, which seemed to Jake to lie directly over the one on the ground floor where they stood. As in the Crone tower, everything was made of stone, but in here the walls were dressed with rich tapestries and banners, of reds, and greens, and deep gold, that glinted in the light of the many torches ensconced in the walls. But the light from the torches wasn't the only light. The spring daylight streamed into the atrium through the most beautiful stained glass Jake had ever seen. This glass took up almost every bit of space on the outside aspects of the tower walls. Such a rainbow of color and light cascaded into the atrium, that the very stone itself seemed alive.

"I could have sworn the outside walls were of solid stone," he whispered to Ureth.

"Your eyes did not deceive you, Jake. This is the Pierglass, found only here and at the king's palace in Marlona. It was a gift of the elves, in their gratitude for Kildraig's confinement, so many years ago. From the outside, it appears to be simple stone, solid and impervious. But from within, as you can see, their ancient craft has rendered the effect of glass, light and airy with all the colors ever known. These fools take it for granted, and half of them think it was some forgotten art of men that made these walls. But if anyone seeks the truth of the old legends, the evidence is here, right before their eyes."

"It's beautiful," said Jake, who never forgot his first sight of the magic Pierglass of Marfang, an oasis of light and beauty in the desert of the struggle to come.

The muttering of the crowd had grown louder. Some of the glances that were being directed towards the Crones were now definitely hostile, when suddenly a fussy little fat man bustled into the foyer from the corridor straight ahead. He had to fight his way through the throng, which parted amiably enough for him, as he approached, crying, "Make way! Make way there! Duke's business. My goodness, don't you people ever bathe? Make way there, I say!"

Jake saw it was the same effeminate little man he had last seen at the dock on the morning of his arrival, when Scarth had refused to hand him over to the Duke's men. Then, he had looked daggers at Jake, but this morning he had fixed a smile in place. Jake sensed that the man was so slimy it was amazing the smile didn't slide right off his face. The man give a little start of surprise at the presence of the Crones, but recovered quickly, and approached the little party as if they were long-delayed dinner guests. Jake's sense of distrust grew even more profound.

"Welcome, welcome, my young Master! And welcome to you, too, Mother Marah and Sister Ureth! And welcome, also to, er, well, welcome to you all. Please, follow me; the Duke and the Council are ready for you. I am Jasper, the Duke's advisor," he continued, as they followed him back along the corridor. "I have the honor of being your attendant, and er, well, your attendant, while you are with us. Anything you need at all, just ask for me, and I will see to it. Yes, we are all most excited that, um, that ALL of you are here, though there might be, well, just one or two more of you that we originally thought. No matter, there are no constraints on my lord's hospitality, none at all. Several important guests have come from far and wide, having seen the signs in the heavens. As you no doubt know, we have a King's Envoy here, with his entourage, and even one of the heathen Sacours too, may the Dancer protect us. Yes, my boy, your arrival in Marfell has caused quite a, um, quite a splash in our world, if you'll pardon the dreadful pun, um yes, quite a splash indeed."

Jasper continued his incessant chatter in this vein until Jake had to tune him out, or slap him. Ureth and the Mother stayed silent, impassive as they walked abreast of him, and Jake followed their example. The crowd remained parted for them, gazing again in silent curiosity, with occasional sidelong glances and shared whispers as they passed. Jake saw some of the women assessing him with a high degree of interest. He knew that look. Being a handsome boy, he had seen it often enough at school. But it wasn't just the younger girls staring at him with that… hunger: yes, that was the word; it was several of the older women too. When he smiled at the girls, they blushed and turned away. He didn't smile at the older women; it was too embarrassing.

Ureth, missing nothing as usual, caught this interplay and whispered in his ear. "Don't worry, Jake. The ladies have simply never seen a man with blue eyes before. You are an exotic curiosity to them, and so they think they might like to bed you. Smile at all of them, as much as you are able, and so repay them for their presumption." So Jake did smile back at all the stares, but there were so many of them that by the time the long corridor ended, at a pair of vast wooden doors, his cheeks were aching. Jasper threw open the doors with a practiced flourish and cried, "The boy Jake, and his companions!"

The Fruit Of The Dendragon Tree

The room he found himself in was vast, with vaulted ceilings nearly thirty feet high. The rear wall was of curved Pierglass, and Jake realized it formed part of the outer wall of the castle. The effect was like walking into a large baseball diamond with people crowded onto the infield. Sunlight streamed in through stone as clear as glass, and winked against the jewels and embroidered finery of the assembled throng. They had left a path, Jake could see, that led up to a broad low dais set against the Pierglass wall. Two thrones sat upon this. The large, golden one, right in the middle of the dais, was empty. It was set upon a slightly raised platform skirted with purple velvet. A tall man with dark hair, and rich clothing of crimson and black, stood next to this throne. A golden mask hid all of his face save his mouth, but Jake could feel the intensity of his gaze as the eyeholes in the mask turned to watch his approach. The smaller wooden throne, sitting to the left of the golden one, was occupied. Jake could tell that the man who sat there was obviously tall, even though seated. He was straight-backed, with black hair and very pale skin, and Jake could feel the intensity of some power in the black eyes that sought his own. He knew without being told that this was the Duke, whom Ureth claimed wanted the kingdom for himself, and Jake dead.

A man in green and scarlet robes stood before the dais, facing the Duke. It seemed that he had been having speech with either the Duke or the man in the mask, for Jake had the strong feeling that his entrance had interrupted their conversation. This man turned to them, and Jake noticed his complexion was much darker than anyone else in the room. He had the tanned skin of someone who never saw winter, black eyes, and hair the color of midnight.

"That's the Sacour," whispered Ureth. "I wonder what he's doing here?"

The Duke's lips writhed in a smile that didn't touch his eyes. The air in the room felt suddenly heavy; all was still with a tense watchfulness that Jake could almost taste by the time Coegun finally spoke. "Sir Jasper, why don't you introduce our visitors properly? Ladies of great rank have graced us with their presence!" His voice was deep and calm, a little like Scarth's voice, Jake thought, yet he sensed of a taint of corruption in the man, and was suddenly very watchful.

"Oh, yes my Lord Duke," replied Jasper. "May I introduce the boy Jake, from er, beyond Tiramonde, guest of the Council and, ah, his escorts, the Lady Marah, Chief of the Crones, the Lady Ureth and their um, assistants, who are here in an, um, I presume an unofficial advisory role- "

"Stop blithering, you silly little man!" said Marah. "We all know that the boy is only your guest at this gathering because you have not yet made him your prisoner, or worse, and that our, "um, er, ah, unofficial capacity" is only because your Duke tried his best to bar us from this meeting! We are insulted, sir," she continued, now speaking directly to the Duke, "to be denied entry as if we were common peddlers!"

But the Duke didn't rise to this direct approach, though Jake fancied he saw a glint of something in the cold gray eyes, before he laughed softly. "Marah, Marah, please do not parody my advisor so unmercifully. Of course you are welcome here. My guards perhaps interpreted my orders in too narrow a sense, so much concern do they have for the safety of my person. I- "

"Of course you don't want us here! Why pretend that you do?" interrupted Marah, as a gasp went up from the assembly. "Your men wanted to take this boy prisoner the night he was rescued from Marfell, naked, defenseless and alone. Is this how you now treat children?"

This time the steel was evident in the Duke's face as he snapped right back: "You may have forgotten, Mother, since you sit up in your cold tower yonder and let events of moment pass you by (another gasp from the crowd, this direct talk was much more fun than the cold diplomacy they were used to), that we have recently been in a state of war and it is better to be too watchful than too welcoming when strangers magically arrive within our borders on an ill-omened night. As for your claim of defenselessness, your child is proficient enough to have cut off my best warrior's hair! Though my men still believe that he received magic help from his Crone minder. So although I don't personally care how many of you attend him here, you will understand why your presence makes my guards a touch nervous!"

The Mother drew a breath as if to speak, but Ureth touched her shoulder lightly and stepped forward, her blue eyes fixed on the Duke's face. "As you clearly value plain speaking, my Lord, let us cut to the chase. There are only two possibilities here. One is that Jake is an accidental imposter, called from his world for no purpose, and brought here against his will and by my error. In which case," and Jake heard the honey in her voice masking the venom underneath, "Your warrior Rand should be made to suffer for the ignominy of losing his hair to an untrained child who, despite the whining of your men, was unassisted by any magic of mine."

But maybe by someone's, thought Jake, for no particular reason.

Ureth flashed him a look, as if she had heard. But she went on, "There is another possibility," she continued. "The boy, if not an imposter, is the Pendraig of legend, here to fulfill the ancient promise. In that case, who could fault Rand? Because if Jake is the Pendraig, then he almost certainly will have access to magic, but not to mine. It will be the Dragon's breath that flows through him, a Dragon's power that sustains him, and not that of a mere Crone!" She almost had to shout the last words, to be heard over the cries of wonder and fear that came from the assembly. Jake caught snatches of conversation: "The Dragon... the legends are true... they must be!... no mere boy could have done that to Rand, I tell you!"

But the Duke was not to be perturbed in his own tower by mere talk of Dragons. He held up a hand, and the noise abated. "Well, Sister Ureth," his mouth curling with contempt as the name passed through it, "So you come straight to the point, as is your wont. Ever you rush to be heard while your betters are speaking. Ever is your rush to act while your betters counsel caution. Yes, we know you acted alone to bring the boy here. Who else would be so rash? Yet there is truth in what you say. And truth in what I say now: If the boy is the Pendraig foretold by legend, then his coming bodes an end to Marfang. And if Marfang falls, who will stand against the Sacours or the Ice folk? And if he is not the Pendraig, then I have a right to discover who he is, and what he is doing within my borders. Perhaps he is a Sacourian spy! No offense (this to the olive skinned man, still standing near the dais, who nodded that none was taken). In any event, I should have him, to better protect this ancient fortress from its enemies."

A general buzz of agreement went up from the crowd at these words. Jake saw more than a few dark looks of suspicion cast his way. He was suddenly very glad that Marah and Ureth and the others were with him. Looking back to the dais, he noticed that the man in the golden mask had moved to the Duke's side. The man appeared to ask the Duke a question, for the Duke nodded, and made a gesture as if to say, "Go ahead."

Golden Mask stepped forward and raised his right arm, palm forward, like a cop stopping traffic. "Enough!" he said, and though his voice was not loud, it rang clear in the confusion of the hall. The hubbub immediately subsided, Jake noticed with surprise. "Peace, my good people! My name is Endil, the Envoy of the King. As Envoy, I bear the king's name, and have forgotten my own. I wear his face, too, as this mask attests, and I carry King Endil's words in my mouth. Hear me!" The room grew perfectly still. "His majesty is grateful," Endil continued in the hush, "for the Duke's continued loyal service and his unceasing care for the safety of our kingdom. He agrees that if the legend of old has come to life in the person of this boy, then his presence here can bring no good to this castle. For as the ancient text says:

> *"He who comes as Marfang's Doom*
> *Before the Dragon Tree does bloom,*
> *With Kildraig's aid the ruby he*
> *Will pluck from Marfang's Dragon tree.*
> *True of heart and brave of sword*
> *He will defeat the Undead Lord*
> *And win the right to pluck his stone*
> *So riving Marfang to the bone"*

The Fruit Of The Dendragon Tree

Hearing the poem, Jake definitely had a better idea of why the Duke might not welcome him with open arms. "Riving Marfang to the bone" didn't sound like a great thing for the people who lived here. It was as Ureth had told him. They all believed that if he did what he had to do to save his Mom, the castle would fall, but how? He still had too many questions, and not nearly enough answers, and he was getting really tired of the whole thing. *Just wait until the damn tree bears fruit, pick one, and get back home somehow. No problem.* But wait, he also had to kill an Undead Lord: what was that about? And how exactly was he to get home afterwards? And if Dad were here too, he wouldn't leave without him.

"There is more, of course," Endil was saying. "Though we needn't recite all the ancient texts here. But the Duke is right. If this lad is the Pendraig, then Marfang is not safe while he is here. If he is not, then he is a trespasser on the king's land (Jake caught the emphasis on the word "king"). Either way, he does indeed present an unknown risk to the kingdom, and the king, ever mindful of protecting his loyal vassals, has commanded me to remove the boy to the royal capital, Marlona. We leave tomorrow. That being decreed, I am honored to represent the king at tonight's feast, which the Duke has most graciously founded."

Ureth realized there was more to the King's Envoy than met the eye. Wasting no time, he had settled what was to be done about Jake, while reminding the Duke who the true ruler was, and the Duke's official place in the overall scheme of things. Ureth could see the Duke didn't care for being described as a vassal, but it would now be impossible for him to disobey the royal order, for order it was, no matter how considerately framed, without declaring himself a traitor. Ureth looked at the Duke. He seemed to actually be weighing the risks of defiance. *Will he declare himself now?* Ureth wondered. Surely he was not yet strong enough. Suddenly she knew he was only waiting for the right moment. His treachery was a foregone conclusion; timing was the only question. Her eyes met the Duke's and he smiled the smile that only reached his lips.

When he broke from the law, who would follow the Duke over their rightful king? Perhaps fewer than might have done, now a King's Envoy had reminded them of their duty. But there would still be many traitors, she knew. Too many of the spectators were observing the proceedings with the calculating looks of carrion birds. The Envoy had turned to the Duke, no doubt expecting his reply of assent. The whole company seemed to hang upon his response. But the Duke did not reply. An angry flush had crawled up his neck. *He will defy the king now*, Ureth thought, *and there will be civil war*. She caught the eyes of the Sacour. He was looking at her intently, and she had the strangest feeling that he could share her thoughts. She shook the notion aside. No man could do that.

"Not so fast!" cried Marah, her voice filling the hall, and what the Duke might have declared was never known. Ureth saw Coegun visibly master himself and look to the Mother.

"Well, Marah?" he asked. "We might have known the Crones would find fault even with a Royal Decree. Whatever designs Ureth or you may have had, the King's Envoy has spoken, and the boy Jake is to return to Marlona with him tomorrow."

"No Coegun," replied Marah, unfazed. "Ureth the Crone may have paved Jake's way, but even she knows the magic that brought him here wasn't hers. The boy doesn't belong to her, or the Crones. As for you and the King, begging your pardons, but you have even less claim to him than we do. You hide in your castles, and you fight over flowers, but you've forgotten the magic of your ancestors. The boy doesn't belong to you either! I say he should go where he will, with any who would give him protection. His father is with the Eldervolk, and I'm sure he wants to see him. Don't you Jake?" The boy nodded. "There you are then," Marah continued. "Give him safe passage to travel to the Bloodwood, and be reunited with his father."

"You speak bravely, O Mother," said Endil. "But you have no authority here. By what right do you proclaim his freedom, in the King's Council Chamber?"

"By the right of the Crones to protect the traveler, which was granted to us before the first stone of this castle was laid, your grace. Though I have to admit, it's a right seldom exercised in these times."

"Perhaps your protection is little used because it is little sought," said the Duke. "It is my men who keep Taumar safe for the innocent traveler!" There were growls of agreement at this from many of the soldiers in the hall.

"I can see that the old knowledge has dwindled indeed," replied Marah. "Ureth told you that Jake came here through a power stronger than yours or the king's, or even the Crones. And until that power is ready for him, I say he must be free to go."

"And who's power might that be?" asked Endil of the golden mask.

"Why, the dragon asleep at the root of this castle, Milord," said Marah. "This lad belongs to Kildraig."

It took some time to restore order after that.

2.

Jake had never seen so much food. Course after course, piled high on gilded platters, made their way to the long tables in the banquet hall. There was roasted duckling; in a sauce Jake had never tasted before. There was chicken, and goose, and venison, and greens. There was a huge baked fish, fresh from the river, which flaked and melted on his tongue. There was soup, and the delicious rolls that he had smelled baking his first morning at the castle. Between courses, there were small, fruit-flavored ices, to clear the palate, and near the end there were pies, gooseberry and rhubarb and apple, with blue veined cheeses, courtesy of the castle goats, and the wine changed with the courses and never stopped flowing.

Jake sat between Ureth on his right, and the Sacour on his left. Marah sat to the right of Ureth, next to the Duke, while Endil the Royal Envoy sat at the Duke's right, in the place of honor. Rand sat next to Endil, his broken arm healed already, no doubt through some potion of the Dendragon flowers. Rand's loose hair, bereft of any rings now, fell to his shoulders. Apart from the single venomous stare he had given Jake in the Council Hall, he had studiously ignored him. Which was fine with Jake. The head table, like the thrones in the Council Chamber, was on a dais at the front of the Banquet Hall. Long trestle tables, set perpendicular to the dais, filled up most of the rest of the space. Jake guessed there were five hundred people, men and women of the town and keep, all eating at once, and the castle servants were constantly running to deliver food and wine to the hungry crowd. Scarth was there, Jake saw, and the old soldier winked at him and smiled. Sathryn sat with her father, relieved of her duties as a kitchen drudge. She also smiled at Jake, and he smiled back, remembering the kiss they had shared that afternoon.

"I may never see you again, Boy From Another World, so take this kiss to remember me by." Jake had needed no further urging. Sathryn was a beautiful girl, no matter what world you came from, and Jake could tell from the glances cast her way that others thought so too. It looked as if she'd be able to leave with her father in the morning. The Envoy had insisted they spend the night at the castle, as guests of the king, in acknowledgment of Scarth's actions on the king's behalf. The Duke had not greeted the warrior, but had agreed readily enough to his presence at the feast. Then again, what else could he do?

Ureth was hardly eating at all, Jake noticed, and she seemed tense. So did the Mother. Neither of them spoke, and he didn't know what to say to the Sacour sitting next to him. But the food was too good to pass up, and the days of Crone fare, together with the relief he felt to leave Marfang, had helped his appetite. He was a little worried about the fruit he was supposed to pick, but there was no sign of it yet. The discussion about his future had raged back and forth for most of the afternoon. Finally Marah and Endil had accepted a compromise that he himself had suggested. "Mr. Endil, sir" he had said, not knowing how else to address the man, "What if I go to meet my Dad with you and Ureth, then both of us can go to Marlona with you?" Endil had pretended to object to this for a while, but Jake could tell he liked the way the idea broke the impasse. The golden mask had faced

The Fruit Of The Dendragon Tree

the mother, and said: "If that's what the boy wants, I can allow it." And so it had been settled, though thunder had gathered silently on Coegun's brow.

"That was well done, Jake," Ureth had said, and Marah had agreed.

"A bodyguard of king's men, and the most powerful Crone in the kingdom should be enough to keep you from harm," she said. Her young eyes crinkled in a smile, and Jake smiled back, surprised at how happy he was to have Ureth along.

"I wonder what's bugging them?" he said aloud now, to nobody in particular, and to his surprise it was the Sacour who answered.

"They are probably wondering how to keep you alive until morning, my young friend. The Sacour rose, and turned to Jake and bowed. "My name is Rajindra Al-Qabir, of the House of Kamal, in the blessed kingdom of Castelfar, washed by the Thunder Falls. I am a wandering mendicant and sometime emissary to the palaces of our honorable enemies of Taumar."

Jake rose and bowed in his turn, though not, he admitted to himself, with the fluidity of the other man. "And my name is Jake Patel, I guess of the House of Patel, from Tennessee, though we came from all over to get there."

"Greetings to you and welcome, my young friend. I am most honored to be meeting you. In one day it is as if the legends themselves have come to life in front of my very eyes, and I am overcome with astonishment. For while it is true that we have crossed swords with the Northern Barbaria- um with our gracious hosts, the legend of the Pendraig is the most exalted myth in my homeland, foretelling as it does the destruction of this magnificent fortress. But I am very curious to hear more about you my son," he went on as they both sat down again. "What is all this talk about dragons and such? I have not heard that part of the legend before. And why, if you are a living legend that threatens his power, would Coegun let you live? And why, if they care about you, would the Crones let you face such an evil creature?"

Which, Jake realized as he started to tell his story, were very good questions.

Chapter 15

*"O Brave new world,
That hath such people in't"*

(Shakespeare: The Tempest)

The Sacour was good company, and Jake enjoyed their conversation. And when they escorted him to his chamber in the Royal Tower he was tired with the particular fatigue that accompanies a happy conclusion to a day beginning in anxiety. But though his bed was comfortable, something of Ureth's tension had infected him. "I don't trust any of this, Jake," she had said. "It's all too easy. Keep your eyes open: there'll be deception tonight, and betrayal, or my Gift is worthless." He was uneasy, and sleep eluded him.

Scarth had overheard her, and offered to guard Jake's door, and Ureth had agreed. "You will see your father soon, Jake," she had said, bidding him goodnight.

"I really hope so," Jake said. "I can't believe he came to get me."

"Can you not?" Ureth replied. "Then you do not know the love he has for you."

"The last time we spoke… I said some pretty mean stuff to him."

Ureth had glanced kindly into Jake's eyes. "That is a wound that can be healed when you see him. In the meantime rest, and know that the best swordsman in Taumar guards your life."

"Let no one in here, Father, unless it's me or Marah," were Ureth's parting words.

"Do not fear, Ureth, the boy will be safe," Scarth replied, and she had withdrawn, together with Marah and Naomi, to their assigned chambers several doors down the corridor from Jake's. And Jake had been left wanting sleep, wanting to leave, wanting his home, and his family.

He must have slept after all, for the sound of his door opening awakened him, and in the light from the hallway he could see Scarth stepping aside as Ureth entered the room and shut the door. His head was throbbing, his mouth dry. The room was cold, a shade less dark than it had been, with the first gray hint of dawn coming through his open window. He could just make out the shadow of the Crone as she approached his bed. He lay still, his eyes half open, wondering what Ureth wanted. The shadow stopped a couple of feet from his bed, and whispered to him.

"Aren't you going to move over? A girl could freeze to death waiting here." But it wasn't Ureth's voice, and when she moved again the faint light revealed Jenny Blackwood next to his bed, smiling at him. He had never seen anyone so beautiful.

"Jenny!" he whispered. "How did you get in here? How did you find me? How…?" But the girl placed a finger on his lips to quiet him, and slid into the bed. She was dressed in the thin burlap rags of a Crone, and he could feel the heat of her body through the rough fabric as she pressed against him. His own body was already beginning to respond.

"Shh, Jake. We don't have much time. You know there'll be trouble if they find me. Which they'll do if you aren't quiet."

"What do you want, Jenny?"

"Do you really have to ask? You must know how I feel about you. And you've wanted me too, you just didn't know it." That must be true, Jake realized. He was achingly aroused. And whatever resistance he might have mounted faded away as Jenny pulled his face to hers and kissed him.

Her kiss was every song he'd ever heard, every poem he had never written. Her open mouth pressed to his ignited a wild tenderness within him and he wanted to possess her and caress her at the same time. He was young, and alive, and far from home and needed no further encouragement to listen with great attention to what his body had to say.

"Let me show you how I love you," Jenny whispered. She placed her hands on his shoulders and pressed him back into the softness of the bed, straddling him. She kissed him again, as she raised the skirt of her tunic and slid down his body. He felt the trail of her wetness as she did so, and the caress of her hair as it cascaded around his face. He inhaled deeply, as if to breathe her in, and when the heat between her legs found what it sought, his hardness strained to find her, and they both groaned softly as she enveloped him in her warmth. He moved within her as she rode him, their lips parting as their thrusts became quicker and deeper. They were ripe, and young, panting full of desire, and when Jake climaxed with a powerful shudder the girl seemed to take equal pleasure from him, her eyes rolling back in her head as she gave a low moan of satisfaction.

Slowly, they came back to themselves. Jenny raised her head from his shoulder, where it had come to rest after she'd subsided, and smiled at him in the growing light. "Thank you Jake. You have given me more than you could ever know." And she dismounted from him quickly, rearranging her ragged attire, the quick precision of her movements forestalling any questions. "I'd better leave, before Scarth gets suspicious."

And then, right before his eyes, Jenny Blackwood turned back into Ureth the Crone. Jake first thought he would throw up, then that his heart would break. Finally, the anger of Ureth's deception took him full force, and he leaped naked from his bed, wanting a fight, but unsure with whom.

The Crone laughed at him, softly. "Oh, please, Jake, don't be angry. You received a gift from me too; don't pretend you didn't enjoy it. Did you really think that Jenny Blackwood could get past Scarth? Please.

The Fruit Of The Dendragon Tree

That girl only plays at being a witch. You've just had the real thing, and we both know you liked it. Or perhaps you'd rather I'd looked like this?" And her features shifted again: her hair changed color, and Sathryn stood before him, smiling in the early morning as she had on the day she'd first met him, what seemed like a lifetime ago. Still smiling, Sathryn became Ureth once more.

Jake found he couldn't speak, there were too many things crowding his mouth to be said. *Jenny cares about me* was one thought. *Jenny's never lied to me* was another. But he could only stare at the witch in impotent rage, weak with confusion whereas a few moments before he had felt as powerful as a king.

Oblivious to his pain, Ureth chuckled as if they had just shared a joke, and turned for the door. She never made it. There was a sudden commotion outside, voices raised in alarm, and the door to the chamber burst open. It seemed as if a crowd of people tumbled inside, all at once, but when Jake could sort them out there were only three: Marah, and Ureth, with Scarth following behind. And when he saw the real Ureth, Jake forgot he was naked, and wondered how he had been fooled by the pale imitation before him. So whom had he been with?

"Naomi!" Ureth cried, advancing across the room. "What are you doing here? Jake! Put some clothes on!"

"It was you, Ureth," Scarth said, appalled. "She looked the very image of you."

Struggling into his clothes, Jake saw Naomi resume her own form, and as she did, he understood how difficult Ureth was to deceive. She was vital and strong, willful and tactless sometimes, but always honest. Truth flowed in her like a wine that lies had no power to dilute, and as Jake saw her and Naomi together he understood that Naomi would never have Ureth's raw power. "What are you doing here, you little fool?" Ureth spat. "Have you gone mad? You know the penalty for breaking the Crone-vow!"

Naomi raised her head in defiance, the wrinkled face on her young woman's body showing nothing but scorn. "Crone-vow? Crone-vow?" she hissed. "I have already broken it, you sanctimonious bitch! I have already lain with him! I WANT to pay the penalty! I am no Crone like you, Ureth, nor you either, Marah! Not for me the long cold years, alone, my heart drying out for want of love! I have had a man, and I will bear his child!"

Marah was faint with horror. "You know nothing of love! Anything based on a lie is no love at all! Do you think I can let you bear a child from this night's… mating? It would be an abomination!"

"Do your worst, you old hag!" screamed Naomi. "You can't touch me and you both know why. Are you really going to murder the baby of your precious "Pendraig"? I'm going home, and you can't stop me!"

But Ureth had recovered enough to be practical. "Nobody's going anywhere if we don't move soon. The Duke's men are coming for Jake. We must leave now. Father, Jake must be protected at all costs. Naomi, whatever happens to you afterwards, you must come with us now, unless you wish to be butchered here. We have to find the Envoy, and get out of this castle now, or die."

She was too late. At that moment, several large, armed men rushed into the chamber. Rand was in the forefront of the intruders, murderous eyes fixed on Jake. Scarth raised his own weapon, and the clang of sword on sword erupted almost before Jake could draw breath.

"Beware Jake! Treachery!" The swords rang louder as two of the Duke's men engaged the merchant and shoved him aside so that the others could reach Jake. One was now before him, with his sword poised to run the boy through. Everything had happened at once, and then it all slowed down. Marah's hand, raised above her head, flew forward toward Jake's attacker, as if throwing an invisible ball. The man staggered, then screamed as a crimson circle of flame exploded in the middle of his chest. His sword swung wildly as the smell of burning flesh assaulted Jake's nostrils, and the boy managed to wrest it from him as the man fell to the floor, already dead. Jake turned to see Rand thrust at Naomi with his sword. But the Mother dove between them, knocking Naomi to the floor, and taking full in the chest the blow that was meant for the girl. Jake heard the whoosh of Naomi's breath as her fall knocked the wind from her, just as Marah's blood splattered his face and shoulder. Rand's sword lodged deep in the Mother's body, and he could not withdraw it in time to parry Jake's slashing blow.

This is what you were born to do. The words came unbidden into a brain that was suddenly ice-cold. Jake could only acknowledge the supreme skill he unaccountably possessed, and now was the time to use it for the destruction of his enemies. Somewhere Ureth screamed in horror, as Marah crumpled to the floor. Somewhere, Scarth's sword rang as it defended Jake from other foes. But the last sound Rand heard, before his mind fluttered away, was the slurp of Jake's sword slicing his neck open. Jake watched the life leave his enemy's eyes, and felt nothing.

He looked for more work for his sword, but there had only been four intruders, and Scarth had dispatched the other two. Naomi lay on the ground, trying to breathe. Ureth was crouched next to Marah, cradling her as one would a child, keening softly to her still form.

"Oh, Marah! Marah! Don't leave me! It is too soon! You're a mother to me! You cannot pass yet, there is too much left to do!" Jake had never expected to see such naked grief on Ureth's face, and his heart went out to her. But Marah was dead. She had been kind to him, Jake knew, kind when many wanted him dead. And she had paid for that kindness with her life. Then Jake noticed that Marah's hair was no longer white, but golden. Her face was no longer wrinkled and ugly, but young, unlined, and beautiful. Only her sightless eyes, which had been the windows to her spirit, had no color of life in them, and it was as if a blood-soaked angel lay dead on the floor.

Scarth coughed, apologetically, from the doorway. "We must go," he said to his older daughter. "Please, Ureth. We must hurry. There are more soldiers on the way."

Ureth looked down at the beautiful face she still cradled in her hands. *Only in death can we be beautiful,* she thought. *I will be the Mother now. By the Dragon, I am not ready.* She looked at Scarth, and for one moment Jake thought he saw the fleeting glance of a little girl wanting her father to fix things. But then it passed, and she was Ureth the Crone again. "I am ready," she said, and stood up.

"We cannot fight our way outside the castle walls, Ureth," Scarth warned.

"We won't have to, I hope," said Ureth. "I made sure the Envoy was placed in a special room, one that has a secret way out of this tower. If we get there safely, we can leave Marfang."

"And then where?" asked Scarth.

"We find the Eldervolk," said Ureth. "We reunite Jake with his father, and hide them both from Coegun until we can decide what to do next."

"There is a lot of ground to cover, and many dangers, before we find the elven caves of Blutwald," said Scarth. "But flight seems our only choice now. Where is this secret passage of yours?"

"Two flights below us," Ureth replied.

"Two flights!" exclaimed Scarth. "Much blood may be spilled, before we win through."

"But we will win, if I am with you," said Jake, and the others looked at him in surprise.

"Are you now sure of who you are?" asked Ureth.

"I'm sure of what I can do," replied Jake. "Where's Sathryn?" Naomi's eyes found his at the mention of her rival, but received no welcome there, and slid away.

"She should already be outside the castle waiting for us," replied Ureth.

Scarth raised his eyebrows at that, but said nothing.

"And what about her?" Jake asked Ureth, meaning Naomi.

"The Mother died saving her life, Jake. Whatever I may think of her, I will not leave her here to be butchered, or worse. Come, child," she said to Naomi, "Your destiny still lies with us, for a time."

The disgraced acolyte got to her feet, and allowed herself to be hurried along, without looking at anyone. Scarth and Ureth led the way. Jake followed with Naomi, bundling her into the corridor.

They met the first group of soldiers at the head of the stairway.

2.

They won through to the second level down, but not before Naomi thought she would vomit from the stench of burned meat. Ureth's hands shot flame again, and another of the Duke's men fell screaming as his chest burst into blue and orange fire. *That made twenty*, Naomi counted. Twenty men had screamed in agony, as Ureth's flame had licked them, and the stench of their roasting flesh mocked her while they died. The Crones were not supposed to take life, but Ureth brought death without pause, her face a stone cold mask. And Jake was the same. He was at the front now, his sword a slashing red counterpoint to the new Mother's deadly flames. He had not spoken since he had left his chamber, and his silence was the most terrible thing about him. Those who managed to avoid the flames felt Jake's sword, and none were spared who stood in their way. Scarth had melted to the rear, awed by the cold fury of the witch he had spawned, and her deadly protégé. And the flame and the sword had carried them to the corridor where the Envoy's chamber was located.

They paused before the door, and Naomi looked back down the hallway. Dead and dying men lay strewn along their path. One of them looked up, and caught Naomi's eye, and on his face was a look of such impotent rage that she shrank back in shame. She had defied the Crone-vow, and used deceit to sleep with Jake, but this… murder that Ureth had caused was beyond her understanding. If the Duke's men had threatened to overwhelm Jake and Scarth, then there were certain kinetic spells that Ureth could have wielded to knock people aside, but she hadn't waited for that threat. She had simply blasted away with fire.

Mistaking Naomi's reaction for fear, Scarth took her by the hand, and whispered, "Don't worry, they won't try anything now, they're too scared."

Is he proud of Ureth? wondered Naomi. And why wouldn't he be? He was a warrior after all. The new Mother was nothing if not powerful, Naomi realized, and her will had no counter now that Marah was dead.

Ureth waved her hand, and the door to the Envoy's room burst open as if it had been kicked. *At least she didn't burn it down*, Naomi thought. Ureth glanced at her, as if she reading her mind. She smiled grimly, but all she said was, "Everybody in," and the company rushed inside.

There were three people in the room, standing to face whatever threat had burst down the door. One was Endil, his mask in place despite the late hour; the other was a royal man-at-arms, no doubt there to guard the Envoy. To Naomi's surprise, the other man in the room was the Sacour, Rajindra-al somebody. Now that was interesting.

"Put up your swords, my friends, we mean you no harm," said Scarth, for the men had drawn them. "Indeed, you are safer here than with anyone, with my daughter's magic shielding you." Naomi thought she heard a note of irony in his voice. "Are you going to ward the door behind us, Ureth?"

"I don't have time," said Ureth. "We have to hurry." She crossed to a small fireplace, set in the corner of the room, against the outside wall. She pressed her hands against the stones, and began whispering to them urgently.

"Well, hurry then," said Scarth. "Though I don't know that Coegun's men will be in such a rush to follow us. I've never seen anything like that, in all my years of fighting."

Naomi could feel Endil looking intently at her, and wondered why. There was something familiar about him, but she couldn't place it. Maybe she'd seen him at home in Marlona, before she'd come to Marfang. But she wished he'd stop looking at her, there were much more important things happening. Without being asked, the man-at-arms stepped outside the doorway to guard the room.

"You don't understand, father," said Ureth, as cracks formed silently around the fireplace, and the outline of a door began to appear. "I'm not hurrying to protect you."

"No? Then why?" asked Scarth.

"I'm hurrying to protect them," said Ureth, gesturing at the doorway through which they'd entered. She meant the Duke's men, Naomi realized. She could see the tears of remorse glittering on Ureth's face, and was glad for her. An open archway stood behind Ureth where the fireplace had been, and suddenly there was no time for regrets. "Quickly, please," Ureth said. "If all goes well we can still escape."

"What about my men?" asked Endil.

"My Lord, I am sorry, but your men are probably already dead," said Ureth. "If you don't leave with us their sacrifice will have been in vain. I know who you are. You must come with us, or every death I have caused this night will have been for nothing."

"If you know who I am, then you know I cannot leave while my men may still be alive," said the Envoy.

"We don't have time for this!" Ureth shouted. Then she put up her hands as the Envoy and the Sacour raised their swords. "No, wait, alright, there might be another way. But you must still come with me first. We'll die if we stay here. Please, we must go!" Scarth and Naomi had already passed through the archway, into the darkness beyond. Jake was waiting for Ureth.

A surprised grunt from the doorway caught their attention. The Envoy's attendant fell backwards into the room, a long, black-fletched arrow sticking from his chest.

"Jonathan!" Endil cried, moving to his servant, but Rajindra the Sacour stopped him.

"Come my friend! It is time to go. Vengeance can be a cold breakfast eaten on another morning, yes?"

A moment passed, while Rajindra looked intently into Endil's eyes, glittering with anger behind the golden mask. *Vengeance*. The word hung in the air like a promise, and suddenly Endil turned and stepped into the black archway. Ureth and Rajindra followed. Jake gave a final look to the doorway where the Envoy's man lay dead. They were coming, he knew, the Duke and his men. They would be here shortly. He could feel their beating hearts approaching, a cloud of rage and hate in the middle distance. How tempting to meet them here, to settle things once and for all. His sword dripped blood onto the floor of the chamber, and his heart sang for more. He shook his head sharply, as if to clear it from a fog. *That's not why you're here*, he thought. Heart racing, he turned and plunged into the waiting darkness.

The floor ahead of him immediately sloped downwards. Despite the light from the chamber behind, it rapidly became very dark, but the floor was smooth, and he walked surefooted. He could feel the others ahead of him, cautious in the blackness. He heard Ureth whisper something, and the tip of her wand began to glow. He knew she did not need the light; she had become like him, invested with the power of the worm beneath the castle. In that moment Jake knew the legends were true. He could feel Kildraig, far beneath his feet, tasting the nearness of his liberation. But the tree had not yet borne its fruit; Jake knew he had to wait, and come back with his father, so it could be plucked. What would happen after that was anybody's guess.

The faint gleam of Ureth's wand flickered in the darkness. In it's light, Jake could see the smooth walls descending at a steep angle. The air was dry, and Jake sneezed once as a cobweb brushed his face, but nothing in that dark place held any fear for him, and he and his companions made good time down the tunnel. After a minute or so, the passage leveled out and ended abruptly on a small patio. A yard or two away, another stone wall faced them. This must be the outer wall of the castle, Jake realized. A large iron ring was embedded in the masonry, at about chest height.

They crowded round Ureth as she grasped the ring. There wasn't enough room for them all on the little patio within the walls, and Jake, bringing up the rear, was still on the sloping portion of the tunnel floor. A tremble in the stone alerted him to their pursuers. "They are coming Ureth," he said softly, and he turned to face back up the passageway. Scarth and Rajindra moved to flank him, swords drawn, and though Jake felt he didn't need the help, he was glad to feel these men beside him.

Behind him, Ureth raised her wand, and a brighter light shone from it, lighting the darkness with a cold blue flame. "Graggath," she said, and Jake felt himself shudder as her magic expanded. He turned his head. Faint lines appeared in the stone behind him, and revealed the outline of yet another door, perhaps six feet by four, set into the wall. Ureth turned the ring, and pushed against it. The door opened without a sound, and they passed outside into the cold air of dawn.

There was no wind, and light suffused the eastern sky, where the warrior moon shone golden as it sank into the approaching sunrise. The Dragon moon had already set. A few stars lingered to greet the day, waiting for the sun to dismiss them. The air was fresh after the dank mustiness of the tunnel, and Jake caught the scent of blossoms on the air. They were near one of the apple orchards, he realized, and it was going to be a beautiful day. A sudden breeze brought the sound of lapping water, and in the growing light he could see the river Marfell, as it parted for Marfang's island.

"I thought you would never get here," said Sathryn from behind him, and Jake laughed out loud, the sound pure and clear in the dawn. He turned to greet the girl, greatly pleased to see her.

"What are you doing here?" he asked.

"Just following orders," said Sathryn, with a wry look at Ureth. "How are you sister?" she asked, though Marah's blood on Ureth's tunic told its own tale.

"As well as can be, considering," Ureth replied. "Did you find the boat?"

"Yes. All ready, just over there." She pointed through the trees. "You knew it would come to this?"

"It crossed my mind. I thought we should be prepared, in any event."

"Well. You thought right then, as usual," said Sathryn. "Come on, this way, I can see you're in a hurry."

"Shouldn't we seal the door?" Jake asked Ureth, as the rest of the party began to follow Sathryn.

"Close it if you like," said Ureth, "If they are rash enough to follow, I shall make them pay."

"Glad you're on my side," said Jake, as he pulled the door shut. Although it lined up perfectly flush with the stone of the wall, it was very clearly a door, perfectly visible in the morning light.

They turned together and ran after the others, catching up to them under the sweet-smelling boughs of the apple trees that ran almost to the water's edge.

3.

Gareth the archer felt as if his chest was on fire, and every breath ignited his lungs as if the very air was lava. His last shot had found its mark, felling the Envoy's bodyguard in the doorway he had guarded. Gareth gasped in pain: his chest HAD been on fire, he remembered. The witch's hands had spurt flame, but his brother, standing next to him, had borne the brunt of it. Gareth could feel the cold stone of the floor against his face. Everywhere else, he burned. He was dying, he knew. A dead man lay beside him, smelling of roasted meat. He recognized the face. Memory returned like pieces of glass restored to a shattered mirror: jagged and unwilling to form a seamless whole. He was Gareth, he remembered, one-time playmate of Ureth the Crone, now a soldier in the Duke's army. *I am a bowman. I can shoot an apple from a tree from a hundred yards. Yes. And my brother was Bal the Boxer, the one who had always shielded me from harm, who had leaped in front of the witch's flame to protect me.* So Bal was the dead man next to him, his chest charred, sightless eyes staring at the direction his soul had gone.

Gareth forced himself to stand. Some deeper taint than a mere flame was working its way into his body. He could feel the darkness of the magic, writhing inwards like a snake. When it reached his heart, he would die. He knew this, and didn't care how. So. Time was short. Death was coming. What could he do to prevent it? Nothing. What could he do to give it meaning? Avenge his brother's life, and his own. *Vengeance.* The thought begat anger, and anger gave him strength. He began to move. He staggered against a wall, but kept his feet. His pain fed his anger, and his anger fuelled his hate. Yes, he hated the witch, had done so since he was a child, and she'd made him laugh like a donkey. He hated all who traveled with her too, and prayed that his heart would beat until his vengeance was fulfilled. He looked down at his brother's lifeless form. A tear rolled down his cheek, its salt stinging the raw burns on his face. For an instant, he had a memory of he and Bal, playing together as boys in his father's sunlit orchards. *We always knew we would be soldiers.* A lifetime of memories crowded in, battles survived, women shared, men of duty, often apart in their service to Taumar. *And though I was with you when you died, my brother, I could not help you. What can a mere man do, against witchcraft?*

Revenge. My brother is dead. I will not cower here like a dog while his murderers escape. Where are they? That door there. They went in there. Gareth staggered down the hall, through the door to the Envoy's chamber. As he stepped over Jonathan's body, someone cried out in pain, and he realized it was himself. Yes, the magic had been here, in this room; the poison in his blood told him he was following its source. Noises reached him from a distance: fellow soldiers, with long swords and keen eyes, guided by the trail of Ureth's fury. But they will arrive too late; already the witch and her party are moving below. He could feel his body growing ever weaker, yet his mind growing in power. Sending forth his thought, he sought his killers. *They have gone through that black arch in the corner of the room. They are descending a steep slope. Keep me alive, Dragonfire! Be the instrument of my revenge, as well as my death.*

Somehow, he was at the bottom of the slope, his travel down the dark tunnel an agony his body decided not to tell him about. He had his bow; his quiver hot against his back. There was a faint outline of a doorway, lit by the dawn, set in the stone in front of him. Scrabbling at the wall, he found an iron ring. He pulled, and the door opened to the morning of his dying. The cool air and the pink sky, left with the pinpricks of a few stars, was a blessing to his eyes. *It's a beautiful day to meet the Dancer*, he thought, unafraid. *I am a soldier of honor, it has never left me, however it may have deserted those I've served.* He looked at the stars once more, rapidly fading in the growing light. *Stars, they say the Dancer dances behind you, and that when we die we join your dance. We'll soon find out.* His spirit felt halfway to the sky already; it would be so easy to lie down here, in the cool green grass of spring, and let his spirit float up to those stars.

Vengeance first, came the thought. With the new power of his mind, expanded by the magic that was killing him, Gareth sensed Ureth and her companions through the trees ahead. *Over there, towards the water. There is a boat.* He reached back to his quiver. *Only one arrow!* He must have spent the others. *Make it count, then. Send it where it will cause the most pain.* He stopped breathing: it hurt too much. *Soon the darkness will come, and the dance will begin. But not yet.*

The shaft against his cheek, he pulled the bowstring taut. *These are my tears, for golden boyhood summers, never to return. A tear for my brother. And one for me.*

The arrow flew. *I missed the witch! Nothing left to live for, then. And even if there was…*

Soldiers poured out of the open doorway behind him. From above, Gareth saw them cluster around his body. Sailing higher, he saw his arrow find a mark after all; a woman staggered and fell. But her spirit remained captive to her flesh, and did not rise to join his own.

Revenge meant nothing now. He was among the stars, joining their dance. And he was Gareth no more.

4.

Sathryn ran with the others, stumbling through the wet grass in the long skirt she had worn to the banquet. They had passed through the orchard, and the scent of apple blossom was sweet behind her in the dawn air. They were making for the boat she had hidden, in a small stand of pines right at the river's edge. For escape had been Ureth's plan, ever since the Envoy had arrived.

"Sathryn, get a boat and tie it on the western shore," she'd commanded the day before. "Jake will leave with me one way or another, but Coegun will not willingly let him go. We'll attend the Council, and make our escape from the guest tower; there is a way out from there. But we'll need a boat. Marfell is too strong for any of us to swim."

So Sathryn had found a boat, and tied it up as she was bidden, as everyone always did when Ureth asked. She gestured to the pines, a little to the left of their bearing, and the others began to move ahead of her as she picked up the hem of her skirt to better navigate the grass. She was a fugitive now, she and her father, caught up in the net of her sister's plans. The Duke would never forgive Scarth for thwarting him, that day at the dock when he'd refused to hand Jake over. But there were a lot more people than she'd bargained for, and the boat wasn't that big. Now she hoped they'd all be able to fit.

She paused for a moment, breathing in the air of spring: the apple blossom behind, and the clean pines ahead. The others ran ahead of her, under the evergreen shadow.

"Sathryn!" her father called, stepping back out from under the trees, to beckon her on. He'd returned for her, she realized, and felt a rush of love for the big, gruff man who'd had no clue how to treat a little girl.

"I'm coming father!" she cried, holding the edge of her skirt up, and running like the little girl she'd been, towards the sound of his voice and the sight of him standing there in the dawn. She had a vivid memory of the time when the sound of him calling her name had been the best-loved thing in the world. She saw him shake his head, and smile at her.

"Come on! We've found the boat!"

She ran faster. But as she ran, she heard a whine, descending from the sky like an angry mosquito. The whine suddenly ceased, to be instantly replaced by the sound of splintering bone as Gareth's arrow crashed into her right shoulder blade, pitching her face down into the grass. The wind whooped from her as the arrow pinned her to the ground, transfixed to the earth even before she felt any pain. But then there was pain; her back was on fire and she wanted to scream, but could not remember how to draw breath to do so. Her fingers scrabbled wildly in the life-giving earth, as she tried to drag herself closer to her father.

"Daddy," she gasped, and fainted.

The others were under the trees, clustered on the river-bank by the boat.

"This boat will not hold us all," said Endil.

Ureth had to agree. The boat was too small for all of them to fit. The wind had picked up, and the river was increasingly choppy. She allowed the problems of transport to occupy her mind, keeping at bay the horror of death she had caused. Jake had untied the boat, and was waiting with Rajindra at the water's edge. Ureth stood higher up the bank, with Naomi and Endil, the Envoy's golden mask glittering under the trees. She looked around. Where were her father and sister? In the distance, she heard Scarth cry out in alarm. *Now what?*

"Jake, you and the others wait here. Naomi, you come with me." Ureth started back through the trees, filled with foreboding. The sound of steel on steel rang out as she and Naomi ran back through the pines, a rain of needles falling as they shoved through the lower-lying branches. Life surged all around, but Ureth sensed Death in the air again. She ran faster.

When she reached the open space between the pines and the apple orchard, Ureth moaned with frustration. Her sister had walked in front of an arrow! There she was, skewered to the ground like a butterfly on a pin, and as always, there was Scarth, getting her out of her mess. Four men with swords were already upon him, and though he could handle those odds, he could not fight them and tend to Sathryn at the same time. More men of the Castleguard poured from under the apple trees. Ureth felt a brush of air as Jake, having ignored her instruction to stay near the boat, surged past her to Scarth's aid. Rajindra followed, sword held high, and Ureth heard the high, keening Sacourian war cry, a sound of the desert out of place in her fertile land. Only Endil checked his run, and stayed near Ureth and Naomi. But Ureth noticed he placed himself between the castle and her acolyte, as if to protect her. Two men had fallen to Scarth's sword, the red of their blood vivid against the green grass. One of the two still fighting Scarth was the Duke himself, Ureth saw, though he seemed to be hanging back, likely because he wanted to fight Scarth alone. Well, he wouldn't get the chance. Ureth raised her hands, and the deadly Dragonfire once again poured from her fingertips, arcing towards Coegun.

The Fruit Of The Dendragon Tree

He let it come. The instant before it reached him, Coegun raised his free hand. Ureth's fire struck his palm, and reflected back towards her, leaving the Duke not only unharmed, but upright and wielding his sword. Ureth barely had time to feel surprise when her own fire struck her with such force she flew backwards and hit the ground, stunned. She heard Naomi scream, but she herself had no breath. The world went black.

Naomi could not believe her eyes. The Duke had bested Ureth! Where had he received the strength to turn away the Dragonfire? He could not wield it himself, she realized; they would all be dead by now if he could. But though he was only a man, he could guard against the Dragonfire, and suddenly, Naomi knew that Ureth had been right to fear this man who so casually reflected death, who had so completely cloaked his evil intent from all except Ureth's most urgent intuition, who even with all her powers had only received the feeblest hints of his burning desire to be King.

Scarth's head whipped around at Naomi's cry, as if he knew his other daughter, the witch, was also in peril. In that instant, the Duke raised his sword and struck Scarth a tremendous blow on the back of the head with his sword hilt. The greatest swordsman in Taumar fell to his knees, and toppled next to Sathryn's prone form. Without being told, the soldiers newly arrived from the castle picked up Scarth and Sathryn from where they lay, pulling the girl's shoulder roughly from the ground as they did so. A red-faced, burly man threw Scarth over his shoulder, and began to stagger back towards the castle under his load. Another soldier did the same with Sathryn, able to make better time with his lighter burden. A large press of guards, thirty or more, rushed forward, desperately parrying Jake and Rajindra's rescue attempt.

Ureth lay still on the ground. She was unburned, but her breath was ragged and her eyes would not open. Behind the fan of his men, the Duke and the soldiers carrying Sathryn and Scarth had vanished under the apple trees. Jake was fighting like a maniac, cutting into the rearguard like butter, Rajindra beside him, piercing the day with his ululating war cry. But there were only two of them, after all. The Duke's men fell back, their numbers dwindling but still sufficient to cover their retreat, until they withdrew through the orchard and reached the postern door.

Naomi heard Coegun's voice, as clearly as if he had been in front of her. *Stay with your mentor, slut.* The words came to her, loud in her mind. *Tell her I will give her father and sister the most painful deaths I can imagine. Then I'll come for her and the brat.* Naomi dropped her eyes and the connection was cut; but in her mind's eye she could clearly see what was happening up at the castle. She saw the Duke escape back up the magic tunnel with both his captives, the secret door closed once more, while Jake hammered upon the stone with the hilt of his sword, over the pile of dead guards who had ensured the Duke's retreat back into his stronghold. She saw Rajindra grab him, and pull him back. Jake resisted at first, but suddenly the warrior in the boy fell away, and he sobbed in Rajindra's arms as if he had lost everything in the world. And Naomi saw the Sacour hold him as if he knew just how the boy felt.

The vision faded, and beside her on the ground Ureth moaned in pain. Naomi knelt beside her, patting her hand, shaking her shoulder, trying to rouse her but not knowing how. Suddenly, Ureth sat bolt upright, crying, and Naomi knew she had seen the same vision of Scarth's and Sathryn's capture. The others returned, walking slowly, covered in blood, none of it theirs. Endil stood aside, and Ureth mastered her tears and stood up.

"He has taken my father?" she asked, her voice as harsh as a raven's cry.

Rajindra nodded.

"And Sathryn too," said Jake.

"Careful, Ureth," said Naomi, as Ureth gasped in pain, trying to walk.

"What is this, Naomi, tenderness?" But then she relented, and said in a different voice: "Agh it burns, it burns Naomi. Those poor wretches I consumed with this weapon, may the Dancer forgive me, for I'm not sure I can ever forgive myself."

"Can you walk, Lady?" asked Naomi. "The boat is not far, I can carry you if you need me to… Oh Ureth! I've been such a fool!" and she started to cry.

"No time for that now, daughter. I burn, but it passes. The Dragon still protects me, for now. We have all been foolish, myself perhaps most of all. And we will pay dearly for our folly, I fear, unless the Pendraig can save us. Do you remember how to get back in the castle through the other Cronedoors?" Naomi nodded. "Then follow the Duke. Try to save my father if you can."

"What about Sathryn?" asked Jake. Ureth just shook her head.

"We can't just leave her! God dammit, she's your sister!"

"Yes, and she loves you, and you her, though we both know there is another you love more! But Sathryn is as good as dead, of this I am sure. It is my father whom we need. Naomi can find her way to the dungeons and perhaps rescue him before they kill him. And we need to leave now, before they decide to come after us again, in spite of the Dragonfire I wield!"

"Where Naomi goes there I go also," said Endil. "If she is to rescue your father, I will help her do this. Besides I must also try and rescue my men. They are under the protection of the king, but who knows what this traitor will do if I am not there?"

"I told you, Lord Endil, your men are dead already. As for Naomi, she will be safer alone. We need you to aid in our struggle here, while there is still a kingdom to rule."

"You do not understand," replied Endil. "But after all, why should you, even though you said you knew who I was? My mask has served its purpose. I am no Envoy, I am King Endil himself, and Naomi is my sister." With these words, Endil tugged at his mask. It came free, and Jake and the others finally saw the face behind. He was a young man, Jake saw, with a pleasant, open expression, notwithstanding the blood that had been shed.

It was a curiosity that of those present, only Ureth and Naomi were his subjects. Ureth knelt, but Naomi was too overjoyed. She simply threw her arms about her brother, and held him as close as skin would allow. "Now I know why you always got between me and their swords! I can't tell you how glad I am to see you, my brother!"

There was silence for a few moments. Jake thought Naomi would break her brother's neck, she was hugging him so hard. He suddenly wanted to be home very badly.

"I did know you, Lord," said Ureth. "But your secret was yours to reveal. I cannot stop you, you are my king, but I need to get Jake to safety."

"Yes, you must go," agreed Endil. "Take Rajindra with you. I will do what can be done here. If Naomi and I can rescue Scarth and Sathryn and escape, we will do so. Then we will make our way to my horsemen, which I have posted a few miles east of here. I wanted to see for myself if I could avert battle with my own subjects, but Coegun has too many men in thrall for that to happen. Now brother must kill brother, and who knows what the end may be."

"And if you don't escape?" asked Jake. "Your majesty," he added after a beat. He had never spoken to a king before.

"My larger army can be here within two weeks, perhaps less, if a raven reaches Marlona with news of my need, or my death. With the help of the Crones, one way or another they will find a way to defeat Coegun."

"No, they won't," said Ureth. "Though they will have to try if it comes to that. I have other plans, though there is no time to share them here. We must leave."

There was no more to be said. Naomi kissed Ureth's hand, and looked up into her eyes, beseeching forgiveness for everything, including the words from the Duke she had not relayed. Ureth smiled sadly, and waved her hand over Naomi's head. "It's all right, Naomi, I know the message he gave you. Go with the Dancer, my daughter. May the Dragonfire protect you from harm, so you can become the mother you were meant to be." Then Naomi and Endil left them, moving swiftly through the cover of the trees, around the castle towards the Crone Tower, from whence, Ureth knew, they could access the inner maze of tunnels that ran through the walls of the keep: the secret passageways of the Crones.

"Let's go, then," said Jake, turning back towards the boat. "Where are we heading, anyway?" he asked, when he realized he didn't know.

"To meet your father in Blutwald," said Ureth.

Jake's heart leaped at the thought of seeing his father, and for one instant that was all he cared about.

"To the Bloodwood we are going then," said Rajindra. "I never thought I would see that dangerous place."

"It's not as dangerous as here though," said Ureth. "Get in the boat, you two, we must be going."

The Sacour got in the bow, rigid with fear at the thought of being out on so much water. Jake took the oars, while Ureth sat in the stern with the tiller. She pushed off, and the swift current carried them downstream some way before they finally struck the safety of the far western bank, away from Marfang's shadow, that reached for them across the water like a stain.

Chapter 16

O spite! O hell! I see you all are bent to set against me for your merriment

(Shakespeare: A Midsummer Night's Dream)

In the beginning, there is pain. The voice spoke in Scarth's mind, as he revived in the dark dungeon. He could not move, because to move was agony. He could not see, because of the blood in his eyes, his own blood, oozing from a gash in his forehead. He could not wipe the blood away because his hands were chained to the wall. Yet as his memory returned, some part of him welcomed his blindness, because some things truly are too terrible to see. At least now her screams were silent.

A father's screams are always ones of powerlessness. And Scarth's cries, wrenched from his throat when they forced him to watch what they did to Sathryn, were those of a father unable to save his child. They had heard his cries, they had laughed, and they had continued on.

Sathryn. She had been his "normal" daughter, by which he meant she wasn't a witch. Headstrong and spoiled, yet compassionate and beautiful, the intuition she possessed was, unlike her sister's, no more than any woman's who could bewitch a man. And though he had always been proud of Ureth's powers, he had quite simply loved Sathryn's more common charms of wit, intelligence, and gentleness.

And now she was dead. And her death was a blessing, because the end of her life had been a horror too awful to contemplate. But they had made him contemplate it; had made him witness her shame, her terror, and her anguish, had made sure he knew how impotent he was to prevent them from killing her just as slowly as they liked. He witnessed his own impotence, the worst kind for any father: his own inability to protect his child.

They had held their swords to her unconscious throat, so that he would not struggle, and they had disarmed him and marched him into the dungeon, shackling him to the wall when they got there. They revived Sathryn with some foul-smelling brew, then cut the shaft of the arrow behind her back, and pulled it from her by the point that protruded from the front of her right shoulder. She bit back her screams until they poured the brew into the wound, and then she did scream, until she fainted again, but whatever demon was in the stuff, it stopped her bleeding very quickly. For a while, Scarth thought this attention boded well for her, but then he realized they simply didn't want her to bleed to death, thereby cheating them of their sport too quickly.

They shackled him to the wall, so that he stood bound before his daughter, and then beat him until the blood flowed from a dozen wounds, and his breath came shallow and jagged from behind broken ribs. They worked him over until he was a ball of pain, and then they stopped. But his beating was just the overture. The symphony had yet to begin. They left him sagging in his chains, unable to fall down, unable to stand, barely able to breathe. Then they turned to Sathryn, and cut off her clothes. Now they held their swords against his throat, so she would not struggle in her turn, and he began to scream at her to try to run, to fight, so that she could precipitate a quick death for herself. But there was nowhere to run. She was no match for even one of them, and the Duke had allowed six others into the cell with him, to enjoy her for their sport. But though they were very experienced at this type of game, her wound had weakened her quickly. When she was too far gone to even show fear, Coegun had taken his sword and casually slit her belly open as she lay on the damp flagstones of the dungeon floor.

Sathryn revived at this fresh agony, and knelt on the cold stone, frantically trying to push her bowels back into her body. When she knew it was useless, she looked at Scarth. And then she spoke the words that truly broke his heart.

"I'm sorry, father," she whispered, and finally, mercifully, she died.

The essence of her was gone, and going, had left an empty, ragged place in his heart. And Scarth filled that empty place with an oath of revenge, though he knew his oath was empty. The Duke had seen the light of hate in his eyes, and laughing again hit him one last time, high on the left temple with the hilt of his sword, and he had started bleeding anew. They had left, leaving him to die slowly, while the blood from his head wound seeped into his eyes. And he had found himself grateful that he could no longer see the horror they left behind.

His position made it difficult to get enough air, but when he tried to draw a deep breath it was as if his broken ribs scraped the inside of his chest, and he gasped his anguish before he could use the extra oxygen. He hung in his pain for what seemed an age, but presently the sound of dripping water gave way to the scrape of stone upon stone, and despite his blindness Scarth knew that someone had entered his dungeon. A breath of air from an open doorway caressed his cheek, and an aura of light blurred the periphery of his vision. He could feel the heat of a torch, and smell the creosote burning. It was a welcome change from the stench of blood and agonizing death that permeated his prison, whoever held it. Someone gasped, and he could hear horror in the voice. He tried to speak, but his mouth was parched, and he only managed a strangled croaking sound.

"Easy, Scarth, we are here to help you." It was a man's voice, young but full of authority. It sounded familiar, but Scarth couldn't place it. "Naomi, try to get the blood off his face, he can't see. I'll get these off." Scarth could feel strong hands, probing at the manacles on his wrists and ankles. The bolts were not locked in place, so the stranger undid them easily, and Scarth immediately pitched forward, gasping in pain as first his knees, then his damaged ribs, hit the stone floor.

"Damn. Sorry about that. Should have realized you'd have trouble standing. Where are you hurt?" But this time Scarth couldn't draw breath to speak, and the stranger's question remained unanswered. Scarth felt another touch, unmistakably that of a woman's, bathing his face with a piece of fabric moistened with the damp from the walls, and feeling his body and limbs. The water stung his eyes, but gradually they cleared, and in the dim torchlight he saw Naomi's young eyes gazing at him from her old Crone face.

"He has broken ribs," she said to Endil, for it was he with her, holding the torch aloft once more. "He has a bad cut on his head, and he's taken a beating. I can cure his physical hurts quickly enough, but he bears another wound that may never heal." He voice was gentle as she spoke these words, and Scarth could hear her compassion. Tears came unbidden to his eyes.

"Do your magic then, sister," said the king, "and may he live long enough to find comfort in revenge."

Something in the young man's voice captured Scarth's attention, and he turned his head to see him better. He had seen that face before, he knew, when it was much younger, and the old king had formally presented the boy as his heir at the royal court in Marlona. "Your majesty?" whispered Scarth. "How…?"

"Shh," said Naomi, as she pressed the neck of a wineskin between his lips. "If we live to escape from here, all will be explained, but living is our first task, and for us to do that you must walk, so drink this, and try not to yell."

Scarth felt his mouth fill with the bitter, acrid wine of the Dendragon flower, familiar to him from previous campaigns. He gagged, despite knowing what to expect, but managed to get it all down. It seared his throat; burning all the way down to his stomach. His chest felt like it caught fire, then his abdomen, followed by his legs and arms, and finally his head. He did moan, after all, but he was still too weak to make much noise. Naomi plugged his mouth with her sponge, and let him bite down upon it as her cordial did its work. Scarth felt his ribs knit once more, stronger than before. The cut in his head closed over; he could feel his skin crawling to fuse itself over the wound, and the blood still in his hair turned to a brownish ash and fell from his body. As his terrible injuries healed, he gasped, and when he breathed, it was as if he inhaled fire, but a fire against which he was proof. His whole body came alive with this inner fire, and absorbed his agony. All his wounds, save the one in his heart, were healed. He could draw breath without pain, yet he had become all the pain ever suffered, and vengeance was his only purpose. In that moment, he was potent beyond measure.

Naomi saw the change in his face, and took the sponge away from his mouth. Something in his eyes must have alarmed her, because she gave a quick glance to the king and muttered, "I hope I didn't make it too strong."

But Scarth answered in his reborn voice, "No, my lady, against our enemies there is no such thing as too strong. I am ready for a hundred Coeguns. He will rue the day when he abused my daughter." He kneeled before the king. "At your service, my Lord, and your family's, while I still draw breath."

"May that be for a long time yet," replied King Endil, drawing Scarth to his feet. "You may well outlive me, given the dragon-draught my sister has poured down your throat! Listen, Naomi," he went on, "Make it known that if I should fall in any coming battle that Scarth shall rule as my regent until the child in your womb becomes a man." Naomi gave her brother a quick glance. "No, don't be surprised. For though you have enough of the Gift to become a Crone, I am not without Sight myself. Why do you think I am here in person, and was not content to send an Envoy who could be easily duped by Coegun? I know the deceit you used to become pregnant, and banished from the Order. If you were so unhappy, you should have sent me word. A Princess of the royal house shall not be held anywhere against her will. Do not hang your head! I am in no place to lecture you, for I too am here in disguise, and also felt that the only way to get what I needed was to lie about whom I really was. But I will be a king without a kingdom soon unless we can escape this evil dungeon. If I am to die,

I would much rather do so in the open air. In which case, sister, your child may grow to be king also. Now show us the way out, so that we may meet our destiny in field or forest, and not in this foul place that has never seen the sun."

Naomi made to move, but Scarth placed a hand on her arm. "If you please, your majesty, may I say goodbye to my daughter?"

Endil nodded. "Yes, my friend. But hurry. And I am truly sorry that we cannot take her with us, nor give her a decent funeral. When we have crushed Coegun, be assured we will properly honor her memory."

Scarth nodded his gratitude, and forced himself to walk over to where Sathryn's remains lay on the floor. A rat, attracted by the blood and offal, had already come to investigate the potential for a meal, and Scarth, having no sword, could only stamp uselessly to drive it away. He knelt beside Sathryn, trying not to look at her from the chest down. Blood had pooled about her body, but a halo of dry stone framed her head, and here Scarth knelt to say his farewell. Sathryn's face was amazingly unmarked, and looked almost peaceful, though her eyes were open in the stare that only the dead can achieve. These he closed gently with his fingertips, and with these same fingers he brushed back a lock of auburn hair that had fallen over her forehead. "Goodbye, my daughter," he whispered in the flickering dark. "If we meet again in the Dance, know that I will have avenged your passing before I arrive." Then he stood and nodded to Naomi, the fire still humming in his veins. There was nothing left to say about Sathryn that could not be better stated with a sword in his hand. He was ready to go.

Naomi motioned the two men into the black opening in the wall, another Crone passage that connected to almost every cell in the dungeons. The dark, secret ways of the Crones, among other things, allowed them to make prisoners disappear from their cells, if they felt their imprisonment was unjust. The belief that this was done by magic only preserved the Coven's mystique. The real magic lay in their concealment, for every doorway was invisible to ordinary people, indistinguishable from the wall into which it was set.

As the three of them entered the dark passage, Naomi waved her hand. *"Celu!"* she commanded, and the opening sealed itself behind them. She moved to the front of the line, squeezing by Scarth and Endil to do so. Endil came next, holding his torch high so that Naomi could see her way. Scarth followed the torch, unsure of their direction as Naomi guided them. He expected to climb, as he knew that the dungeons were below ground level, but they did not. Instead, after a few turns they descended rapidly before proceeding along a dead straight tunnel that gleamed black and glossy in the light of Endil's torch. There was no pursuit, not that he expected any, and they were alone in this dark avenue beneath the earth. The tunnel was cool but dry, odorless, and devoid even of rats. They did not speak.

Presently, the tunnel began to rise again, more gently than it had delved downwards. The air grew warmer. Naomi came to a halt in a small cylindrical vestibule made of stone, with an iron ladder set into its wall. Peering upwards, Scarth saw the ladder end in a wooden ceiling roughly ten feet above his head. An iron ring protruded down from this ceiling, which was obviously the doorway out of the tunnel. Naomi scaled the ladder quickly, as silently as a cat. She turned the ring, and pushed against the ceiling. A square of blue appeared as the trapdoor opened, and light spilled into the darkness of the tunnel. Endil motioned Scarth to precede him, and when the king had followed the big man up the ladder, he doused his torch in the grass. Naomi pulled hard against a bush lying on its side, camouflaging the top surface of the trapdoor, and Scarth moved to help her. Together they maneuvered the bush upright, closing the way into the tunnel from above. *"Celu!"* she said again, and suddenly the bush was just a bush, indistinguishable from all the other bushes that dotted the stand of trees in which they found themselves.

Scarth looked to the west, and saw Marfang, sitting on its island in the river. The sun was low in the sky, but still above the horizon. Fingers of shadow reached towards them from the castle. They had come out on the eastern shore of Marfell, Scarth realized. That would explain why they had gone downward from the dungeon: they had needed to get low enough to cross the river underground. Well enough, Coegun would not immediately think to look for them here. But if they were to rejoin the others headed for Blutwald they would have to cross the river again somehow.

"So there you are," croaked a harsh voice from above. "I've been waiting all day for you." Scarth looked up, his hand automatically reaching for the sword he did not have. A raven was sitting on the branch of an oak tree, laughing at them.

"Well met, master Blackbird," said Endil, "If we'd known we were making you wait, we would have stopped for some tea."

"Yes, well, don't let it happen again," retorted the raven, cheerily. "And don't be calling me a blackbird, either, your majesty, you well know that's an insult we reserve for use among ourselves. But tell me," he went on, "Where is your daughter Sathryn, Master Scarth? She was not with the group that fled with Ureth across the river."

Endil replied for Scarth, who suddenly found it difficult to speak.

"Sathryn was killed by the Duke, Dobrun. My sister and I were able to rescue Scarth only after she was murdered. What of my men? Any word of them?"

"No, your majesty, I'm afraid you must abandon them to their fate. We are too few to attempt a rescue, and it's not as if you can just walk up to the castle and ask Coegun to hand them over. It seems he has finally shown his true colors."

"He has indeed," replied Endil. "But you can imagine it hurts me, Dobrun. I've known most of those men since I was a boy. They depended on me, and I've let them down."

"I know, Lord," said the raven, and Scarth could hear the kindness in his voice even through the harsh croaking. "But if you were to try to free them, you would die. Men would remember you forever in song, and think in private you were a fool, for abandoning the rest of your kingdom over wounded pride and personal loyalty. The rest of your subjects depend on you too. You can do them no good rotting in one of Coegun's dungeons."

Endil gave a bitter laugh. "It is well said that a raven will always speak the truth, even if it is not what you want to hear! Guide me then, Master

Bird, and tell me where I can find the force that I sent after me, in case I found my Duke indeed had designs upon my throne."

Dobrun ducked his head to one side, and looked at the king out of one wise eye. "As indeed he does, your majesty, more's the pity. Long has Coegun eyed your crown, and you are wise to be cautious now. He has many followers, not all of them human, and blood will be shed before long, never fear. I believe you will get your wish to do battle with your enemies very soon. Three hundred of your finest horsemen set out for Marfang after your departure, as you commanded. They are camped not three miles from here, in some woods to the northeast. If you seek my counsel, lord, I would hasten to them and cross Marfell to the north, at the ford of Avon-rhyd. From there, it is an easy strike across the veldt to the southern border of Blutwald."

Endil turned to Scarth. "Seers are all very well, but they have an annoying habit of doling out counsel as one would bread to a beggar. Half the time you have no idea what they're talking about, or why you're doing what they tell you to do!"

Dobrun chuckled good-naturedly, and began to reply, but before he could do so Naomi intervened. From the flat tone of her voice, Scarth knew she was speaking with the Sight, as Ureth did on occasion. Her eyes stared into the middle distance, unblinking, and the hairs stood up on his scalp as it always did when Ureth told him things. "The Undead wait for you, brother," began Naomi. "They are in league with Coegun, and already taste the blood for which they everlastingly thirst. He has promised it to them, promised the blood of his own people, if they help him take your throne."

"The Undead?" Scarth was incredulous. "If they even exist, they are imprisoned in Blutwald. They cannot come out, the Waterstones prevent them!"

"The stones have been moved!" said Naomi. Scarth didn't understand why her words hung in the air like an accusation.

"You mean he's moved the Waterstones?" he asked, "Coegun has?"

"Yes," said Naomi. "And you helped him do it."

The Fruit Of The Dendragon Tree

Scarth opened his mouth to protest, but then stopped, remembering. He had been paid much more than usual for his last trip for the Duke, the one where he had picked up Jake. They had only moved by night, with less crew and more soldiers than was usual. They'd told him the cargo was secret, and important to Taumar, and to the Duke. And the money had blinded him, and silenced him, the money and the sight of the golden dragon badge that Rand had waved under his nose to appeal to his sense of brotherhood. He had been duped, Scarth realized, led astray by easy money and an appeal to his nostalgia for his days a soldier. He had helped betray the kingdom, however inadvertently. How they must have laughed at him! He flushed with shame, and didn't know where to rest his eyes. He didn't dare look at his king.

Naomi rested a gentle hand on his shoulder. "He fooled us all, Scarth, all except Ureth, and we wouldn't listen to her. I even came to think that she was my enemy, if not an enemy to the kingdom, with her single-minded obsession with Coegun. It's all so obvious, now that he has shown himself, though he was able to mask himself with magic we didn't know he had. But she saw more clearly than all of us, trusting to her inner knowledge. And when she could get no help, in her desperation she did all that she saw left to her. As did I. So now Jake is here, waiting for the tree to bear fruit, and I carry his fruit within me. And even the ravens don't know how it all will end."

"And the Undead?" asked Scarth.

"We have defeated them before. We shall do so again," said Endil. And Scarth knew that whatever happened, Taumar had a king worthy of the name. At least for the moment; but he put that thought aside.

Endil directed the raven to fly ahead of them, and give word to his troops that he was on his way. This Dobrun did, and they followed the line of his flight to the northeast. Presently, they neared the woods that Dobrun had told them of. Scarth knew them well. It was a pleasant place, with many open spaces under the trees, where his wife and he had shared many picnics in the early days of their courtship. He was a soldier then, already famous for his ability and courage, but that never impressed his wife, which is why he had married her. Ureth had been conceived here, Scarth remembered now. Funny, he hadn't thought of that in ages. Where had the time gone? Ureth had been born, the baby with years in her gaze. Then Sathryn had arrived, the death of her mother, but the light of his eyes for so many years. Life had moved on. Scarth had become a merchant. The Crones had taken Ureth, and Sathryn had grown into the beautiful young woman whose ravaged remains lay in the castle behind him. And now he was walking with the king to meet the Undead in battle. Life was strange.

The last rays of the sun were warming their backs when Scarth saw horsemen come out from under the trees ahead. There were three of them, leading three riderless horses. One of the riders held the king's banner aloft. Scarlet and gold and brave it shone in the sunset, and the golden dragon that was its blazon rippled as if in flight. Scarth felt his blood stir at the sight. He had fought many a battle under those colors, spilling Sacourian blood at the top of the Thunder Falls, and even in the hot sands of their desert country, far to the south. Then he had put away his sword, and turned to more peaceful pursuits. But the Sacours never rested, and the Duke won fresh glory with their defeats, and Taumar rejoiced in its strength, never knowing its greatest enemy lay within its greatest stronghold, and masqueraded as its hero. And for Scarth the time for a sword had obviously met him again, yet he faced this truth with dread, not because he thought his skill was rusty, for it was not, but because the blood he would spill would be that of his own countrymen, younger men than he, the children of other fathers, whom he had risked his life to protect.

The colors came nearer. There had been a time, Scarth remembered, when he had fought away from the vanguard, and near that banner. The Sacours had taken it into their heads to attack the colors, and Endil's father had placed some of his best fighters near his flag as a result. Their desert foes were valiant, but were no match for Scarth and his men, who sang as they killed all who came near. It was only afterwards, remembering the bravery of his enemies, that Scarth felt there should be an end to war. It had gone on for hundreds of years, for

The Fruit Of The Dendragon Tree

the Sacours coveted the Dendragon flowers, which Taumar jealously guarded. Flower petals and juice came with a price that the Sacours found excessive, and always there was conflict over this precious, life-giving commodity. Scarth suddenly remembered that Endil had been in private dialogue with the Sacourian delegate the previous night. He wondered what THAT had been about. Perhaps he should ask. But then the riders met them, still some distance from the woods, and in the confusion of formal greetings and mounting of horses he missed his chance. They rode into the trees with the last of the daylight, and Scarth found himself among the familiar controlled bustle of a military camp, with the smells of wood-smoke and horses, and unwashed men ready for battle.

2.

"Where has he gone?" Duke Coegun almost screamed the question at the king's man, battered and bleeding and kneeling in front of him, with no time to have been properly tortured. Not that it would have mattered, thought Coegun, as he sank his sword into the man's throat, murdering the last of Endil's brave entourage. There is a look that comes into a man's eyes when he knows he is going to die, a look that says he has nothing more to give you, and wouldn't give it if he could. Better to kill such men quickly, and he had. It appeared that none of Endil's men had known they were traveling with their king. The golden mask had even fooled his entourage, and they had taken him for a Royal Envoy, just as he had wished. Coegun had known immediately, of course. So transparent a deception could not shield the truth from someone as adept in the Craft as he. Fools! They needed his leadership to protect them from themselves.

He looked around. The sandy practice ground near the Dendragon tree was covered with the blood of the king's men. Their bodies lay in the sun, soon to be fodder for the ravens already gathering atop the crenellated battlements, far above. His men stood by, waiting for his command. The courtyard was otherwise deserted. The inhabitants of

Marfang knew better than to be seen when their duke was in a killing mood. They feared him, and that was good. That was power. *Think!* He had gone to the Envoy's room after he realized Ureth and Jake were headed there. But Endil had not been there. Instead, Coegun had seen the golden mask flashing in the dawn, as he had been beaten back inside his castle.

That had been too close for comfort. Ureth's bolt had nearly undone him, he admitted to himself, if no one else. But he knew the reflection of her power back on herself had also weakened her for a time. Magic thus stalemated, the furious little battle outside the castle walls had depended on force of arms. Coegun shuddered. He had almost lost that battle too. Scarth, the Sacour, and the boy Jake, arrayed against him at once. Where had the brat learned such skill with a sword? It was lucky they'd had the girl. Their foes had been careful not to kill her by accident, and so had ensured her capture. And Scarth's too! What fun they had had with that ripe little peach, and what pleasure it had been to rob the greatest swordsman in all Tiramonde of his manhood, by raping and murdering his daughter right in front of his eyes! That was power too. Coegun smiled as he thought of it.

He turned to one of his men. "Get rid of these bodies. Perhaps Scarth knows where the king is headed." The man saluted, and did as he was bid, signaling several others to help. Coegun laughed in the late afternoon sun. It was good to be alive, when so many enemies lay dead. It was especially good when they were dead because of you. It would be fun to pay the merchant another visit. He was strong, and would bear more pain well. Just then, Coegun caught sight of Jasper, hurrying across the courtyard towards him. The fat man minced his steps, and held a scented handkerchief against his face to ward off the odor of death. But Coegun knew that despite his feminine ways, Jasper was no stranger to blood, and had spilled much in his service to his Duke. He hurried up now, picking his way daintily among the dead bodies. Another man was with him, carrying a lit torch that burned weakly in the sunlight, and Coegun recognized the warder of his dungeons. The man looked terrified. Coegun began to feel uneasy.

The Fruit Of The Dendragon Tree

"What is it, Jasper?"

"It's your captive, Scarth: he's disappeared from his cell."

"What do you mean, disappeared?" Coegun growled, looking at his jailer. The man quailed under his glance, and could not meet his eyes, but answered bravely enough, considering what he guessed might be in store for him.

"I swear to you, my Lord, he did not escape through his cell door. I had to unlock it myself to enter."

"Why were you entering his cell? I gave orders to leave him until I returned."

"I, I'm sorry, milord," the man was stammering in fear now. "But I thought I heard v-voices from the cell, and I knew that Scarth was alone. I went to fetch the key, and when I returned, I found the cell empty. There was n-no way he could have got past me unnoticed."

This much was true, Coegun knew. He had designed the dungeon himself. There were no nooks and crannies where a would-be escapee could hide. And the jailers were not allowed to walk about with any keys on their person. Every cell had its own key, and every key hung on its own hook at the entrance to the prison cellars, identified by a special code known only to the jailers. It was like an underground lodge for travelers that would not be leaving, save at the pleasure of the landlord, and Coegun's lieutenants called it "The Duke's Inn," a name that did not displease him. The locks to every cell were specially made to be proof against picking, from inside or out. And in the unlikely event that a prisoner did escape his cell, the system ensured that he (or she) couldn't release any other prisoners to help him. So where was Scarth?

"Take me to the cell. And pray that I don't find anything amiss."

The terrified man bowed, and scuttled back the way he had come. Coegun, Jasper, and two men-at-arms followed in his train. When they arrived at the cell, the jailer unlocked it, and Coegun went in with his men. It was true: Scarth was not there.

"Walk with me," said Coegun to his frightened jailer, still carrying his torch. Nobody else spoke. The Duke's anger permeated the dark room, like the miasma seeping from its walls. Sathryn's body, partially obscured by feeding rats, still lay on the floor where they had left it, but her father was no longer there to be tortured by the sight. Coegun approached the spot against the wall where they had beaten Scarth. The manacles were still set into the wall, but their bolts had been drawn back and they were unbroken. *He had had help, then.* The Duke grabbed the torch, and began to inspect the walls more closely. Then he paused.

"Jasper, tell me what you think of this." The fat man moved over to his lord. The others could tell that even he was nervous. Coegun raised the torch higher, and pointed at the floor. Chipped stone fragments lay near the wall, at a spot roughly five feet from where Scarth had been shackled. The wall itself looked intact. Coegun pressed his hand against the stone in several places. Nothing gave, but on the last push the slightest puff of stone dust caught the torchlight. It was enough.

"There's a door there, my Lord," whispered Jasper.

"I agree," said the Duke. "A secret door, laid in my own castle. So the rumors of the Crones' perfidy are true! Master Jailer!" he said to the abject warder. The man started, but could only manage a small moan of fear in response. "Tell me, how is it that there are secret ways out of my prisons that you do not know about?"

"I, I, d-don't know, m-my lord," was all the jailer could manage.

"Hmm," replied the Duke, in his silkiest voice. "Perhaps further reflection will bring you to an answer. Put him in those irons," he added, gesturing to his two soldiers.

The man whimpered, already limp with fear. He knew he would receive no mercy. The soldiers chained him unresisting to the wall, and the Duke stepped close.

"Perhaps if you call loudly enough, the Crones will hear, and rescue you too. But then again, I'm betting they won't. In which case, only the rats will hear your cries. I wonder if they'll have the good manners to wait until you are dead, before they start feeding on you?" Coegun laughed, and his cruel mirth echoed in the dungeon. He left then, with Jasper and his soldiers, and the jailer cried out his despair. But no one heard him except the hungry rodents.

Chapter 17

This is my beloved son, in whom I am well pleased

(Matthew; 3:17)

"May I ask why we're just standing here? I'm freezing!" Rajindra was soaked, having borne the brunt of Marfell's choppy waters from his seat in the bow. Jake and Ureth finished drawing the boat up on the west bank of the river.

Ureth didn't answer. She was still reeling from the revelation of the Duke's power. The strength of the Dragonfire she had wielded seemed remote to her now. She felt weak and less sure of herself with each passing moment. Was Coegun too powerful to be stopped, after all? Had she done the right thing by sending Naomi back into Marfang? What if she lost her too? What if Endil was captured? Ureth had known that Naomi was the king's sister: one didn't become a Crone without surrendering every detail of one's life to scrutiny by the sisterhood. And she had not been blind to the "Envoy's" true identity, though the Golden Mask had done its work well enough to fool others. How like royalty to be so in love with intrigue! But there was nothing more she could do for them now. They would either escape or not, with her father or not. But Sathryn would not escape Marfang, this Ureth knew in her bones. "Good-bye, sister," Ureth whispered. "Forgive me."

She looked at the others. Jake was pale, but looked unharmed, and Rajindra was shivering. What had he been doing with the king? Ureth wanted to ask him, but there was no time for that kind of discussion. They had to get moving. Coegun would come after them in force, once he had finished with her sister. And if he caught them in the open veldt they would be slaughtered. They had to reach Blutwald before he could do that. The forest would hide them, or the elves would protect them. But somehow, she would have to get Jake back to Marfang when the Dendragon tree bore its fruit. And no one alive knew when that would be.

"We should move, Ureth," said Jake. She looked at him, the ghost of a smile in her eyes. The boy was a leader, and didn't even know it.

"You're right Jake. Blutwald it is."

"Werewolves and Vampires, and Elves, oh my?"

Ureth didn't get the joke, Jake saw, and answered him seriously enough. "Yes, Jake. Let's hope we find the latter before we meet too many of the first."

"Let's go then," said Jake, and they turned westward, away from the light dancing on the cold river, into the rich veldt that lay between the Marfell and the dark forest to the north and west.

The going was easy. The land rolled away from them in a gently undulating sea of green, as far as the eye could see. Here and there, lonely homesteads dotted the landscape in regular squares of brown earth. Sometimes, especially to their right closer to the river, a group of buildings huddled together as a village, small hubs of people where the homesteaders could go to trade food for other necessities and the small luxuries of farm life. But Ureth kept them to the wild green fields, far away from village or farm, and they met no one. She set a brisk pace all that morning, as the sun rose in the sky and warmed their bones, but Jake had no trouble keeping up. His sadness for Scarth and Sathryn aside, he had never felt healthier in his life, and it was a relief to be finally away from the castle that had been his prison for the past while. There was no conversation among the companions, they moved in purposeful silence through the waving grass, and disturbed nothing but the occasional dragonfly.

They came to a stream about noon, and drank their fill. Rajindra had a wineskin, which he filled with water, and the trio moved on again after a short rest. They had no food, but Jake realized he wasn't hungry. He was different, somehow, he knew. Food and drink had no meaning for him, and fatigue was something others felt. It was with some surprise that, when Ureth finally paused for the day in a small hollow near another stream, he saw it was almost dusk. A few trees stood around the hollow. He and Rajindra began to collect firewood. When they had made a small pile, with some reserve nearby, they looked expectantly at Ureth.

She pointed her hand at the wood. "*Admani!*" she cried, and there were instant tongues of flame, licking eagerly at the wood.

"Cool trick," said Jake. "Bet you'd make a heck of a girl scout." Then he remembered the fires that had killed the Duke's soldiers, and regretted his levity.

Ureth didn't mind. She looked at him and smiled, and sat down to watch the fire. He did likewise, and Rajindra sat next to him and began to talk.

"Well, we certainly walked a long way today, didn't we my young friend? What a pace you set us, Mistress Ureth. I don't suppose you could perhaps conjure any food out of thin air, to eat by this excellent fire?"

Ureth smiled again. "I'm afraid not, Rajindra. We Crones are used to eating very little, and often don't think of the need for others to eat. It makes us welcome guests, but not very sought after hosts."

The Sacour chuckled. "Well, never mind. I have some foodstuffs in my pouch here," and he patted a small leather satchel that Jake now noticed for the first time. He wore it like a fanny pack, and kept it closed by two leather straps, fit into metal buckles that looked as if they might have been gold. "I always think it's a good idea to carry some food with you, especially if traveling in a country where most people think you are an enemy. Come, you two, eat with me. I have plenty for us to last for several days." He handed Jake and Ureth each a two-inch cube of something dense and slightly crumbly. Jake sniffed it. It smelled like bread, and suddenly he was starving. He pushed the whole cake into his mouth. It burst into flavor, filling his mouth with the taste of honey, and pastry, but with the consistency of steak.

"Careful, careful, my friend," said the Sacour, laughing. "You have just gobbled up a whole day's rations in one fell swoop! Here, have some water to wash it down! If I'd known you were so hungry I would have offered you some sooner! How do you like it? That is the marching food of the army of the sultan, and I made this batch myself, before I set out here on my journey."

"It's delicious," said Jake, his mouth full. He swallowed, and turned to Ureth.

"Why did Naomi deceive me? What did she really want, anyway?"

"She wanted to stop being a Crone," replied Ureth, "without having to accept the dullness of mind that comes with the surrender of the Gift. She needed to lie with a man, and have his baby. The sex act gets her expelled from the order, while motherhood keeps her fully alive. But no man in our world would lie with a Crone. And I can't imagine she appealed to you as she looked. She must have appeared to you as someone else. Someone you cared about very deeply. She came to you as Sathryn, didn't she?"

But Jake shook his head.

"Don't lie to me Jake," said Ureth in a low voice.

"I'm not lying!" cried Jake. "She didn't come to me as Sathryn!"

"Then who?" asked Ureth.

"She came as his Q'ahemba gahallah," said Rajindra, with wonder in his voice.

"The Kemba a who-who?" asked Jake.

"The Q'ahemba gahallah," corrected the Sacour. "The Gauntlet of God. What some would mistakenly call your soul mate."

Jake didn't know what to say. Naomi had come to him as Jenny Blackwood, but Jenny couldn't be anything like his soul mate. Could she? He had barely noticed her until the night she had sent him to Tiramonde. It would have made much more sense for Naomi to disguise herself as Sathryn. At least they'd kissed each other. But then

The Fruit Of The Dendragon Tree

Jake thought back to the previous night in the castle. There had been something very right about being with "Jenny" like that. He stirred uncomfortably as his body remembered his desire. He looked up. The campfire was burning low. Rajindra was looking at him intently, though Ureth seemed to have forgotten all about him. She was gazing into the flames. Jake wondered if she was trying to determine what the future held for them all. He thought she should give it up. Nothing had yet happened how she said it would. There were the dead to prove it.

"She came as Jenny," said Jake. But though Ureth nodded, she still didn't look at him or speak.

"So tell, me, Jake, about this young girl," said Rajindra, after a small silence.

"What do you mean?"

"Do you love her?"

"I dunno. I didn't think so."

"You don't know? The Q'ahemba Gahallah is too important a thing to be ignorant of, my friend."

"If you say so."

"Well, but I do say so. And there are many poets of my people who are saying the same, and many Rishis, and many young men and women, who have not yet tasted the bitterness of disillusion with their mates. So I would be in good company by saying so. But until you say so, you have not yet loved."

"Don't tell me about love! Love was what brought me here."

"Ah, yes, the love of a son for his mother. Who can deny this bond? And if I asked you if you love your mother, would you say 'I dunno'?"

"I guess not." He looked up. "I mean, no. I would say I love her."

"So, we make progress. And again, I ask you. Do you "love" the girl that Naomi pretended to be?"

"I don't think so. But I don't have anything to compare those feelings to, you know? I mean, I haven't known her that long, and I don't know that many girls, so what do I know?

"Yes, I see your problem. Your ignorance is abundant, but at least you are honest about it. This is the first step to wisdom, and let me tell you it is a step that many men never take. It may surprise you to know that many older than you also never know love, not the real love. But "love" is too trite a word for what we Sacours mean by Q'ahemba Gahallah. If you were a young man of my people and I asked if this young peach of a woman was your Q'ahemba Gahallah, you would know what I meant."

"But we don't have a word like that. So I don't know what it means."

"It is the dance that occurs very rarely," said Rajindra, "and then only if you are lucky, or cursed, or perhaps even both. Many confuse it with a once in a lifetime romance, but it is not that. Seeking other people to complete them, they search in vain for this connection all their lives, and count the life well lived, even if their desire is not achieved. But Q'ahemba Gahallah is not the bond that requires another person to complete you. It is the doorway through which you complete yourself. It is the relationship through which you meet your destiny. It is always a challenge, and may last for a lifetime, or only five minutes."

"Tell me."

"Your Q'ahemba Gahallah always presents you with a choice. She will offer you your heart's desire, and if you take the offer the price will be much steeper than you expected to pay. But not taking the offer will seem like a worse choice still. Was it like that for you with this Jenny?"

"I guess," said Jake, thinking of Jenny's offer of help, which he felt he couldn't refuse.

"Ah my friend, you guess too much and commit too little. When you find Q'ahemba Gahallah, you know it. I am sure the witch Naomi was able to look deep into your heart, and chose the one she found there for a reason."

"He makes sense Jake," said Ureth, finally lifting her gaze from the fire. "If she deceived you by posing as your Q'ahemba Gahallah, it would explain why you lay with her without question. And when she bears your child, it will bear watching."

Jake thought again of Jenny. He HAD gone with her from his house, and did as she bid him, strange as it was, without asking many questions. And when he thought it was Jenny who had come to him at Marfang, he had accepted her again with desire. Was she the person who had led him to his destiny? Was that the same thing as love? Jenny had certainly launched him on a completely unexpected path when he had followed her to the woods, and stood in the pentagram. But he was tired, and suddenly wanted to see his Dad very badly. Forgetting about Jenny, or perhaps not, he poked the fire with his stick in irritation, and the sparks flew upwards into the cold clear night air, to wither into nothingness on the breeze.

He awoke the next morning to the sound of Rajindra singing. Jake groaned, and sat up. The sun was a pink promise in the eastern horizon, and dew lay thick on the grass. The Sacour was shaking it from his cloak. Ureth was standing nearby, looking back along their path.

Rajindra saw that he was awake, and offered him another portion of the Sacourian travel cake. Jake gladly had a morsel, and washed it down with some water from Rajindra's wineskin.

"Good morning, my friend. Did you sleep well? The grass is very wet this morning, but a finer bedding cannot be found outdoors, this I know from many years of travel!"

"Morning, Rajindra. Sorry if I was a pill last night."

"Do not be troubled, please. I myself am sorry if I caused you undue distress. It is simply that when the truth hits you, sometimes you want to spill it into the world, and forget that the world is often not a ready vessel for the truth."

"Well, if you're finished apologizing to each other, we should get a move on," said Ureth sharply.

She took the lead. Jake followed with Rajindra behind him and humming some repetitive bit of verse as they strode across the lush green grass. The dew dried quickly, and well before noon the morning was hot. At midday, they stopped near another small stream, and drank and rested. Ureth and Jake shared more of the Sacour's rations.

"How much of that stuff do you have left?" Jake asked Rajindra, meaning the travel cakes.

"Oh, we have sufficient for at least another four days, five if we are careful, I think."

"That should do us just about right, then," said Ureth, who had barely spoken a word all morning. "In four days, we should be in sight of Blutwald, and near the elves."

"And to others less kindly disposed to us," said Rajindra, meaning, Jake imagined, the werewolves and vampires Sathryn had told him about. A shadow fell across his mind, as he thought of her, and he shivered in the warm sunshine.

"Yes, Jake, she is dead," said Ureth, and he was surprised to see unshed tears well up in her eyes. "She died yesterday afternoon, and my father was powerless to stop it."

"I'm sorry," said Jake, and didn't know what else to add.

"We will be dead too, or worse, if we do not keep moving," said Rajindra. "The Duke will send his men after us soon, if he hasn't already. We must be under the Bloodwood's eaves, and safe with the elves before they catch up to us."

"Let them come," said Ureth, and her voice was grim. But she turned and began to walk again. Jake shuddered, remembering the men screaming in Marfang, as Ureth's fire burned them alive. The smell of roasting meat haunted his nostrils for a moment, and the remnants of the cake in his mouth suddenly felt like ash. He swallowed hard, and began to walk as well.

The great western veldt of Tiramonde, breadbasket of the Kingdom of Taumar, lay all around them like a green sea. Small streams cut through the land, irrigating the earth, which was brown and fertile under the grass. Still, they met no one. They passed occasional copses of trees, and the landscape fell into a rhythm that Jake came to find predictable: grass, trees, river, grass, trees, river.

The Fruit Of The Dendragon Tree

Late in the afternoon, Rajindra halted, and pointed back the way they had come. "They follow," he said. A flash of metal glinted in the sunshine, far to the south. They began walking northwards once more, hastening their pace, only to halt again a few minutes later as a raven flew up to them, flying steadily from the east.

Ureth stopped to wait as the raven landed in front of her. The newcomer looked intently at Jake for a moment, before speaking to Ureth. "Well met, Ureth," he said, and Jake thought his voice was as harsh as a raven's would be. "Warriors approach you from all four points of the compass, with you in the middle. Endil lives, and has escaped Marfang with your father and Naomi at the head of a company of horsemen. They hurry to you from the east. Dynan's folk also hasten to meet you from the north. This boy's father is with them, and anxious to see his son. But Coegun himself leads a small force of soldiers pursuing you from the south, and a large force of the Undead race towards you from the west. You cannot reach the forest now. Turn east, towards the ford of Avon-rhyd-"

"Is my Dad ok?" Jake interrupted. The knowledge that his father had come washed through him, and flushed away any residual taint of anger from their previous meeting.

"He is well. He has killed the werewolf king," replied the raven, and Jake saw Ureth share a quick glance with the bird.

Jake didn't know what the look meant, and didn't care. He could only think of seeing his father again. "Are you going back there?" asked Jake.

"Yes," replied the raven. "I was to find you and report back your position to Dynan and Coblyn, who lead the elven warriors."

"Can you give my Dad a message?" asked Jake.

"Jake, this is a Royal Courier, not your personal carrier pigeon," began Ureth, but the raven waved a wing at her.

"If either this lad or his father is who you think he might be," croaked Dobrun, for it was he, "then whatever they have to say to each other could be of great importance. Tell me your message, Jake, and I will see it safely delivered. A world can change on a word."

"Tell him," began Jake, but then words failed him for a moment. What could he say? How could he undo the accusations he had hurled at his father's head? And even if his father should have been at home, earlier on that fateful night that Jenny had sent him to Tiramonde, what if he had been? What if they hadn't fought? Maybe Jake wouldn't be here now, trying for one last chance to save his mother. He had a sense that destiny could alter on the slightest shift in circumstance, and that the words that came out of his mouth could be powerful beyond measure. "Tell him," he began again, "tell him I'm sorry. Tell him I can't wait to see him. Tell him… that I love him."

"It is well spoken that the tree bears its own fruit," said the raven in his croaky voice. "I will be sure to tell him your words. He asked for them to be his words to you also, if I met you on my travels." And Jake felt his heart warm at the truth he heard in the raven's voice.

Dobrun then had a short dialogue with Ureth in his own language. It was strange to hear her speak in the harsh, guttural tongue of the raven, but they didn't talk long enough for Jake to come to understand what they were saying. Presently the bird flew away to the north, and the companions turned east, heartened by the knowledge that reinforcements awaited them ahead.

They moved quickly, the afternoon growing ever more breathless and still. The cloud of dust to the south that marked their pursuers came inexorably closer. It seemed to Jake that the daylight began to fade earlier than usual, and when he looked back he saw a towering bank of clouds hastening from the west to receive the sun before its time. Lightning flashed within the anvil they made in the sky, and long afterwards Jake heard a peal of thunder. Dark sheets of grey hanging from the clouds' underbelly spoke of heavy rain. A ribbon of black shadow raced along the ground towards them underneath the clouds. *Those must be werewolves*, Jake thought with a shiver.

The storm clouds hastened closer. A dust cloud ahead spoke of other horsemen, hopefully the king's. They hastened their pace, trying to gain the protection of Endil's cavalry before the Duke's soldiers or the Undead could catch them. Suddenly, the first drops of rain began to fall, triggering the unmistakable scent of hot earth quenching its thirst. Lightning flashed again, the thunder rolling more quickly: giving voice to how much closer the storm had come. Rajindra looked back and gave a cry of alarm. "Hai! Hai! Run! The Wolves are almost upon us!"

Jake glanced back too, and saw that the Sacour was right. A group of werewolves, twenty to thirty strong, had separated themselves from the main force, and closed to within two hundred yards. Jake could see their fangs gleaming in the dull light. He looked to the south. The green banner of Marfang streamed from a lance near the front of a tightly packed group of riders. *That would be the Duke*. He wanted to stand and fight.

Not yet. The dragon's voice whispered in his brain. *I will unleash you when it is time. But not yet.* Jake turned and ran after the others, but drew his sword nonetheless. He noticed Rajindra had done the same. Jake passed him, running easily. Then he passed Ureth. Thunder crashed immediately overhead, and the earth shook with its own thunder of hoof beats. In the near distance he felt the pounding of more horses. He looked up and saw the king's cavalry, a few hundred yards ahead. A red and gold banner, not green, flew in the breeze of their passage. Surely they were too far. The earth thrummed as if it wanted blood as much as water. The urge to stand and fight was now nearly unbearable. *Not yet*, the voice spoke again, so on he kept. He looked left, to the north. And there were elves, eyes bright, running to meet them. But they were too far as well…

"Jake, keep going! We are not safe yet!" He heard Ureth shout as he slowed, and he knew then she would never leave his side. But the voice inside him spoke one last time. *No Jake. Stand and fight. And meet your destiny*.

He listened to the inner voice, even though he knew it was not his own. And he met destiny also; though whether it was his own or not he was never afterwards sure.

2.

Scarth found time to have speech with the king late that first night. Endil was being attended by only two retainers, whom he waved away as the big warrior approached and asked for an audience.

"How may I help you?" he asked Scarth, pouring him some wine into a wooden goblet.

Scarth hesitated. He didn't know how to ask the question he had without it sounding like a criticism, and this was his king, after all, not to mention a man to whom he owed his life. But his sojourn in Marfang had made him wary of men in power, and he needed an answer to a troubling question.

"My Lord," he began, fumbling for words, but then his soldier's directness took hold, and he found his voice. "My Lord," he began again, "When we came for you in Marfang, thinking you were an Envoy and not the king himself, the Sacourian delegate was in the chamber with you."

"And you want to know why," said Endil, finishing the unasked question.

"My Lord," began Scarth again, but Endil held up his hand for silence.

"I understand," said the king, "that on a night of treachery you would find it curious, to say the least, that your king, while pretending to be something less, should be closeted in secret discussion with an emissary from our ancient enemies."

"Well, yes," replied Scarth, thinking he would never be so eloquent as a noble. He was glad not to be.

"It's simple, really," replied Endil. "We were discussing peace."

"Peace, my Lord? But they have always fought us. They lust for what we have, and chafe against the price we ask for it, and fight us when the chafing grows too much. We fight, we bleed, we die, and the Dendragon flowers remain ours. If they want their petals and their juice, they can come and try to take them, as they have always done, and we will repel them, as we have always done."

The Fruit Of The Dendragon Tree

"Spoken like a true warrior," said Endil, his voice grave in the firelight. "You have always done your duty to Taumar, and none can deny it. But what if there was another way?"

"What other way?" said Scarth, who was beginning to feel out of his depth.

"What if we gave them what they wanted? Think of it!" Endil continued, as Scarth stirred to protest. "We have more than enough Dendragon extract every year to supply Taumar and the Far Kingdom, but we extort the Sacours' gold to pay dearly for that which grows in abundance in our own land, through no ingenuity or effort of our own. We grow wealthy upon the back of their desire to also live long and healthy lives, yet we have done nothing to bring this gift to the world. It is mere luck that the Dragon flowers grow at Marfang and not Castelfar, and we both know it. What if we didn't gouge the price, and simply charged them the cost, say, of a bushel of wheat, what tally of lives would we save for both sides, what richness of life could we gain through peace? How would all Tiramonde be enriched, and not just Taumar, if we showed such generosity?"

Scarth didn't know what to say. The idea was startling in its simplicity, but so radical. So much of Taumar's energy went into defending it from the "Sacourian scourge" that it was hard to imagine life without that constant threat of conflict with their southern neighbor. What would peace look like? What would sharing their wealth feel like? What would the world be without the need for swords and warriors? He looked at his king, and saw there the face of radical compassion, and knew that his ruler was a very dangerous man.

"It can be done, can't it Scarth?" asked Endil.

"I believe it can, Lord," replied Scarth, and he knew it to be true.

"Will you help me?"

"Lord, you rescued me from the pit. I swore my service to you. I will do whatever you ask in what remains to me of my life." And this was true also. But then he laughed, under the stars, and the truth of his laughter also surprised him, he who had thought never to laugh again.

"What is it?" asked Endil, smiling in the night.

"Coegun would piss himself if he knew what you were planning!" said Scarth, as he continued to chuckle.

"Then we should ensure his death, and save him from incontinence," replied Endil, and the two men laughed together, drawing curious glances from the nearby soldiers.

They set out early the next day, and the young king led his men with an economy of words that appealed to Scarth, veteran of many campaigns. They were about three hundred strong. The horsemen of Marlona sat tall in their saddles, and each carried a long wooden spear, a sword, a shield, and a quiver of arrows on his back. Some carried their bows over their shoulders, but most left them unstrung and tied to their saddles. Endil had given Scarth a sword and a shield, and sworn him back to service as a member of his own bodyguard. Scarth had a horse too, a black one, with a white diamond on his brow. All the horses were black, or chestnut, and their dark manes tossed in the breeze of their passage.

The company did not sing, nor did they speak much amongst themselves, or to Scarth and Naomi. The girl rode with Scarth, and told him that this group of men was aware of her brother's journey to Marfang, and of his ruse of pretending to be mere Envoy, unlike the bodyguard that had gone with him to Marfang. They had been ordered to follow at a safe distance, in case of problems, and attempt a rescue if needed. Scarth also learned that though most of the men took the Duke's treachery as a blow, they did not see it as a fatal or completely unexpected one. Ambitious nobles had challenged more than one king in Taumar's history, and Endil would likely not be the last ruler to which this happened. Coegun was powerful, and a gifted general, and the lust for power was ever the shadow of such men. But the king's men were loyal, said Naomi, and would fight against Duke Coegun when called. Many of the men now traveling with the king had friends or relations among Endil's bodyguard at Marfang. Vengeance for those deaths alone would be sufficient cause to fight against Coegun now.

The Fruit Of The Dendragon Tree

As for Coegun's own obvious magic powers, who knew its scope, or its limits? Perhaps only Ureth, and she was far away. It was clear Ureth believed Jake could be the Pendraig. Scarth knew the legend of the imprisoned dragon, of course, but he didn't believe it to be literally true and didn't know anyone besides Ureth who did. Even Naomi seemed unsure. The dragons, if they had ever existed, were all dead now. Whatever power his daughter hoped to unleash from beneath Marfang, he hoped it wouldn't require sacrificing Jake. Scarth had grown fond of the boy in the few times they had met. He had spirit, and certainly someone had taught him to be an amazing swordsman. Scarth believed Endil would need good swordsmen soon.

They crossed the Marfell in the late morning, at the ford of Avonrhyd. The waters of the ford swirled about the horses' knees, but everyone made it across safely. And early that afternoon, while to the west Jake and his companions loped through the long grass on foot, Endil's men came upon a homestead, by the chance of their route the first they had seen. It was a typical veldt farm, Scarth saw: a lone house in the middle of a vast sea of grass, with a few acres of cultivated land surrounding the dwelling. From the fresh furrows in the rich dark earth, Scarth guessed that the farmer had recently completed his spring planting, and the first shoots of green, already poking through the ground, supported this conclusion. A path wide enough for a cart led through the neatly ploughed field to the east of the farmhouse, and out of respect for the farmer's crop King Endil led his soldiers two abreast along this. On his right was his company commander, a taciturn but able man named Alun. Behind these two rode Scarth and Naomi. The rest of the company strung out behind, their shadows dark in the afternoon sun. Looking up, Scarth saw wispy clouds of mare's tails racing high overhead.

"Looks like rain later," he said to Naomi, but her eyes were elsewhere.

"There's something funny about that scarecrow, brother," she called to Endil, and the king held up his hand to halt his column of men. Their dust caught up to them, and settled where they stood, and on the nearby edges of the fields. Scarth looked north of their path to where Naomi pointed. A scarecrow dangled from his cross, garments fluttering in the breeze. The head was covered by a broad-brimmed hat, which had been pulled down almost to the shoulders. A cloud of flies hovered above, and a large vulture stood nonchalantly on the manikin's right shoulder, tugging at something underneath the hat. The bird pulled something red and fleshy looking from under the shadow of the brim, took a speculative look at the company, and flew off with a single derisory caw, its spoils dangling from its beak.

"That's no scarecrow," muttered Scarth, who was already moving, with Endil, Alun and Naomi close behind.

It was worse than he thought it would be. They had impaled the man on the upright part of the cross, and driven the post between his legs up through the middle of his torso. The crosspiece had been thrust sideways through his chest at the level of his armpits. The body itself had been ravaged by what looked like the bites of a huge dog. The head was missing; the hat simply rested on the top of the upright pole, which exited the body where the neck had been. Scarth had seen many savage things on the field of battle, but this was something different. This was an inhuman degradation. He felt cold in the sunshine, and Endil shivered next to him, as if in support.

"Werewolf," said Naomi flatly. "Or werewolves, more likely."

"How do you know?" asked Alun sharply, before he caught himself. "Your Highness," he added, after a small pause.

"I know because I have been trained to know," answered Naomi. "Ureth taught us to know such things, because she believed we would have to face them. And I came to believe that she was just power-hungry, and after the Mother's position, and so I refused to hear her. But I do remember this. It is the werewolf crucifixion, and they do it to say they are free, and don't need to eat the meat they are killing." Scarth heard the girl's voice become more monotone with every word she uttered, and knew she was moving into the trance of Sight.

"The werewolves are ranging out from under the eaves of Blutwald," Naomi went on. "The Waterstones have been moved, and they are free.

The Fruit Of The Dendragon Tree

The vampyrim walk with them, and they too drink the blood that the werewolves spill. They walk to aid Coegun, who believes he can rule them, and he will reward them with the blood of his own people, in return for the throne." Naomi shook herself slightly, and Scarth knew the trance had left her. She looked at them, then at the farmer's house. "They will have left one alive to tell the tale," she said, in her normal voice. "They want us to follow, and give them battle."

"They will have their wish," growled Endil, and Scarth heard the pain of a good-hearted young king who had failed to protect his people. He could understand that pain. The king turned to Alun, and pointed at the farmhouse. "See if there's anyone alive in there."

There was, but only one. They found four more corpses, all children, none so brutally ravaged as the farmer, but all drained of blood, meaning, as Naomi told them, that vampires had been with the werewolves on this raid. There was a chill in the air, and Scarth shivered again. Naomi nodded at him.

"Your senses do not deceive you, Scarth," she said. "Wherever they go, the vampyrim leave that coldness behind. They suck the life from others and give nothing back, and submit to no will but their own." Scarth thought of the children dying, the horror of their last moments as their blood drained into the maw of some Undead creature, and then his fear left him. Grief and horror fused inside him, and forged a slow-burning anger waiting to flame. He itched to wield a sword again.

The farmer's wife sat on the earthen floor of her little home, her youngest daughter's head in her lap. She was pleating the little girl's hair, which Scarth saw was a lovely auburn color above the white face, drained of blood. "It's her birthday today," said the grief-stricken woman. "I have to finish her cake."

"Tell us," said Naomi gently. "Tell us where they went, and if you can, how long ago they were here."

The woman looked deep into Naomi's eyes. "They went west, milady. They went west after they were finished here, and my family was alive at dawn." Tears welled up in her eyes then, and she started to cry, great, heaving sobs that racked her body, and jerked the dead little girl's head as it lay in her lap, the burnished hair flopping on the floor.

Endil detailed four men to look after the widow, and bury the dead. "Stay with her through the night," he ordered. "Then take her back to Marlona." The men demurred at this: they had come to fight, after all, not play bodyguard to a farmer's wife, no matter what horrors she had witnessed. But Endil planned to ride on immediately, and would not leave the widowed woman alone. "Your swords may get just as bloody as ours if any of these brutes return," he told them. "And I will need more men in any event if I have to besiege Marfang. You will have the honor of raising them for me, and bringing them back to Coegun's castle. This woman will be our witness to the horror he has unleashed. Perhaps now those whom the Duke's legend blinds will see him for who he truly is. Do not grumble! Your journey may be no safer to the east than ours is to the west. Keep your swords ready and pray to the Dancer for Taumar, indeed for the whole of Tiramonde, for these fell beasts, roaming at will, upset the balance of the world that has been preserved for so long."

With that he left them, and all the others followed, spread out behind, no longer worrying about the crops in the field, for no one would harvest them now. They galloped west, as thirsty for revenge as a vampire for blood, and the shadows grew long as the four men and lone shattered woman left behind buried the dead, and denied the vultures their feast.

3.

The river of this story flows more swiftly now. Four groups of fighters clashed on the veldt that day, and many songs have been sung of that meeting, but I was there and can tell you it was not like the songs. I ran with the elves, and we traveled swiftly, some six hundred strong, from beautiful Kyphala-dyn and out from the forest as silently as ghosts. We pressed southwards across the green carpet of the veldt, and all was still before us. Dynan led us, but I traveled with Coblyn and Keffyldyn, ever forward of the main body of the force, and they had to slow me down more than once. The werewolf taint in my blood sang strange songs to me under the stars, and I could tell when any of them passed near. We met none: they feared the elves too much, but there was another danger too, colder, less wild, and much more evil.

"It is the vampyrim that you sense," said Coblyn when I mentioned it to him. "They are fewer than the wolfen, but more deadly. They run before us, goading the werewolves, drawing us along until they feel they have sufficient numbers to give us battle."

I shivered, my blood singing to me of danger to the south, danger to my son, whom I was sure was near, and I ran more urgently to protect him. I was never sure afterwards how long our journey took. One day seemed to flow into the next; elves don't require sleep as mortal men do, and I myself was now something in addition to human. I could rest my brain and dream even as my body loped through the grass like a wolf. But I do remember a night when the yellow light of the full Warrior moon, that the elves call Dyndraig, poured from the sky. The elves had made a rare pause to rest and regroup. A stream flowed through the grass, and I moved forward with Coblyn and Keffyldyn to drink the silvery water. The moonlight warmed me, and I drew in its strength and growled softly at the sky. Coblyn gripped my arm, and I shook myself, seeing the nearby elves glancing at me strangely. "Are you all right?" Keffyldyn whispered, and I nodded, not trusting myself to speak, unsure what my voice would sound like. The moment passed, and I was David once more. But the wild has never been far from me since, and I knew I had become something far different from the bookish academic who drank Scotch by firelight in his snug suburban study.

I remember next it was daylight, the end of a beautiful spring afternoon. We were a dense force of elven valor, leavened by a centaur, and a lone wolf. Thunderclouds gathered high in the western sky, and rushed towards us as we sped southwards. I was running free, out in front with Keffyldyn nearby, and Coblyn was racing to keep pace with us. I could smell Jake on the westerly breeze that gusted ahead of the approaching storm. He was the blood of the covenant I had made with my wife, and I was the bringer of death to anyone who might harm him. Such is a father's vanity, because we can rarely protect our children from the world. I could scent danger on the wind also: there were many werewolves ahead, and cold vampires too, thirsting for blood. I could feel them chasing my son, and I snarled and ran faster. The ground began to tremble with the advent of horses, and looking left, to the east, I saw hundreds of horsemen racing to join us. A red and gold banner streamed amongst them, catching the rays of a sun soon to be consumed by storm. I saw a small group straight ahead, running due east towards the horsemen. Another company of riders, roughly thirty strong, and riding under a green banner, approached from the south.

My heart leaped, for at the head of the small company was my son. A sword flickered in his hand. An old woman kept pace with him as he ran, while a brown-skinned man with flowing black hair brought up the rear. A vanguard of werewolves loped ahead of a larger horde that chased Jake and his companions from the west. Three of the beasts put on a sudden burst of speed from the forward group, straight towards my son. I howled in warning: we were too far away to help. Jake stopped and looked towards me, then turned with his friends to fight. The brown-skinned man took one in the throat with his sword; the old woman stabbed at the air, and another burst into flame. But Jake leaped almost to the shoulder of his werewolf, and slashed downward, decapitating the brute in one flowing, graceful offering of death.

I howled again, and beside me Coblyn roared, and we ran even faster, as if that were possible without wings, Keffyldyn thundering beside us. More dark shapes poured along the ground, werewolves and vampires together, ten of them, fifty, a hundred, always coming to where Jake wielded his sword. But we joined them after only a heartbeat, six hundred elves, three hundred horsemen, a centaur, a Crone, and me: whatever I was. Coegun and his men (for I learned later who rode under the green banner) withdrew very quickly. He was no coward, that Duke, but he was no fool either, and he retreated to Marfang to make us fight him there. I have always believed that, if we had met him that day, a larger part of the evil of that world would have perished, and much of what came later might have been avoided. But he fled, and the storm broke above us, and lightning smashed down to the ground where we fought. The sky was black. A tree exploded to my right, horses screamed, and the vampires hissed like the rain that fell in sheets.

My sword danced in my hand, and the wolf in me knew how to use it, and I brought death with every stroke. But it was still a battle: werewolves are unutterably savage, and the only way to kill a vampire is to behead it, and they don't usually stand still to let you do this. One in particular, their king himself, laughed as all others fell or fled before him. He laughed as he killed. He laughed as Dynan faced him, and he laughed as he plunged his sword into the heart of my brave elf friend. And that was how Dynan the elven prince, who carried starlight in his hair, and who had welcomed me to Tiramonde in friendship, died as thunder crashed to mark his passing. I raged at this, and avenged myself on the three werewolves and one vampire who had surrounded me. But revenge can never bring back a life that is lost, and I mourn Dynan to this day.

The creature laughed at my rage, and was still laughing as Jake beheaded him from behind. The head rolled away, a grim smile still etched on the cold, white face. Smoke poured out of the body from the neck, finally liberating the captive, tormented spirit from the curse of not being able to die. I could see Jake's face as he dealt that death, could see he realized in that moment that there are worse things than dying, living as a vampire being one of them. But my compassion for the torments of the Undead cools when I think of Dynan, and I hope there is a special hell for vampires who finally let go of life.

I found Jake again that evening, on the battlefield of a different world, over the body of my dead friend. We had both become warriors under the moons of Tiramonde, and together no enemy could withstand us. We hugged in the rain, as only men can who have faced death, caused death, and have themselves survived the day. They told us we covered ourselves in glory, and struck such terror into the hearts of both werewolf and vampire that none would come near where we were, but all I remember now was the rain on my cheek mingling with my tears as I held my son. They say that our small force of elves and men was outnumbered five to one that day, and killed at least twice our number before the others fled. But only the scribes and the poets will tell you they know what happens in a battle; to those that were there its scope is limited by what you can see, and hear, and smell, and feel. Or like me, you don't remember even that, yet afterwards you find yourself still in your body, and alive. The poets will scribble of the ebb and flow of momentum, and the decisions that won or lost the thing, and they are not above lying to suit their purpose. But they know nothing of the stench of blood, and feces, and vomit, as men and other beings die around you: the clamor without, and the stillness within. I know we made no decisions that day. We found evil in the grass. We met it head on, with no sense of who should go where and do what. We had a victory, and lived to fight again.

I held on to Jake as if I would never let him go, and in truth I didn't want to. We were covered in blood, little of it ours, and the rain washed most of it away. "I'm sorry son," I said. "I never meant to hurt you."

"It's OK Dad," he replied. "I'm sorry too."

But time goes on, the world turns, rain stops, battles end, and even the dead are not dead forever, as I have come to know. Keffyldyn came up to where we stood, accompanied by the woman I had thought was old, but whom I could tell was young despite her wrinkled skin. It was her eyes. I'll never forget the first time I saw those eyes, young in the ancient face. And with the centaur and the witch was the swarthy man who had been running with Jake. So it was there, on the veldt of Taumar, that I first met Ureth the Crone, and Rajindra al-Qabir, Prince of the Sacours.

I had no sense of the tapestry that would be woven by the meeting of these strands, though Ureth's eyes captivated me, for they would not leave my own. "My name is David Patel," I said, when Jake introduced her.

"It's an honor to meet you," she replied, and I could tell she meant it, though I didn't yet know why.

Chapter 18

"This time," said the Voice, "I will grant you the most difficult dream of all."
"Am I to be a leper?" asked my spirit, ready to be brave.
"No," said the Voice. "This time you will be a King,"

(The Dynfarch Wisdom, Book 2: The Flame of Ysgith)

Night had fallen, and David and Jake discovered the work of victory, that must be done after battle. The dead werewolves and vampires were tossed into a shallow pit that men and elves had dug together. Finding and burying the vampire heads was a grisly business. Another pit was dug for the fallen men and elves. These two pits were covered over with wood gathered from a nearby stand of trees. A pair of great fires were set atop the burial mounds, lit from the soaking wood by Ureth's fire, and the soldiers of both elves and men gathered upwind of them, while their leaders spoke. Jake stood with his fellow escapees from Marfang, while his father stood nearby with Keffyldyn and a tall elf that David introduced simply as Coblyn, but whom the other elves seemed to treat with a mixture of sympathy and affection. "He's a prince among the elves," whispered David to his son. "He'll be the next in line for the throne now that his brother Dynan has died." His voice trailed away, and Jake could tell that his father had held Dynan in high regard. They couldn't speak more, as the impromptu battle council began.

Endil stood silently in the firelight, waiting for the warriors to become quiet. Jake saw Naomi standing with him, seeming younger almost by the minute. He assumed, correctly as it turned out, that she would look more and more like her true age as her pregnancy progressed.

"We await your orders, Lord," said Alun of the king's bodyguard. "Are we to go to Marlona?" There was a murmur of approval at this, and it was clear that many of the men would rather retreat to the capital than fight Coegun.

But Endil would not hear of it. "We cannot go to Marlona now!" he cried. "To do that would mean abandoning all of Taumar west of the river to the Undead. We have won this battle, but many escaped us today, and there are more of them, who have waited for ages in the forest, hoping against hope that the Waterstones that contained them would one day be found, and moved, thereby letting them roam free. The Stones are in Marfang now; we must rescue and replace them, and banish the Undead once again from the veldt before they lay it to waste. It was Coegun who conspired to bring the Stones back to his castle. He wishes to rule Taumar, and thinks he can use these creatures to that purpose. But he cannot squint far enough past the glitter of his own ambition to see that in the end they will rule him instead. No, my brothers, we must attack Marfang now, while Coegun is unaware of the victory we had here today, and that elves and men have united once more to banish darkness from Tiramonde forever!"

There was a roar of approval at this speech, but Coblyn, not under the authority of Taumar's king, said: "But we are few, Lord Endil, and even with we elves you number less than a thousand. Everyone knows that Marfang's garrison can match our numbers. If our initial assault fails, and we are stuck outside the castle walls, all Coegun has to do is wait for the rest of the werewolves and vampires to arrive. He can then meet us in open battle with the odds in his favor, the elite warriors of Marfang in his vanguard, and the Undead behind. Surely we should retreat to the Bloodwood where they still cannot find Kyphala-dyn, and wait there for the reinforcements that you sent for, instead of committing to a desperate siege with too few soldiers."

"There will be no reinforcements, Prince Coblyn." It was Ureth who had spoken, with the voice of the Sight. There is always a silence when this voice is heard, and it was into silence, broken only by the crackling of the funeral pyres, that she spoke once again. "I see a widow woman, standing by the grave of her child, screaming at the vampire leering on top of it, waiting to drink her blood. I see four brave men, dead in a field, bloody swords in their hands. There are six dead werewolves nearby, but a dozen more howl to the moon, waiting to feast on the hearts of their enemies, so as to gain their courage. The soldiers' bodies will be devoured, and the graves the king told them to dig will be desecrated, and the reinforcements they were told to raise from the empty-throned castle in Marlona will not be sent until it is far, far, too late." The men and elves remained silent about her, and Jake could see the scene in his mind's eye, so clearly did the voice of the Sight paint the vision of what it described.

"We could send a raven," said Jake, and though there was a murmur of agreement Ureth shook her head.

"Even if we sent a raven," she said, "it would take at least three weeks before a force of sufficient size to besiege Marfang could arrive at the castle. And Coegun and his fell allies would by then have walked over our corpses, carrying the Stones across the river, to give those who came to our aid savage defeat in the North March. This I have seen, and you can believe it to be true. No my friends, the matter has to be decided sooner than that. We are alone in this fight. We are alone, and have to do what is necessary and just, or die in the attempt of it. If we win, there will forever be songs of your valor, and if we lose, there will be few songs ever again, for the alliance that has been formed in the name of Coegun's ambition will grow in power until the whole world has been overrun."

"How did this happen?" asked Scarth. "I have known the Duke since he was a boy! It's true he has always been harsh and cruel, but under him we had victory, and safety from the Sacours, and grew rich upon their desire for the Dendragon flowers. Taumar was the blessed kingdom, the jewel of Tiramonde. How did we come so close to the brink of catastrophe without knowing the fall that loomed ahead?"

"How did it happen?" Ureth's voice was soft, barely heard above the twin pyres. The night had deepened, and men had to struggle to see her. But such was the truth they heard in her voice, that no man questioned it. "If we wish to see who is to blame, all we have to do is look in the mirror. We valued comfort and security more than justice and truth. We valued the strength of arms of those who swore to protect us more than the strength of their character. We valued the ease of peace through a sword more than the difficulty of peace through generosity and forgiveness. And we forgot, if in fact we ever knew, that if you tolerate the evil of your protector because he fights your enemies, one day you may find that your protector is the worst enemy of all."

"We cannot dwell upon this," Endil said. "We have to look the moment squarely in the eye and fight, or run. The weapons a ruler uses define the character of his kingdom. We know what weapons Coegun is willing to use: the Undead who suck the blood of children, and ravage any corpse they find. But we know who we are! Here, with you men at arms are the elves, who have always stood for the light. Here is a centaur, wise with laughter. Here is a boy from another world, come to try to save his mother. Here is his father, who loved him enough to follow. Here is your enemy, a Sacour, who yet fights at your side, a Crone who has the arts of healing, and a princess who carries a babe of royal blood in her womb!" He carried on above the approving murmurs of the crowd. "With whom would you rather stand? And what if you die? Would you want to live in a world fashioned by the sick ambition of a man who would perpetrate such evil upon his own people merely to further his own grasp of power? We are more than Taumar!" cried the king. "We are Tiramonde!"

"Tiramonde!" cried the crowd, men and elves together.

"Life for our world!" called Endil, his voice young and clear in the firelight.

"Life!" cried the throng, with one voice.

"Life!" they called again, and Jake felt chills down his spine.

The Fruit Of The Dendragon Tree

The crowd erupted in cheers, and men banged their swords on their shields. The fires grew taller. The din was terrific. Jake moved closer to Ureth. Naomi was standing near her, and on an impulse he took her hand. "Take care of our baby!" he shouted, over the noise of the cheering warriors. "And of yourself too!" he added, not sure if she heard him.

But she smiled, looking ever more like the young girl she truly was, and he was glad for her, even though she had tricked him. "You be careful too!" she replied, and he nodded, smiling back at her. He caught the Sacour winking at him. He was glad of the firelight, so the man would not notice his blush. *I thought you were Jenny,* Jake thought to himself, looking at Naomi. *I thought you were Jenny, and you came to me as her and no one else. How did you know to do that, when I didn't even notice her in my heart? What have you awakened in me? What will I say to Jenny, if I ever see her again?*

But the centaur had come up to him, and nudged him gently in the ribs. "Well child, you did well today."

Jake was glad to see him. "Thanks Keffyldyn," he answered. "I got lucky, I guess."

"Don't be too modest lad," said the centaur. "You did well enough and no mistake. That's no more than the truth. It's not over yet, though. Today was just a skirmish. That fine speech by the king? Someone always bleeds after speeches like that. Just make sure it's not you, alright?"

Jake chuckled. "I'll try, I promise."

"Aye well, I'll be there to see that you do, never fear." He looked over to where Ureth and Scarth were speaking with David. "Now let's go talk to your father. He didn't come all this way to have you whinnying with me all night."

The rest of the night passed quickly, and they sat around a small campfire, talking until the dawn. David told Jake how Jenny had woven the spells a second time for him to come to Tiramonde, how Dynan and Coblyn had found him in the forest and set out with Keffyldyn to ensure that Jake was safe. Ureth spoke of the Duke's treachery, and

Scarth and Sathryn's capture during their struggle to escape. Endil spoke of his plans for peace, and Rajindra of the welcome they would receive in his desert kingdom.

"For," he said, "we too are tired of the endless shedding of blood. There is much we can learn from each other, and together who knows what greatness we can achieve?"

"Let us hope all men think the same," said Scarth, before telling of his rescue by Naomi and the king. Of Sathryn and her fate he would not speak, but all could see the nature of her death written on his face, and Jake felt his blood boil.

Ureth nodded at her father's words, as if something missing had been found, and when Keffyldyn raised an eyebrow at her expression, she answered his unspoken question: "I understand even more now why Coegun wants to become king. If there is peace, then his importance as a warlord, and the prominence of Marfang as the guardian of the Dendragon flowers, are both diminished. If he is king, he can ensure there is no peace, and keep both his purpose and the need for his type of power alive."

"I think you're right," said the centaur.

"But Endil said it was a secret," said Scarth. "How would Coegun know?"

"I think," said the king, "that given the magic we have seen him use, he may have access to other secrets also. Many envoys traveled back and forth before my meeting with Rajindra was arranged. Who knows how one of them could have been compromised, or even bought? Gold has its own magic, as we know."

"What I don't understand," said Jake, "is why we are turning around to go back to Marfang again."

"This is an eminently sensible question," agreed the Sacour. "I am seeing much more of your fair country than I thought I would."

"We have to go back, Jake," answered Scarth. "It is as King Endil said. Coegun has to be defeated, before he breaks out across the river with the Undead."

"We could not stay at Marfang, Jake, because you would have been killed," said Ureth. "But even more importantly, you had a destiny to meet outside its walls, a prophecy that had to be fulfilled. You had to vanquish the vampire king in battle, and this you have done. It was long foretold among the Crones that the slayer of the vampire king would be the one who could pluck the fruit of the Dendragon tree, the Pendraig. It has also been long foretold that a visitor from another world would receive the werewolf king's sword after this battle, and change it back to its original steel and gold. It is said that the one who returns the sword to its original beauty will become the king of all Tiramonde, and bring justice to all our peoples." As she spoke, Ureth drew a stone sword from beneath a bundle of rags next to her.

"Coblyn retrieved this sword after the skirmish in Bloodwood, where he, Dynan, and your father killed the werewolf king and his bodyguard," continued Ureth. "Thanks to you David, its owner had no further use for it. More than a thousand years ago, during the time of the Dragon Wars, Nablut the vampire king turned the first King Endil into a werewolf and his sword into stone. Thanks to you, Jake, and you, David, both of them are now at their long-awaited rest. For you beheaded Nablut in battle, Jake, as was foretold by legend. And David, you killed the first Endil, the werewolf who wore a circlet of gold around his brow, though you knew it not. I hope he kept a sufficient remnant of his humanity to feel relief at his death."

There was a small silence after Ureth stopped speaking. Jake imagined the first King Endil's long life as a werewolf, hiding in the forest, in thrall to a vampire, shunned by his people. Outliving everything except their fear and hatred. He shuddered, remembering Nablut's death, and the understanding that had flooded through him then, as it did again now. *Maybe there are worse things than dying.*

"But I don't want to be the Pendraig," he said. "And I sure don't want to be king. I don't belong here. I want to go home with my Dad, and have my old life back."

"But, my friend," said Coblyn, who hadn't spoken much. "Destiny has nothing to do with what we desire. I am now the future king of the Eldervolk, but the price for that has been steep: do you not think I would rather have my brother here alive? Only you have slain Nablut, and so you only may pluck the fruit of the cursed tree of life, whose offshoot flowers have been the cause of so much bloodshed. When you do, maybe your mother will live, but Marfang will fall and the Duke with his castle, and we will have to deal with the consequences."

"Take the sword, Jake," commanded Ureth. And despite his misgivings he did so, grasping the thing by its stone hilt and holding it high, to catch the first rays of sunshine that was sparkling the dew into diamonds. A sudden gust of wind tugged at the smoke from the fire, and it writhed around Jake as he stood near, snaking up his arm and the sword blade before vanishing into the clear spring morning. The stone blade gleamed red for a few seconds, but that was all. The moment was gone, and Jake felt vaguely foolish as he stood there. The sword was still stone, and he lowered it slowly until its point dug into the soft earth.

"Well, I guess I'm not your king then," he said, confused by relief and disappointment.

"I don't understand," muttered Ureth. "The prophecy is clear. There is no doubt in my mind that you are the Pendraig. How can the sword not come to you?"

"Because 'Pendraig' is not the same as 'king'," said Keffyldyn, taking the sword gently from Jake's hand. "And you, Ureth, haven't considered all possibilities. There's a legend of a vampire, and one of a werewolf, and maybe they're not the same one. There's more than one visitor from another world among us. Stand please, Lord David, and take this sword from me."

David looked bewildered for a moment, then struggled to his feet. Jake could tell from the way he rubbed it that his father's back was hurting, from having sat on the ground all night. He met his Dad's eyes, and shrugged. Keffyldyn's tail swished as he handed the sword to David. "Hold it high, wolf-slayer," said the centaur, "and let it catch the light."

The Fruit Of The Dendragon Tree

2.

I did as he asked, and so I sealed my doom. But doom is relative, I've discovered, and rarely permanent, and I've had a long time to get over mine. As soon as I touched it, the cold stone in my hand began to grow warm, and the hilt became suffused with a golden light that seemed to soak up the morning sun. I raised the sword high, and flakes of stone along its edge turned to smoke, and fell to the ground as ash. Ribbons of silver striated the blade, as stone turned to steel, and a bright white light surrounded the sword as it quivered in my hand. A high-pitched hum, like that from a tuning fork, began where the blade met the hilt. The music entered me, and I laughed in the dawn as a king should laugh, when he has received the token of his kingship. The light circled my head, and clothed my body, and for a moment I wore a crown of light, and robes of light, and very nearly felt as if I myself was made of light. The humming faded, the light subsided, and I felt no more or less than David again. But I held a beautiful sword in my hand, with a golden hilt, and a fine steel blade, where before there had only been dead stone. I knew I was the future king of all Tiramonde, and that I could never return home. But even kings don't know how everything will happen, which is useful for keeping them humble, I think.

There wasn't a lot of ceremony afterwards. We had to get moving, and I wasn't king yet. Endil and Naomi didn't look happy, but I pointed out that I was the future king of Tiramonde, not the present one, that Endil ruled Taumar, and that my claim to any throne would not be revealed until its time. There was no argument, and I was in fact being wiser than I knew. I did accept a scabbard that Coblyn found for my new sword, which for no reason I knew I decided to call *Ysgith*. Coblyn eyed me curiously when I said this aloud. I know now that "Ysgith" means "fang" in the werewolf tongue, which probably explains things. Then we busied ourselves with the task of readying nine hundred warriors to march. I think we were all confused by what had happened, Jake and I not least. As could be expected, perhaps,

Keffyldyn and Coblyn recovered the quickest. Centaurs and elves have no agenda but the truth, and though Ureth was entirely noble she couldn't help admit that her calculations had been slightly off. Even when everything about a prophecy comes true, things rarely happen like people imagine. And if you've tried to engineer a particular future it can be a blow to your ego if the ensuing reality doesn't quite match up to your vision. So it was always difficult for Ureth to understand that the Pendraig and the king were two different people, even though the two legends had played out exactly as they were written.

A couple of spare horses were found and Jake, Coblyn and Keffyldyn rode with me when we started. The rest of the elves were on foot, and we proceeded at their pace, but I knew the horses would tire first. I was interested to see how much Jake liked the centaur. Even when he was being wise, Keffyldyn could make my son laugh, but then that is a centaur's gift; no matter how bleak a situation is they can usually find some humor in it, and though we rode to a fight we were certain to lose laughter was never far from our lips. Ureth, Naomi and Scarth joined us, and the six of us rode together behind Endil's banner. I understood that the king had never intended to bring a besieging force, only a vanguard should he have needed immediate protection. And even with the elves, each worth about five human fighters, it was clear that we had no chance to liberate Marfang through force of arms. Just what we were going to do when we got there seemed less clear, but Scarth took this uncertainty in stride. I came to like him a great deal; the bonds of fatherhood bound us, and of loss: the ones he had already suffered, and the one I believed would soon be mine. A werewolf army followed us. I could feel them, and we would sometimes glimpse their scouts far off on our flanks, or behind us in the distance. The vampires never came close enough for me to feel, content, as they must have thought, for their wild servants to shepherd us to Marfang, and to our ending.

When we grew tired of riding, Coblyn and I walked with his elven soldiers, but though I could have run all the way to Marfang I would take to the horse again so that I could be near my son. He had changed in the time he had been gone; when he wasn't being entertained by Keffyldyn there was a quiet air to him I had never seen before. We spent more time together during that ride than we had in ages. We spoke as equals, and Jake was more open with me than he had ever been, as if he too realized how precious a gift that time was. I learned a lot from him, mostly that children carry their wounds in niches of their hearts that can be secret even to them, secret certainly from the parents who have wounded them, however inadvertently.

"Do you think I was wrong to come here?" he asked me, on the second day. We were riding together, apart from the group, and could speak privately. "Do you think I was wrong to risk my life, and now the lives of a lot of other people, to try and save Mom's?"

I didn't know what to answer, so I settled for the truth. "I don't know son," I said. "I understand how much you love your Mom, how much you don't want her to die. I do know I couldn't let you be here by yourself; I had to come and find you. Jenny told me we could try and bring you back, but I think in my heart I just wanted to find you. Hell, maybe we both secretly wanted to escape life back home, maybe that was part of it. Who knows? I'm no shrink. If you were wrong, then I was wrong too. But right or wrong, we can't do anything about it now. We've made our choices, and we have to see things through. We are here, and apparently the stuff of legends. You are to pluck the fruit of the Dendragon tree, and I am to become king of all Tiramonde."

He thought about this for a while, and I was worried he would argue with me about it, because of course if I became king I wasn't going back with him. But he didn't say anything about that, and I never knew what, if anything, he felt about it at the time. He was a teenager after all, by definition self-absorbed, whatever wisdom he may have acquired.

"Do you know why I had to try?" His voice sounded funny as he asked the question. I looked at him, and could see he was close to tears. I was about to say something again about how much he loved Mary, but suddenly I knew there was more, and simply shook my head.

"I thought if she died, it would be my fault."

I was gloriously unprepared for this. "What?" I said, not sure I had heard him correctly.

His words came in a torrent. "After she was diagnosed, I heard you arguing with her. You guys hardly ever argued, but you did after we knew she was sick. You told her how you'd worried she would get sick all along, how the doctors had told her not to get pregnant, how with her family history of breast cancer it was a bad idea for her to try and have kids. 'I knew this was going to happen,' you said, and she didn't disagree, she just said how badly she'd wanted a child, how even if it meant she could die she'd wanted that, and how happy she was that she'd had me, even if she died young, how much I'd meant to her. 'The price was too high,' you said…" he stopped, and I could see the tears on his face now, the effort it took for him to keep his voice steady.

"Jake, listen…" I began, but he cut me off with a wave of his hand.

"No, Dad, you listen. I have to say this. 'The price was too high' you said, and at the time I thought you meant me. Heck, at the time you probably did mean me. I thought I was the price that was too high. I even agreed with you. And even though I knew I was wrong, I told myself that you would rather have that other woman than be with me after Mom died. So if I could save Mom's life, if she could die of something else, get hit by a bus, die any other way than this one, then it wouldn't be my fault. Then it would be ok, everything would be like it was, that then…"

"That then you would be worth it," I said, and my son, whom I loved more than anything in any world, for whom I would pay any price, burst into tears. I moved my horse closer to his, and awkwardly, because it is an awkward thing to do, I hugged him to me as best as I could while we rode side by side. I could feel the truth of his words deep inside me. I wonder now if I hadn't known the truth of them even before he'd spoken.

"Jake, you are so worth it. Your Mom knew what she wanted, and was willing to pay any price to have you in the world. She is at peace with her going because of the joy you brought her. I love you so much," I said into his hair, as his head jogged up and down on my shoulder while we rode.

"I know," he said. And suddenly we could see the funny side of that comment, and for this, and the difficulty of holding our position, we shared a small chuckle together.

"Yeah?" I said, teasing. "How do you know?"

Jake grew serious again, and wiping his eyes with his sleeve sat up alone on his horse, relinquishing his contact with me: a suburban American kid who had become a warrior of prophecy in another world. And I, of the wolf and future king, rode beside him. Then Jake gave me a smile to break my heart, but in a good way, you understand, in a very good way. "You're here, aren't you?" he replied, and smiled once more.

I nodded, not trusting myself to speak, and indeed we spoke no more about it. Instead, as men do, we rode on in silence, on to our respective destinies, to shed blood for reasons that no longer applied.

Chapter 19

When all swords are drawn, blood will be spilled.

(Sacourian proverb)

Ureth became distant, never speaking to me directly, and rarely meeting my glance, which was a change from the first night we'd met, when she wouldn't stop looking at me. Keffyldyn brought the matter up late that second day, as we continued through the rich, cultivated lands of Coegun's duchy.

"You've upset Ureth," he said in his matter of fact way, absently stroking my horse's ears as he walked alongside.

"How so?" I asked.

"Well, she had very tidy ideas about her prophecy. Now it wears two faces, and she doesn't know what to think. Ureth is many good things, but she doesn't like surprises. Never knew a Crone that did. You're a threat to her plans."

"How? I know that I'll probably never even get home again. And I'm OK with that, as long as Jake can. I only care what happens to him. As long as he picks that magic fruit, and somehow gets it home to save Mary, everyone gets what they want most."

"Well, that's exactly why you threaten her, child. You want to protect Jake."

"Of course I do! I'm his father! Ureth cares about Jake herself, I can see it in the way she talks to him."

The Fruit Of The Dendragon Tree

The centaur slowed his pace a little, and my horse did also, not wanting the ear-scratching to stop.

"You don't know, then?" asked Keffyldyn.

"Know what?" I sounded angry, as men do when they are suddenly afraid.

"Do you know what'll happen when Jake plucks the fruit?"

"Yes, he said that when he plucks the fruit this dragon underground the castle will be freed. He'll escape his prison, and destroy it in the process, and with it the power of the Duke. That's the legend anyway."

Keffyldyn continued to walk alongside, but his face was still. Only his eyes moved, as they kept on mine. "Aye, that's true enough, I suppose. But that's not all, lad, not by a long shot. Tell me, what do you think will happen when a dragon that's been imprisoned for a thousand years is suddenly free, and encounters the descendants of the very folk that imprisoned him?"

"Jake said that Ureth believes that in his gratitude for his release the dragon will kill the vampires and werewolves."

"Well, she could be right about that," mused Keffyldyn. "The Dancer knows the dragons hated the Undead. But I doubt he'll stop there, child. I doubt that very much. Kildraig may grant Ureth that one favor, and I shudder to think how that bargain was achieved. But he'll go his own way on all else; you mark my words. Anyone standing outside the castle when that dragon is released will be lucky to get away with their lives, very lucky indeed."

"You believe in this dragon then? This Kildraig?"

"Believe in him, David? Believe in him? I should say I believe in him! I've met him! I helped put him underground, fractious worm that he was! Still is, no doubt. I bet his temper hasn't improved with nowt but slugs to eat for the last millennium!"

"Met him?" I said, disbelief stretching my tone. "But that would mean you're more than a thousand years old!"

"Well, by the Dancer, you addle-headed foal! Of course I am! Closer to three, if you really want to know. I've known most of the elves riding with us since they were imps! Coblyn's a baby, at five hundred years, but most of the rest of them are a respectable age. There's nothing overly special about living a long time, as I'm sure you humans will discover if you ever get the hang of it. Though you'll probably muck it up, like everything else you touch."

I was reeling. Three thousand years! In our world, Keffyldyn would have witnessed nearly all of recorded history. He could have met Caesar, and Christ. He could have met the Buddha. I shook my head. No wonder he called me "child".

"No David," he went on in a gentler tone. "The history of centaurs and elves, though fascinating, isn't relevant to you at this point. And even though Kildraig will be a royal pain in the arse if he gets loose, Ureth's probably right in thinking that we'd be better off worrying about one dragon than a horde of vampires and wolf-creatures running amok. And you threaten to upset the whole precarious apple cart."

"But how do I do that?" I asked again. "I totally want to help Jake get to that tree and pick its fruit. I don't know how we're going to fight our way through all the Duke's soldiers to get him there, but I've seen enough to know that if anyone can do it, we can."

"Oh, I know, child," replied Keffyldyn. "Nobody questions your courage, nobody at all. And if it were just a question of fighting through to the tree, I'm sure we could figure out a way to do that. But that's the piece you don't know about, the piece where Ureth can't count on your help, and maybe not even on Jake's either, now that he's proven himself to be such a bonny fighter-"

"What are you talking about?" I snapped. It's not typically a good idea to be rude to a centaur, but Keffyldyn didn't seem to mind. "How is he going to pick the fruit, if we don't get to the tree?"

"He has to approach the branches from the roots, David. He has to meet the dragon face to face. He has to go through water to meet the fire. It's all in the prophecy." Keffyldyn looked into my face, his emerald eyes full of ageless compassion. We'd stopped walking, and the column was passing us by. "For all Kildraig wants to be free, he won't let just anyone pick his fruit. He can't allow that. If someone NOT the true Pendraig were

The Fruit Of The Dendragon Tree

to harvest the tree, the dragon would be trapped below ground forever. That wouldn't do him much good, would it? The dragon has to consent to his rescuer. The Pendraig has to meet him face to face."

"I see," I said, very calmly, though my mind was in a whirl. "Well, Ureth is right to think I might try and put a stop to that. She's crazy! Why does she think she can put Jake in that kind of danger? Who does she think she is?" Strange as it may seem, as long as I was by his side I had no worries for Jake if it came to combat. A sword was a blur in his hand, and I was now savagery personified. I doubted anything could touch us. But for him to face a dragon underground, alone, that was something else. That was a battle where a sword was useless. "I won't allow it!" I said to Keffyldyn, beginning to turn my horse, planning to have it out with Ureth there and then. But Keffyldyn took hold of the bridle with his hand, and of my eyes with his own.

"Aye, David. She told me you would say that. Which is no doubt why she's wanted to keep you in the dark as long as possible. And you may well have a few choice words with her about that. But that's not all that's got her upset."

"Why should I care about her being upset?"

"Ah, don't be too hard on Ureth, child. There are not many I'd like beside me in a tight spot more than her, let me tell you. She'll be a fierce friend to you one day, I imagine, if you both live long enough. No, you see, she's always believed the Pendraig would also be the future king of Tiramonde, uniting this kingdom with the desert, ending war, and ushering in some sort of golden age among humans, though as I said before, knowing humans as I do you'd find some way to foul up paradise itself. But now she's not as sure of her ground as she used to be." He saw my glance, and hurried on. "It's the prophecy, lad. If Jake meets the Dragon, passes muster and picks the fruit, he can fulfill his heart's desire: he can go back home to his mother, your wife, and save her life. Our world is also saved, disregarding the minor problem of one very angry dragon. But if he doesn't, nothing comes true, Kildraig stays underground, the Undead rule, and all of you probably die. Quite a different outcome, understand?"

Keffyldyn looked at me, and I knew what Ureth had been worried about. "She's worried I might try to stop him, isn't she, when I see how dangerous it'll be for him? And I'm her future king, which limits what she can do to stop me getting my way."

"Aye, child. Ureth was so sure of herself before, sure enough to challenge everyone she knew, break every rule she lived by. But now, you carry the sword she was sure was your son's. She was wrong about that, and doesn't know what else she might be wrong about."

I fingered Ysgith's hilt, and was silent.

Eventually, Marfang came in sight. Even from a great distance, I could see why men thought the place was impregnable. The castle sat upon its throne of rock, massive and tall, dividing the river that parted at its feet. A wind blew from the west, bringing up clouds and the threat of more rain, and flags fluttered on the battlements, green and black and brave in the gray light. I could see why the ruler of such a place could start getting delusions of grandeur. We kept on, the castle growing larger with every step, and the men fell silent as we approached. The Undead army followed us, no longer trying to hide themselves, and our scouts came back to report at least five thousand werewolves shadowed our rear and right flank. A few didn't come back at all, and we heard their death screams across the cultivated southern veldt. After this, Endil kept his force consolidated. We knew what was out there.

The countryside was empty. With the wisdom of peasants, the smallholders who farmed the duchy had smelled trouble brewing, and most of them had retreated farther south, to evade the tides that shaped their little world, hoping to return once the danger was over. But a few came to meet us, carrying pitchforks and scythes, understanding that if our small force was defeated then their danger would never be over. We rode through the town opposite the fortress. This too appeared deserted. I knew that Scarth's house was here, but he did not speak of it. Hoof beats clattered on cobblestones as we approached the river more closely. We descended to a small harbor on the edge of town, where a series of four stone quays jutted out from the riverbank and into the western side of the forked river, serving as a partial breakwater. A few barges sat untended at their berths, and one or two smaller boats bobbed slightly in the gentled current. I noticed some rapids downstream. Endil halted his force on the riverbank, and we looked across the water to Marfang, grim and contemptuously unassailable in the fading light.

Three old women emerged from one of the small boats, throwing off the skins under which they had been hiding. Ureth dismounted with a small cry, and ran ahead to embrace the women. They were too far away for us to hear their speech, but presently the four of them walked back to where we stood, the horses uneasy due to the unsettled weather, or perhaps the scent of werewolf on the wind from the empty town at our backs. The skin on the back of my neck tingled.

"It is as I feared, Lord," said Ureth to Endil, her face ashen with grief. "Coegun has overrun the Coven. The Crones are no more."

I looked at the three women. Despite the wrinkles on their faces, I could tell that two of them were still young. The other was older. Her hands trembled, and the younger two had to help her along as they walked. Endil spoke to them. They shrank back from him at first, but a gentle murmur from Ureth seemed to calm them, and they answered his questions readily enough. I gathered the two young ones had been with Ureth the night she called Jake from our world, and my interest in them quickened at this, but it soon became apparent that their magic hadn't helped them in the struggle against the Duke's men.

"Why didn't the Sisters defend you?" asked Endil, and I had learned enough by then to know he was speaking of the three older Crones, who thought Ureth was insubordinate.

"We couldn't," said the old woman, in a trembling voice. "At first we didn't because of the law. Then, when we saw he meant us murder, we tried, but we could do nothing. He was too much for us."

Endil looked a question at Ureth, and she tilted her head at the old lady. "Lord, this is Sister Hane, of whom you have heard me speak." She turned to Hane, and touched her gently on the shoulder. "Do you mean the Duke, Sister, that Coegun was too much for you?"

The old lady nodded. "He led the charge himself. Somehow he has come to know our secret ways in and around the castle, because he posted men at all of them. When I sent the young ones to flee, they died by the sword. When he came at us in the tower, and we tried to fight him, we died too, by sword and by fire. Bolt after bolt of Dragonfire we threw at him, but always he reflected it back on us, and we died burning. We died screaming. Myself he merely threw against the wall with a buffet of air that would have felled a horse. I was winded and could not move. Elbeth and Rathe tried to help me, they stood in front of me to protect me, but he just laughed, and used their fire against them. They screamed, Ureth, they screamed, the Dancer help me, I will never forget how they screamed as they burned." Tears were running down the old woman's face, and Ureth took her in an embrace and let her sob for a time. The men stood about awkwardly, and in my mind I could see the horror of the last moments of the Crones, as they burned or bled in their cloisters of stone.

"I can't believe no one tried to help you! We have pledged to honor the Crones since time out of mind!" cried Scarth, "I still know some of the men in that garrison; there are some good men there."

Hane just shook her head. "How many times have we seen good men follow bad leaders? And some did try to save us from butchery, but Coegun's followers cut them down. He exploits men's fear, to make them malleable, and he rewards their greed when they do what he wants. He has promised them land and gold if they serve him, and death if they do not. And he keeps both promises."

There was a pause. "Are you hurt, Sister?" asked Scarth, and I could tell the question pained him. "Did they…?"

"He didn't touch us," Hane said. I could have sworn there was a shadow of a smile around her lips. They were resilient, these Crones, no matter what else you said about them. "I'm sure we don't appeal to him, old and wrinkled as we seem. He let me live. He let these two live also, to attend me. And he sent me out to find you, saying that you drew near. I asked him how he knew, and he said the Waterstones had other uses than keeping the Undead at bay. He said to be careful that they did not find us first, so we hid on the boat. I guessed he must have moved them, the Stones I mean, and looked in one. The Undead have left Blutwald then?"

The Fruit Of The Dendragon Tree

Ureth nodded, somehow following the rambling thread of Hane's conversation. "They follow us. He wishes them to break us here, before the walls of his castle. Then he plans to march with them across the river, and take Marlona. He would become king of Taumar, supported by the vampires and werewolves from whom the Stones and the Elves have so long kept us safe. Fool! Little does he know he would soon become their servant!"

"Perhaps," said Hane. "But his magic has grown deep, Ureth. He is very powerful." She looked glum for a moment, then brightened as a though came to her. "What about Jake?" she asked. "Is the Pendraig with you? Did he kill the vampire king?"

Ureth nodded. "Yes, Sister, the Pendraig is here. And yes, the vampire king is dead." But she looked at me directly for the first time in two days, and I knew, thanks to Keffyldyn, that there was much she wasn't saying. It's funny how you can sometimes speak the truth, and still mean something very different from what your audience hears.

Hane paid no attention to me. To her, I was just another armed man on horseback. But her eyes found Jake, sitting near me atop his own horse, and she spoke directly to him. Her voice was filled with sudden hope, arising from the ashes of despair, and Jake and I both knew that such a hope, if strong enough, can make a man travel between worlds. No doubt it did the men nearby good to hear her conviction, as they drew close to a battle in which they were hopelessly outnumbered. But her voice was weak, and fled downstream with the wind, and few heard her words. As a battle speech it was a failure, despite the passion that was written on her face. "Jake, you have a destiny here! Ureth was right; Coegun is the greatest evil that we face! She was right to bring you here to save our world! Remember your heart's desire! The Dendragon Tree has borne its fruit. Only you can pluck that fruit, and release the dragon. Only his power can save us now. Fight for the Pendraig, oh men of Taumar! Fight for him, and for our freedom!" Her voice rose to nearly a shriek as she struggled to be heard, and suddenly she stopped, panting, looking a little crazy with her white hair awry in the breeze, and her cheeks flushed. Nobody said anything, and someone's horse whinnied in the silence of anticlimax. I could see that Jake was embarrassed. It was a sad way for more than a thousand years of history to end.

The moment didn't last, however. A warning shout came up from the elves at the rear of our force, and we whirled around to face the danger. A few hundred werewolves poured along the streets that led to the harbor, and fell upon the elves guarding our rear. Whether by accident or design, I could see that our position gave us something of an advantage. Despite outnumbering us nearly seven to one, the wolves and vampires could not attack in full force. They had to come down the narrow streets to the harbor, thereby limiting the numbers they could throw against us at any one time. They faced elves who had been warriors for thousands of years, and their first assault receded like foam on a beach.

The logistics for survival rapidly became clear. Endil and Coblyn positioned their forces in the harbor square, with the greatest concentration of soldiers at the opening of the streets that led to the quays. There were five of these, arranged like spokes around half a wheel. Three came roughly from the west, or inside the town. One led in hard against the bank from the north, or upstream, and one from the south, or down. Four long warehouses stretched between each avenue. It was no place for cavalry. We dismounted, and picketed our horses close by the water, along the northernmost of the four piers that jutted into the river. The animals were shy of the swirling waters, but glad enough I think to be away from the enemy. Marfell was at our backs. We placed roughly a hundred soldiers at the entry of each of the roads, and about fifty in front of each warehouse, to guard against any infiltration through the buildings themselves. The rest of our force, about two hundred in all, remained in the square itself, ready to give aid to any sector that needed it. This area became Endil's command center, and Coblyn was there with him as leader of the elves. I too was there with Jake, and Rajindra, Scarth and Keffyldyn stayed near us. Naomi and the two young acolytes tended to Hane, while Ureth paced among us, unspeaking and grim.

The sky was overcast, though the threatened rain had not yet arrived. The night gathered round, and Endil ordered torches lit in the square. By their light we could see dark shapes harrying our lines, charging up in snarling fury, and falling back when the thrust of steel grew too intense for their liking. The elves, stewards of the forest, had taken over the front of our lines; their enmity for the fell creatures that attacked us was long and deep. Swords grew red with blood, and the corpses of the wolf-men piled higher, forming natural barricades across the openings of the roadways. One or two vampires lost their heads, and their death shrieks curdled our blood, as the smoke of their long-imprisoned souls finally departed their bodies. Our own casualties were light, and things seemed to be going better than we had hoped, or at least so it seemed to me.

But we had ignored the river. Or at least, we hadn't put enough men to watch it. It is said that the vampyrim could not cross water, and that the werewolf will shun it, so our eyes were turned to the battle in front, and not the river behind. But this was a bad assumption, as we learned that night to our cost. A large band of the wolf-men, several hundred strong, had exited the town upstream of the harbor. They braved the icy waters of Marfell, keeping close to the bank, and let the current carry them to the outthrust piers of the harbor. No doubt several of them drowned. In the end, it didn't matter. Enough of them remained. Pulling themselves out of the river, they ran along the piers almost unopposed and attacked us from the rear. At the same time, several loud explosions rocked the quay. The vampires had their own brand of witchcraft. They had brewed some devilry, and the warehouse roofs were on fire. Meanwhile, the werewolves had been busy inside the buildings. They had loosened the wall structures, and instead of coming out through the windows and doors, they simply pushed the walls facing the square down from the inside. These four walls fell among us almost simultaneously, bursting into flame as they hit the ground, werewolves, elves and men dying under the fallen, burning timbers, Hane and the two young Crones among them. More werewolves and vampires poured into the square from where they had gathered in the warehouses, and more followed from the avenues that now had too few warriors to defend them.

It was the chaos of battle: we were surrounded, and the wolf howled in my blood.

I began to thoroughly enjoy myself.

Chapter 20

*And they said to one another, Behold this dreamer cometh.
Come now therefore, and let us slay him, and cast him into some pit,
and we will say,
Some evil beast has devoured him…*

(Genesis; 37: 19-20)

"Come, Jake, we must leave." Ureth tugged at his sleeve. He withdrew his sword from a dying werewolf, and looked at her in disbelief.

"Are you crazy? I'm not leaving my Dad!"

They looked over to where David stood, near the front of the melee. Ysgith flashed in the firelight, and another vampire head rolled to the ground. Scarth stood on his right. To the left of these two, Endil, Coblyn and Keffyldyn were also hard at work. Jake and Ureth were some distance away, on one of the piers. They had raced there with Rajindra and Naomi, to help repel the werewolves attacking from the water. A large group of men and elves had gone with them, and they had cut swiftly through the first wave of assault. The rest of the attackers died as they tried to climb the piers. Their job done, the soldiers who had been with them had run back to the harbor square, to buttress the ranks that had been thinned by the assault on their rear. Jake shrugged Ureth's hand from his arm, and turned to rejoin the others. But Ureth caught hold of him

The Fruit Of The Dendragon Tree

again, and the steel in her grip surprised him. He stopped, and turned to look at her.

"We must leave," she said again. "It is time for you to do what you came here for. Your father is more than capable of handling himself."

Jake looked at the square. Ureth was right. There was a space around David and Scarth where the werewolves were afraid to go. Even the vampires were wary of them. Wherever the monsters threatened to overwhelm the defenders, there went Scarth and David, and the attackers fell back. But the enemy's plan had worked. The line that the elves and men had to defend was much broader, now that the Undead had access to the square through the buildings. Slowly, inexorably, the line of defense was shrinking, and the brave men and elves were being pushed by sheer weight of numbers ever closer to the water.

"It's over, Jake," said Ureth. "If you don't do what you came here to do, your father will die, the dragon will stay entombed, and those fell creatures will rule our world. You can stay and fight next to your father, and die, or you can come with me, and give all of us some last gleam of hope that we can undo what Coegun has started."

"I. Can't. Leave. My. Father!" Jake shouted. "Not again! He came all this way to get me!"

"Jake, your father came to get you, but he knows in his heart that he will never leave our world. Do you think he wants you to die next to him? Or do you think he would want you to live?"

"I know! But I can't leave him here to die alone, so far from home!"

But Ureth could see the hesitation in his eyes, and she pressed her advantage. "Do you remember the bargain you made before you first got here? That you didn't care who had to die? A lot of people have died already! And everyone on this wharf could be dead soon too! Are they really going to die for nothing, or are you finally going to think of something else besides your own pain?"

Jake recoiled as if he had been slapped. He took another long look at his father, fighting with a sword on a world far from home, fighting as if he had been born to it. Who knew? He probably had been. He looked back at Ureth. "Let go of me," he said to her, his voice flat with anger, and she did so, knowing she had won, hating herself for the hard choices she always seemed to be bringing him.

And then the Sight descended upon her, unbidden. "The Pendraig must release the Dragon, or the King will not live to be crowned…" she began, in the monotone of Vision. But Jake simply pushed past her, breaking the trance.

"Yeah, yeah, whatever," he said, and stalked over to where Naomi and Rajindra stood waiting on the pier. "Let's go," he said, and Naomi hurried to where one of the boats was tied against the quay, on the downstream side.

Naomi untied the boat, and clambered into the bow as the others scrambled to get aboard. It was a much larger craft than the one in which they'd left Marfang. Jake and Rajindra each took a heavy oar, while Ureth grabbed the tiller. "You will have to row hard," she said. The current is strong here."

"Where are we going?" asked Rajindra.

"There," said Ureth, jerking her head towards the castle.

"Ah," said Rajindra. "We are jumping out of the cooking pot and into the fire, I think."

"Probably," said Jake. "Save your breath and row."

Despite the current, and the inexperience of the rowers, the crossing didn't take long. The din of battle on the western bank carried clearly over the noise of the rushing water, but Jake could not see what was happening. When he glanced behind him over his shoulder, Marfang remained dark and silent in the night.

"Do you think anyone in the castle can see us?" he asked.

"Good point," said Ureth. She made several circular gestures over her head with her right hand, then thrust her hand towards the bow. "There, now we'll just look like the river to anyone watching. Keep on your oar, Jake! It's hard enough doing magic and steering the boat, without you breaking rhythm as well!"

"If you were any sort of witch, you'd just fly us over," muttered Jake. Rajindra chuckled softly. Ureth glared at him, but if she'd heard she gave no other sign.

The Fruit Of The Dendragon Tree

They beached upstream of the castle, at the middle portion of the island where trees came close to the water. The boat clunked against the small rocks that formed the shoreline, and Jake got out and helped Naomi to dry land. She seemed to be in pain, and gasped when he pulled her close to him to stop her from stumbling. His hand felt something warm, and came away from her side wet with something.

"Ureth!" he whispered, "I think Naomi's hurt!"

Ureth came up swiftly, and felt for the wound. "It's not deep," she said in a low voice. "Naomi, did you see what struck you?"

The girl nodded. "It was a werewolf," she said, as Rajindra gave a low hiss. "But he didn't bite me! He just got a claw on me as I gave him a strangulation curse. I'm all right, really, it's just a scratch. There is no shadow in my blood, I swear it."

Ureth gave Naomi a searching glance, then nodded as if coming to a decision. "Rajindra, you stay here with Naomi and guard the boat. We might need it later. If I don't come back in an hour, leave without me. You know where to go." The Sacour nodded. "Jake, you come with me." She took him by the arm, and began to lead him away. They were soon in the thick of the orchard, Rajindra, Naomi and the boat already lost to view. The noise of battle on the far bank was very faint. Jake wondered if his father was still alive. He hadn't even been able to say goodbye. *That's twice*, he thought.

"Where are we going?" he asked, as Ureth led the way through the trees.

"Not we," said Ureth. "You. I can't go with you, Jake. Only you can enter the castle the way I will send you now."

"Why?" asked Jake.

"Because only you are the Pendraig," said Ureth. "Only you can meet the dragon."

The Dragon. Well, there it was. It was why he had come after all, wasn't it? He had taken the only chance to save his mother's life. And Ureth had taken the only chance to save her kingdom. She was right. A lot of people had died so that he could get this chance at beating death. He hoped his Dad would make it, hoped he could find his way back home too. But in his heart he knew that his father would never come home. The thought brought tears to Jake's eyes, and he dashed them away angrily as he followed Ureth through the woods. It was quieter under the trees; the noise of battle on the far bank was now just a whisper above the rustle of the river, chuckling to his left. The wind kissed the treetops, and every now and then a sliver of moonlight would lance through the boughs, as the clouds overhead grew taller and taller in the night, towering for a storm. Castle Marfang brooded to his right as they passed. Jake could see the occasional flicker of a torch on the battlements through the treetops, but Coegun held his troops in check, the very stones of his fortress constrained by waiting.

The apple blossoms that fluttered to the ground in the breeze of their passing were white as snow in the moonlight, and as silent. Their scent was sweet in the night air, and the reek and clamor of battle seemed very far away. Jake wished he could pause and enjoy the quiet, but Ureth pressed on, and the urgency of her will was like a rope, pulling him along behind her. He didn't yet understand that moments of peace were often like this: transient gleams of light among the shadows, effervescing like sea foam as one journeyed from one dark shore to another. Soon he began to get his bearings. Here was the track upon which they had raced, it seemed like years ago. Here was the bridge, that he had so narrowly won against the surprisingly fast witch whom he now followed. And here, at last, was where he realized he had known he would return all along, the dark, silent trees from which no light nor sound readily escaped: the glade of the Imperviata, gateway to the dragon's lair.

Ureth paused by the edge of the swift flowing spring. Jake remembered how the water bowed up from its source in the river, before delving deep underground, no one knew where. He came up beside her, panting slightly at the quick pace she had set. Ureth took his hand and crouched by the water, tugging him down with her, and he knelt beside her, his scabbard scraping against the bare earth. The air here was as close as he remembered it. Lightning flashed outside the glade, and thunder rumbled an answer, still far away. But under the Imperviata it remained as dark as a cave.

The Fruit Of The Dendragon Tree

"Jake, I need to tell you two things," said Ureth, and he waited in silence for her to begin. "First, despite the fact that your father restored the sword of stone to its previous glory, it is you who are the Pendraig. It is you who slew Nablut the vampire king, and I believe you have the courage to meet Kildraig face to face."

She was silent for a time, and though it was dark, Jake thought he caught the gleam of a tear on the witch's withered cheek. "And the second thing?" he asked, anxious to get things over with, wherever they would lead.

"Yes," answered Ureth, and her voice sounded husky in the close air of the glade. Crones didn't cry, did they? But it was too late to ask. "The second thing is, that despite the fact your father is supposed to become the future king of Tiramonde, and you are the Pendraig, remember that prophecy is always manifested by intention. We control nothing, but direct everything."

"What do you mean?" asked Jake, abrupt in his desire to finish.

She sighed gently in the darkness. "I mean, that whatever happens, remember you always have the power to choose."

Jake was suddenly afraid. "What do you see, Ureth? Tell me!" He wanted to shout, but the heavy air allowed no volume but its own. It took his words away and muffled them close; his impatience was swaddled and his anger was swallowed, and a slight shock of electricity tingled his scalp as lightning again flashed outside the still glade.

"I do not see everything, Jake," answered Ureth. "And I may have said too much. But take heart. Love has a way of completing unfinished business. And you and your father love each other even more than either of you know."

Jake knew it was useless to ask for more. *It doesn't really matter anyway*, he thought. He was here, where Ureth's gamble, and his own bargains with God, had put him. A mother lay dying, a dragon lay sleeping, and a father fought so that a son could save the one by waking the other. It was time.

"Tell me what to do," he said.

2.

We fought, and continued to die. There were just too many of them. It all became the same, after a while. The vampires hissed, and the werewolves snarled, swords lifted and thrust, we took a step backwards, and blood ran red upon the stones. A slip in the blood, and a wolf-creature rips out the throat of the man next to you. Avenge that death, and another feral monster lunges to fill the breach. Repeat this enough times, and lose nearly half your force, and retreat becomes automatic. King Endil, dreamer of peace, died somewhere in that time, and a howl of triumph went up from the Undead when his banner fell. They swarmed to the spot, pushing us away, and hacked him to pieces. We were too busy surviving to feel horrified.

I remember hoping that Ureth would use some of her famed Dragonfire to burn the werewolves. I looked around and instinctively knew she was gone, and Jake with her. I had come so far to find my son, but had lost him to the witch once more. I could imagine how difficult his choice had been, but I could not protect him anymore. We were at the foot of the three southward piers now, our force split accordingly. Roughly two hundred elves were with us in the middle, about a hundred men battled on the piers to either side. Coblyn, Scarth and Keffyldyn were all on the middle pier with me. I couldn't see Rajindra. Maybe he'd gone with Jake. I hoped so. He deserved better than to be here. The fighting grew a bit easier again, as the front narrowed to the widths of the three piers. The wolf-men pressed their attack, but we held, aided by our desperation. Some of them jumped in the river and swam, attempting to climb up the pilings and engage us from the water once more. But we were ready for them this time, and that gambit came to nothing.

There was a sudden tacit pause in the action. We panted on the piers, and held our swords at the ready, daring the Undead to come and get us. They stayed on the shore, none willing to be the first to taste our steel, and jeered at us to fight them. "Come my lovelies!" they howled. "It won't hurt for long! We'll only bite enough to change you, then you can live forever, wild and free!" There was more besides, none of it tempting, except perhaps to me, who could feel my blood keening to their call. But there's much more to life than living forever, and it was easy enough to stay with my friends.

Then the Undead turned to the horses. We had left them on the northern pier, and thought them safe. But now their terrified whinnies rent the night air, as the werewolves found easier meat than men with swords. The wolf men love horse, and our poor beasts were like us: trapped between the enemy and the river. Many chose the river, and were carried downstream, to drown in the rapids or swim ashore, I never knew. Many tried to fight their way out, brave hearts undaunted by the terror on land, and all of these died screaming. Some died on the pier, eyes wide with terror, as the wolf creatures swarmed them. The tears were wet upon my face as I witnessed this horror, and I remembered how much my Mary loved horses. There are those who doubt the existence of evil. But they have not felt the shadow song dancing in their blood, nor seen the horrors of that night. Indeed, the sight of those noble beasts dying was too much for some of the men, who rushed ashore to try and help the animals, and died for their pains. Only a token force of the enemy remained at the shoreward end of our three piers, just enough to keep us honest, and on our narrow causeways. But Scarth was not prepared to have us sit there, and die piecemeal. The king was dead, but Taumar's greatest warrior still lived, and Endil's soldiers were happy to follow him

"To the boats!" he commanded, and we obeyed, numb with fatigue, and grief, and terror. We on the middle pier filled two of the large barges, the men on the outside piers took up one apiece, and four vessels in all shoved off from the wharf and into Marfell's swift current. The wolf-men jeered, and howled their scorn, but they let us go. The ones who had been guarding us ran off to get their share of horseflesh.

"To the island, my friends, to Marfang!" Scarth's voice rang clear and true across the water, and my heart lifted, because I knew that Jake must be on the island; perhaps I would find him there. The elves in the ship's belly pulled on their oars, and our barge thrust its way across the river, fighting to make landfall before the current pushed it irrevocably below the island.

Lightning flashed in the west, and thunder rolled in the sky. I looked around. The barge downstream of us was not aiming high enough to make the island. It was clear the men upon it had had enough of the fight, and who could blame them, given the horrors we had seen? It was not mortal men whom we faced, after all. The vessel pointed her bow downstream, and ventured to escape by daring the rapids. But a sudden, angry buzzing filled the air, and bolts of flame arced into the sky, raining down upon the fleeing craft. Forty arrows made their target, and she caught well, blazing in the night. I looked to the west, and saw a cluster of grim vampire bowmen, setting their arrows alight by some art I could not discern, and launching them at the helpless barge. Men were jumping overboard, many in flames. These drowned very quickly in the icy, swift-flowing rapids. Others were slightly more fortunate, at first. They were stronger swimmers, and they bobbed up, trusting to their ability to fight the current. But the vampire bowmen would not even let these go in peace. Flight after flight of fire arrows flew into the water around these men, some of them finding targets outright, others hitting the water. By now I was certain that magic was in play, for the very water ignited, as if the arrows cast a spreading taint of burning oil, and men caught fire as they swam, and when they submerged to try and douse the flames, they burned all the brighter, in cocoons of flame that glowed under the waves until the life force of those it burned was extinguished.

"Row!" bellowed Scarth, and our oarsmen needed no further urging. The two barges upstream stayed with us. They could see what was happening to the other boat, and pulled hard to avoid a similar fate. But the vampires didn't fire upon us, and I wondered at this, wondered in fact why they hadn't sent any arrows among us while we had been fighting on land. And then I knew. We were going where they wanted us to go. I looked at Keffyldyn, and I could see that he knew it too. Marfang had always been where our steps would lead us; it was where our enemy's purpose, and our own, would have us arrive. So be it. I looked to the castle. It towered over us as we approached, blacker than the black night, dark and forbidding and impregnable. I wondered vaguely if Coegun would come out to fight us, or whether he would simply let us starve in some kind of pitiful reverse siege, where the ridiculously puny force of his attackers would eventually run out of provisions. But I didn't think so. One way or another, I felt, the thing would be settled soon.

We landed about halfway along the island, three barges abreast, running aground on the rocky shore. We jumped out and regrouped quickly, but there was no pursuit from the river, and the castle remained silent and watchful. Suddenly, Rajindra was among us, the Sacour pushing through the press to get to where I stood with Scarth. The three of us laughed, and embraced like brothers, and laughed again. Even Coblyn smiled, his first since his brother had died.

"I thought I asked you to stay with the boat," came a voice, and suddenly there was Ureth, coming out of nowhere, it seemed. But she too was smiling, with real pleasure at seeing us all alive, though her glance when it rested on me was thoughtful, and she would not meet my eyes.

"So you did, lady," said Rajindra al-Qabir. "But I thought I should come and see my friends. The way things had been going, I wasn't sure I would get another chance."

"It was a close thing," agreed Scarth, and our smiles faded once more in memory of just how close it had been. "Our king is dead. But we are here!" he called, and the men around us growled in acknowledgement. "We still live!" he cried, and the growl came once more. The elves stayed silent. They are not a race that requires pep talks. Lightning flashed again, much closer now, thunder following almost immediately. The first drops of rain began to spatter around us.

"Well, what now, my friend?" asked Keffyldyn, looking at Scarth. "I don't fancy standing here in the rain. I can't do a thing with my tail once it gets wet."

But Ureth answered for her father. "Jake is inside, or will be soon if all has gone well. He will need a diversion. We can enter the castle and create one. A few of us can open the gates to let the rest of us in."

"Well lass, that sounds like a grand plan," said Keffyldyn. "Should we ask Coegun for a cuppa tea while we're here?"

"Love you as I do, this is no time for your banter, Keffyldyn," said Ureth. "Listen to me, Father! I deliberately left open the door that we used to leave the castle. A few of us can enter that way. Once inside, we can make our way along the ground level passage that ends within the gatehouse. The wall there swings open. Coegun has it lightly guarded, and once inside we can open the gate for the others."

Keffyldyn, for once, was silent. Scarth and Coblyn looked at each other. They nodded, as if coming to an agreement. The wind was picking up, and the rain was spattering harder. Soon it would be a true downpour. "The Dancer guide our steps!" said Scarth, and embraced his daughter.

"What about me?" asked Naomi. "My brother is dead and the child I carry is heir to the throne of Taumar." She looked hard at me as she said this, but it wasn't the time to argue the finer points of succession.

"I hadn't forgotten," said Ureth dryly. "Rajindra will wait with you in the apple orchard until I come for you. She looked at the Sacour, who bowed slightly in agreement. "Whatever happens, stay among the trees until I return. Don't forget what happened to Sathryn."

"Yes, Mother," said Naomi, and it took me a second to realize she meant the term literally.

Then the Sacour, and the woman who bore my grandchild disappeared into the night. All my family was now gone from me, in all the worlds I knew. But I was sufficient to my own purpose, and I was content.

"Let's go," I said to Coblyn, and he nodded again.

"About bloody time and all," muttered Keffyldyn, but if anyone heard but me, they gave no sign.

We arrived at the magic postern door with no trouble. The rain muffled the sound of our approach, and Scarth and Keffyldyn dispatched the two guards outside before they could raise any alarm. Thirty of us entered the castle with Scarth, and he told the rest to make their way to the gate, and wait for it to open. "If we do not let you in within an hour," he said, "then we have died in our attempt, and I release you from any oath you have sworn to keep faith in this struggle. Make way to rescue us, or make your escape, it will be all the same to us by then."

Coblyn nodded. "We'll be there. Ureth will not lead you astray."

"Aye," said Keffyldyn to me softly, with a swish of his tail in the dark. "Ureth will be proved right, as usual. That's what I'm most afraid of."

But we spoke no more. Lightning flashed once and thunder crashed above us immediately. The heavens opened. I went inside with Scarth's group, glad to be out of the rain. So much for heroism. There were four elves with us, the rest were men. Despite his remarks about his tail getting wet, Keffyldyn stayed outside with Coblyn's group. It was almost pitch black inside the castle walls, and I wondered how we would find our way. I closed my eyes, to find out what I could sense without sight. The wild wolf ran in my blood. In the darkness, a brief vision flashed before my eyes. I saw myself fighting a man near a large tree, enclosed by a pond. I saw my son standing by the tree. Keffyldyn was shouting something at him, but I was too busy to notice what he said. The vision faded as quickly as it had come, but I felt strangely lighter. I was suddenly sure I would see Jake again, and my friends, and my heart lifted. I opened my eyes, and a faint silver light glowed about us. Someone moved, and then I understood. It was the starlight of the elves, which they carry in their hair, and which is always their light in the darkest of places. And they shared their light with us, in the darkness of Marfang castle.

The passage split just inside the door, one path going up a ramp, and it occurred to me that Jake had escaped the castle by this very route. But we took the level path that hugged the inner face of the castle wall, and made good time even in the dark. As far as I could tell, the corridor went straight for a while, then turned sharply to the left. Very soon, we came up against a wall, and the passage ended in front of this in an alcove large enough for five or six men to stand abreast. In the faint light, I could see Scarth pressing against the wall. It gave slightly, with a soft grinding sound of stone on stone.

"Get ready, men," he said, and the hoarse echo of his command ran around the walls of the alcove. Those few who had sheathed their swords now drew them again, and the whisper of undressing steel echoed with us also. I looked around. We were ready. Scarth pushed again on the wall. It gave easily, sliding open upon a central pivot that made two aisles out of our secret tunnel. We streamed along both sides of the open door and found ourselves in a storeroom. Burlap sacks were piled against one wall. Spears and swords lined another, arranged neatly in racks, looking well-oiled, and ready for use. There was a faint smell of sawdust, and something else, some sweet odor that I couldn't identify. A stone staircase in the far corner led up to a massive wooden door.

Ureth looked around, and upwards. "We're in the lower level of the gatehouse, if I'm right in my reckoning. That door should lead us into the archway right behind the castle gates. Let's hope we are able to swiftly open them to our friends outside." She vaulted up the stairs, closely followed by Scarth, and a pair of elves.

The rest of us lined the stairs in twos and threes, waiting for the door to open. I was just behind Scarth and the two elves, neither of whom I knew. A large brass doorknob was set in the door, and this turned easily under Scarth's touch. Fresh air gusted into the musty storeroom as he opened it slightly. Thunder boomed again, and I heard the hiss of rain upon stone as the storm outside continued unabated. Scarth opened the door wider, and the wind thrust down the stairs as it eddied under the gateway. As we moved forward, lightning flashed again, and a sound like a giant hand ripping the sky filled our ears. I looked past Scarth and the two elves in front of me. A man had turned to see us exiting the storeroom, and Scarth stopped his cry of alarm with a sword in his throat. A few other guards had congregated under the gateway, no doubt to escape the rain, but we were pouring out of the storeroom now, and these men also died, some before they had even lifted their swords.

"Open the gates!" called Scarth. There was no need for quiet, the storm raged about us. Sheets of water pelted the inner courtyard; I

The Fruit Of The Dendragon Tree

doubt we could have been seen from there even if someone had been looking. Soon Coblyn, Keffyldyn, and the rest were pouring in from the wet night outside. There were about three hundred of us left now, of the nine hundred that had first battled on the veldt. Nearly six hundred had died since then, not counting the horses. There was just room enough for us all under the vast archway that lay above the gates of Marfang, and we huddled there out of the storm as if taking a collective breath before our final strike. Keffyldyn had fought his way toward the front, and was pressed close against me. He smelled like a wet horse, and I told him so.

"What did you expect, child? It's not a fit night for man or beast, and I'm one of each, so I know."

At that moment, the rain stopped as if someone had turned off a tap. Thunder rolled, but was already retreating. The clouds raced overhead as if late for an appointment, and pale light grayed Marfang's inner court. But this was not the presence of noble elves, lighting the way to our final battle. It was the dawn.

Chapter 21

...the soul of man is immortal, and sometimes it comes to an end –which is what they call death- and sometimes it is born again, but it is never destroyed;

(The Dialogues of Plato: Meno)

The water was cold at first, but as the current drew him swiftly downwards it grew warmer. Jake had relinquished his sword, and was naked except for the thin cotton undergarment he had worn since his escape from Marfang. Now he was trying to get back into the castle, or at least under it. He had undressed and given Ureth his clothes and his sword. If either of them felt self-conscious at his near nakedness, neither of them had mentioned it.

"I'll be underwater," he said. "Clothes will only slow me down. And if I do meet a dragon, I'm not sure what I can do with a sword, anyway."

"I dare say you'd know best about the clothes," she had muttered. "But are you sure you don't want the sword?"

"I don't need it," he'd said. "If it comes to me fighting this Kildraig, then we've all lost anyway."

So she'd taken the sword from him also, and bidden him farewell. He'd jumped in the pool, and only had time to snatch a deep breath, before the strong current had borne him under its surface. Down and down he went, past fronds that brushed against him in the blackness, rushing downward beneath the roots of the Imperviata. The pool narrowed to a tunnel, and the tunnel bored downwards also, and still down into the depths of the earth he surged, without exertion, and strangely without fear. All of his life thus far seemed to have led to this: to meeting himself in a dark place, waiting for the light to find him.

He expelled a little air from his lungs, and felt rather than saw the bubbles race past his cheeks in the speed of his descent. His ears popped, but there was no pain, and still he dove. He brushed against nothing now, his way was smooth, and his only worry was if he would be able to hold his breath long enough to get to where he was going. The current carried him down, warm as bathwater now, and it seemed almost as if he could see. He raised his head to peer forward. Yes, there was a whiteness ahead, like foam, almost as if…

He burst into air, in the midst of a cataract, tumbling through space in the dark. Over he rolled in a somersault, completely disoriented, still falling. Somehow, he caught a breath and aligned himself with the water once more, and when he hit the deep pool into which the waterfall poured, he was only slightly winded, and managed not to swallow any water. Still, he was tumbled underneath the cascade for a few seconds, roiled in the underground pool as Marfell poured in what she would share from above, until he could swim out from underneath, coughing and retching as some water finally found its way into his windpipe. He surfaced, and was surprised to find he could see: that is, he could see the white foam of the cataract pouring into the underground pool, and he could see the edges of the pool, starkly outlined above him as he swam. A dull, reddish gold light came from above, and there was a strong smell of sulfur, like that of an underground hot spring. There was another odor too, but he couldn't place it. It was brighter on the side of the pool farthest from the waterfall, and he swam towards that side with the easy strokes of the excellent swimmer that he was.

When he got to the edge, he was surprised to find it was very smooth stone, almost slippery, but it was dry enough on the flat surface a foot or so above the water, and he climbed out without much difficulty. The rock under his feet was very smooth, which he had not expected. He lifted his eyes, and looked forward. The glow was brighter now, and he could clearly see he was in a vast underground cavern. It spread to either side, black beyond the reach of the golden-red light that spread above him. He looked up, and before him was a hill, smooth as glass, fretted by what looked like long ribs of rock. The smell of sulfur was stronger here. The glow was pulsating from atop the hill, but it seemed to be in some sort of mist, and behind it was only blackness.

It was warm in the underground cave, despite his standing there soaking wet. But he shivered once, for he knew he was not alone. A dry chuckle rattled from the hilltop, and the hill of glass shuddered in the undulating light.

"So Hatchling, you have come at last." The voice came out of the blackness above him, large, sibilant and deadly. The glass hill moved again, and what he had thought were rocky ribs fanned away from each other, then closer again, as the dragon flexed his wing. Jake somehow knew in a flash that the other odor he'd noticed was the stench of captive snake. He felt terror clutch at the pit of his stomach, but found he could not move. Where was there to go, anyway?

"Where are you? I can't see you!" Somehow he had found his voice, and if it was a touch squeaky in the darkness, he didn't think anyone would blame him.

"But I can see you, and the sight displeases me," replied the voice. "This is what they have sent to me, after all this time: a mewling boy, unarmed, with not even eyes to see what awaits him in the dark? No wonder they are desperate, if you are all they can manage to scrape up to fulfill their most powerful legend. Where is your sword, boy?"

"A sword wouldn't have done me much good underwater, now would it?" Jake was suddenly angry. He sensed it was foolish to anger a dragon in his lair, but he was past caring. There had been so much blood already spilled. Ureth was right. A lot of other people had paid for his dream of saving his mother. "If you don't like it, feel free to fry me!"

There was silence for a beat, then a low hissing laugh came from the blackness. "I like your spirit, Hatchling." Something moved behind the pulsating light atop the hill of the dragon's wing, and Jake saw two huge yellow eyes staring at him from behind the mist, which was really smoke

The Fruit Of The Dendragon Tree

trailing from the Dragon's nostrils. The light was coming from the eyes, and the small fires that emanated from his nose when he breathed. The head towered above Jake, easily thirty feet in the air, and Jake knew that he would be dead in a flash if the Dragon so decided.

"Tell me," the Dragon was speaking again. "What is your name?"

"My name is Jake Patel," answered Jake. "What's yours?"

The dragon had clearly decided to be amused, rather than annoyed, at Jake's impertinence. He laughed again, more loudly this time, and the sound was like an old steam locomotive, chuffing at a station. Perhaps he was just happy to have company, Jake thought. After all, he hadn't spoken to anyone for a thousand years. He must be lonely. And at the thought of such a long time underground, cut off from the world outside, in the dark, alone, for a thousand years, Jake felt a pang of sympathy for the huge creature. Whatever he had done, he had certainly paid a price for it.

"Well met, Jakepatel," said the dragon, running Jake's two names together. "But you will have guessed that I knew it already. And I strongly suspect you know my name too, for Ureth would not have sent you here without teaching you my legend. She is nothing if not thorough, that one, and a nice bit of woman flesh as I've enjoyed in a long time. But enough of that!" the dragon continued, as he saw Jake's look of puzzlement, "My name is Kildraig, short for Erchylldraig, which means "Terrible Dragon" in the old tongue. They were accurate but not very imaginative, the Old Ones, though they were clever enough to imprison me here, that I grant you."

"Well, pleased to meet you, I guess," said Jake. "You sound pretty philosophical about it."

"Are you?" said the Dragon. "Do I? You may be pleased to have met me, Jakepatel, once all is said and done, but then again, you may not. And if I sound philosophical, I've had a thousand years to do nothing but think. But tell me," Kildraig asked again. "Where is your sword? It is the token you are the Pendraig. Did you not kill the vampire king? Did you not grasp the werewolf's sword, and turn it back from stone? Are you not the future king of Tiramonde?"

Jake didn't know why Kildraig was obsessing about his sword, and for a moment he didn't know what to say. If he admitted he wasn't the future king, Kildraig might decide to roast him on the spot. But on the other hand, Ureth had convinced herself that he, Jake, was the Pendraig. Somehow, he in turn had to convince the dragon of the same thing.

"I killed Nablut the vampire king," he said. "And so I am the Pendraig. Ureth said it was so, and I guess she knows more about that stuff than I do."

"Truly, if you killed him, then you are he," replied Kildraig, and though it took Jake a moment to work out the pronouns he figured he was off to a good start. "But was there not also a sword of stone? Or did the witch tell you to leave it behind?" A great gout of flame shot out of his nostrils as he said these last words, and it grew uncomfortably hot in the dark cavern.

And so there it was, thought Jake. For some reason, Kildraig wanted that sword for himself, and he was getting pretty pissed off that Jake hadn't brought it. For a moment, he thought of running, but decided again there really was nowhere to go. Gulping slightly, he tried to ask a conciliatory question.

"May I ask, why do you wish the sword?"

"No you may not!" snarled Kildraig, openly angry now. "It is not for the likes of you to question the motives of those such as I! I am Kildraig the Black, and my purpose is my own! Thus it ever has been, and thus it ever will be!" The great voice thundered now, and Jake covered his ears. The huge wing, folded before him on the mouth of the cave, flapped once, and the resulting buffet of air toppled him backwards, almost into the pool. Fire and smoke cascaded upwards into the high vault of the underground dungeon, and Jake gagged at the resulting reek of sulfur. Some time passed, and the air cleared slightly. Kildraig's breathing slowly returned to normal, which is to say it reverted to hissing wisps of smoke with only a hint of flame, and Jake felt he had better say something.

"There was a sword," he said softly.

"What's that, Hatchling? Speak up, boy, I can't hear you!"

The Fruit Of The Dendragon Tree

"I said, he did have a sword, the werewolf king, I mean. And yes, it was made of stone. And Ureth did give it to me," he went on hurriedly, as an ominous glow began to build behind the mist of Dragon's breath. "She thought something would happen when I took the sword, but nothing did. And she eventually realized that though I was Pendraig, I was not the future king. So the sword was not mine to keep."

There was a silence. At least, it got as quiet as it can get when the largest fire-breathing dragon ever known is stuck in a cave with you. Jake could hear the small chugs of Kildraig's breath as he wrestled with the same thoughts Ureth had had. Jake realized that Kildraig had assumed the same thing as Ureth: that the Pendraig and the king of prophecy were one and the same person. And he arrived at the truth more quickly as well. "You killed Nablut, so it's true, you are the Pendraig," he said. As for the sword, it's your father's, isn't it? The sword turned back from stone when your father held it. He is the future king of which the legend speaks."

"Yes, it did," said Jake. "Turn back from stone, I mean. That's what happened when my Dad held it."

"So where is it now?" Kildraig's voice was silky, as if he had never been angry.

"The last time I saw it, he was killing werewolves and vampires with it," said Jake, recalling with a twinge that he had left his Dad fighting by the water's edge.

"I hope he leaves some for me," said Kildraig to Jake's surprise. Seeing his expression, Kildraig went on. "They are disgusting creatures, even more so than humans or elves. They are neither living nor dead, but they need the blood of one to delay the release of the other. I would gladly slay every last one of them, for my own sport, if ever I was free of this place."

"Isn't that what I'm supposed to do for you?" asked Jake.

Kildraig chuckled again. "It may be what you are supposed to DO, hatchling, but even I don't presume you do it for me! Even though my spirit flows through your sword hand, and none may touch you in battle, I expect no gratitude from you! What was your bargain? You don't care who has to die, so long as your mother can live? Tell me, have you learned yet to be careful what you wish for?"

Jake hung his head. "They might have died anyway," he said. "Coegun is evil. Ureth did know. And war would have come anyway."

"True, Hatchling, true," rumbled Kildraig. "Let others torture themselves with questions of what might have been. We can only deal with what is. Your mother still lives, though Death waits at her door like an impatient suitor."

"Mom's alive?" breathed Jake. "You're sure? I'm not too late, after all?"

"Of course I'm sure, Hatchling," and Jake caught a definite note of irritation in the Dragon's tone. "Do you take me for some wizened Crone, denying herself of all of life's pleasures, subjugating her body for the sake of some second-rate parlor tricks that I could gift to you in an afternoon?"

Jake didn't know what to say to this, so he waited for Kildraig to speak again.

"Yes, your mother lives, boy. She lives, and above us your father fights, as savagely as the werewolf whose blood runs in his veins. Ah, you didn't know that, I see. You should ask him about it when next you get a chance to talk. Ureth I do NOT see, she must be hiding somewhere. I'll find her, never fear. But enough talk. I have desired company, it's true, but I crave my freedom above all. The earth is my sanctuary, but the air is my delight, and fire is my weapon. Free me, Hatchling, it is time!"

"Only too glad to," said Jake, somewhat disbelieving things could be that easy. "Just tell me what to do."

Kildraig grunted in satisfaction, and turned his head towards the end of the cavern opposite the pool. "Walk that way, Hatchling," he commanded. "A little to the left! Yes, now straight ahead! Do you see the door, set into the stone?" The dragon breathed a little harder to give Jake some light.

Jake thought he did see something, and made towards it. As he drew close to the end of the cave, he spied a round wooden door, about the size of a sewer cover, set at roughly the height of his chest into a vault of stone that ran from the cavern floor, up a spine of rock, disappearing into the blackness above.

"Open it, Hatchling, it should come right away from the rock."

The Fruit Of The Dendragon Tree

Jake pulled on the round piece of wood. It wasn't heavy, and he lifted it easily from the rocky spine against which it sat. A rushing sound met his ears, and he saw water racing upwards in the opening the door had concealed, very little spilling out as it channeled towards the outer world, against the law of gravity.

"It's magic, Hatchling," chuckled the dragon. "And a bit of clever plumbing. The river flows under the Imperviata into the pool behind you. The water from the pool is forced upwards in this tunnel to the pool of the Dendragon Tree. That pool is drained in turn at the same rate back to the river. Everything returns to its source in the end."

Jake didn't reply. Gingerly, he placed his hand into the upward-flowing stream. The force of the current was very strong, and sprayed out from under his hand as if he had interrupted the flow of a giant hose. Which is probably exactly what he had done, he reflected, as he drew his hand away.

"So this will float me up?" he asked Kildraig.

The dragon chuckled again. "Well it won't float you *down*, Hatchling. But if you're asking if you'll float up safely, rather than get stuck inside that tube and drown, that I can't answer. No one has ever tried, you see. But I do know that if you don't try, then you're stuck down here with me. And it's been a thousand years since I've eaten man-flesh. Or anything else, for that matter."

Jake shuddered, seeing Kildraig's point. Some joke about being stuck between rock and a hard place tried to come out, but he wasn't Keffyldyn, and his words died unspoken. So here was his choice: to be eaten underground by a dragon for certain, or to try and regain the open air and possibly drown. It wasn't much of a choice when he put it to himself like that. It was in fact easy to be brave when one had run out of choices. Without looking back at Kildraig, he took a deep breath, and stuck his head inside the rushing plume of water, stretching his hands to the side in the torrent as he did so, and feeling the sides of the tunnel. He pushed out and down against rock, and simultaneously kicked hard against the floor, and was pulled upward, banging his knees against the doorframe for his trouble. He kicked again, against this, and was away.

Once he was completely in it, the current bore him swiftly upwards. Fearing again that he would run out of air, he scrabbled and kicked against the smooth rocky sides of his watery elevator. Up he went, his way clear, with no rocky outcroppings to snag or injure him. It was pitch dark at first, but soon he saw a pale light above him, and he could see bubbles in the water as he moved upwards. He was running out of air, he realized, and forced himself not to panic. His mother would die if he did not live; he had to make it, for her sake.

His lungs were on fire, demanding that he breathe, even though there was nothing to inhale but water, when all at once the light that fell around him spread away, and he knew he was in the Dendragon pool. Up he went, a few more feet, and his head broke the surface of the water. Gasping for breath, he saw with surprise that he was in daylight. He had been with Kildraig longer than he had thought. Heavy gray clouds streamed away overhead, and gray light bathed the gray stone ringing the pool of the Dendragon Tree. The surface glimmered like silver milk in the dawn light, here and there disturbed by droplets of water falling from overhanging branches of the tree, telling the tale of the recent storm. Jake had surfaced within the pool, and, still breathing heavily, he moved towards the bank of the small verdant island, upon which stood the tree, to catch his breath. He clutched at the grass, but it was slippery after the rain. He clutched at a chocolate brown root of the Dendragon Tree, and pulled himself up. He smelled earth, and rain, and the dawn breeze. He had met the dragon, and he was alive. There was a noise of battle close by, and Jake remembered he had no sword. Then he heard his father calling his name.

2.

The battle in the castle was worse in some ways than the one at the dockside. We had gained the inner courtyard with ease, but afterwards paid for this advance with many lives. As soon as the rain stopped, the arrows started, flight after flight from men atop the crenellated walls, shooting into the press of us, huddled in the gateway, from their high perches. Ureth burned a few, but could not get them all.

The Fruit Of The Dendragon Tree

We were fish in a barrel no matter what we did, but we might as well have died moving as standing still. "To the Tree!" cried Scarth, and we surged farther in, and the rain of arrows ceased as we moved deeper into the courtyard. I felt once more that we were being shepherded where Coegun wanted us to go, but it was either move, and perhaps die later, or stay still, and die for certain. One or two men broke ranks, and tried to run back to the safety of the gate-house, but a storm of arrows cut them down, and in any case, the Castleguard had poured out from the other side of the gateway from which we had entered, cutting off our retreat. The only way open was forward, and so that is where we went. It was not far, and without the arrows most of us that had gained the courtyard survived the journey across it, although it seemed to take forever. The space between my shoulder blades tingled, as if expecting an arrow's kiss, but we made the small pool safely, and ringed ourselves around it, as if to guard the tree that stood within. It was clearly an old tree, but its bark was a rich dark brown, and its leaves were a dazzling emerald color that glittered like jewels after the rain. But the most arresting thing about the tree were the large, spherical fruit that hung among the leaves, gleaming red and gold in the morning, and more fragrant than any apple tree back home. The sight of them made my mouth water, and I realized I was desperately thirsty.

"Don't drink the water!" criedUreth. "David! It's enchanted!" I ignored her. We were going to die anyway, and I wasn't worried about what the water could do to me. It was delicious, and I felt immediately refreshed, as if I could fight again all day.

None of the others followed my lead, thirsty though they must have been, and Scarth looked at me as if wondering if I'd grow three heads. Then his brow cleared as if he had read my mind. He smiled, "It may not matter soon in any case, Ureth. Drink if you wish, my brothers." But old superstitions die hard, especially among soldiers, and nobody followed my lead.

We were ready to face death now, but nothing happened for a time. We stood about the pool, still nearly three hundred strong, with our backs to the enchanted tree. The archers on the walls had their bows trained upon us, but did not shoot. We waited, and so did they, wondering what would happen next. The dawn grew brighter, and a hint of blue streaked the morning sky. A raven cawed from somewhere above, and as if that was a cue, the sound of trumpets rang out, harsh and clear. We heard the tramp of feet, and from every side the courtyard began to fill with Coegun's troops. They marched towards us, greaved with iron, carrying heavy wooden shields and long bright swords. Many had spears tipped with gleaming metal, but these stayed back and let the swordsmen approach us.

A tall man with a white horsetail arranged above the crest of his helmet walked next to a standard bearer who held aloft the flag of Marfang castle, green and black in the sunrise. A bodyguard of a hundred or so men followed close behind these two, and they walked up to where Scarth and Ureth stood with me, Coblyn and Keffyldyn.

"Well, Sir Merchant," said horsetail, and he made the term a sneer, "You seem to have a renewed craving for my hospitality. It seems you took a long walk to and fro, just to return here once more. If I had known you would miss me so much, I could have entertained you as I did your daughter."

I felt Scarth stiffen next to me, and I thought he would lunge straight at Coegun, for it was obviously he, but Keffyldyn put out a restraining arm and spoke instead. "No child, it's not your hospitality we're after. Though what we seek is here, it is not yours."

"What do you mean?" asked Coegun.

"Ah, so you're stupid as well as ugly, Duke Coegun. I should have guessed that. Would it help if I drew you a picture?" Several of our men were smiling now, Coblyn was grinning openly, and I could see Coegun pressing his lips together in fury.

"Why do your betters let you speak for them, horse-man?" growled the Duke. "After all, what is a centaur but the result of a soldier growing too fond of his mare?" But his insult was ineffectual, for the fear he used to rule Marfang held no power over Keffyldyn.

The centaur chuckled. "Oh child, you'll have to do better than that, I've been better insulted by a spavined mule! But to put you out of

The Fruit Of The Dendragon Tree

your misery of confusion, we've come to collect one of those lovely fruit behind me," and he jerked his head backwards in the direction of the Dendragon Tree.

"Well," said the Duke, recovering his composure, "Stupid as I am, even I know you aren't the Pendraig, Keffyldyn, so how do you propose to pick my fruit when the prophecy would forbid it?"

"No child, the Pendraig will pick the fruit, never worry your small brain about that. Yes, the Pendraig will pick that fruit soon, we're just here to see him do it."

"Well then," said Coegun, looking at me, "As I don't see the brat I suppose you must mean his father here, and so I suppose I'll be killing him. And you," he ended, looking back at the centaur.

"That's two 'supposes' in a row lad. Don't hurt yourself." Centaurs have a knack of getting in the last dig before a fight. Coegun gave a snort, and drew his sword. His bodyguard pressed forward, their swords ringing as they left their scabbards, and just that suddenly the fight was upon us.

They had honor, of a kind, the Duke and his men. Coegun could have ordered his archers to shoot. But I think he truly believed he was better than any warrior there, certainly better than Scarth, and this was his chance to prove it. In any event, the archers watched as the battle joined, and steel rang upon steel within the precincts of Marfang, the first time in her history that had happened. We fought against many superior numbers, such as we had faced upon the banks of Marfell, but this time there could be no escape. Surrounded by swords, it could only be a matter of time before Scarth's great strength failed, before my wolf song was silenced, before Coblyn stared at the sky with always-opened eyes, never again to glimpse the magical trees in the elven caves of Kyphala-dyn. Even Ureth and Keffyldyn could not escape, I knew, they would die here beside me guarding my body with their own, until even they too succumbed, and Coegun gained mastery of the kingdom, and then the world.

But I was wrong, of course, which is why you are reading my words, long though they may have been in coming to you. A murmur started among the men and elves ranged around the pool. The murmur built, and soon there was no mistaking what they were saying, even the Duke's men were saying it.

"The Pendraig!" they cried. "The Pendraig is come!" I wanted to turn, but the Duke had targeted me from the beginning, and was in front of me now, as vicious and skilled a fighter as I had yet encountered. I let him press me backwards, until I felt the low parapet against the backs of my legs. I jumped up, and swung my sword at Coegun's head. My blade bit into his helmet, just to the side of the horsetail crest, and he fell sideways, the helmet rolling in the dust. He lay still on the ground, a streak of blood along the top of his head. Someone kicked his hand, and his sword came free. The rank of men and elves closed in front of me, and reckless of other danger I turned to see my son. Jake stood under the Dendragon tree, pale but alive, and I thought my heart would burst with joy.

"Jake!" I called, for the pleasure of saying his name. He smiled at me, and though the moment was far too brief, all the love we shared flowed between us in that instant. It was as my vision had showed me, and it was enough.

"Pick the fruit, Jake!" I cried. "Pick the fruit and save your Mom!"

"Look out Dad!" he cried, and I whirled to face the battle once more. But I was too late. Coegun was somehow in front of me, grinning through the blood that streamed down his face. His sword was already entering me before I could bring mine up, and I felt it tear inside me, deep in my body, hurting far too many things for me to think I would survive. He made to withdraw his sword, but the wolf sang in my blood one last time, and I snarled and held his right hand fast with my left so that he could not pull out.

Scarth's sword finished him; flashing down it seemed from the very sky, taking Coegun's head from his body like weeds under a scythe. I saw the head topple backwards in the dust, I felt his hand grow weak, and the momentum of my pull sent me backwards over the parapet. I felt the silence as Coegun's men saw their leader fall. My own fall seemed to take forever, and I remember Keffyldyn screaming at Jake, "Pick the fruit, Jake!" and as I fell I smiled, for the quest was done.

The Fruit Of The Dendragon Tree

I splashed into the milky water, and it closed over my eyes. I felt the Duke's corpse fall next to me, and I let go of his lifeless hand. The pain was beginning now, and it was with an effort that I sat up in the water, shallow near the parapet. Blood streamed away from me, and this time I knew much of it was mine. I looked at my son, unarmed under the magic tree, wrestling with his choices. He wanted to come to me, I could tell. He ached to come to me, and put me back together. One of those fruits could do it; I could see that thought in his eyes, despite my desire that he made all the sacrifices worthwhile by carrying out his promise to save his mother.

Jake reached up and plucked a low-hanging orb from its branch. It came away easily in his hand, that much I saw, but then Keffyldyn was splashing next to me in the water, and he and Coblyn were gently lifting me up and out of the pool. They couldn't lay me down, as Coegun's sword had gone all the way through, and the point was sticking out my back. So they propped me against the outer wall of the parapet, and stayed with me until the end. I saw elves and men clustered around, all fighting forgotten. With Coegun gone, there was no will strong enough to keep good men in treachery, and any of the bad men knew they were outnumbered. I felt all this with clarity, as one does when one is dying, and the truth of it warmed my heart, though the rest of me was cold.

"Is Jake ok?" I whispered, and Keffyldyn nodded. I could see he was crying, and I thought my heart would break for the years of sadness I saw in his eyes. That was where the humor came from, I realized, his knowledge that life was sad, but had to be lived in any event.

"Aye, lad. Let's hope the fruit can do its work."

"Yes," I managed in a whisper. "Let's hope."

"Don't try to talk, David," said Ureth, hoping, as humans do, that she could disbelieve the evidence of her eyes, and her long experience as a healer. Coblyn held my hand, but didn't speak. Elves didn't say much at the best of times, and this wasn't one of those times.

"It's OK," I whispered, looking at my elf-friend, who had greeted me to his world with an arrow, and who would now see me out of it.

My sword Ysgith was still in my right hand, and I moved it ever so slightly so that it tapped against the blood-soaked earth.

"You guys are good friends," I said. I saw Keffyldyn nod, and felt his horse-sized tears fall upon my chest. I saw Scarth smile. I saw Coblyn, with the starlight in his hair, and I saw the sky above his head, blue in the morning. Then I saw Jake, bending over me, holding the fruit of the Dendragon tree. My eyes closed.

Chapter 22

That which is not, shall never be; that which is, shall never cease to be

(The Bhagavad Gita)

I saw nothing for a time, though time had ceased to have any meaning. I rose above the stars, and walked in a hall of light. Mary was there, and smiled at me. She was young, and happy, and bore no trace of any disease. I ached to go to her, but she shook her head slightly, still smiling, before some force more powerful than my desire tugged me back, to where existence is dense and material.

I woke to the sweet taste of the Dendragon fruit, luscious in my mouth, and Keffyldyn saying, "Easy does it child, don't choke him!"

My chin was wet with juice, and I opened my eyes to see my son's gazing at me. "Hi Dad," he said.

I felt wonderfully alive, and my body had no memory of any wound. They had removed the sword from me and I sat fully upright, pulling Jake's head to mine.

"Don't feel bad," he mumbled. "I think Mom would understand."

"She does," I whispered. "She does."

"You saw her?" Jake asked, and I nodded into his chest. He didn't ask me how, and I wondered if anything would ever seem strange to either of us again.

"Kildraig lied to me, then," he said finally, and helped me up.

"Well that's a huge surprise," said Keffyldyn. "Come, children, we must leave. He'll be here soon."

But it was too late. A loud splitting sound came from behind us, and I whipped my head around to see the pool steaming, and the island within it tilting at a crazy angle to one side. The Dendragon tree was being upended, its roots pulling the island with it as it toppled over, spilling fruit into the courtyard. Its topmost branches trapped a number of men and elves beneath it as it fell; they died as the top of the tree accelerated towards them, crushing them beneath its weight.

The ground was shuddering violently now, and looking up, I could see the walls of the castle waving like wheat in the wind. Cracks began to flow up and across the walls, and the sound of splitting stone echoed in my ears. The ground below the pool was sinking, forming a pit from which billowed steam and the stench of sulfur. The tree was being dragged down into the earth, the bodies of the men and elves it had crushed still tangled in its branches like obscene fruit. I saw Coblyn fall, and strike his head upon the low stone wall around the pool, and Keffyldyn stooped to help our friend.

"Get away from the Tree!" shouted Scarth, and those standing nearby needed no further bidding. They turned to flee, but it was difficult to walk, let alone run, on the shaking terrain. More and more of the ground was sinking; the tree had completely disappeared, and steam and smoke belched through the gaping hole in the earth. A few people fell, yelling in fear, and Coegun's head rolled into the pit.

"Follow me, children!" yelled Keffyldyn, and I looked to see the centaur carrying Coblyn in his arms. We staggered after him, and managed to reach the gate wall of the castle in a few seconds.

"Don't go too near the walls, Keffyldyn!" cried Ureth, and a big slab of masonry fell into the gateway arch as the castle walls began to collapse. Marfang was massively strong, but the stone was rigid, not built with earthquakes in mind. The walls began to crumble, falling in huge chunks into the courtyard, and without. Suddenly, the whole entry side of the keep gave a mighty groan, and fell outwards. Piles of dust billowed into the air, and men screamed in pain and fright. The earth was cracking, stone was breaking, and the castle died about us. "Through there!" called Scarth, and as the centaur hesitated, the big man pointed ahead. "Through there!" he cried again, meaning the gaping open space where the castle wall had been, and Keffyldyn lunged forward, his strong horse's body picking its way at a trot through the rubble-strewn remains of Marfang's courtyard.

There was a great roaring behind us. I looked back, and saw huge gouts of flame, spewing skyward from beneath the earth.

"The Dragon! The Dragon comes!" Men were calling, and many fell to their knees, as if in supplication for their sins, for which they knew they'd receive no forgiveness. Others followed us out as best they could, elves and men together, Scarth shouting encouragement. Keffyldyn had passed beyond the line of collapsed wall by now, and was negotiating the toppled stone lying about the greensward of Marfang Island. Some had rolled all the way into the orchards, some into the very river itself. The ground still quaked and shuddered, and the castle continued to disintegrate.

"To the boats!" called someone nearby, and others heard the man, and took up the cry.

"To the boats!" men echoed, and they ran, the remaining elves, leaderless, among them in the panic.

But Ureth touched Keffyldyn on the shoulder, and pointed to the apple orchard where we had left Rajindra and Naomi. "We have to find them!" she cried. "There's a boat there too!" So we headed that way, cutting across the stream of men and elves racing for the dubious safety of the barges.

2.

But I had recently returned from the dead, with the expanded awareness of the reborn, and so it was that for a brief time I could feel within my own body, and see with my eyes, how Kildraig the Black fulfilled the legend of the Pendraig, and emerged from his thousand-year confinement hungry for freedom, and for meat. The Dragon roared in triumph, and with rage, and his fire erupted from beneath the earth like a volcano. He thrust his head and shoulders through the opening above him, and turned his head to the left, where he saw a number of elves and humans running away. He breathed at them, a long, lazy exhalation that sent a river of flames snaking along the ground. The fire licked at the bodies of the fleeing, and took hold. They danced in the flames, and screamed as they danced, and then they died. A large piece of wall fell across the dragon's shoulders, and he bellowed in surprised fury. But then he laughed, as he saw the archer who had fallen from the wall trying to scrabble away, with two broken legs, from where he had landed. I shuddered as I felt the worm's delight.

Raw or cooked? Kildraig wondered. *Raw for now*, he thought, and thrust his head forward to grasp the man in his jaws. He was still alive as Kildraig began to swallow. That was certainly a good way to have them, the dragon remembered, as he devoured his first food in a thousand years. You could taste the fear still fresh in their blood.

Kildraig writhed upwards, belching flame, and squirmed farther out of his hole. He freed his wings, and flapped them once; just to make sure they were working. It was pure joy to feel them beat in open air once more. A thousand years! There was a debt to pay. Up he surged, using his gigantic hind legs. Down he beat with his tail. The ground shuddered and groaned as it collapsed around him. His wings thrust again, and suddenly he was in the air. A lazy flick of his tail, and an entire castle wall crashed to the ground, men screaming and dying below the cascading stone. He descended once more, ravenous for the taste of fresh meat, and gorged himself on the dead and wounded, feasting on their terror as much as their flesh. They were so puny, these men! How dare they imprison him, and refuse him the homage he deserved! And as for the elves, how arrogant they were, with their eyes bright with wisdom! He would deal with them also!

His hunger slaked for the moment, Kildraig took to the air once more. Beneath him, the river glittered, reflecting the sun in diamond flashes that hurt the eyes of the long-imprisoned worm. High and higher he flew, looking for the one who had brought the Pendraig.

The Fruit Of The Dendragon Tree

Ureth, where are you? Come to me my love!

But she would not answer. He sent her pleasure, then he sent her pain, but she would not be lured by the one nor compelled by the other, and Kildraig knew he had lost that particular morsel for the present. *How delicious it will be to have her, in the end, especially after she has played so hard to get!* She couldn't hide from him forever; she was bound to him in ways she did not understand. But there was still so much fun to be had! *Look at those stupid werewolves, down there on the jetty, waiting for Coegun to lead them! Ah, yes, now they understand! Coegun is dead, you fools! Now he can never break the thrall that the vampires have over you! But I can, because I loathe the vampyrim more than anything that walks, so at least as you die you will know that your slave-masters die with you!*

Down he flew, in a rush of flame that ignited the very air before it, like a comet within the envelope of the world. Out gushed his fire, flooding among the fell creatures that ran as panicked as any human to escape his wrath. Again and again Kildraig spewed his flame among the Undead, until he could see none alive. He did not eat the werewolves, or the vampires. Death was what he brought them. They could rot for all he cared. All the lower town was afire, and just for sport he torched the upper town too. The few humans that had hidden in their houses to escape the battle at the water's edge died within them screaming, or else ran out into the flame-soaked streets and so ended under the sun of a new ruler. Oh yes, there was a new ruler now! And he would demand tribute!

Sighing with pleasure, Kildraig soared higher, and looked down at the river once more. He spied two barges, pulled up onto the eastern bank, and a stream of men and elves running, away eastward into the veldt. Time to pay them a visit as well. He would leave one or two alive, so that his tale would grow in the telling, and others would know what to expect. Fear was always such a productive seed to sow among one's enemies. With a lazy flap of his wings, he began his descent. *These will taste better cooked*, he decided, and he came upon them breathing fire.

3.

"This is becoming a story too often told!" exclaimed Rajindra as I came back to myself. The river tossed us about, large waves breaking randomly into the craft from the bow, or crashing over the sides in foamy torrents that threatened to swamp us. This was the third time he had crossed Marfell in a boat, Rajindra said, promising us it would definitely be his last. Naomi huddled with him in the bow, drenched to the skin. She had already vomited once, and periodically gave a dry heave when the yaw of the craft became too much.

Ureth sat in the stern, trying to steer. Scarth, Jake, Coblyn and I each had an oar, and we were making rapid, if erratic progress across the river. Wherever my mind had soared with the dragon, my body had gone on well enough without me. Keffyldyn stood amidships, desperately trying to keep his balance as our craft pitched about. Coblyn looked pale, no doubt from the nasty gash in his head, but appeared to be holding up otherwise. We were heading to the western bank. Kildraig had flown east, and even from far away we could hear the screams of men and elves as they died on the eastern shore. I vaguely remembered that Ureth had woven a chameleon spell about us. Anyone looking would only see a large log, she had said, albeit one traveling upstream, but she probably needn't have bothered. Kildraig would be busy for some time. Ureth looked at me in curiosity, but if she knew where my thoughts had been she gave no sign.

South of us, the town of Marfold burned, the flames pale in the bright sunshine, the smoke black as it rose into the sky. But Jake looked at me and smiled as he rowed. Despite all the horrors of the past few days, Kildraig's escape, and the knowledge that his Mom had died, the anxiety of the past year had melted from his face. I smiled back. *He's a great kid, Mary,* I said to my dead wife, though dead was hardly how I would have described her at our last meeting. *I know,* she said in my mind, and that was the last time she talked to me, at least while I've been awake.

The Fruit Of The Dendragon Tree

Ureth gave a low moan, and faltered at the tiller, but when I looked at her she was smiling, almost as if... but then, her expression of pleasure changed to anguish, and she moaned again, this time in pain. I realized what Kildraig was trying again, but the moment passed, and Ureth steered us straight once more, giving me a rueful smile. Day had fully stolen back the night when we finally landed a mile or so above Marfang, the boat clunking against the rocky shore. The riverbank was steep, and we clambered up to find ourselves in a ploughed field, with the green shoots of the farmer's early crop pushing through the earth. I was reminded of that other homestead to the north, with its grisly scarecrow, and wondered if any of the Undead were nearby. I sent forth my thought, but could feel nothing.

"No, David," said Ureth, sensing what I did. "Kildraig has done that for us, at least. There are no werewolves or vampires left alive, or if there are, they are too few in numbers and too far away to be a burden to us. As long as we stay hidden from the dragon, we will be safe enough."

"And at what price, Ureth?" asked Naomi. The girl looked pale and miserable, though otherwise none the worse for wear. But her pretty face was marred by scorn and contempt. "The Undead are vanquished, but my brother is dead, and Taumar is without a king. The elves have lost their prince, Marah is gone, and the Crones are no more. The town of Marfold is destroyed, Taumar's greatest fortress lies in ruins, and the Dendragon flowers are surely lost to us, unless you think Kildraig will let us keep on harvesting them. Thanks to you and Jake, he rules here now. At least Coegun was human!"

"He wouldn't have been for long!" retorted Ureth. "Do you really think the Undead would have let him rule them? No, he would have become one of them, vampire or werewolf, and that shadow would have grown until all the world was in darkness!"

"And this is your idea of light?" Naomi countered. She was nineteen years old, a princess and the mother of the Pendraig's child. Ureth was her superior no longer.

"It's all she had!" cried Jake, coming to Ureth's defense. "Sometimes you have to use poison to kill a cancer!" He looked at me as he said this, and I knew my son had learned a great deal since he had left home.

"Don't talk to me of necessity, Jake Patel!" said Naomi. "You failed in your quest to save your mother. You had everything you needed, yet couldn't do what was necessary!"

"Did you not hear David?" asked Scarth. "Jake's mother was already dead-"

"He didn't know that!" Naomi retorted.

"But if he had picked the fruit and gone home, both his parents would now be dead," said Ureth.

"None of you get it!" Jake cried. "I had to do what I did, don't you see? I finally understood that my mother's dying wasn't my fault! She was *willing* to die to have me in her life. She knew what she wanted and was willing to pay the price. But I couldn't leave my Dad to die here, alone, so far from home. He had a sword sticking out of him, right in front of me, and I couldn't leave him a third time, I just couldn't!"

"Enough, children!" said Keffyldyn, shaking the water from his coat. He put his hand on Jake's shoulder, and another on mine, and I felt as if my son and I were connected through the centaur's compassion, that I could feel flowing from his touch. "What's done is done. We have all made our choices Naomi; you should understand that as much as any of us. But what we have to decide right now is where to go, and quickly, before that miserable flying worm remembers he hasn't seen us among those he has eaten."

There was a silence while we thought this over. The river breeze was cold on my wet skin, and I shivered despite the growing warmth of the day. All I knew for sure was that nobody was going to separate me from Jake again.

"I must go to Marlona," said Scarth, finally. "Endil made me his regent, and I must go there to ensure whatever stability I can now that he is dead."

"That's true," said Keffyldyn. "But Kildraig will look eastward first for the remnants of the army, to eat his fill after going so long hungry. Come northward with Coblyn and me to Blutwald. The dragon won't expect you to go that way, and the elves can hide you for a time, until it is safe to travel east again."

Scarth and Coblyn agreed to this readily enough, and Keffyldyn looked at the Sacour. Rajindra said, "I must go home. My people need to know of the great calamity that has befallen here. There will be those among them that will wish to invade. These must be made to see the folly of such a course, especially now that the prize they have always coveted, the Dendragon flowers, may be even less accessible than before."

The centaur nodded, but didn't reply, and suddenly I knew where the rest of us were going, too.

As if she had read my thoughts, Naomi gave Ureth a twisted smile, saying: "So, we are going to the land of the Sacours?" She looked somehow defeated, as if her outburst had drained her of any defiance.

Ureth nodded. "It's the safest place for the baby. And for you."

"We will be safer among our enemies than among our own people in Marlona?"

Ureth nodded again. "You will." I knew she was suddenly too tired to speak more. Too tired to explain the years of court intrigue that awaited the bastard son of the orphaned princess and the Pendraig. Too tired to explain the prophecy of Ysgith, the sword of the king who would unite both kingdoms, and how the unborn child traveling with them could finally help fulfill that vision of peace, and how he never would if the plotters and schemers ever got wind of the idea. I knew what Ureth thought as clearly as if she had spoken, and wondered from where my sudden gift came. But I had been wounded by werewolf and by sword, I had drunk from the enchanted pool of the Dendragon Tree, and been brought back to life by its fruit. I had returned still living from the Dancer's dance beyond the stars, and any or all of those things were likely enough to endow me with insight denied most men. And perhaps Naomi retained enough of her own Gift to discern the situation also, because she went willingly in the end. For Ureth was right. It was much better for my grandchild to grow up far from home, to befriend the people his own folk would brand as enemies. To grow to manhood without the sycophancy of those who pretended to be loyal, while secretly plotting his downfall, so that they could sate their own lust for power. All this had been in Ureth's visions, I saw, but she was tired of explaining them. And now she didn't have to, at least not to me.

Rajindra spoke to Naomi instead. "You will be an honored guest in my house, my lady, and your son and his father and grandfather shall be as my brothers. Your boy will learn to read, and write, and ride a horse, and the finest swordsmen will teach him the noble arts of battle. I myself will teach him to read the stars at night, and the stories they tell us. He will be a prince of the desert and the oasis. And neither he nor you shall want for anything." Naomi said nothing, but bowed her head as graciously as she could manage. A tear fell onto her sleeve, but Rajindra pretended not to notice.

We made our farewells to Scarth, Coblyn and Keffyldyn. I looked at Scarth. He had killed his daughter's murderer, but his eyes betrayed the emptiness of the dish called vengeance. I told him, "Wherever she is, my friend, it is better than here." It could have been a platitude, but he could see in my face that I spoke from having walked in the hall of light myself, and so I think my words offered him some comfort, however small. "Good-bye, Coblyn," I said to my elf friend. He pressed an arrow into my hands. It was black, and a shiver went down my spine as I recognized it.

"This arrow welcomed you to Tiramonde, David Patel," said Coblyn. "If you ever have need of me, let it fly, and I will come to you as soon as I am able."

"Better do it in an empty field," said Keffyldyn. "In case you're as bad with a bow as you are with a sword. We don't want you shooting anyone by accident."

Despite everything I laughed, and the centaur laughed with me, ruffling my hair as if I were a boy. But then he was three thousand years old, and I knew I must seem like a baby to him. The three of them left us, jogging northwards under the sun. I knew they would be safe, and that I would see them again.

The Fruit Of The Dendragon Tree

The rest of us headed south, giving the burning town as wide a berth as possible. The countryside was empty. Several miles below the rapids, the river curved west to join us, and we drank, for the sun had been hot upon our shoulders for several hours. When we started south once again I looked back. Marfang had disappeared, and a dark pall smudged the sky to mark where Marfold lay burning. But here bulrushes grew in the water, and the chatter of river birds came from among the reeds. There was a small splash downstream, and I saw a pair of young otters, playing in the spring morning. I pointed them out to Jake, and he smiled with me at their antics. Small life went on, despite the events that witches and dragons had put in motion.

We followed the river south for many days, living off small game and fish, until one morning a fine mist towered above us along our path, and Rajindra told us we were nearing the end of our journey. Later that day we came to the edge of the impossibly tall cliffs that marked the boundary between the kingdoms of Taumar and Castelfar. Marfell cascaded over this precipice in a rushing torrent known to the desert people as the *Jalapat Gajarnam*, the Thunder Falls. The roar of water made speech impossible. Rajindra led us a mile or so southwest along the cliff edge to what he called the *Ananta Sopanam*, or Endless Stairs. These were cut into the cliff face and descended forever down to the green valley floor far below. I looked, and saw a ribbon of green bordering the descended Marfell as it flowed south to the ocean, the burnt yellows and browns of the great desert stretching east and west and south as far as the eye could see. We could only descend in single file and I hugged the cliff wall, trying not to think about the terrible drop to my right.

And so we came to the place of our waiting, the years of waiting before prophecy could be fulfilled. We lived in Rajindra's household, and true to his word he provided us with everything we could desire, for as a prince of the ruling family he was a man of influence and prosperity in his own country. Above us, in Taumar, the dragon ruled, and the people of the veldt awaited the coming of their king, and paid uneasy tribute to the worm while their nobles cowered in Marlona.

Coegun's cancer had been defeated, but Kildraig's poison lingered, and Naomi was right: the price of liberation from the Undead had come steep. While nobody knew how it could happen, all of us knew that Kildraig would have to be defeated for there to be true peace.

In the meantime my grandson was born, and looked at me with Mary's blue eyes when first I held him in my arms. He stared at me in recognition, and squeezed my finger with his tiny hand, before his eyes shifted to the unfocused gaze of the newborn and the moment passed. But I knew what I saw, and he was even more of a delight to me than he would have been otherwise. Sadly, Jake and Naomi remained ill at ease with each other. But then deceit is never a helpful way to begin parenting, and Naomi's ruse carried its own price in that marriage. For they had to be married, Sacourian law is very strict on that point and there was no way Jake would abandon his son. Naomi named the boy Endil, after her brother, and Jake didn't object. Ureth took a real shine to the baby, and was often with him.

We grew close, my son and I, and he drew much comfort from my retelling the story of seeing his mother after I died at the Dendragon pool. He'd made an excruciating choice that day, for he truly hadn't known Mary was already dead when he held the fruit of the Dendragon tree to my lips, forced it into my mouth, and brought me back to life. Of course, for all we knew we could not return to our world, but that didn't bother either of us as much as we thought it might. Jake fretted sometimes about Jenny Blackwood, but it was Mary who had been the center of our lives, and I truly believed I'd seen the light of her soul shine from little Endil's eyes, and that she lived with us through him. Still, we faced enormous consequences for our choices, and I knew Jake couldn't easily explain his decision to save me, even to himself, so I never asked him to repeat the why of it. His words on the bank of Marfell, the day we escaped the dragon, had cost him enough.

One day when Endil was three, Ureth disappeared without saying goodbye, and when Rajindra asked me where she had gone, I told him, for she and I had become connected in ways that needed no speech.

"She has gone north, to find her father, and the elves. She will return for Jake and me one day, when it is time."

Ureth did come back, as I predicted, though not for several years. Endil came to fetch me before she arrived, though I too had already sensed her approach. The pair of us waited for her at the west gate of Rajindra's compound, while the dust settled in the sunset. She smiled when she saw us, her young blue eyes sparkling in her ancient face, and she embraced the boy who was already growing tall. Then she led me to my destiny, which was foretold so long ago, though the price of it was also very high. Even now, I may venture out at the night of the full Dragon moon, to howl my grief in solitude. I tell no one of these wanderings, or of the wild dance in my blood that echoes in me at these times, like drumbeats in the hills of my soul.

At least I have my memories, of two worlds, and my loves that have transcended time and space are with me still. I'm sure, after I have set down this much, that the scribes will demand more of me for their history. But I am old, and old kings need their rest, even if their dreams are sometimes troubled.

So for now I must sleep.

The End

Afterwards, life imitated art

I started drafting rough passages for *The Fruit Of The Dendragon Tree* in mid 1998. My son, whose middle name is Jacob, provided the name for my character, "Jake." My real son was about seven years old at the time, but the fictional Jake jumped into life already and always aged seventeen.

As my career in corporate America moved along, with extensive travel and increased responsibilities, my writing languished.

I hated being apart from my family as much as I was, and grew acutely conscious that my dream to finish a novel remained unfulfilled. I finally left the corporate life in late 2005, to finish work on *Dendragon*, which by now had lain dormant for over four years. My own son was now fourteen, catching up to Jake who was still only having his first interview with the chief Crone, Marah, and David his father had only just left our world to find him.

I worked on *Dendragon* steadily, beginning in January 2006, and attended the San Diego State University Writer's Conference in January of 2007 for the first time, where I met editor Pat LoBrutto.

Though *Dendragon* was nowhere near finished, Pat liked the premise and the writing thus far, and I subsequently hired him as an editorial consultant. Pat works as an author's advocate with agents once a book is completed, which is why I chose him. Plus he's a great editor, which doesn't hurt.

I plugged away and finished the first draft of *Dendragon* later in 2007, returning to San Diego in January of 2008, where I met Pat once again. At that meeting, we changed the ending to the first draft, which I had already sent to him. He liked it well enough, but pointed out that it was far too long, and I spent most of the rest of 2008 "murdering my darlings." This is a writer's best exercise in ego reduction.

By the summer of 2008, the book was finished, with a different ending than I had first imagined, and Pat deemed it saleable, so I began to contact agents with whom he facilitated introductions. I also began outlining the sequel to *Dendragon*, which I planned to call *The King Of Tiramonde*. I received my first two rejections from agents, but wasn't discouraged: I knew it was a numbers game, was confident that the book was publishable, and figured it would only be a matter of time until someone agreed to represent it.

In July 2008 my son turned seventeen, the same age as Jake, the character to whom he had lent one of his names. That August my wife found a lump in her left breast, and was subsequently diagnosed with breast cancer, which was the same disease I had given, long before, to Jake's mother Mary in *Dendragon*. Life had now imitated art in a very personal way.

My own mother, who had lived in western Canada since my father died, was also diagnosed with a cancer of unknown primary two weeks after my wife's diagnosis. The two most important women in my life therefore both had cancer at the same time, but my Mom died quickly, in late September 2008.

Mom's last coherent words to me were: "I can see your father, and he wants me to go with him. I hope he knows what he's doing." I held her hand as she took her last breath, as Jenny did with Mary.

The day after she died, I was lying on my Mom's couch in her apartment in Penticton BC, while my sister searched for some paperwork. I forgive any skepticism about this, but I felt Mom's fingers graze the back of my neck, just at the hairline, where she used to tickle me when I was a boy. She was indescribably happy, and wanted to tell me, and she did. Then she was gone. This was very reminiscent of David's experience at the end of *Dendragon*, which I had written about two years before.

Soon after, my wife began chemotherapy treatments. These ended in late December 2008, but by then she had lost all her hair and truly looked like a cancer patient. She also was very tired, had little appetite, etc. but it was amazing how she kept on pushing herself. She has since made a full recovery and her prognosis is excellent. We pray it remains so.

With all that had been happening at a personal level, my creativity well had run dry, and *Tiramonde* came to a standstill. In February 2009 I returned to the SDSU conference for the third time, where I was honored to receive an Editor's Choice Award for *Dendragon*. I received further agent interest, but still no commitment for representation.

In August 2009, almost exactly a year since my wife discovered her lump, I suffered a heart attack. I too made a full recovery, but I had still not managed to acquire an agent for *Dendragon*, and it felt in my body as if too much time was passing. I finally decided in January of 2010 to self-publish, and mentally committed to sharing my royalties with various breast cancer charities my wife and I had already been supporting.

The day after I made these decisions, I was offered steady writing work for a financial consulting firm, and restarted work on *Tiramonde*. The universe can reinforce your choices in powerful ways.

I have been occasionally astonished at the eerie way in which my own life subsequently manifested some of the themes and situations I wrote about in *The Fruit Of The Dendragon Tree*. I sometimes joke that I will be very careful with what I write about next time! I don't have any wisdom to offer about the apparent symmetry, but I do know these two things:

Life is precious, and worth fighting for with every ounce of our strength. At the same time, as Jake discovered, there are far worse things than dying, and the light does wait for us afterwards.

Peace be with you.

Paul Deepan
Tennessee
May, 2010

Words Of Thanks

I would like to thank my wife and sons for the gift of indulging my compulsion to write this book, even though it meant they made a lot of sacrifices. Guys, I know it wasn't always easy, so I will always be grateful you found the patience to let me tell my story.

Thanks to Mrs. "Beetle" Ross, for reading *The Narnia Chronicles* and *The Hobbit* aloud to a bunch of kids in a sun drenched classroom in Port-Of-Spain, Trinidad back in the day, and to my boyhood friend Keith MacDonald, who pretty much made me read *Dune* and *The Lord Of The Rings* later on when I was living in Ottawa, Canada. I was never the same after those childhood experiences.

Thanks to Heidi Montijo, for reminding me not to give up on my dream, and to Vish Deepan, Laurie Parker and Pam Huette, for the encouragement to keep going when I needed it. Thanks to all the members of Faith Leaders 2007-2008 (you know who you are), for all those same reasons.

Thanks to Dodge Rea, for formally introducing me to my Shadow, which let me bring Kildraig alive.

Thanks to my editor, Pat LoBrutto, for his insightful suggestions regarding the manuscript, all of which improved it significantly.

Thanks to Jim Minz, editor at Baen Books, for the award.

Thanks to the folks at Outskirts Press, for their professionalism and help in getting this book in print.

Thanks to Lori Macdonald and Sid Coe, for "walking around the structure" with me, and to Matt Ladisa, for being the first "non-industry professional" to read the manuscript and make encouraging noises.

Thanks to all of you who bought this book, and so donated toward Breast Cancer research, education, and support.

Thanks to Indra, Vera, Archie and Alma, beloved fathers and mothers, dancing in the light.

Thanks to Richard Phillips, for the light at the end of the tunnel.

Thanks be to God.